This call may be monitored to ensu ... rvice. Can you afford it? Can you afford *no* ... eam puff. He's like a Nerf manager. A) Da ... heck one. He melts under pressure. He ala ... es of workplace horror, he goes apeshit w ... iews any change at all as a threat. He fucks up majorly in the face of last-minute change and takes everything personally. I love my desk. It loves me. I am it and it is me. Do you meet/exceed expectations? Uh-oh . . . Warren's gone into his foxhole again. Enter your four-digit PIN number and press "OK." Don't imagine for even one second that I'm not watching you. What's the most outrageous thing you ever got away with expensing? How many Post-it notes do you have to have stuck in your cubicle before you start to look like you no longer have your shit together . . . five on your monitor? . . . twelve or more within your total work environment? People notice these things. How old were you when you learned what cc and bcc mean? I prefer bleached paper to recycled paper. It looks nicer. I am evil. I remember being in the Delta business class lounge at San Francisco's airport. I was using my laptop at a desk, and every other minute there'd be a *vzzzt* noise and my screen would go snowy. It turns out that the luggage x-ray machine was maybe a foot away from my head on the other side of the wall. Delete all. I used to hate delegating tasks, but then I got smart and realized that having other people do my work leaves me more time for golfing and whoring. Is your boss a soul-raping machine? We are pleased to offer you a smoke-free environment. Raise your production quota. File an accident report. Generate a shitstorm. I babysit a laser printer for a living. A four percent raise is an insult, you suck-ass butt-licking hornbag of a remora fish. There's a name for women who shoot the shit with the senior men in the company and who view other women in the company as an embarrassment and threat to their power agenda: they're called *successful*. Hey, we're all going down to the food court for lunch—me, Denise, Leon and Rob. Want to come? I think Mitsuko is on sick leave with mono. Murray, I can't help but notice that you parked in an executive spot this morning. I know it was just an accident, but the guys upstairs get really prickly about parking. And how's that Excel project coming along? Hey, you miserable cum Dumpster, thanks for passive-aggressively micromanaging what used to be an okay job. Please listen carefully as menu options have changed. 1-800-Go-FedEx. I used to work at this company that announced it was going out of

JPod

JPod

a novel by

Douglas Coupland

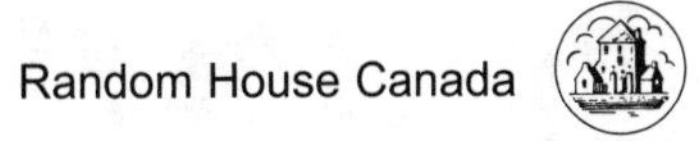

Random House Canada

Published in 2006 by Random House Canada, a division of Random House of Canada Limited. Distributed in Canada by Random House of Canada Limited.

Random House Canada and colophon are trademarks.

www.randomhouse.ca

This book is a work of fiction. Names, characters, places, and incidents either are the product of the author's imagination or are used fictitiously. Any resemblance to actual persons, living or dead, events, or locales is entirely coincidental.

Library and Archives Canada Cataloguing in Publication

Coupland, Douglas
jPod / Douglas Coupland.

ISBN-13: 978-0-679-31424-0
ISBN-10: 0-679-31424-5

I. Title.

PS8555.O8253J66 2006 C813'.54 C2005-906077-8

Jacket Design: Will Webb
Text Design: Douglas Coupland

Printed and bound in the United States of America

10 9 8 7 6 5 4 3 2 1

“Winners Don’t Do Drugs”

William S. Sessions, Director, FBI

FINAL

FINAL.FINAL

final.FOR REAL

FINAL.version 2

absolutely.FINAL

FINAL.2

FINAL.3

FINAL.3.01

FINAL.3.02

FINAL.working

1ne

2wo

3hree

4our

5ive

6ix

7even

8ight

9ine...

...*Best!*

...*Dream!*

...*Ever!*

Play as Gene Simmons
Play as Iron Man

watch_me_xplode

332 of 438 comments

Universal Goo

Chihuahua Death
Drive the hot dog wagon onto the hockey rink
Fatality gap
Do the Boneless

Want to take your business to the next level? Use new strategies to improve your income, and locate parks and truck stops where purchased orgasms are a snap. Make your elevator banter funny but not witty. Get free publicity even though you're promoting nothing. Business network with scary people you don't respect and whose haircuts obviously cost way more than your own. Establish credibility for tasks you hate performing. Clarify values but remember, a million times nothing is still nothing. Read business magazine articles written by children and adults who've never owned businesses. Get more referrals by grooming better and by shooting out more pheromones; basically, don't wash your perineum, that little strip of skin between the genitals and anus. This goes for both sexes. Sex is everywhere in even the drabbest office environment. But then, so is death. Find the middle ground. Overcome objections by pretending you have a non-existent education. Nobody will ever check your credentials unless you run for public office or become head of a school; the secret message is "don't aim for the top—aim for someplace two notches below the top." Having said this, you will still become bitter for not having made it to the top. Even when life is good, it isn't really good. Get commitments, then let people down. Increase sales and get nothing for it. Sell more with your Internet marketing and your website, but don't show too many teeth in your press photo. Make spelling mistakes in your resumé and then wonder why nobody calls you. Play Freecell and contribute nothing to the world but have fun doing it. Yes! You can improve your marketing strategy and your sales, but people will find you kind of boring while you're doing it, and if it works out, people will still think you're not that nice person who showed promise in high school. Also remember that high school is a North American obsession. Europeans think this obsession is juvenile, and the moment you use a high school metaphor, their minds will wander. They're just jealous. There is a much better way to market your products and services, but it's maybe *too* fresh, and maybe you're not ready for that new freshness. If you want to grow your business with less wasted effort, then you're living in dreamland. Whether you're just starting out or you made a million from your business last year, it's all kind of scary and futile, isn't it? There are simply too many people on earth. Oil is going to run out in your lifetime. What's your follow-up strategy to increase sales and profits? Honestly, if you haven't joined a local Kiwanis-type organization, then do it right now. Most of the business decisions in your city are made by older guys who eat mediocre chicken dinners in hotel ballrooms and then go off and have naked whipped cream go-kart rides. It doesn't matter how savvy your proposal is, if the guys in the fezzes have chosen Murray to take over the lease to that office space you were eyeing, then you're totally fucked and Murray will get the lease. One person's testimonial: "Requests for my services went up by 300% as a result of working with Ken, because he's way better-looking than the earnest blank before him, Ron. We fired Ron under the pretext of catching him swiping Post-it notes and bond paper from the storeroom, but really it was because he was boring, didn't like golf, and Tracy at the front desk thought he was, quote, 'Kind of pervy.'" If you're trying to stay more focused on what you do, then simply do what most genuinely successful people do, which is take Ritalin. Most people think Ritalin is a kiddy drug, but what it actually does is allow you to stay focused and stop your mind from wandering. Hi, I'm Denise from HR. This morning I crumpled up a piece of paper and then I held it in the palm of my right hand and I looked at it and I thought, "Denise, this is your life. This is as good as it gets." Hi, I'm Jeremy. I'm that high-energy new guy they stole from Remtech across the Parkway. I'm young, smart, good-looking and I'm using ever-escalating amounts of crystal meth to make me seem more alive than you. I'll either end up winning everything or be found holding up a cardboard sign and talking to myself at the Exit 23 off-ramp. Hi, I'm Rick and I hate everything in the world because I lost everything I owned in the tech bubble in the late 1990s. I really thought I'd be on a beach right now. Instead, I piss in the men's room urinal and have to listen to Jim in the stall beside me flip through the sports pages. It's all he does. I don't know how he gets away with it. He's there for two hours a day. Please turn off all cellphones and personal computer systems. Engineers aren't funny or cute or nerdy. They're damaged. I might be damaged, but they're way more damaged than in any other division of the company. I resent the fact that nerds are somehow cool. They're just losers. Would you like another transaction? People say that everyone can be a success, but you look at the numbers and no, the world is way more about failure and compromised standards than it is about winning. The older the culture is, the less cutesy it is about saying, "Well, you're a winner because you tried your best." Can you imagine a Chinese person saying that? They'd just think you're a loser and buy all of your goods at fire sale prices during your bankruptcy yard sale. You're always hearing about "following your dream," but what if your dream is boring? Most people's dreams are boring. What if you had a dream to sell roadside corn—if you went and sold it, would that mean you were living your dream? Would people perceive you as a failure anyway? And how long would you be happy doing it? Probably not long, but by then it's too late to start something else. You're fucked. Communists are smart in some ways. They actively discourage hoping or dreaming. At least that way, when you finally get a shitty little AM radio after being on the waiting list since 1988, you'll feel both cheered and kindly towards the regime in power. Okay, I'm kidding. The only way to the top is killing and greed. Okay, I'm kidding. But killing helps. Greed kind of helps, but it looks ugly, and at parties people avoid greedheads, so there goes your social life. Life is a contest between you and everyone else. Don't you get an empty feeling in your soul when you have a blank to-do list? Hasn't it been a long time since you had a flying dream? Workshops and seminars are basically financial speed dating for clueless poor people. TV and the Internet are good because they keep stupid people from spending too much time out in public. There are too many old people coming down the chute in the next few decades. Heaven help you if you can't hold your job act together. Put a smile on it, or it's cat food for dinner tonight. A decade of cat food is 3,652 cans. Incorrect password, please try again. People who advocate simplicity have money in the bank; the money came first, not the simplicity. Invitation to All Staff Members: Thursday bowling, pizza and drinks, sponsored by the company. Black lights and music galore. Dancing and bowling shoes provided. Bowling Skills Not Required!!! People who use the phrase, "In these changing times, when the only thing that's certain is change itself" are idiots. Think about it and read the following sentence: "In these static days, when the only guarantee is stasis itself . . ." You see what I mean. Sometime when you're all alone in a room, ask yourself if what you do for a living can be done by someone in India. If there's even a flicker of doubt, then you have to admit that you're doomed. Which is more humiliating: losing your job to a robot, or losing your job to someone who lives in a country whose standards of living you consider inferior? You can't fake creativity, competence or sexual arousal. If you have none of these three attributes, then pack it in right now. Go sell roadside corn in India. Your call is important to us. As you know, Jessica is away for two more days—could you please be sure all of your dirty dishes are put into the dishwasher (not the sink) before the end of the day so that when Katie or Kirsten comes down to turn it on, it is ready to go. Nobody has ever been happy in a job they obtained by first handing in a resumé. Most people have no idea how to politely answer a phone. The English do, and it's been their only major business advantage for the past two centuries. Using the keypad, spell the last name of the person you wish to speak with. Women can discern shitty clothes at thirty paces. Even seasoned recruiters base their first impression on the basis of fuckability. The second thing they look at is whether you're competent, and the third thing they see is whether you're creative in disguising your lack of competence and/or fuckability. A big Thank You to everyone who participated in Jeans Day this year. We

did really well and were able to raise $230.00 for the kids. My friend Josie used to apply for jobs she had no interest in getting, and she liked to mess with people's minds. She'd talk about cramps and abusive boyfriends and her daydream about one day breastfeeding her baby and she always got offered the job. Most people are at their most robotic when interviewing, which is obviously ironic because you're trying to put forth the most concentrated essence of yourself that you can. Most resumés are as boring as yours, and nobody ever reads the second page. There are people out there who will hate you for the way you use your knife and fork. Put the word "implement" in your resumé and you won't get phoned back. College will guarantee you a higher life-long income, and friends made in college last longer than those made in real life. Men turn bitter around forty. The easiest way to get a job is to fill in for women on maternity leave. They almost never come back. Watch out for post-grad students. They wreck more marriages than drugs and alcohol combined. Needy people never last more than two years at any job. I used to get straight A's my whole life, and then in college I started getting D's and it was like morphine. It was great. If someone's bothering you at work, ask him or her to make a donation to a charity. Keep a can and donation envelopes in your desk. They'll never bug you again. It works.$$$$$$$$$$$$$$$$$
$$
$$
$$
$$
$$
$$
$$
$$
$$
$$
$$
$$
$$
$$
$$
$$
$$
$$
$$
$$
$$
$$
$$
$$
$$
$$
$$
$$
$$
$$
$$
$$
$$
$$
$$
$$
$$

$$
$$
$$
$$
$$
$$
$$
$$
$$
$$
$$
$$
$$
$$
$$
$$
$$
$$
$$
$$
$$
$$
$$
$$
$$
$$
$$
$$
$$
$$
$$
$$
$$
$$
$$
$$
$$
$$
$$
$$
$$
$$
$$
$$
$$
$$
$$
$$
$$
$$
$$
$$

ramen noodles, ramen noodles, ramen noodles, ramen noodles, ramen noodles, ramen noodles, ramen noodles
ramen noodles, ramen noodles, ramen noodles, ramen noodles, ramen noodles, ramen noodles, ramen noodles
ramen noodles, ramen noodles, ramen noodles, ramen noodles, ramen noodles, ramen noodles, ramen noodles
ramen noodles, ramen noodles, ramen noodles, ramen noodles, ramen noodles, ramen noodles, ramen noodles
ramen noodles, ramen noodles, ramen noodles, ramen noodles, ramen noodles, ramen noodles, ramen noodles
ramen noodles, ramen noodles, ramen noodles, ramen noodles, ramen noodles, ramen noodles, ramen noodles
ramen noodles, ramen noodles, ramen noodles, ramen noodles, ramen noodles, ramen noodles, ramen noodles
ramen noodles, ramen noodles, ramen noodles, ramen noodles, ramen noodles, ramen noodles, ramen noodles
ramen noodles, ramen noodles, ramen noodles, ramen noodles, ramen noodles, ramen noodles, ramen noodles
ramen noodles, ramen noodles, ramen noodles, ramen noodles, ramen noodles, ramen noodles, ramen noodles
ramen noodles, ramen noodles, ramen noodles, ramen noodles, ramen noodles, ramen noodles, ramen noodles
ramen noodles, ramen noodles, ramen noodles, ramen noodles, ramen noodles, ramen noodles, ramen noodles
ramen noodles, ramen noodles, ramen noodles, ramen noodles, ramen noodles, ramen noodles, ramen noodles
ramen noodles, ramen noodles, ramen noodles, ramen noodles, ramen noodles, ramen noodles, ramen noodles
ramen noodles, ramen noodles, ramen noodles, ramen noodles, ramen noodles, ramen noodles, ramen noodles
ramen noodles, ramen noodles, ramen noodles, ramen noodles, ramen noodles, ramen noodles, ramen noodles
ramen noodles, ramen noodles, ramen noodles, ramen noodles, ramen noodles, ramen noodles, ramen noodles
ramen noodles, ramen noodles, ramen noodles, ramen noodles, ramen noodles, ramen noodles, ramen noodles
ramen noodles, ramen noodles, ramen noodles, ramen noodles, ramen noodles, ramen noodles, ramen noodles
ramen noodles, ramen noodles, ramen noodles, ramen noodles, ramen noodles, ramen noodles, ramen noodles
ramen noodles, ramen noodles, ramen noodles, ramen noodles, ramen noodles, ramen noodles, ramen noodles
ramen noodles, ramen noodles, ramen noodles, ramen noodles, ramen noodles, ramen noodles, ramen noodles
ramen noodles, ramen noodles, ramen noodles, ramen noodles, ramen noodles, ramen noodles, ramen noodles
ramen noodles, ramen noodles, ramen noodles, ramen noodles, ramen noodles, ramen noodles, ramen noodles
ramen noodles, ramen noodles, ramen noodles, ramen noodles, ramen noodles, ramen noodles, ramen noodles
ramen noodles, ramen noodles, ramen noodles, ramen noodles, ramen noodles, ramen noodles, ramen noodles
ramen noodles, ramen noodles, ramen noodles, ramen noodles, ramen noodles, ramen noodles, ramen noodles
ramen noodles, ramen noodles, ramen noodles, ramen noodles, ramen noodles, ramen noodles, ramen noodles
ramen noodles, ramen noodles, ramen noodles, ramen noodles, ramen noodles, ramen noodles, ramen noodles
ramen noodles, ramen noodles, ramen noodles, ramen noodles, ramen noodles, ramen noodles, ramen noodles
ramen noodles, ramen noodles, ramen noodles, ramen noodles, ramen noodles, ramen noodles, ramen noodles
ramen noodles, ramen noodles, ramen noodles, ramen noodles, ramen noodles, ramen noodles, ramen noodles
ramen noodles, ramen noodles, ramen noodles, ramen noodles, ramen noodles, ramen noodles, ramen noodles
ramen noodles, ramen noodles, ramen noodles, ramen noodles, ramen noodles, ramen noodles, ramen noodles
ramen noodles, ramen noodles, ramen noodles, ramen noodles, ramen noodles, ramen noodles, ramen noodles
ramen noodles, ramen noodles, ramen noodles, ramen noodles, ramen noodles, ramen noodles, ramen noodles
ramen noodles, ramen noodles, ramen noodles, ramen noodles, ramen noodles, ramen noodles, ramen noodles
ramen noodles, ramen noodles, ramen noodles, ramen noodles, ramen noodles, ramen noodles, ramen noodles
ramen noodles, ramen noodles, ramen noodles, ramen noodles, ramen noodles, ramen noodles, ramen noodles
ramen noodles, ramen noodles, ramen noodles, ramen noodles, ramen noodles, ramen noodles, ramen noodles
ramen noodles, ramen noodles, ramen noodles, ramen noodles, ramen noodles, ramen noodles, ramen noodles
ramen noodles, ramen noodles, ramen noodles, ramen noodles, ramen noodles, ramen noodles, ramen noodles
ramen noodles, ramen noodles, ramen noodles, ramen noodles, ramen noodles, ramen noodles, ramen noodles
ramen noodles, ramen noodles, ramen noodles, ramen noodles, ramen noodles, ramen noodles, ramen noodles
ramen noodles, ramen noodles, ramen noodles, ramen noodles, ramen noodles, ramen noodles, ramen noodles
ramen noodles, ramen noodles, ramen noodles, ramen noodles, ramen noodles, ramen noodles, ramen noodles
ramen noodles, ramen noodles, ramen noodles, ramen noodles, ramen noodles, ramen noodles, ramen noodles
ramen noodles, ramen noodles, ramen noodles, ramen noodles, ramen noodles, ramen noodles, ramen noodles
ramen noodles, ramen noodles, ramen noodles, ramen noodles, ramen noodles, ramen noodles, ramen noodles
ramen noodles, ramen noodles, ramen noodles, ramen noodles, ramen noodles, ramen noodles, ramen noodles
ramen noodles, ramen noodles, ramen noodles, ramen noodles, ramen noodles, ramen noodles, ramen noodles
ramen noodles, ramen noodles, ramen noodles, ramen noodles, ramen noodles, ramen noodles, ramen noodles

Click here.

Part One
Never Mess with the Subway Diet

"Oh God. I feel like a refugee from a Douglas Coupland novel."

"*That* asshole."

"Who does he think he is?"

"Come on, guys, *focus*. We've got a major problem on our hands."

The six of us were silent, but for our footsteps. The main corridor's muted plasma TVs blipped out the news and sports, while co-workers in long-sleeved blue and black T-shirts oompah-loompahed in and out of laminate-access doors, elevated walkways, staircases and elevators, their missions inscrutable and squirrelly. It was a rare sunny day. Freakishly articulated sunbeams highlighted specks of mica in the hallway's designer granite. They looked like randomized particle events.

Mark said, "I can't even think about what just happened in there."

John Doe said, "I'd like to do whatever it is people statistically do when confronted by a jolt of large and bad news."

I suggested he ingest five milligrams of Valium and three shots of hard liquor or four glasses of domestic wine.

"Really?"

"Don't ask me, John. Google it."

"And so I shall."

Cowboy had a jones for cough syrup, while Bree fished through one of her many pink vinyl Japanese handbags for lip gloss—phase one of her well-established pattern of pursuing sexual conquest to silence her inner pain.

The only quiet member of our group of six was Kaitlin, new to our work area as of the day before. She was walking with us mostly because she didn't yet know how to get from the meeting room to our cubicles. We're not sure if Kaitlin is boring or if she's resistant to bonding, but then again none of us have really cranked up our charm.

We passed Warren from the motion capture studio. "Yo! jPodsters! A turtle! All *right*!" He flashed a thumbs-up.

"Thank you, Warren. We can all feel the love in the room."

Clearly, via the gift of text messaging, Warren and pretty much everyone in the company now knew of our plight, which is this: during today's marketing meeting we learned we now have to retroactively insert a charismatic cuddly turtle character into our skateboard game, which is already nearly one-third of the way through its production cycle. Yes, you read that correctly, a turtle character—in a *skateboard* game.

The three-hour meeting had taken place in a two-hundred-seat room nicknamed the air-conditioned rectum. I tried to make the event go faster by pretending to have superpower vision: I could see the carbon dioxide pumping in and out of everyone's nose and mouth—it was purple. It made me think of that urban legend about the chemical they put in swimming pools that reveals when somebody pees. Then I wondered if Leonardo da Vinci had ever inhaled any of the oxygen molecules I was breathing, or if he ever had to sit through a marketing meeting. What would that have been like? "Leo, thanks for your input, but our studies indicate that when they see Lisa smile, they want a sexy, *flirty* smile, not that grim little slit she has now. Also, I don't know what that closet case Michelangelo is thinking with that naked David guy, but Jesus, clamp a diaper onto him pronto. Next item on the agenda: Perspective—Passing Fad or Opportunity to Win? But first, Katie here is going to tell us about this Friday's Jeans Day, to be followed by a ten-minute muffin break."

But the word "turtle" pulled me out of my reverie, uttered by Fearless Leader—our new head of marketing, *Steve.* I put up my hand and quite reasonably asked, "Sorry, Steve, did you say a *turtle*?"

Christine, a senior development director, said, "No need to be sarcastic, Ethan. Steve here took Toblerone chocolate and turned it around inside of two years."

"No," Steve protested. "I appreciate an open dialogue. All I'm really saying is that, at home, my son, Carter, plays SimQuest4 and can't get enough of its turtle character, and if my Carter likes turtle characters, then a turtle character is a winner, and thus, this skateboard game needs a turtle."

John Doe BlackBerried me: **I CAN'T FEEL MY LEGS**

And so the order was issued to make our new turtle character "accessible" and "fun" and the buzzword is so horrible I have to spell it out in ASCII: "{101, 100, 103, 121}"

ORIENTAL
NOODLE SOUP

NISSIN

70622 03503

2¼ oz. x 6 CUPS

Chicken Flavor

• • •

Back in our cubicle pod, the six of us fizzled away from each other like ginger ale bubbles. I had eighteen new emails and one phone message, my mother: "Dear, could you give me a call? I really need to speak with you—it's an emergency."

An emergency? I phoned her cell right away. "Mom, what's up? What's wrong?"

"Ethan, are you at work right now?"

"Where else would I be?"

"I'm at SuperValu. Let me call you back from a pay phone."

The line went dead. I picked it up when it rang.

"Mom, you said this was an emergency."

"It is, dear. Ethan, honey, I need you to help me."

"I just got out of the Worst Meeting Ever. What's going on?"

"I suppose I'd better just tell you flat out."

"Tell me what?"

"Ethan, I killed a biker."

"You killed a *biker*?"

"Well, I didn't *mean* to."

"Mom, how the hell did you manage to kill a biker?"

"Ethan, just come home right now. I'll be there in twenty minutes."

"Why doesn't Dad help?"

"He's on a shoot today. He might get a speaking part."

She hung up.

• • •

On my way out of the office, I passed a world-building team, standing in a semicircle, staring at a large German-made knife on a desktop.

"What's up?" I asked.

"It's the knife we're using to cut Aidan's birthday cake," a friend, Josh, replied.

I looked more closely at the knife: it was clownishly big. "Okay, it's hard-core *Itchy & Scratchy*—but so what?"

"We're having a contest—we're trying to see if there's any way to hold a knife and walk across a room and not look psycho."

"And?"

"It's impossible."

A few desks away, Bree was showing someone photos of her recent holiday visiting Korean animation sweatshops. She was bummed because she couldn't get into North Korea: too much legal juju. "It's a real blotch to have on your passport. I just wanted to know what it's like to be in a society with no technology except for three dial telephones and a TV camera they won from Fidel Castro in a game of rock paper scissors."

Bree is right. For those of us who are too young to have visited Cold War East Germany or the USSR, North Korea remains as the sole boutique nation with a quack low-technology dictatorship. "Owning a 56K floppy disk can land you two decades of hard labour."

I suggested North Korea should change its name to something friendlier, more accessible.

"Like what, Ethan?"

"How about Trish?"

"As in Patricia?"

"Yeah."

"I like that. It's fresh."

"Thanks."

• • •

Through a rare and cheerful accident of freeway planning, I can get from the campus to my parents' place by making two left turns and two right turns, even though they live 17.4 miles away in the gloomy evergreen cocoon of the British Properties. I find this elegant and pleasing.

When I pulled into the driveway, nothing seemed out of place. It could easily have been 1988, right down to the 1988 Reliant K-car wagon. Inside the front door, I heard Mom call from the kitchen, "Ethan, would you like a sandwich? I have egg salad."

I walked into the kitchen, unchanged since Ronald Reagan ruled Earth. My brother, Greg, and I once found a pile of cleaning products that predated bar-coding on a hallway shelf. "No sandwich, thanks, Mom. Am I, or am I not, here about a dead biker?"

Mom cut her own sandwich in two. "I know for a fact that your diet is appalling. Greg tells me that all you eat is Doritos and fruit leather."

"Mom, the *biker*?"

"I was going to eat my sandwich, but okay, Mr. Impatient, follow me."

We walked out of the kitchen and down the main hallway, past my old bedroom, over which my beer-bottles-of-the-world collection had once stood sentry—a room that now housed Mom's sewing machine, her cigarette-making machine and the machine she uses to roll up old newspapers to convert them into fire logs. Where my bong once sat now rested a balsa wood mallard duck, sitting in a basket of silk freesia.

Farther down the hall we descended a set of stairs into the back hallway, rife with the aroma of mildewed sporting equipment, and from there, down another set of stairs that led into the basement proper. Mom reached into a basket and handed me a pair of Ray-Bans and put a pair on herself. She said, "I'd lower the lights, but it confuses the chlorophyll cycles."

Mom also keeps her grow-op at nearly a hundred percent humidity, and I hate humidity. Humidity feels like hundreds of strangers touching me.

At the far end of the basement, where the air hockey table had sat dormant for decades, amid a cluster of astonishingly fertile female plants decked out in coloured ribbons (Mom's genetic bookkeeping system), lay the beefiest, scariest death star of a biker I'd ever seen. "Holy *crap,* Mom, you've done some weird stuff in your life, but this tops it. What happened?"

"I electrocuted him."

"You *what*?"

"I rigged up this corner of the room so that if I ever got into trouble, I could electrocute anybody standing in that puddle." I looked down—the biker *was* lying in a puddle.

"You set up a death trap in your own house?"

"This is a grow-op, dear. I'm not raising miniature ponies down here."

"So why did you electrocute him?"

"His name is, or was, Tim."

"What did young *Tim* do to you?"

"He was trying to extort me into giving him a share of the crop."

"How much?"

"Fifty percent."

"What an asshole."

"It really was an accident, Ethan. I wasn't sure if it was going to get ugly, so I arranged things so that he was standing in the puddle. And then his cellphone rang, and I had a panic reflex and flipped the switch."

I wanted to know what sort of ring tone a biker would select for his cellphone, but that could wait until later. I stared down at Tim. He looked heavy. And his—for lack of a better word—*deadness* was hard to absorb.

Mom said, "If you could drag him through the door into the carport, together we can probably lift him into the wagon."

"What then?"

"You tell me, Ethan. You're the family genius."

"Why couldn't you call Greg?" My brother is a hot-shot real estate sales guy.

"Greg is in Hong Kong on business."

Here's the thing: How *do* you get rid of a body? Pretend that right now you have a corpse in your house. It's like trying to get rid of a side of beef with nobody knowing. It's hard. "Mom, do you have a carpet you want to get rid of?"

"Why a carpet?"

"The Sikhs are always rolling up the dead bodies of unwilling brides from arranged marriages and tossing them into the Fraser River. Maybe we can do that."

Mom looked disappointed.

"What? What's wrong with that idea?"

"What's wrong is that wherever we put the body it has to *stay* where we put it. I wouldn't want Tim floating to the surface. I think we should bury him."

"We could roll him up inside the carpet *and* bury him."

"Okay. Let's get the carpet from your father's den. I've always hated it. It reminds me of your grandmother."

We went upstairs. Dad used to work for a marine engineering firm. When he was laid off, he got into acting, mostly TV, but lately he'd been copping a few brief non-speaking roles in U.S. theatrical releases. Okay, he gets tiny crappy non-speaking parts in TV commercials where he always seems to be left on the cutting-room floor, as well as gigs as an extra in crowd scenes.

In his den, all of his old ship models and nautical maps had been dumped off the shelves and heaped in a corner in favour of framed headshots—colour and B+W, serious, lighthearted, "The Lover," "The Sad Clown," "Good Cop Gone Bad—" as well as pictures of Dad shaking hands with a galaxy of made-in-Vancouver actors carted up to Canada to max out tax credits: Ben Affleck, Mira Sorvino, Kirk Cameron, Lucy Lawless, Raffi and various Muppets way down the Muppet food chain, like Cookie Monster. There was a new one of him with Uma Thurman. "What was she like to work with?" I asked Mom.

"Apparently a dream. She signed his cast and crew jacket."

Some of Dad's ballroom dancing outfits were draped over an armchair, awaiting dry cleaning.

"What your father sees in that horrid dancing I'll never understand." Mom pointed to a braided rug beneath Dad's desk. "That was a wedding present. It's given me the heebie-jeebies for decades. Is it big enough to hold Tim?"

"I think so."

She bent down. "Lift up the desk, and I'll pull it out from under the legs."

I lifted the desk, and in so doing, toppled a five-hundred-thick pile of headshots of Dad as a Nazi. Mom puffed. "Got it."

We rolled up the rug and lugged it downstairs, where we made a biker-wrap sandwich out of Tim. I dragged him out into the carport—man, was he heavy—and I got oil stains on the carpet.

Mom was holding open the wagon's rear door. "Come on, Ethan, show a little respect."

"You electrocute the guy where my air hockey table used to stand, and you ask me to show some respect?"

"You and your brother never played air hockey after the first Christmas weekend."

"Well, it kind of sucked."

"Well, *I* kind of drove all over town trying to find a place that wasn't sold out of them."

With one big huff, I lifted Tim into the back, but he fell out with an unnerving thump. "Ethan, get him in the car."

I did that, and we backed out of the carport and driveway.

"Okay," Mom said, "let's find a nice big hole."

"Just for the record, Mom, this whole thing is creeping me out."

"Men should never discuss their feelings, Ethan."

"I thought women are supposed to like guys discussing feelings."

"Good God, no."

• • •

It's strange how everything in the world changes the moment your focus becomes extremely specific. *Hmmm . . . is that a good place to bury a body? No, soil's too thin.*

Mom suggested Stanley Park, on the edge of downtown. "If there was ever a place to dump a body, the park is it. At this point in history, there are probably more bones there than soil."

So we drove to Stanley Park, but there were way too many people walking around. We headed back to the North Shore and checked out jogging paths and some of the smaller municipal parks, but even there, people and dogs abounded.

Around six it started getting dark, and I had an idea. "Let's drive up to those monster houses Greg is always selling. We'll put Tim in the foundation of one of the construction sites."

"I don't know . . ."

"The bonus is that we don't have to dig a hole. Instead, we get to fill one in a bit."

"I see your point."

We ended up on the winding treeless roads of West Van's bizarre Canterbury neighbourhood, a rainforest bulldozed to make way for jumbo houses that resembled microwave ovens with cedar shake roofing.

"Who lives in these things?" Mom asked as we drove.

"Greg says it's mostly sports stars and abandoned Asian housewives sitting out their three-year sentences required for citizenship."

"There. Let's put him down there." Mom was pointing at a freshly poured concrete foundation for a house in the twenty-thousand-square-foot range. It had been framed in with two-by-sixes, and from the skeleton I could tell the style would be best described as Sailor Moon's Breezy West Coast Hideaway. The house was on the highest street. There was nobody overlooking us.

Mom's spot selection was good. The basement concrete had been poured and coated with vapour barrier tar. The hole was obviously slated to be backfilled with dirt within a day or two. In it there were a few tatters of tarpaper, a tuft or two of pink insulation and a Wendy's wrapper.

We removed Tim the Biker from the car and ever so casually carried him to the front door area like he was a futon. With a one-two-three, we lobbed him in. We both pretended not to hear the gentle cracking noise.

I said, "Perfect shot. Come on. Let's cover him up."

We entombed Tim using the greyish-orange dirt from the excavation. It went far more quickly than I'd expected, five minutes, maybe.

Mom looked a bit dizzy as we walked back to the car. When we drove away, she sat like a preteen caught shoplifting at Wal-Mart. Her hands were folded in her lap, and her head was down. She sniffled once, twice, and then came the tears, in floods.

"Mom?"

"Ethan, could you pull over?"

I did.

She turned to me, red-eyed. "I didn't tell you everything."

"Oh?"

"I'm telling you because I can't tell your father."

"Tell him what?"

"I quite liked Tim. He was a troubled soul. I thought I could help him."

This was a conversation I wasn't prepared to continue. I said, "Mom, let's turn on the radio. We can discuss this later." I turned on the AM radio, and the music that came on was French. "Mom, you listen to the French station?"

"*Oui.* Sometimes."

From the speakers came the sound of accordions.

"Mom, what's with French music? All the songs have the same title." As we drove home, I composed a mental French song list that went like this:

Ça va, ça va
On qui peut
Ma vie
Le Métro, c'est où?
C'est ça
L'amour, c'est bien
Le bon cowboy
De bon Métro
C'est comme ça
J'ai un rêve
Quelle heure est-il?
Nous nous allons
Dit donc!
Chanson des Métros perdus
Amour des rêves
Où?
J'ai mal à la tête
Nous sommes perdus (Avez-vous une carte?)
J'ai une carte
Passé composé
Le pamplemousse et la grenouille
Le ça

UnknownSender@UnknownDomain.org

Greetings to you. I am Mr. Macaulay A. Ofurhie from the office of the Department of Petroleum Resources, DPR, Nigeria. I write to solicit your cooperation in the execution of this entreaty.

Without any prejudice to the foregoing, the DPR is the presidium petroleum Inspectorate and directorate of the Nigerian oil and gas industry vested with the following responsibilities: supervising all petroleum industry operations; enforcing safety and environmental regulations and ensuring that those operations conform to national and international industry practices and standards; keeping and updating records on Nigerian petroleum industry operations as well as rendering regular reports on them to Government and relevant Agencies; verifying and processing all applications for payment/debt claims and licenses so as to ensure compliance with laid-down guidelines before making recommendations to Government and relevant Agencies as well as providing estimates and projections for work plans, scheduling methodology, bid documents and to prioritize, distribute and award contracts for the development of oil and gas projects.

To the main purpose of writing you, following a summarized breakdown of the fiscal expenditure by the DPR for the past four years and as reported to the government and relevant agencies, showed that the total project contracts awarded to both local and foreign firms amounted to over five billion US dollars and 52% were awarded to foreign firms/multinationals. The crux of this letter is that along with contracts cleared for pay-off is an acclaimed sum of US$38.6million US dollars which has been approved for pay-of by the Federal Ministry of Finance (FMF) alongside with other beneficiaries whose applications are been process. The finance/contract department of the DPR deliberately over-invoiced most of the contracted projected and DPR motivated projects. Consequently in the course of disbursements, the department was been able to accumulate US$38.6million US dollars, as contained in its records and that of the FMF's suspense account with the Debt Reconciliation Committee (DRC). Respective application for payment will not last more than two weeks. Hence, as the Coordinator of this project is to solicit your unalloyed cooperation and assistance to enable us pull out $3.6m into acclaimed foreign beneficiary account owned by your good-self and covered by a foreign company/business name to be used. This business is 100% fool proof, genuine and risk-free. Hence the need for strict and absolute confidentiality till the end is all Important because members of the office the office of the DPR involved in this business are personalities who have attained impeccable track records of probity in the Civil Service of Nigeria and as such are not permitted to operate Foreign Account in discharging their functions as members of the DPR. Furthermore, sharing of this fund after remittance into your provided bank account will be done as follows: 70% for us, 25% for you the account owner and 5% to cover contingencies expenses and to be reimbursed immediately. Confirming your faithfulness to this entreaty and your unalloyed cooperation to consolidate this transaction as proposed to you, please endeavor to reply immediately with your contact/postal address; telephone and fax lines for further briefing.

I thank you for your attention and anticipated co-operation as I am looking forward to hearing from you.

Kind regards,

Mr. M. A. Ofurhie
Office of the Director, Department of Petroleum Resources.

• • •

Back in jPod, Mark accidentally tipped over John Doe's stack of Tom Clancy novels, and it was one of those things that got slightly ugly.

"Look, John, I said I was sorry."

"You should treat books with more reverence."

"You've actually read all of those?"

"Yes. So? What was the last book you read?"

"Book? As in paper and ink and everything?"

"Yes."

"Hmmm . . . it was the manual that came with my microwave oven. I was trying to figure out how to make it tell me the time in the European mode. You know, 18:00 instead of 6:00."

"Could you do it?"

"Yeah, but I used up three sick days nailing it."

"What about fiction?"

"Novels?"

"Yeah."

"Ummmm . . ."

"Just as I thought. You're an emotional blank."

"Oh, *please.*"

"Too close for comfort?"

"This is stupid."

Mark went to his desk, but John started heckling him from the other side of the wall baffle. "*Mark's an emotional blaaaaank. Mark's an emotional blaaaaank.*"

This was driving me nuts. "Both of you stop it. Neither of you are emotional blanks."

Harrumphs from both cubicles.

"And to prove it," I said, "I'm going to draw up a

standardized list that itemizes everything that's special and unique about all of us here in jPod."

"I can't imagine Mark's will be too long," said John.

"Manners, please."

And so I made up a quick template and standardized our personalities on paper. Anything to get out of doing my actual job.

Living Cartoon Profile No. 1

Name: Casper Jesperson

Name people actually use: Cancer Cowboy, or simply Cowboy
Reason for unusual name people actually use: Grew up in an agricultural region and was told by well-meaning mother who didn't want him to smoke that the local cowboys were all dying of lung cancer
Smokes: Yes
Non-work e-name(s): xtinctionevent@mindlink.com
Preferred room temperature: 71°F
Favourite game: Doom 3
Preferred *Simpsons* character: Duff Man
Preferred karaoke song: "Dust in the Wind" by Kansas
Food group most prevalent within work cubicle: Skittles, with the green ones removed
Most disturbing trait: Is not suicidal, but really enjoys thinking about death, and, to be frank, is actually kind of looking forward to it

Living Cartoon Profile No. 2

Name: Brianna Jyang

Name people actually use: Bree
Most evident pathology: Makes no bones about the fact that she wants to sleep with almost every guy she meets, but only once
Does she actually do this?: We're not sure
Non-work e-name(s): boxofpaperclips@hotmail.com
Preferred room temperature: 65°F
Favourite game: The original PlayStation Tomb Raider
Preferred *Simpsons* character: Edna Krabappel
Preferred karaoke song: "My Heart Will Go On" by Céline Dion
Does this song make her mushy?: Yes
Does this mean she's a crying drunk?: Yes
Food group most prevalent within work cubicle: A low-fat oat muffin that she eats, one molecule at a time, over the course of an eighteen-hour workday.
Does this frighten and annoy her co-workers?: Yes

Living Cartoon Profile No. 3

Name: John Doe (yes, legally, as of three months ago)

Birth name: crow well mountain juniper (all lower case)
Name people actually use: John Doe
Reason for spooky birth name and subsequent selection of John Doe as a real name: Grew up in a lesbian commune and was home-schooled until the age of twelve. Never saw a TV set until age fifteen. Wants to be statistically normal to counteract his wacko upbringing.
Non-work e-name(s): johndoedammit@aol.com
Preferred room temperature: 62°F ("I may have grown up in a lesbian commune, but I think we truly are overdependent on climate control systems in our society.")
Favourite game: *The Simpsons* Hit & Run
Preferred *Simpsons* character: Groundskeeper Willie OR Lard Lad
Does he watch too much TV, specifically *The Simpsons*, to compensate for his media-free upbringing?: Yes
Preferred karaoke song: None
Reason for having no preferred karaoke song: Grew up without pop culture or music: "I just don't get it—but I'm trying, I really am."
Food group most prevalent within work cubicle: M&M's (which is based on statistics on items most commonly eaten out of hotel mini-bars)

Living Cartoon Profile No. 4

Name: Brandon Mark Jackson

Name people actually use: Mark
Reason for boring name people actually use: Entered jPod only three weeks ago
Non-work e-name(s): bmarkjackson@earthlink.com
Preferred room temperature: Haven't yet discussed this, but I'm guessing 72°F
Favourite game: Baldur's Gate
Preferred *Simpsons* character: Fast-food guy with cracking voice OR Moe Szyslak: opposite ends of the food-and-beverage industry labour cycle
Preferred karaoke song: Has yet to show any musical verve
Food group most prevalent within work cubicle: None
Does he think we don't notice this?: Yes
Is his office freakishly clean with no evidence whatsoever of an interior life—not even so much as a snapshot or anime knick-knackery?: Yes

Living Cartoon Profile No. 5

Name: Kaitlin Anna Boyd Joyce

Name people actually use: Kaitlin
Was she at the meeting today with Steve Who Turned Around Toblerone in Two Years? Yes
Do we know much about her yet?: No. She joined jPod yesterday.
Non-work e-name(s): C13H20N2O2.HCL@shaw.ca
Preferred room temperature: Haven't discussed it, but I'm guessing 72°F
Favourite game: Yahoo! Games.com's TextTwist (spied on her)
Preferred *Simpsons* Character: I'm guessing Lisa
Preferred karaoke song: I'm hoping it's one I really like
Food group most prevalent within work cubicle: Gum
Does she notice me?: To be honest, I think not
Will I let her see this particular character report?: No way

Living Cartoon Profile No. 6

Name: Me

Name on birth certificate: Ethan Harrison Jarlewski
Name people actually use: Ethan
Non-work e-name(s): snacklover@gmail.com
Preferred room temperature: 68°F, and I hate hate hate humidity
Most creative thing ever done: An old operating system I invented when I was in high school. I called it Mentos.
Favourite game: Chrono Trigger on Sony PlayStation, a delectable console RPG with art by Akira Toriyama, sound by Yasunori Mitsuda and Nobuo Uematsu
Preferred *Simpsons* character: Kang and Kodos, the aliens
Preferred karaoke song: None
Reason for not having a preferred karaoke song: I live in fear of karaoke. Even thinking of it in this detached neutral listing format causes me to worry that I might somehow even unintentionally lure karaoke into my life.
Food group most prevalent within work cubicle: Kettle Chips with cracked pepper and lime, even though I suspect they give me bad dreams. Went through a Jell-O Pudding Snacks phase last fall, but now can't even look at the stuff.
Does he consider himself normal?: I used to, but now I wonder. Or rather, I think I'm still normal, but everyone around me is going random. Now I look at most people like recently lit Roman candles, unsure if they're about to go off, or if they're merely duds.
Does he enjoy his job?: The greatest challenge is to have a job without actually doing work, which is really hard to pull off in a company where workspace productivity is measured with just about every conceivable form of metrics
Does he take satisfaction in his approach to work?: Yes

• • •

"Ethan, your description of me makes me look like a goof."

"Mark, all I did was collect the data and present it."

Mark was peeved. "Ethan, there has to be more to my life than this."

"Why can't you just be happy as a shallow cartoon glyph of a human like everybody else here?"

"You don't understand—I'm *me*—I have a *soul*."

"Mark, I think you're obsessing on this whole individuality thing. Revel in your averageness the way John Doe does."

On the other side of my wallboard, John Doe gave a muffled, "Amen."

"No. I want to improve my profile now. I demand to be more than just a cartoon character."

"Okay, then, please tell us, what is the single event that most changed you as a person?"

"That's easy. Six years ago I was doing the please-my-parents thing, landing a degree in biological sciences. I had a part-time job in the beetling pit."

"What's that?"

"It's where they take a dead animal and put it into this big stainless steel cone-shaped pit full of starving beetles, and after a few days, there's nothing left except bone-dry bones."

I thought of Tim the Biker's graceless burial. Where are these beetling pits when you need them?

Bree's head was above the wall partition. "You never told me about any beetling pit."

"Bree, by the time we got to your place, we'd only said eleven words."

I said, "Bree, please, I'm doing an interview here. Mark, how was the beetling pit the event that changed you most as a person?"

Mark turned to me. "It was the part of my life that made me realize something had to change in my universe. I was studying biology, as I was saying, to please my parents, and I don't think there's ever been a happy person on earth who chose an education and a job to please their parents. Then, one day, I got notice that the building I lived in was being torn down for condos, so I tried to find a place to live, but I screwed up and didn't find a place in time. When I asked my folks if I could live in the basement, they said *no way.*"

"You were a problem child?"

"No. They turned the house into a B & B, and my room was gone."

"What happened then?"

"I was going to crash on a friend's couch, but first I had to put all of my stuff in a U-Store-It place over by the Second Narrows Bridge. It was late on a Friday afternoon, and I was the first client in this new patch of mini-units they'd built. I was glad, because it meant the place was clean, and I didn't have to worry if Jeffrey Dahmer had ever stored his boyfriends in my unit. But then the lights went out, and when I went to check the switch I accidentally clicked shut the big roll-down door; it locked, and because the place was new, they hadn't properly installed the fail-safe unlocking switch. I was stuck in there with no lights. When I tried pounding on the door, there was no one to hear me. It was pretty bad."

I stole a line from my mother: "Boo hoo. What then?"

"I tried to be all Boy Scout-y and positive, but after about nine p.m., I realized I was screwed."

"Can we speed this up?"

"Okay. I was in there for four days without light. The only thing I had to drink was a bottle of Gatorade autographed by John Madden. I had to eat the gum from my sacred collection of twelve factory-sealed boxes of 2003 Upper Deck SP authentic NFL cards, with one autographed and sequentially numbered rookie card per box, including autographed cards from Bart Starr, Donovan McNabb, Jerry Rice and Joe Montana. I was going to use them to fund my retirement."

"How long did the Gatorade last?"

"Almost fifty hours."

"And the gum?"

"Almost seventy-two hours. It was a long weekend."

At this point, all the heads in jPod gophered upwards, making *oooooohhhhhh* sounds.

"Mark," I asked, "so how has that changed you as a human?"

"It's kind of weird."

"We wouldn't *possibly* want to hear something weird, Mark."

"Since then, I need as many edible objects around me as possible."

"Huh?"

"Like my futon. It's from this place in Finland. Cost me $2,500, but the entire futon is edible. They market them to Japanese people who are worried about earthquakes and being trapped alive under rubble."

"Go on."

"My apartment is like Willy Wonka's factory. You can eat my chairs."

"But, Mark, your cubicle is entirely devoid of stuff, let alone edible stuff."

"So it would appear, but you see this stapler?" Mark held up a generic stapler. "It's made of marzipan. I bought it online from this geek shop based in Palo Alto. And these pencils here? Chocolate."

Silence passed over us. We could never look at the world the same way ever again.

"Mark, I think you can safely consider yourself a member of jPod."

• • •

Sidetrack: Cowboy was cleaning out his hard drive and found some old penis enlargement spams he'd saved from 2003. All of us got sentimental for that brief historical moment when a fresh young Internet promised us a better tomorrow with all of the free Viagra, Ambien, Vicodin, OxyContin and enlarged members we were willing to accept.

How come you don't see dildos that are 5 or 6 inches long?

I know you're good looking. You probably have money and a nice car. But I would bet you have one that is small to average size. How do I know? Statistics. On average, men are from 5 to 6.3 inches. And don't tell me you haven't measured it, because every guy does at some point.

I used to be small—so small I'm too embarrassed to even type it. I was like you ...thinking that it was the love that counted, or that money was all that I needed. How wrong I was! I found that out when my wife of a year packed up her bags and divorced me, yelling as she walked out the door that I was the worst guy she had ever slept with, because my unit was too small to get her off.

Right then and there I decided that I had to do something. But I didn't know where to look. That's when I came across an email telling me that I could gain 3 inches in 3 weeks.

Desperately wanting to try anything, I said to myself "What the heck, it's cheap, and who knows, it might work." It MIGHT work? How about growing 3 inches in only 2 weeks! Now Im the proud owner of an 8.3 inch unit.

Anyway, I just recently saw my ex-wife at our favorite hang out. She told me she still loved me and that she wanted me back. I took her to my house and her eyes almost popped out when I pulled down my pants. Then I told her to get out of my house. As she was walking out the door (crying) she asked me why didn't I want her back, I replied "Baby, I have a huge (actually gigantic) new gun that's loaded with bullets, and its hunting season!"

So, if you like being small (or average), then delete this email. On the other hand if you want to be Better-Than-Average then visit the link below and try it for yourself.

• • •

I played this truly evil welcome-to-jPod prank on Kaitlin while she was away from her desk. I popped the M and N keys off her keyboard and switched them. I can't wait to see the mirth and mayhem that ensues.

• • •

Okay, so around nine at night I finally got down to work, trawling through Google for data on turtles. Then my father phoned. From the odd background noise, I guessed he was calling from a location shoot.

"Dad, where are you?"

"I'm waythefuck out in Cloverdale."

"Is it a Western? I hear yee-hawing in the background."

"Sort of a Western—it's about ranchers, but they get invaded by aliens."

"What do the aliens do?"

"They inhabit the cattle, but then they get stuck inside them. So the ranchers suddenly discover their cattle are displaying highly intelligent behaviour, and every time the price of beef comes up, the cows go apeshit."

"What's the budget?"

"Crap."

"Why are you calling?"

"Because I want you to come out to the shoot."

Cloverdale is a half-hour drive, but because it's in the Fraser Valley it feels like three hours away. Los Angeles seems closer to me than Cloverdale does. I'm a bad son. I didn't want to make the drive. "Dad, I have to finish scrubbing up some 1980s motherboards I bought on eBay."

"Ethan, I'm in love."

Dad using an expression like "in love" was a wallbuster. "Oh," I said.

"That sounded judgmental."

"Well, this is a pretty weird thing to be hearing. What about Mom?"

"Just come out here and watch the dailies with me."

"Dad, you're an extra in a movie about aliens invading a cattle ranch. Why would you be allowed to watch the dailies?"

"Today I finally got my first speaking part. I thought it'd be a good day to tell you about other changes in my life, too."

I heaved out a lungful of air. "Okay. Tell me where you are."

"I'll pass you along to Sharon here. She's a teamster, and handles anything to do with vehicles."

Sharon's directions were eerie, a mirror image of the two lefts and two rights I took to get to Mom's. I took two rights and two lefts and arrived at Dad's shoot. I parked my car and got shuttled to the trailers. I opened the door to Dad's trailer, expecting to find him in a makeup bib drinking bottled water. Instead, he was French kissing someone who appeared to be Ellen Kovacs, who had been two years behind me in high school.

"Dad?"

It was like a French farce, the two of them separating and trying to appear chaste, smoothing their hair and pulling down their shirts. "Don't worry," I said, "there's no judging going on here."

"Son, this is Ellen."

"Hi, Ellen."

"Ethan, you look just the same as you did in high school."

"You two went to school together?"

"She didn't tell you?"

Dad said, "We're in love. Weird, huh?"

"You know what? You got me on the wrong day. I've actually seen weirder."

Dad still felt the need to justify his love. "Ellen here's in charge of set-dec for this production. She's got a head on her shoulders."

I needed to change the subject. "How's the shoot going?"

Ellen said, "Actually, not too well. We had to do this scene supposedly set in New Mexico, which is impossible to fake in Vancouver, at least on our budget. So we hosed this whole field and ravine with zinc isocyanine, which gives a nice rusty colour, but I don't think the salmon will be hatching in the nearby feeder stream for a few years to come."

"Isn't she talented?" Dad asked.

"Yes, Dad, she certainly is."

Ellen said, "I have to prep for tomorrow. It's a long day's shoot. The mother ship arrives above the ranch."

Dad said, "That's okay. We've got the dailies to watch." he turned to me. "Come on. Let's go check them out."

The lovebirds kissed goodbye, and I followed Dad to another trailer filled with cables and screens. We arrived at an exquisitely bad moment—flubbed shots; a hair trapped in the gate; a failed mike contact. Men in suits sweated vegetable oil as they watched what was, to even the most uninitiated eye, money flittering away into nothing. Dad asked the director, "Matt, can you—"

"You got axed, Jim."

"Huh?"

"Your line is gone."

"Dad, I think we should leave."

As we walked back to the extras' trailer, Dad kept saying, "It was supposed to have been my speaking part."

"Dad, I'll drive you home."

As I gave him a lift, I wondered if there was a more subjective, non-Einsteinian theory of time that could explain how I was able to cram so much weirdness into one day—Steve; turtles; dead bikers; philandering parents. The day felt like two or three days crammed into one. I wondered, if you're an incredibly famous rich person who does more in one day than I do in a month, does your perception of time's passing go slower or faster than it does for me?

Finally I broke the silence to ask Dad what his line in the movie had been.

"Goddam aliens!" he roared with astonishing anger. "Did a good job, didn't I?"

"Dad, I'm the one who's supposed to be looking for approval from *you.*"

"We're all adults now, and by the way, we're two people in a car, not one, so let's stay in the commuters-only lane."

"But there's no traffic."

"Think big, Ethan. Your head's always locked in a little cupboard, like boxed-up Christmas decorations in the middle of July. You have to open up your mind about stuff . . ."

During this lecture, I realized Dad was doing something to his shoe. "Dad—are you rubbing a vitamin E capsule on your shoe?"

"So what if I am?"

"Why are you doing that?"

"Keeps the leather alive—vital."

"That is so stupid. What are you doing with a bunch of vitamin E capsules, anyway?"

"I found them in the Fraziers' garbage."

The Fraziers live three doors down from my parents.

"You *what*?!"

"I was trying out my new pedometer, and I saw that the Fraziers had thrown out a perfectly good bottle of vitamin E capsules."

"Dad, I can't believe what I'm hearing. You stole vitamin E from the Fraziers' trash to rub onto your *shoe*?"

"No sense it going to waste."

"I guess not, but doesn't Mom's grow-op clearing God-knows-how-much per year render vitamin E theft kind of silly?"

"We have to save all of that money."

"Why?"

"In case you or Greg is in some other country and needs major surgery. Appendicitis can bankrupt you, especially in the States."

"Dad, I could accept Grandma or Grandpa stealing vitamin E capsules—what with their being members of the Greatest Generation and living through the Depression and all. But you?"

"It wasn't theft! Once trash is on the curb, it belongs to everyone."

"Even in my darkest moment, I would never pilfer vitamins from the neighbours' trash can."

"We like ourselves, don't we?"

"Yes, Dad, we do like ourselves."

Painful silence.

More painful silence.

The effort of not discussing Ellen amplified the silence

further. I broke down. "Did they throw out anything else good?"

"An umbrella, a nice black one, with a malacca cane handle and just one of the spokes shot."

"Isn't that something."

We pulled into the driveway. Not twelve hours earlier, I'd dragged Tim the biker into Mom's car.

Suddenly, I felt profoundly tired. I felt like I'd just been tossed into a construction site hole.

I drove home.

• • •

When I arrived in jPod the next morning, I found that my keypad's keys had been rearranged in the following configuration:

1234D67890
QWFRTYUIP
A5SHOLEKJG
ZXCVBNM

Kaitlin also won't acknowledge my presence. *Fascinating* . . .

• • •

The first turtle meeting was scheduled for one, and I hadn't yet given it three brain cells worth of thought. I was in denial over the turtle as a concept. Here we have a genuinely non-lame skateboard game for PlayStation, and they add a *turtle* to it? All morning I hung around the cafeteria, pretending to be busy, but actually playing Tetris with my back against the wall. At noon I went upstairs and was sitting down in my cubicle when suddenly I smelled something.

"The Taint!" I yelled.

John Doe's head popped up. He said, "You're right—'tis the Taint!"

My voice was loud enough to escape jPod's remote grotto and reach the cubicles in the main work area. "The Taint! The Taint!" Heads and bodies appeared as if on cue in a Broadway musical: The Taint? *The Taint!*

A minute later the mob zeroed in on Mike, a coder, who sullenly pulled from a drawer beneath his hard drive the crescent-shaped corpse of a partially eaten Quarter Pounder with Cheese and a scraggly bale of cold, dead fries.

"Mike, I can't believe you brought the Taint into our office."

"It's their french fries. They're the only fast-food place that doesn't put that disgusting batter on their fries. I went home to get a disk, and I saw their drive-thru sign and . . . I was weak."

"Silence! Let the shunning begin!"

Mike knew the rules, and he broke them. And so, for the rest of the day, he was shunned by everybody in the company.

Back in jPod, Bree said, "Maybe McDonald's food is the way it is because Ronald is lonely."

"Lonely? He's asexual."

"That doesn't mean he's not lonely. Maybe he needs a cat."

"I bet he's into water sports."

"No, that'd mess up his makeup."

"I think he's probably bi-curious."

"Bi-curious? How can he be bi-curious? By now he's at least fifty."

"He's from a different era. They didn't discuss certain topics back then."

"Well, then, how does he stay so young-looking?"

"Steroids. Botox. Happy Meals."

"But all those kids' birthday parties must leave him pretty haggard."

"I wonder what he'd be like on a date."

"Well, you couldn't really go to a movie with him, because everybody would recognize him. No privacy. It'd be like dating Spider-man."

"Where do you live if you're Ronald McDonald? He must be loaded—Bel Air? I mean, he can't even go out for a coffee without looking like a flashing red light."

"Maybe he takes off his makeup and wears sweats."

"No, I don't think so. If you're Ronald, then part of the whole metaphysical proposition is that you can never 'go civilian.'"

"I agree. On *The Simpsons,* whenever you see Krusty the Clown, even if he's in a Jacuzzi or as a baby, he's always got his full makeup on."

"I bet Ronald drinks."

"All clowns drink. They need to blot out the ravages of terrifying children for a living. I wonder what you say to your parents: 'Mom, Dad—I want to be a clown. I'm going to Clown School, and you can't stop me.'"

"Can you imagine the annual family Christmas card photocopied mail-out? *Dan broke his arm skiing in February, but six weeks in a splint and he's tickety-boo. Laurie got her accreditation and is now a fully qualified dental hygienist. Mark brought shame upon the family after he signed up for the local community college's Clown Program. He says the program will put him into the clown fast track, but he's now dead to us.*"

"I bet Ronald is home as we speak—it's his day off. He's in his bathrobe and staring out the den window at his immaculately maintained front garden. He wonders if it was all worth it—the fame, the money, the fries—and then he has this moment when he realizes that this is all he'll ever be. It shocks him—the purity of the emotion. He has to sit down in an armchair. He reaches over to the bookshelf and, from between a row of comic books, he removes a bottle of Scotch."

"And just then, the Hamburglar walks in wearing a pink nightie."

"We need to find him a mate."

"Let's all write to Ronald to explain why each of us is his ideal mate."

"Who chooses the winner?"

"We'll vote." I went first.

• • •

Hi Ronald,

You may or may not remember me. I'm Ethan—you gave away balloons at my seventh birthday party, and my mother says you were able to get the orange drink machine working again with just a paperclip and the wits God gave you.

Ronald, I hear you're looking for a mate. I may not be the best candidate, as I'm straight and, well, too much makeup is always a bit of a turnoff. Maybe you're straight, too. Maybe we're just two lost souls trying to make a go of it in this great big nutty world.

Be all of this as it may, I'm supposed to plead my case. I am nearing thirty, and I make $41,500 a year (Canadian) as a programmer, *but* they've dangled this huge carrot in front of me, telling me that I can become an assistant production assistant if I learn to integrate programming skills with art skills plus skills in managing people. The irony is, assistant production assistants make way less, even though they're higher up the food chain. In any event, this is all to say that I have good prospects as a provider.

Ronald, do you play computer games? I know that the cooking of your french fries is regulated by a special deep-frying computer run by proprietary McDonald's software that beeps once the fries are golden yellow. So I think maybe you're more computer savvy than people give you credit for.

I'm single at the moment, but have had two reasonably longish relationships. Both ended because they simply weren't The One, which is such a corny notion. It always leaves you with a niggling unease that the relationship you're in is merely love's calorie-reduced version. It also would have helped if they cared about my work. It's not like I'm married to my job, but a little "Honey, how was your day?" goes a long way. Speaking of work and relationships, I'm currently more attracted than I acknowledge to Kaitlin, who's new to jPod. She's a programmer and she's . . . just nice to look at. But wait, I'm supposed to be wooing *you.* What else can I add that would make you desire me? Oh, I know—I like both helium and balloons. What a blast it would be to mate with someone who has the entire global helium cartel in his big yellow pockets.

That's about as gay as it gets, Ronald.

Pick me! Pick me!

Ethan

• • •

Naughty Ronald, you mayonnaise-guzzling bun pig . . .

It must be hard to live at the top, what with Wendy and Burger King always waiting to knife you in the back. I say to you, smother them in melted cheese while they pray uselessly to their cardiac gods!

I am Bree, and when I was sixteen I worked in a McDonald's in Richmond, BC (which was, BTW, the first non-US McDonald's ever). I was fired because I was never meant to be working in the service industry, which is an elliptical way of saying I dated all the guys on the staff at once, thus triggering a mass-quitting saga. That, and I also reconfigured the french-fry computer to make a ringing doorbell sound instead of beeping, which is how I turned on to technology.

Here's a confession: everyone thinks I sleep with anything with three legs, but the fact is, I don't do it that much, and when I do, it's only to confirm that I don't like it that much—which means I'm maybe into gals instead of guys. That's my challenge for the next year. Are you into gals who like gals? To be honest, I look at your public persona and say, "Okay, Bree, this guy's into Smurfs or something, not women." Or am I wrong? I mean, Ronald, let's face it—what's with you? How do clowns replicate? Do you have parents? A family? Do you believe in God or a political party? After you've taped your TV commercials, do you go back to your toadstool and kick back a box of wine? Part of me is happy to think of you as a mere cartoon, but the more genuine Bree says there has to be something more primal and demanding and blood-and-guts at the centre of it all.

I work in a cubicle farm called jPod with a small handful of geeks. It's called jPod because of a computer glitch that put six people whose last names start with the letter J in the space that was supposed to have been a rock climbing wall, but which got cancelled because it was too twentieth century. Once you're in jPod, there's no escaping. I tried for months, and simply gave up. Kaitlin's new here. She'll try hard to get out for a while, and then she'll simply accept her fate and try to get on with life as best she can.

Oof.

I'm tired and a little bit lonely. What a no-hope statement from a twenty-six-year-old woman. I suppose next it's ten cats and my head in the oven.

Call me.

Your little tease,

X

Bree

• • •

Dear Ronald McDonald,

I'm Mark. I can't believe I'm actually writing this letter, but I talked to this guy downstairs in HR, and he says it's part of the lifestyle here, and I should take part, since it can't hurt me and will help me bond with the others. I'm supposed to ask you (oh God, this is stupid) to choose me over the others to be your mate. And I've been thinking about it, but it's maybe not a good idea we get together, since you seem to kill everything you touch. In all your old commercials, you were romping through french-fry patches with your fellow spokesmascots, but you think I haven't noticed that the french-fry characters vanished a decade ago? Or that nobody's seen that website with JPEGs of the Evil Grimace weighing nine hundred pounds, wearing a diaper and living in a failing mobile home community north of the Mexico-Arizona border? What about Mayor McCheese, unrecognizably bearded and detoxing from pickles in a Las Vegas homeless shelter? Every day, when he prowls the city's alleys, crows and jackdaws bite away at his bun face. How could you allow these creatures to just vanish like that? Don't tell me that it wasn't your decision to make, because I *know* you have clout with the people there. I once saw a video of you golfing with Ray Kroc, so don't go pulling the "No Clout" stunt with me. Maybe you were jealous of those characters sharing your limelight, but I don't think so.

As I'm supposed to be winning your matehood here, I ought to be more cheerful. Okay, here's something: I think it was really brave of you to invest so heavily in purple restaurant furniture in the 1970s. You go, clown! Sex would be a problem because, sorry, I'm not into you. Maybe it's a clown issue. Maybe it's me never knowing whose party you've been attending. How about if I offer to be your friend instead?

Mark

• • •

Hi Ronald.

I'm John Doe, and I think I could help change your life in good ways. I come from a freaky upbringing myself, so I know how it must feel to always be the different one. The thing is, I was stuck being in the family I was in, but what about you? How does it work with clowns—are you born with your face made up? Did you get your mother's red nose and your father's Raggedy Ann hairdo? Is clowning something that is thrust on you at birth? Do other clowns hate you because of your fame and success? Do you have friends?

Let me be your friend. I'll bring over a loofah and a bottle of Noxzema, and we'll take off your paint. If it turns out that you're really Liv Tyler, we can even make it, too.

But otherwise, the sex thing? Look, it's not like I have trouble with same-sex relationships—my mother is the biggest raging dyke on the planet, and I love her to death. When I was growing up, she made this big stink about how I had to call her a dyke, and nothing else—even in high school—and because of it I was always being sent home. She really liked that, though, because she relished the fights she had with school staff. It was only after I escaped from home that I discovered, thanks to the miracle of satellite TV, that the real mother I always wanted was, in fact, Lindsay Wagner of *The Bionic Woman*—not as she appeared in her TV series, but rather as she appears in car commercials two decades later: calm and confident; the sort of mother who'd buy you Count Chocula *without even being asked to do so.*

No, I got the scary, crazed dyke mama, *plus*—over the course of seventeen years at home—Joan, Nancy, elan (all lower case), Georgia and Sunn, more often than not overlapping.

So, if there's something you want to tell me, I'm the one with ears. Have you considered gender reassignment procedures? You have to take hormones for years, and then they gradually "regenderize" you. Georgia was regendered.

As for me, I want to look as average as possible. I'm difficult to locate in a crowd because I wear only khakis and a solid-colour buttoned shirt that, scanned in Photoshop and desaturated, lies between twenty-five and thirty percent on the grey scale. I keep myself nine pounds overweight and drive a white Taurus, which everyone says looks like a rental car, which makes me happy. I'd never eaten any of your narrow but tasty range of burger-type products until I was seventeen, in the McD's outlet on the other side of town. I ordered a cheeseburger—it was also my first non-vegetarian experience—and it was *wonderful.* I didn't even puke. Thanks for turning me on to cow.

It was actually my love of cow that made me leave home. I kept tasting it in my dreams. My mother had some weird voodoo dream scanner, and she could tell I was being non-vegetarian even while I slept, and come morning it was wheat germ and stern lectures on slaughterhouse procedures. Did you know that a cow enters a meat-processing facility at the top of a seven-storey building and that, as it gets more and more processed, it goes down the building floor by floor? Not only that, but there's a thing in abattoirs called the Chute. Every time they find a diseased lung or something, it goes into one of a succession of seven funnels in the building's centre. By the time you're on the first floor, the Chute is filled with this monsoon of inedible cow remnants, which are then blenderized into pet food smoothies. I mention this because, here at work, we call our in-house memo system the Chute. So, you see, Ronald, even when you don't think you're giving to society as a whole, you continue to do so—when you cause us to reformulate our personal relationships to carnivorism and the Chain of Meat—a distant cousin of the food chain.

BTW, what's the deal with these salads you're selling now? It kind of rubs me the wrong way. You're about cow, dammit, not leaf. Anyway, send me an email or even phone me. It's area code 604, and the number itself is a seven-digit prime which, when squared, is two digits short of being a factorial. Are you up to that challenge? Let me help *you* become the Power Clown you *know* you can be.

John Doe

• • •

Just before the turtle meeting, I went on eBay and bought a Benelux keyboard. Belgian keyboards are totally from hell. For whatever reason, they scramble the character keys even more randomly than a QWERTY keyboard. Thanks to UPS, it ought to be here the day after tomorrow, and Kaitlin shall meet her match. God, I love the twenty-first century.

I just heard her on the phone with someone in HR, trying to get out of jPod. Good luck.

"What do you mean it's not possible?"

[HR staffer]

"Do you mean not possible now, or not possible *ever*?"

[HR staffer]

"I'm a super-experienced character animator, and I've worked at two other big companies, and none of them would ever have stuck me in this chunk of Siberia with a clump of whacked-out freaks."

[HR staffer]

"Okay, that was harsh, but look at my position."

[HR staffer]

"Call Allan Rothstein. He hired me. There's no way he'd have hired me and then stuck me in jPod."

[HR staffer]

"I know Allan Rothstein is busy, but he wasn't too busy to hire me, so I'm sure you can speak to him and clear this up."

[HR staffer]

"When *does* he get back from the Orlando studio?"

[HR staffer]

"Who else can I speak with?"

[HR staffer]

"They can't *all* be in Orlando. There's a meeting here soon, and *some* of them have to be here for that."

[HR staffer]

"You don't understand. The people in this place you stuck me in perform tasks completely unrelated to mine. I'm a character animator; I have to be with my team."

[HR staffer]

"Oh. How did people ever get out of jPod in the past, then?"

[HR staffer]

"They don't?"

[HR staffer]

"What do you mean, just be quiet and try to make peace with it?"

[HR staffer]

"My last name actually begins with the letter B. I'm Kaitlin Boyd."

[HR staffer]

"Boyd is my stepfather's name. Well, yes, on official forms, it's Joyce."

[HR staffer]

Kaitlin hangs up.

[Sound of phone keypad buttons being pushed.]

"Hello, Allan? It's Kaitlin Joyce calling. Sorry to call your cell number when you're away. But your cell number was on your card, and . . ."

[Allan Rothstein]

"I'm going into a meeting soon, myself, sir."

[Allan Rothstein]

"I'll be quick, then. Your HR people put me in a place called jPod. Can you please call them and have me moved to the team's character-animating pod so that . . ."

[Allan Rothstein]

"What was that noise you just made?"

[Allan Rothstein]

"No. You distinctly said something like, *uh-oh*."

[Allan Rothstein]

"I know you're busy, Allan, and, like you, I want to get to work, but I . . ."

[Allan Rothstein]

"When are you back, then?"

[Allan Rothstein]

"Okay. I'm sorry to have called you on a semi-holiday."

[Allan Rothstein]

"I'll make the best of the situation until then."

[Allan Rothstein]

"Goodbye."

Kaitlin hangs up.

• • •

Ronald,

This is Casper Jesperson, a.k.a. the Cancer Cowboy, and I have to ask you, mister, what do you think happens to you after you die? Which is a way of asking, do you believe in something specific, or a warm cosmic glow, followed by the total extinction of your being? Do you go to church? It's hard to imagine you there, no offence, and if you went, you'd probably be thinking about life and death in the Clown Universe, that great balloon-twist in the sky.

I come from a farm community, and when I was maybe seven I went to a party at a friend's place. There was a clown there, juggling navel oranges, and while he was doing it, I went out and looked inside his car by the dog kennel, and there was McDonald's trash all over the floor, front and back, and fifty aluminum beer can empties on the floor of the passenger seat. On the dashboard was a Tom Clancy novel (that's how I turned on to him) with all of the yellow ink sun-faded out of the cover (but not the cyan or magenta), as well as the wet, pulpy stump of a cheap and recently extinguished stogie. There was other crap, too—pizza flyers, a copy of *Oui* magazine opened to a woman sitting spread-eagled, wearing a bandolier of machine gun bullets. It's kind of haunted me my whole life, that car.

So imagine you've just finished scaring kids at a birthday party—you're still in your clown makeup and you get in your car, and maybe it doesn't start right away, so you say *fuck fuck fuck* a few times, which is like a magic phrase that starts it. You pull out of the driveway in reverse, way too quickly, and once you're on the main road you floor it because you have to get to your favourite cocktail lounge to put your birthday party money on a greyhound race. But when you get there, the bar is closed because some pipes burst, and suddenly you can't place your bet, which gives you Clown Rage. You need a drink, but you're a clown, and you can't go into just any bar. Nonetheless, a bet is a bet, so you decide to drive over to the next town and put your money down there. In between the two towns, you stop the car, get out and go to the trunk, where you get your de-clowning makeup remover. Your stomach lurches because you're hungover, and you haven't eaten in a day, and there you are, scraping off the white guck with nothing around you but the sound of the wind whistling over the alfalfa stubble, and maybe a crow on a fence that's curious as to whether your paper towel is edible.

You hear a car approaching, but you pretend you're too busy to look because, from experience, you've learned that making eye contact with adults when you're in clown drag is risky. So your head is in the trunk, and you're scraping away, when without you even knowing what it is, a baseball bat held by a sixteen-year-old kid on meth clubs you on the head and you die. Where do you go from there?

Yours from Planet Earth,

The Cancer Cowboy

• • •

When Mark asked Kaitlin where her letter to Ronald was, she said, "Don't you people have anything better to do with your lives?"

I poked my head up and said, "I can think of no better thing to do."

She said, "Here's what I think. Mark and *you*"—she almost spat out my name—"*Ethan,* are the same person. To read your letters, there's no difference between you, no shred of individuality." (**NOTE:** I deleted the passage on Kaitlin from my publicly released letter.)

"Well, Kaitlin, if you're such an individual," I shot back, "put your words where your mouth is."

"What a witty comeback. Even John Doe's letter had more edge than yours."

John Doe's head popped up: "Then I have failed. I strive for averageness in everything I do."

"I have an idea," Bree offered. "If Ethan and Mark are so similar, we might as well arbitrarily assign them distinct personality traits. I know—Mark, from here on, you're to be called 'Evil Mark.'"

"Why do I have to be the evil one?"

"Because your email address is so dull—bmarkjackson@earthlink.com? We really have to zap your brain with defibrillator paddles to get you up and running."

"If I'm evil, then what's Ethan?"

"Ethan is good."

"This is so 'Spy vs. Spy' arbitrary."

"Which spy did you vote for?"

"The black one."

"There you go. Evil. You are pure evil."

"Just because I didn't root for the white one?"

"It's more complex than that."

Chorus: "Mark is evil! Mark is evil!"

Kaitlin said, "This is so stupid."

I said, "Kaitlin, before you go name-calling, pony up. Send us all a letter to Ronald that says 'Kaitlin,' and only Kaitlin."

"If it gets you off my back, I'll do it."

• • •

It's weird, but every time I visit the Drudge Report website, I'm the fifty-millionth person to visit it, so there must be a software error on their part, because how could they possibly have more than one fifty-millionth visitor? And I can't wait to see what my prize will be.

• • •

Dirk, who's a friend of mine from Hewlett-Packard, sent me photos from his trip to Nagoya, using the Kodak EasyShare photo display system. Using its interface, I felt like I was time-travelling to 1999. I half expected a pop-up window to tell me to submit my mailing address so that they could snail-mail me a 56K floppy. And *then* I got to thinking about it . . . Kodak still *exists*? Even seeing its name makes me feel like I'm at a garage sale. I bet they stopped hiring young people in 1997.

• • •

While Kaitlin was writing her letter, my phone rang. "Your father is acting weird around me," Mom said. "Did you tell him about Tim?"

"Of course not."

"Why is he acting so strangely, then?"

"Maybe *you're* the one acting weird, and he's just feeding it back to you."

"I just drove up the hill to make sure Tim's body was still covered up."

"And . . . ?"

"They've already backfilled the area."

"That's a relief."

"I miss him."

"Mom, not here, not now."

"Can I come see you?"

"At *work*?"

"Why are you so surprised?"

"Mom, you never even came to elementary school or high school . . ."

"I always thought you should have a space in the world that was entirely your own."

"I always thought you didn't care."

"Nonsense. What time should I come visit?"

"You can't. I have meetings."

"Meetings? Who are you—Darren Stevens? I'll pop by. It'll be fun."

"Mom—"

She hung up.

• • •

Dad phoned a minute later, his voice kind of distant and calling-from-a-tin-can-y.

"Dad, you sound all funny."

"I'm dying my eyebrows black, so I have to hold the receiver away from me."

"Why?"

"I'm auditioning again."

"What movie this time?"

"Something about a radioactive teddy bear that saves Halloween."

"How do black eyebrows fit in?"

"If I get the part, I get to be a father taking his kid trick-or-treating dressed as Abraham Lincoln."

"So what's up?"

"Your mother is acting weird."

"Maybe *you're* the one acting weird, and she's just feeding it back to you."

"You're not going to mention Ellen, are you?"

"No."

"She's hot, isn't she? Ellen, that is."

"Dad! Do not talk like that to me. She was too young for *me* to dance with at the Z95 noon-hour Beat Breaks in high school."

"Discussing women makes you feel weird?"

"Discussing women with my father? Yes. It does. Dad, is there anything else? I've got this meeting . . ."

"Gee. You have a job and I don't."

"Dad, let's not go there again."

"Just kidding. You couldn't get me back into an office chair for a million bucks. I should have been an actor all along."

"Dad, I really have to go."

"*Hasta luego,* cubicle boy."

• • •

Ronald Darling,

I've just been transferred into a new game development pod, which is truly the pod of the corn. Part of their tribal lore is that I have to write you this degrading letter, which is so stupid, because how many times have you and I already had online sex—three hundred? They don't even think you're real, which pisses me off no end. And I know if I try to discuss our forbidden love, we'll both be mocked and shunned.

All I want to be is in a living room with the lights on low, and the battery in my laptop hot and aroused, with you and me talking smutty across the ether. Tonight I'm yours, and yours always. But Ronald, darling, next time don't let the Hamburglar into the dialogue box. He totally kills the mood. Three-ways are for tramps.

Your McSlut,

Kaitlin

Closed course
Professional driver

High-Speed CMOS Logic

Introduction to Algorithms

VHDL Made Easy!

$M_1, M_2, M_3 \ldots \infty$

SANFORD No. 81803

EXPO

WHITEBOARD CLEANER

8 fl. oz. (237 mL)

bezierkurv
chunkylover53
darksideofaplanet

~~Bwoonhilda~~
Bwoonhilde

Kill the wabbit

• A 1-terabyte disk for
(get this) only US$699.00!

• • •

Meeting time:

Steve, the guy who turned Toblerone around in two years, tries to be one of the people. He's always hanging around with the cool crowd on a project, and he socializes with them off-hours, so he can say, "Hey, I'm hands-on in the trenches with my team!" of which there are now fifty-six members. As production speeds up, dozens more will pile on as senior management weighs in with all kinds of random, last-minute features. Steve is the only suit in the room and, thanks to Bree's mastery of Google, all of us know it's a $2,200 suit.

"*Be* the turtle!" Steve said.

Nervous titters.

"*Think* like a turtle."

Nervous titters.

"My friends, you *are* the turtle."

Fake contemplative silence peppered with ironic gasps.

"You, over there—" Steve pointed to a world-object texture map artist named Marty Choy, who I worked with two games ago. "When you think turtle, what do you think of?"

Silence. Marty couldn't believe that he, of all people in the room, had been chosen. "Reptile . . ." he said.

"Exactly!"

"Really?"

"Yes, really. Now, you, over there—" Steve pointed to a guy who I think was in either an AI-SE or a Tools SE on hockey titles. "When you think of turtles, what do you think of?"

"Konami's arcade and console games based on the Teenage Mutant Ninja Turtles franchise?"

Steve looked gratified, but then a serious expression came over his face. We were all hoping that the random selection of audience members was over.

"Everybody, I must say before we go any further, that the Teenage Mutant Ninja Turtles characters®, including Raphael®, Michelangelo®, Leonardo®, Donatello®, and April O'Neil® are all registered trademarks of Mirage Studios, and anything we say or do is in no way based on or disparaging of this fine intellectual property."

Dead silence.

"Come on, team—let's talk turtle here. I can't take unless you give."

Someone I couldn't see on the other side of the room volunteered, "Turtle shells don't require many polygons to render. So it won't slow gameplay much."

Another voice said, "That's like Keanu Reeves's black dress/cloak thingy in *The Matrix*."

A different voice yet: "Really?"

"Computers were way slower back then. They used the black cloak to shorten render times."

"Let's get back on track," Steve said.

Kaitlin, going for broke, asked, "Steve, we're at milestone five, and you want to dump a charismatic turtle into an action-sports game? How can you wreck a third-person skateboard game like this? Who's going to play it, Teletubbies?"

Then everyone began to cluster-dump on the turtle idea. Steve remained serene through it all, then held up his hand for silence. "This is all well and good. I encourage vigorous debate and the exchange of ideas—who wouldn't? It's what democracy is based on. I like the fact that all of you are so vocal here this afternoon. But the point of this meeting is that my son Carter loves the turtle character in SimQuest4, and if Carter likes turtles, every kid in the world is going to like turtles. So the fact is, a charismatic turtle character is going to be in the game—that's been decided at the upper levels—so today we take the first steps as a group to flesh out our turtle."

Silence.

"On a constructive front, the game has also been renamed BoardX."

Evil Mark turned purple and shot up his hand. "Why?"

"X says to the world, hip and daring—punk and funk. It tells the world we're not just some average game."

Just then there was a gentle knock on the door. What sort of chowderhead would risk management's ire by intruding in the middle of a grok? The door opened, and in walked Mom.

"Can I help you?" Steve's voice was pleasant.

"Why, yes, I'm looking for my son, Ethan." She spotted me. "Oh hi, dear."

"Mom—?"

Everybody began chanting *EthanEthanEthan* and *Mama's Boy*. I'd have been legally entitled to have a stroke at that point, but I figured, high school was over a decade ago. I stood up and went over to her. How did she get through security? Why wasn't she accompanied by a guard, or wearing a laminated security pass?

Steve said, "Is everything okay, Mrs.—"

"Jarlewski. Carol Jarlewski. Yes, and thank you for asking. I was at home this morning, and I realized that I don't really know much about where Ethan works or what he does. I thought I'd see for myself. Sorry for interrupting your meeting . . ."

"Steve. Steve Lefkowitz."

They shook hands. Mom showed not a twinge of uneasiness at standing before a group of fifty-six geeks. "My! Look at all of you clever young people. What are you doing today?"

Everybody giggled, and Steve, a master of timing, said, "Carol Jarlewski, what do you think of when you think of turtles?"

"Turtles? Well, I think that turtles have to be intelligent creatures, because in evolutionary terms they go back farther than just about every other animal. They're good at surviving. And they're cute, too. Sort of cheeky. My sister and I found one in the pond back when we were kids, and it winked at me. Saucy little things."

Steve looked at all of us. "And you thought turtles weren't hip."

This was now out of my hands—not that it was ever in them.

"Everybody, let's have Carol sit in on the meeting," Steve announced. "Her outsider perspective might add something valuable to our quest." People actually clapped.

And thus Mom took her seat near Steve's podium and spent the next two hours beaming at me and offering the occasional idea, some of which were good. "Those skateboard monsters are always spray-painting everything, including the Edgemont Village SuperValu's walls, and in my opinion they all deserve a few months in jail. But why not make your turtle's shell a surface on which players spray-paint clues? The turtle can't see what's on his back, so one of his goals is to locate reflective surfaces throughout the game, while his competition is trying to wreck those surfaces."

John Doe also lobbed out an idea that stuck. He suggested

that a universally appreciated buddy-type personality was that of Jeff Probst—"charismatic host of TV's still-sizzling long-running reality show *Survivor*." I'm not sure if John Doe was kidding, but everybody clapped, and suddenly Steve said, "Hey—this sounds like an idea with legs."

At the end, when I asked Mom if she wanted me to take her on a tour, she said, "That's okay, Ethan. Young Steven here is taking me."

Steve didn't even look at me. His eyes were all on Mom.

I schlumped my way back to the pod.

• • •

Random note from today's meeting:

Fresh New Lucky Charms Marshmallow Shapes . . .

. . . Masonic emblems
. . . witch-dunking stools
. . . stepmothers
. . . PayPal logos
. . . anal beads.

God is an Xkb state indicator

God is a Window Maker docked application

God is a multi-platform Z80 cross-assembler

God is a lightweight XML encoding library for Java

God is a programmatic API written in C++

God is Oracle's OCI8 and OCI9 APIs

God is a configuration backup utility

God is Web-based groupware and collaboration software

God is a graphical editor for drawing finite state machines

• • •

Kaitlin was on the phone again, trying to extract herself from jPod. Cowboy was over by a ventilation unit, having a smoke. One of jPod's quirks is an air intake duct in front of which you can puff away on anything. Hell, you could let off an Exocet missile, and it'd suck everything up and away in a jiffy.

"If that had been my mother who showed up today, she'd have made a big deal of telling people she doesn't shave her armpits," said John Doe.

Bree said, "If that was my mother up there, she'd be asking every guy in the place what his salary was, and what his career prospects were."

Evil Mark said, "If that was my mother up there, she'd be drunk."

Kaitlin slammed down the phone in disgust. She looked over at us and put her face down on her desk.

As we'd all gone through the same responses when we were put into jPod, we felt sorry for Kaitlin. She needed a bit of quiet time.

Respecting her need, we entered work mode. The mood grew nice and quiet as we checked to see what was falling down the Chute. After maybe fifteen minutes, Cowboy piped up, "You know, I'm so sick of cigarette smoking's negative image problems."

There was a chorus of jPod agreement.

He continued, "I have a suggestion. Let's take a minute-long break and blithely pimp for the tobacco industry."

"Okay," Bree said. "But first I could sure use the smooth clear taste of a Marlboro Light."

"Me? I prefer Virginia tobacco. *Mmm*—nothing like a Rothmans to make the afternoon sweeter."

"But you know," said Mark, "I think there's nothing like menthol for a fresh smoking experience."

I asked, "What's the deal with menthol cigarettes? What sort of person smokes regular cigarettes for years and then suddenly says, *Gee, this isn't satisfying enough. I need something more from my tobacco*?"

Bree said, "My mother quit smoking in the 1980s, and then three months later they test-marketed lemon-flavoured cigarettes and she couldn't resist. She's two packs a day now."

I added that if Big Tobacco came up with orange-flavoured cigarettes, I'd probably start smoking.

Bree said, "Chocolate for me."

"I'd like roast beef–flavoured smokes," said John. "Nothing like a touch of cow to perk up a dragging day."

Evil Mark said, "Me, I find that the toasted tobacco flavour of a 100-millimetre-long More helps me to think better."

Bree asked, "More? Are those the skinny brown cigarettes?"

"Yup."

Cowboy said, "Me? I'd like to try one of those lady's cigarettes."

Bree added, "What kind of woman would look at a cigarette and say, *Finally, someone out there is addressing my feminine tobacco needs*?"

"Actually, I did just that last week."

"Cowboy, you're a guy."

"But I wanted to see, you know, what a woman's cigarette might be like."

"How did it taste, then?"

"It made me feel, you know . . . *fresh*."

• • •

As I walked past Evil Mark's cubicle, he moved quickly to get something off his screen.

"Porn?"

"Ha ha. Yeah. Uh. Don't tell anyone."

"That wasn't porn you were looking at. It was something else."

"Ethan, it's none of your business."

"Porn degrades everybody, Mark."

Evil Mark snorted.

"Okay, I was just trying to PC you into coughing up the truth. So what was it you were looking at?"

"Nothing."

"If it was nothing, you wouldn't be overreacting like this."

"I'm not overreacting."

Behind his cubicle wall, John Doe said, "I think he's overreacting."

"Evil Mark, are you into terrorism or something? Stock scams, maybe? Industrial espionage—passing along confidential in-house documents?"

"Leave me alone, okay?"

"Evil Mark, we're on to you now. We *know* you're up to something."

John Doe added, "We will crush you like a bug when we find out what."

"It was nothing! Just go and feed yourselves on a wide array of products containing high-fructose corn sugar. *Zheesh.*"

"That wasn't funny, Evil Mark. It sounded fake and hollow. You're terrible at being ironic, and you've been rehearsing that line, haven't you?"

"I am *not* evil."

"People don't get nicknames for nothing, Mark."

Mark was beginning to lose it for real. "Bree arbitrarily chose 'evil' out of nowhere."

"Was it really so arbitrary, Mark?" Bree asked.

"You people are nuts."

"Let's look at the facts: a) boring email name; b) chose the black spy over the white spy in 'Spy vs. Spy'; c) could easily have confessed to having porn on his monitor, but instead chose to pretend it was nothing, *meaning,* it wasn't porn, but something too shameful to let his compassionate pod members in on."

Kaitlin put her head above her wall. "You people are totally fucking crazy. How can you live like this?"

"Like *what,* Kaitlin?" I asked.

"Like people damned forever to a shady armpit of an entertainment empire too cold and indifferent to even try to rescue people from a clerical spreadsheet error that assigns employee seating."

This stopped everything dead.

"Kaitlin"— and you have to remember, this was me, someone with an embryonic crush on her—"I don't think you quite understand the ramifications of being in jPod."

"What's with this whacko jPod shit?"

From all of us: "Ooooooohhhhhhh . . ."

"She really doesn't get it, does she?"

"Poor girl."

"She still thinks there's hope."

"Just tell me this: How did I end up here, huh?" Kaitlin asked. "Because if I'm here, it means somebody else had to leave."

She'd crossed the line. "We can't talk about that," I said.

"What do you mean, you can't talk about that?"

I headed to the snack machines as the others scampered back to their chairs.

"Augh!" Kaitlin screamed, jumping up onto her desktop, sending her Aeron chair into her hard drive, giving it a good bang. "Stop right now, all you assholes, and tell me what's going on here!"

Bree said, "This is so *Pulp Fiction.*"

Cowboy said, "They didn't tell you, huh?"

"No! As far as I can see, nobody tells anyone about anything in this place."

"Well, you're right about that."

Silence.

Kaitlin said, "What? Tell me something. *Anything*!"

"It was helium."

"Excuse me?"

"It was helium. Marc Jacobsen used to have your cubicle."

"You've lost me here."

This was going to be difficult. I said, "Marc was a really nice guy. He was actually a world builder for Xbox games."

"What does he or helium have to do with anything?"

Even Evil Mark had been here long enough to know that this was delicate.

"This isn't the best time and place to be telling you this," I said.

"Telling me WHAT?"

Bree stepped in. "Marc was really sweet, and totally into the games, and really wanted to make people's lives better. And he was the only staffer who was never guilted into coming in on weekends during crunch times, so that shows you how good he was, and how much clout he had."

"Helium? Everybody—*helium*?"

I took over. "Marc was at his sister's birthday party, and he was in charge of party tricks, and so he rented a helium canister from a novelty supply company. He was at the party making twisted balloon animals when he decided to suck back some helium so he could speak in a Donald Duck Munchkin voice."

"*And*?"

"So there were maybe a dozen kids there—eight-year-olds—really easy to entertain. He put his lips onto the helium canister's nozzle and sucked in about a gallon of helium . . ."

"And?"

Silence.

"And?"

"Let Google help us here," said John Doe. "'If the concentration of oxygen falls below eighteen percent in the body, symptoms and signs of asphyxia occur. Helium gas can entirely displace available oxygen. If this continues for even a few seconds, asphyxia and death can occur.' Sure, we all want to sound like Donald Duck—but is it worth the price?"

Kaitlin said, "Uh-oh."

"Exactly. In front of all these kids, Marc keels over, turns blue and dies."

"Oh God. When did this happen?"

"A few months ago."

"And his desk has been empty all this time?"

"That's life. One moment you're mimicking Munchkins, the next, birthday cake is digging its way into your nostrils."

Kaitlin said, "What about Evil Mark? He arrived here only a little while before me. Why didn't he get this Marc guy's old cubicle?"

"Evil Mark? They just came in here one day and installed another cubicle, and then he showed up."

The look on Kaitlin's face said it all. For the first time, it was sinking in that jPod was real, and that she was a part of it, and that there was no escaping her destiny. "I think I'll just sit down now and see what's coming down the Chute," she said.

And with that, jPod fell silent.

Afrikaans
Albanian
Amharic
Arabic
Azerbaijani
Basque
Belarusian
Bengali
Bihari
Bjork
Borg
Bosnian
Braille
Breton
Bulgarian
Canadian
Catalan (lisping)
Catalan (no lisping)
Chinese
Cockney
Coleslaw
Croatian
Czech
Danish
Danish (cherry)
Dutch
Elmer Fudd
English (helium)
Esperanto
Estonian
Faroese
Finnish
Fortran
French
French Canadian
Frisian
Galician
Georgian
Greek
Grover
Gujarati
Gym mat
Hebrew
Hindi
Hungarian
Icelandic
Ikea
Indonesian
Interlingua
Irish
Italian
Japanese

Jif
Klingon
Korean
Kyrgyz
Latin
Latvian
Lion King
Lithuanian
Long Island
Lowly Worm
Macaroni
Macedonian
Malay
Maltese
Maltese (on novocaine)
Massachusetts
Müslix
Nepali
Noodle
Norwegian
Nyorsk
Occitan
Ontario
Oriya
Pebbles (Flintstone)
Persian
Pig Latin
Pig Latin (stoned)
Pitcairn
Polish
Portuguese (Brazil)
Portugese (Portugal)
Punjabi
Rastafarian
Romanian
Rotarian
Russian
Sailor Moon
Scooby-Doo
Serbian
Serbo-Croatian
Shoe
Shrink wrap
Sinhalese
Slovak
Slovenian
Snoopy
Spanish
Spice rack
Stepford
Swahili
Swedish

Tagalog
Tamil
Tang
Telugu
Texan
Thai
Tlön
Toast
Turkish
Turkmen
Twizzlers
Ukrainian
Urdu
Uzbek
Vanna White
Vietnamese
Welsh
Welsh rarebit
Xbox
Xena
Xhosa
Yabba Dabba Doo
Yiddish
Zulu

• • •

The rest of the afternoon passed without incident, mostly with me going around the building, massaging egos and putting out fires. If I'm ever going to become an assistant production assistant, then this is the way forward.

I got back to jPod around seven, and my message light was blinking, so it had to be Mom or Dad. Dad said, "Ethan, it's five to seven. Call me the moment you get this."

I called him.

"Thank frigging God," Dad said. "Get over here."

"What's going on?"

"Just come, right now."

"Did Mom find out about . . . ?"

"No. Just get over here."

And so I drove to the house. Dad's car was in the carport, and there was a small silver Suzuki Sidekick parked out front, which I assumed belonged to Ellen, as every single woman I've ever met who does set-dec work in film drives one of these things or something similar. I parked behind it, only to see Ellen walk across the lawn towards the creek, naked. Dad opened the door.

"Ethan—help me grab her."

"I'm not touching her, Dad."

"She's high as ten kites."

"It doesn't matter."

Before she fell into the creek and cracked her skull, Dad headed across the grass and lifted her up like a set of heavy golf clubs. "Upsy-daisy." Ellen kept moving her limbs as if she was still walking, which was more than slightly disturbing. He carried her in the front door, yelling over his shoulder, "She went downstairs and took the biggest bud off The Dude. Smoked the whole frigging thing."

"Oh shit. How are you going to explain that to Mom?" Ellen had mutilated Mom's favourite and oldest plant, called The Dude, even though it's a female.

"You tell me. I'm screwed." I followed him down the hall to Greg's old room.

"Ellen and I stopped by to get my Abraham Lincoln hat for my audition, which was set for six o'clock. I gave her a tour of the basement, and then the phone rang, and by the time I got back downstairs—*pow!*—she's baked, and there goes my Abe Lincoln role, stupid bitch. So I laid her down on your brother's bed so I could figure out what to do next, which was when I called you. Next thing, I look out the front window, and she's off sleepwalking towards the Brodies' breakfast nook." Dad was slipping a T-shirt and a pair of sweat bottoms onto Ellen, who was moaning. "Where's your mother?" asked Dad.

"No idea. She came out to visit me at work today."

"She *what*?"

"Exactly. She said she wanted to see where I work."

"Why would she do *that*?"

Just then we heard Mom's car pull into the carport. Dad looked at me. "Ellen's your new girlfriend. End of story." We hightailed it to the kitchen.

From the back door, I heard, "Ethan? Is that you?"

She came into the kitchen. "Oh hi, dear. Didn't get enough of me at work today, huh?"

"I just thought I'd come see how you guys are doing."

Both of them were squinting at me, wondering if I was about to blow their secrets. I glanced at Dad. "I also have a new girlfriend, and I thought I'd introduce her to you."

"A new girlfriend? Finally—the possibility of grandchildren."

"I also have bad news for you, Mom."

". . . *Oh*?" At this point, bad news could mean many things. "Like what?"

"I showed Ellen your business downstairs, and she picked a bud off The Dude."

"She *what*?"

"It happened before I could say anyth—"

"Ethan, you *know* how I feel about The Dude. And I was trying to get a nice shape back to her after all the clones I made this season." She sat down heavily in a kitchen chair.

Dad said, "Kids. All they do is wreck stuff."

"Where *is* your new girlfriend, dear?"

"She's in Greg's old bedroom."

"Why?"

"She's kind of baked."

"So let me guess, then—she smoked the bud?"

"Kinda."

"Ethan, how *could* you go out with a druggie? Did she steal my earrings, too? Should I check my jewellery to make sure it's all there?"

"You're making too big a deal of this, Mom. It was a first date. Last date, too."

Mom stood up and began removing dinner ingredients from the fridge and freezer. She turned around. "You know what, dear? I don't want to see your girlfriend or know her name. This is your get-out-of-jail-free card. Just pack her up and take her away. I think we've all learned our lesson for the day."

Dad turned to me. "Ungrateful little bastard." He winked. "Come on, I'll help you get her to the car."

Dad and I lugged Ellen out to her car, plunking her in the back seat along with a one-third-empty box of Dad's headshots, which he made me promise to drop off at his agent's. He wrote down Ellen's address. "Just park it in her garage. When she wakes up, she'll figure things out."

"What about me?"

"Oh, right." He reached into his pocket. "Here's a twenty. Take a cab, but keep the receipt, as I can claim it on taxes."

So I drove Ellen to her condo in Kitsilano, not far from the beach, and put her inside on her bed. I cabbed to pick up my car, then finally got home to my dishevelled but lovable three-storey dump in Chinatown. When I got the door open, a wave of relief flooded me. I could have a long bath and forget turtles and bodies and Steve and Dad and Ellen and . . .

I turned on the light to find maybe twenty stick-thin Chinese people huddled on my floor: men, women and children. I dropped my keys and turned around, only to bump into my brother.

"Greg, what the hell's going on in there?"

"Chill out. They're friends of mine. I just needed a place to put them for a few hours."

"What do you mean, friends? They look like refugees."

"They *are* refugees."

"What the hell are you doing with—refu*gees*? And in my place, too."

"I owe a friend a favour."

"What kind of friend is that?"

"Stop acting like a little girl. They're only here for a few hours, and then they ship out."

"I—" Words failed me. Meanwhile, I looked at the refugees. "Shit, Greg. I gave you a copy of my key for emergencies. Don't get me caught up in your weird business shit. And why aren't you in Hong Kong? Mom said you were in Hong Kong."

"I told them not to touch any surface or object, and trust me, they won't." The refugees looked at Greg in a way that said he was alpha dog, and not to be crossed.

"There, look—they're not even sitting on your furniture."

"What's that smell?"

Greg barked a question in Mandarin, and a woman replied.

"They've been shitting in a cardboard box off the kitchen. They didn't know how the toilet worked."

"Get them out of here now, or I phone the government."

Greg turned frosty on me. "That's not something that's going to happen, Ethan."

"Wait a second. These people aren't really refugees, are they?"

"That depends how you define 'refugee.' And if you mean 'noble fellow world citizens searching for a better life on a new continent'—"

"Greg, you're people-smuggling."

"Keep your voice down. I'm not the one who's people-smuggling. My friend, Kam Fong, is the, uh, businessman here. He messed up a connection, and I owed him one."

"How did they get here?"

"A truck dropped them off six hours ago."

"You're the world's biggest asshole."

"Ethan, it was either that or have my real estate licence revoked. Kam Fong is well connected."

"Kam Fong? Isn't that the name of the guy who played Steve McGarrett's sidekick on *Hawaii Five-0*?"

"It is. Isn't that a gas?"

"Have these people had anything to eat in the past week?"

"What am I—a flight attendant? How should I know?"

"They have to eat something. They're so skinny."

"I'd order pizzas, but all that dairy's not a good idea."

"Where are they from?"

"Fujian Province, northern China."

I went online to search for takeout. Stir-fried clams, lychee nuts, squid with pineapple, prawns, crab, whelks and radishes. "Okay, asshole brother, you're spending ten bucks apiece for dinner for everyone here."

"Ten bucks?"

"Either that, or I call the RCMP."

Greg went to pick up the food, and I orchestrated a hygiene pageant. Two weeks in the hold of a container ship leaves the modern traveller a bit . . . fragrant. I got a conga line going in and out of the shower, and I put their dirty clothing in the washer and gave them my own clothes to wear. The hot water ran out quickly, but nobody seemed to mind. I felt like Elliott from *E.T.* handing out Reese's Pieces.

Greg came back an hour later carrying a Santa's toy sack worth of Chinese food, and he was surprised to see them all in their new duds. "Check out the makeover," he said. "It's like casual Friday at the Asian Studies department of a Midwestern university."

"Just put out the food."

He did, and a feeding frenzy ensued. "Jesus, Ethan, just look at these guys chow down."

"Greg, what or when was the last time these people ate—a dead seagull somewhere off the coast of Guam?"

"Relax."

"How can you be a part of this? It's just—inconceivable you'd get wrapped up in it."

"Don't be so self-righteous. The people in this room

probably made the shoes on your feet, the computer you just turned on, the glass in the windows, the light bulb in that lamp, and just about everything else in here. It's okay if these people are across the ocean in a sweatshop working for fifty-nine cents a day, but heaven help us if we have to actually deal with them in real time in our part of the world."

"Your social conscience is making me teary."

"Look, I sell Vancouver condominiums to global pirates from Hong Kong or Taiwan who need a crash pad if China goes ballistic. And tonight it was either bring these folks to your place, or let them starve and shit themselves in a Maersk shipping container over by the Second Narrows. Don't be so pissed off. Here—" He handed me a wad of twenties. "Let them keep your old clothing. You go buy some new stuff."

"I can't take this money." I turned around and gave the pile of twenties to a scrawny young guy wearing my Nine Inch Nails FRAGILITY V. 2.0 tour shirt. "Take one and pass it along." He quickly caught my gist.

The doorbell rang, and everybody stopped as if a DVD's PAUSE had just been hit. Greg answered—it was one of Kam Fong's henchmen. He and Greg had a whispered argument. When it was over, the henchman motioned the Chinese out of the house and into the truck. Aside from the food trash (two dozen completely licked-clean paper plates) and a cardboard box full of shit outside the back kitchen door, it was as if the place had never seen a soul. Greg said, "Okay, then, you're right, this was a pretty big imposition on you. Let me pay you back."

"How?"

He looked around my place. "Ethan, your furniture is

total crap. I'll have Kelly from my office send you some pieces left over from our display suites."

"I don't want or need new furniture."

"Don't be stupid. Your furniture is college-grade, and you're pushing thirty. Collectively it spells out L-O-S-E-R."

"My furniture isn't crap. At least my place doesn't look like I ordered the whole thing from a Delta Airlines SkyMall catalogue."

"Gee, that one sure stung. How are Mom and Dad?"

"Busy."

"I'm off."

After I closed the door behind me, I went to the washer and took out the first big load of smuggling-wear—cheesecloth-thin knit shirts too flimsy to buff a car with—profoundly depressing—and I wondered what I was going to wear now.

I put the wet clothes into the dryer, and an hour later, as I removed them, I got to thinking of how you'll sometimes be at a friend's place, and they loan you a jacket or sweater, and how extra-great those garments are to wear because they come with a pre-built aura—and how you even sometimes plan on keeping the sweater or whatever because suddenly it feels so . . . *yours.*

I picked a shirt from the laundry basket of Downy-soft clothes. Voila! My new look.

Within an hour I was asleep.

• • •

The next day in jPod, Bree and Cowboy saw me in my smuggling-wear. "Dig the threads, Ethan. Begging for spare change at stoplights?"

"It's—a long story. Where's John Doe?"

"He went out last night to tag grain cars with some guys from IT and never came back. Hey, word has it that corporate really loves the idea of the turtle character based on beloved reality TV show host Jeff Probst."

I grabbed an apple granola bar and a banana in the snack room, and then sat down at my desk. I needed to somehow put the day into focus. I decided to research the life and career of Jeff Probst, host of TV's long-running reality TV hit *Survivor,* as well as . . . well, just see for yourself:

Jeff was born on November 4, 1962, and began his career in the early 1990s, bringing us laughter and song as a VH1 veejay. From there, Jeff became host of the informative mirthfest that is VH1's *Rock & Roll Jeopardy!,* but only after he'd hosted and made guest appearances on many network TV shows. Yet it was as himself, "Jeff Probst," that Jeff entered our collective hearts as the crusty but fair host of the long-running king of reality shows, *Survivor.* There, Jeff outplayed, outlasted and outwitted all of the naysayers and doom-mongers, and showed us that with pluck, fortitude and a honey bronze tan, one can be both God and the devil, choosing the next soul from the hinterlands to be catapulted into exciting millennium-style fame—and a higher tax bracket!

FUN FACT: Jeff is an accomplished director of art house films. His 2001 thriller, *Finder's Fee,* netted Jeff awards for Best Picture and Best Director at the Seattle International Film Festival. First step Seattle—next stop . . . *the world!*

Bree saw that I was researching Jeff Probst. "Hmmm. I wonder if Jeff Probst has his own specific kryptonite—something that makes him self-destruct."

"What makes Jeff blow up? Bad room service. Or players who quit the game before the game tosses them out."

Bree asked me what my own kryptonite was.

"That's easy—meetings. Yours?"

"Microsoft press releases."

We looked at some JPEGs of Jeff. "If Jeff were a turtle, he'd be on the side of the forces of good, right?"

"Can skateboard games embody morality?"

"I don't think so."

The fluorescent lights flickered for one hundredth of a second, which told us that the render farm a floor up had kicked into operation for the night. "Have you looked in the snack room lately?" I asked.

Bree said, "I never go there. Vegan."

"I forgot. Did you know we have an entire Frigidaire stand-up model dedicated only to condiments and spreads?"

"Huh?"

"Kraft Golden Italian Dressing, gallon-sized, Adams Peanut Butter, HP Sauce, marmalade, Annie's Natural Raspberry Vinaigrette . . ."

"How do you re*member* all that shit?"

"Brain wiring. I've always been able to remember brand names."

"I have this theory about smart people. If you're smart, you're either the only person in your family who's smart, *or* everybody in the family is smart. No in-between."

I considered this. "I think I come from the everybody's smart category. But they don't apply their smarts to . . . *larger picture* pursuits. That includes me."

"My sister works at the World Bank," Bree said. "My older brother's finding a cure for Alzheimer's, and my younger brother played viola at the White House two years ago. They all have trouble with me and gaming."

There was an awkward moment as the two of us considered our lives from a long-term perspective. Then Bree said, "You know, if the company wants to get better work out of the staff, they should follow Jeff's unwritten laws from *Survivor.*"

"Like what?"

"They should starve us. Starved contestants make for better shows, always, so it might make for a more zestful office lifestyle as well. Management could leave bottles of Scotch along the hallways here, like Mario coins. Booze could really loosen us all up. Let's face the truth—drunk people are more fun, and they're much better at telling the truth than sober people."

"And we should be able to vote one person out of the company *every single day,* so that there'd be all these massive intrigues as everybody tries to figure out who's ganging up on who."

"Forget about our office for a second. Do you know what they ought to do on the real *Survivor*? They should forget about the tropics. Make them play in Romania. Romanians will do anything. No more weepy crap about, *We were friends—how could you have abused our friendship?* They'd be slitting each other's throats."

We heard a cat yowl from behind our cubicle wall: Kaitlin. "You people are driving me absolutely fucking *crazy.* All you ever talk about is junk."

I looked over at her—brown hairs Van de Graaffing from her forehead; a pimple she'd been hoping nobody would notice caked in skin product; small, perfect teeth. I was wondering what her kiss would taste like, when she picked up a Clive Cussler novel that everyone in the pod had read, and hucked it at the wall by the air intake.

Bree encouraged her. "You throw that book, Kaitlin! Get it all out!"

She gave another snared-in-the-leg-hold cry, then hurled an N64 development folder from 1998, followed by a hardcover copy of *If They Only Knew,* the 1999 autobiography of World Wrestling Federation sensation Chyna.

After this, she seemed as spent as Mr. Burns handing a shovel to Smithers after throwing a handful of dirt onto a grave, and she spoke in the one-word sentences used by exhausted slaves: "All. I. Want. To. Do. Tonight. Is. Design. A. Realistic. Looking. Waterfall. Ripple. Texture. Is. That. Too. Fucking. Much. To. Ask?"

"I think we should all get back to work," I said.

a pair of oversize

green foam latex

Incredible

Hulk

boxing

gloves

with built-in
Hulk
noises

All new company passwords must contain at least one character, integer and symbol:

~~happycamper~~

~~happycamper5~~

~~happycamper*~~

happycamper*5 ✔

This fridge belongs to the company.

Anyone using this fridge automatically agrees to obey all rules for fridge usage dictated by the company.

“Usage” is legally defined as “the moment somebody opens the door up until the moment the door is once again shut.”

lens

urethra

womb

tail

eardrum

mustard

bun

pseudorandom number generator

//

Texture diffuse:

DiffuseMap

Float amount = 3.0i

LightMap

[. . . n_x, n_y, n_z, x, y, z, r, g, b . . .]

• • •

I was about to get to work when I decided that I needed, nay, *deserved* a nap after the previous freaky day, so I crawled under my desk, with a Yellow Pages as a pillow, and conked out for an hour or so. I woke up with my neck feeling cricked and spina bifida-ish. I grabbed an orange juice and went back to my desk. *Ahhhhhhh* . . . I have to say, smuggling-wear is actually quite comfy—soft, with no hems or waist-bands to dig into the skin.

I began fielding Chute-mail from various levels of producers, and was feeling calm and good, when Gord-O, a senior development director, came rumbling towards jPod. "Ethan, word upstairs is that you're thinking of switching to the production career path."

"It's true."

"Very well, here's the Costco card. I'm going to need you to pick up some DVD-Rs for weekend builds. The Physics SEs want to look at THUG2, so pick up the Xbox version of that. And we're out of Cheerios. Pick us up a couple dozen boxes in a ratio of three boxes of Honey Nut to one box of classic Cheerios."

Such is the life of a young techie dreaming of being a genuine future production assistant: one moment you're trying to round up a selection of C++ fantasy castles to appease an angry fartcatcher in Development, the next you're stuck in traffic with enough Cheerios on the back seat to make the car rattle like maracas going over a speed bump.

En route to Costco, I was phoned by John Doe for details on an upcoming Tetris tournament, but we got side-tracked and ended up discussing work. The big discussion around the office is how to alter BoardX's development cycle to accommodate Jeff the Turtle. "John, this is no Japanese curry–induced bad dream. It's really happening."

"Stop saying that, Ethan!"

Bree then called. "Ethan, did you hear about Adam?"

"No, what?" Adam is senior animator from the company's jock set.

"He got really drunk last night and then went on the treadmill. His anti-chafing nipple tape came off, he freaked, and he ended up whacking his head on a stainless steel bowl filled with bottles of mineral water," Bree said.

"Ow."

"Ten stitches. On the way to the hospital, he started screaming in Jeb's Saab, so Jeb reached into the glove box and got out a can of Solarcaine and started spraying it on Adam's face—which promptly caught on fire from a spark from Jeb's cellphone battery charger. Not a trace of eyebrow left."

"Wow."

"Everybody in his pod is shaving off their eyebrows in sympathy."

Tetris Challenge
Tonight, 7:00

Merlots
vs.
Zinfandels

S
Z
T
L
J
Q
bar
square

• • •

My prank Belgian keyboard is in the belly of an Airbus 320 somewhere over the North Polar ice cap, huddled in its little box, wondering if its new owner will love it or not. I've only ever flown across an ocean once, to London with the school band. The entire experience was wasted on me. Mostly I remember that never-ending in-flight information screen that tells passengers how far they've come, and how many miles remain. It's so sloooowwwwwwwwww. Stare at it intently enough and time goes backwards. And do we really need to know that the outside temperature is –59 degrees Fahrenheit? Does this information comfort us with the knowledge that should we crash and somehow survive, death by exposure will be swift and merciful? Also, Celsius conversion seems unnecessary, as around –59, electrons probably crawl to a stop, like Ping-Pong balls on a basement floor. Okay, I know it's 222.6 degrees Kelvin, –50.56 degrees Celsius.

• • •

My phone rang. "Hello, dear."

"Mom. Hi."

"Did you get your girlfriend home okay?"

"Yes. Yeah. Fine."

"She hacked off such a huge chunk of The Dude. It's good to know you've dropped her. You *have* dropped her, haven't you?"

"Uh, yeah."

"You hesitated there for a second. I heard it."

"I was closing windows on my screen."

"Young Steven took me on a tour of the entire facility, you know."

"*Steven*? We call him Steve here."

"Lovely man. He turned Toblerone around in just two years."

"Yes, he did do that."

Silence.

"Ethan, I need your help."

A loaded pause. "Again?"

"My spreadsheets."

Relief. "Okay. Sure."

"Are you free later this afternoon?"

The moment Mom asked if I was free, Gord-O walked into my cubicle and pointed his index finger at me, meaning, *Come talk to me, right now rather than later.* "I can find the time."

"Make sure that time is four o'clock. *Please,* honey?"

"Well . . ."

"I'll make your favourite dessert."

She hung up.

Gord-O asked, "What's with the ragamuffin fashion look?"

"Gord-O. Hi. How can I help you?"

"You get a lot of personal phone calls, Ethan."

"In three years, I've had six personal phone calls, and somehow you're always right there when they happen. Are you stalking me?"

Gord-O ignored me. "The level builders just got a call, and the exec group is on their ass saying they need a better castle model."

"I found maybe four dozen pre-modelled castles, ranging from a molecule-perfect rebuilding of Mad King

Ludwig's Bavarian hideaway to a do-it-yourself plywood backyard kit. What do they want?"

Gord-O repeated himself. "The level builders just got a call, and the exec group is on their ass saying they need a better castle model."

"Gotcha. I'll look again." I actually don't mind scouring the Internet, finding stuff. In my brain it doesn't feel like work.

"And, Ethan, next time remember the ratio of Honey Nut to classic Cheerios is three to one."

"They were out of Honey Nut."

"To be merely good enough is to never succeed." With a platitude as his last word, Gord-O left.

I heard Kaitlin's disembodied voice from over the cubicle wall. "Ethan, what exactly is your job description?"

She speaks.

"One minute you're supposed to be optimizing code, the next you're bulk shopping for Cheerios. Doesn't this place have free cereal already?"

"Last year Gord-O's team ate too many Cheerios, so Accounting got on their case, and they still ate too many, so then Legal had to draw up a brief outlining the company's free Cheerios policy. Since then, they've had to buy their own."

"And you have to get them?"

"I look upon my job as apprenticeship rather than servitude."

"If you ask me, you're living in Schmucksville."

"Schmucksville?"

"It's a retro reference to 1960s Catskill comedy routines."

"Huh." I tried to think of something witty to say.

Kaitlin asked, "So what *is* the real deal with your ragamuffin look?"

"It's"—how to explain?—"hard to explain."

"You look like Elizabeth Smart's kidnappers."

Her phone rang and I went off in search of more 3-D clip art castles. By three-thirty I was able to squeak out of the building on the pretext of buying Honey Nut Cheerios. Mom was in the kitchen, drinking tea and reading the *Province*. "Hello, dear. You're wearing . . . rags."

"It's the new look."

We went into Dad's den, where Mom had a G4 all set to go. The spreadsheet problem seemed easy to fix. "I think you just have some fields crossed. Which part is giving you the biggest problem?"

"I'm trying to track THC counts, along with the genetic ancestry of the plants."

"I see what it is—genetics are logarithmic, whereas potency counts aren't."

"I'm glad someone here understands it. I'll go get you a nice big piece of double-frosted chocolate devil's food cake."

"I thought you were kidding about that."

"Nothing's too good for my baby boy."

Mom has a pretty good system for tracking the genetic histories of her crops. It involves an alphabetizing scheme wherein each female plant is assigned one upper case letter, which is followed by an upper or lower case letter, depending on whether the plant was a clone or a genetic male/female cross. Td, her favourite, was The Dude, a mutant THC miracle of genetics, and, to be honest, it bugged me, too, that Ellen had given him a pruning.

Mom's plant names reflect her somewhat random TV watching habits. Surrounding The Dude were:

CL	Cloris Leachman
Ee	Emilio Estevez
Fb	Fantasia Barino
MK	Mary-Kate Olsen
Bb	Bo Bice
BbG	former UN secretary-general Boutros Boutros-Ghali
LL	the nightingale of Glasgow, "To Sir with Love" songstress Lulu

• • •

Gord-O saw me walking into jPod.

"Where were you?"

"I was out looking for Honey Nut Cheerios, but Save-On was sold out, too. The guy there said that Martha Stewart used them in a program about homemade energy bars, and they've been out for a week."

"Oh."

Am I good, or what!

Everyone in jPod was beavering away, and my entrance generated no enthusiasm.

The phone rang, as I suspected it would: Dad. "My Ellen problem is solved. I gave a producer I know twenty-five grand in cash from my Hummer fund, and he's sending Ellen to Toronto tomorrow for ten weeks to work on a Hallmark Channel movie."

"That was fast. Hallmark has a channel? The greeting card company?"

"Whoops. I meant Heartland—the chick flick channel."

"Dad, if you want a speaking part in a movie so badly, why don't you find a producer and give him or her some

Hummer money, too?"

"That would be cheating. I have to *earn* that speaking role. And by the way, your mother says you're wearing rags."

• • •

Okay, I know I have to address the ragamuffin issue.

Here's the deal: when it comes to duds, I'm really sick of everybody trying to be different from everybody else. In the end, everybody's simply buying their outfits from the same selection of stores at the same mall. I'm also not stupid enough to think that wearing random thrift-store clothing makes me a rebel or an outsider. *Gee, is that a 1997 Chilcotin Rodeo T-shirt you've got on? Wow! Out of 5.5 billion people on the planet, you differentiate yourself from the rest!*

So, when all those smuggled Chinese people had to abandon their clothes at my place, it was like my fashion gift of the gods. Indeed, the gods had handed me a look on a platter. And the thing is, once you establish a look, and once everybody recognizes that look as *your* look, you never have to think about fashion again. It's pig laziness on my part, but so what.

• • •

The rest of the evening was quiet.

Turtles.

Jeff.

Deadline.

Efficiency.

Lots of efficiency.

Too much efficiency.

A sense of unease . . . a wave of paranoia.

A slight gust of chilled wind.

Cowboy said, "Do you feel something weird?"

Cap'n Crunch granules of sleep fell from the corners of my eyes into my keyboard, into the seven-key cluster of

UI
HJK
NM

I said, "No."

Cowboy said, "I feel chilled or something."

Kaitlin, surprising us all from behind her cubicle wall, snorted and said (without standing up), "You feel chilled because you have no character. You're a depressing assemblage of pop culture influences and cancelled emotions, driven by the sputtering engine of only the most banal form of capitalism. You spend your life feeling as if you're perpetually on the brink of being obsolete—whether it's labour market obsolescence or cultural unhipness. And it's all catching up with you. You live and die by the development cycle. You're glamorized drosophila flies, with the company regulating your life cycles at whim. If it isn't a budget-driven eighteen-month game production schedule, it's a five-year hardware obsolescence schedule. Every five years you have to throw away everything you know and learn a whole new set of hardware and software specs, relegating what was once critical to our lives to the cosmic slag heap."

Cowboy considered this. "So, then, what's wrong with that?"

"What's *wrong* with that is that you might just as well be

tyrannized cotton-mill workers in rural Massachusetts in the nineteenth century. You might as well be stitching Nikes together in some quasi-corrupt archipelago nation in Asia in return for badly ventilated dorm rooms and $1.95 a day."

Silence.

Loaded silence.

Cowboy said, "Do you have to be so political about it?"

Kaitlin heaved a generic world-weary sigh. "Cowboy, let's look at you—tell us what your character is."

Cowboy fumbled. "Well—"

"I'm listening."

"I think I'm an okay-enough guy."

"Gee. That's fascinating."

"Let me think."

"Take all the time you want."

After thirty pregnant seconds, Cowboy said, "This is stupid. Why should I have to sit here and define who I am?"

"There you have it, Cowboy."

"Have *what*?"

"What you have is the fact that if you don't have a character to begin with, everything and nothing is in character."

"That's really fucking depressing."

"And what if it is?"

"It's like *Melrose Place*."

"*Melrose*?" said Bree. "That was a hundred years ago."

John Doe got excited. "I watched the whole series on DVD. Remember when the script writers couldn't come up with personalities or characteristics for the characters? They simply made them all go psycho, one by one."

Bree nodded. "It worked, didn't it?"

Evil Mark added, "I liked that show."

I said, "I never watched it. It felt target-marketed."

"Aaron Spelling made so much money with it," said Kaitlin. "But didn't you notice that, when they started, they were all twentysomething slackers looking for meaning in life, living in a motel-like complex with a swimming pool in the centre?"

Bree said, "That's exactly like the characters in Douglas Coupland's 1991 novel, *Generation X*."

"Exactly."

"So they ripped Coupland off?"

"That's harsh and actionable. But who are we to say?"

"Sounds fishy to me."

"If I were Douglas Coupland, I'd have sued the pants off Aaron Spelling."

"Me, too."

"So would I."

Finally something we all agreed on.

Lovely pod

jPod は幸せな場所である。jPod
スペースで、また、幸せな彼できる。幸せがありなさい。jPod
がありなさい。

jPod is a happy place!
You can be happy, also, in the jPod space. Be happy. Be jPod.

Let's Working!

私達の落ち着いたオフィスの環境の嬉しい事の大きい変化を見本抽
出しなさい。それらは友人でありたいと思う!
それらはよい時、余りにほしいと思う。

Please sample a large variety of our serene office environment joyful things.
They want to be your friend! They want your good times, too.

jPodding work style は友人を作り、幸せな人生を
楽しむ方法である!

jPodding work style is a way to make friends and enjoy the happy life.

Zaxxon
Manufacturer: Sega/Gremlin
Year: 1982
Class: Wide Release
Genre: Space
Type: Videogame

Conversion Class: Sega Zaxxon
Number of Simultaneous Players: 1
Maximum Number of Players: 2
Gameplay: Alternating
Control Panel Layout: Single Player Ambidextrous
Sound: Amplified Mono (One Channel)

• • •

Kaitlin's dissection of Cowboy's personality made me begin to have doubts about my own personality. Prior to Kaitlin's rant, I thought Cowboy was the quirkiest person I knew. And now he was suddenly just a Lego mini-fig. (Okay, maybe John Doe is the quirkiest person I know.)

But honestly—*do* I have a personality? Do any of us? I scoured my life and saw no overriding purpose, just my love affair with computer games—my old SOL and the 8808s in particular. If nothing else, I was pleased to be able to earn a living within an industry that's increasingly more corporate and bland and soul-killing, but . . . *but* then I got to wondering if I even possessed the ability to fall in love with another human being and . . . I began to feel like such a *module,* especially compared to Kaitlin, who was such a firebrand tonight. I couldn't help but wonder what she's like when she removes all of her brakes.

I was having this crisis of faith while parked outside my Chinatown shack. Then, while attaching The Club, I looked up and saw that the bathroom window upstairs was open, the nylon Union Jack curtain billowing from within. I always keep that window shut (pigeons) and was curious as to what was going on. I put my key in the lock, opened the door, and realized that all of my old furniture was gone. In its place was strange, ornate, gilded, swan-crested, diamond-tufted black and red leather junk—the sort of stuff I'd expect to see in the living room of, say, North Korean president Kim II Sung. It was disturbing and garish and way too big for my place, like adult furniture in a tree fort. In a corner I saw some boxes that held my flight simulation software, but everything else was new. I wasn't hallucinating—it really *was* my place.

There was a sofa made of curlicued gold wood, upholstered with baloney-coloured fabrics patterned with Chinese mountainscapes. At one end were a matching club chair and a glass coffee table—a lens of blue tinted glass held aloft by worshipful egrets. My framed Offspring poster had been replaced by an oil-painted fantasia of kittens frolicking amidst Louis XIV mirrors and vases filled with blue Himalayan poppies. In what was now the dining room (but what had been the gaming room) sat a glistening black lacquered table with matching chairs for eight. My bedroom and the spare room were similarly decked out.

This was Greg's doing.

Fortunately, his cell number was pencilled onto the kitchen wall, just above a brand new plum-coloured breakfast nook table inlaid with a mother-of-pearl scene depicting Marie Antoinette in her garden throwing lawn darts at poor people.

"Greg."

"Tell me how much you love it!"

"I . . ."

"Yeah?"

" . . . I don't know where to begin."

"Isn't it great? Kam Fong is rewarding your hospitality for helping him with his, um, *shipment.*"

"Greg, I told you I've got no interest in dealing with people-smugglers, and I don't want their free furniture."

"Grow up. For the people being smuggled, it's all just one big adventure, and they'll be telling their grandkids about all of your old shitty furniture and your dorky slackersomething clothes."

"Greg . . ."

"And by the way, what's with the Union Jack flag curtain? Only junkies use flags as curtains."

"I . . ."

"Junkies with *lice,* Ethan."

In the background I heard my father shouting, "Who's that?"

"It's Ethan."

"Greg, are you over at Mom and Dad's?"

"I came for dinner here and thought I'd spend the night, too. I'm bagged. By the way, why is there lipstick on my old pillow?"

"It's a long story. What's everybody doing up so late?"

"Dad was on a shoot and came home too stoked to sleep. There's a live feed from the Perth-Fremantle ballroom dancing semifinals coming in, so Dad and I are watching it. You know how he gets during semifinal season."

Dad is a ballroom dancing fanatic. I spent my preteen years being abandoned on the sidelines of dance club floors while dad studied and practised. Mom won't go near a dance floor. I heard a wash of flamenco music. "Where's Mom?"

As if on cue, Mom said, "Greg, is that Ethan?"

"Yup."

She took the phone. "What do you think of your new furniture?"

"It's . . . overwhelming"

"I think your brother is just a dreamboat. And aren't you lucky his friend, Kam Fong, has such a generous heart and gave you such an amazing array of luxury furniture? You must have done a terrific job helping him redo his accounts and balances spreadsheets."

Words failed me and then re-entered my life. "Yes, I certainly am lucky."

Mom was on to a new topic. "Ethan, I need your help tomorrow. I have to make a collection."

"Mom, I have a job."

"Nonsense. I'll phone young Steven and tell him it's important to me that you take the afternoon off."

"You're still talking with Steve?"

"Of course. I made him a pie today, too. He works so hard, and hard workers need treats every so often."

Mom handed the phone back to Greg. I looked around me and noticed something else. "Greg?"

"What, bro?"

"Everything here is on . . . an angle."

"Oh, *that.* Yeah. Kam brought in his feng shui guy."

"Thanks."

"Ethan, you sound pissed off. This is the last time I ever try to help you out. *Ooh, look at me, I'm an information worker. My job is clean and environmentally friendly and futuristic—*"

"Greg—" Experience has taught me to simply ride out Greg's diatribes until they stop.

"Hey, Ethan, you know the guy who stood in front of the tank in Tiananmen Square? He's the guy who hot-glued the faceplate over the keypad in the phone you're using."

"Greg, I have to go."

He changed his tone. "Hey, speaking of sweatshops and toxins, I'm flying back to Hong Kong tomorrow. Want anything?"

I thought about this. "Can you pick up an assortment of bootlegged games for me? I've got a bet going with Cowboy that he can't properly detect bootlegs. Just buy a bunch at random. Nothing over two bucks."

"Done."

• • •

Mom's pie worked. The next day I left jPod at noon and passed Steve's Touareg by the main security booth down the hill. He gave me a rehearsed-looking thumbs-up, and that was that.

At Mom's we switched to her K-car wagon and drove out into the Fraser Valley amid a chilly monsoon. I was wearing another outfit cobbled together from smugglees' remnants. Mom took one look at it and said, "Oh, Ethan. You're dressed like a newsie in a Broadway show."

"I told you, it's my new style."

"How am I going to make a collection with you dressed up like a ragamuffin?"

There was a twenty-mile patch of fashion-induced tension before Mom stopped editorializing about my personal style. We were headed to Maple Ridge, a suburb on the city's easternmost extreme—largely built overnight, with overtaxed roads that burped along at a speed best described as digestive. The clouds were so dark it felt like we were night driving. Mom gunned the engine and cut off an impatient Prelude driven by a baby boy with a new driver tag in his rear window.

"Tell me more about this Jeff Probst celebrity. What do you think he's like in real life?"

"Jeff Probst?"

"Yes, Steven has got me intrigued."

"Well, he hosts this show where he's always having to deliver bad news to people. He's like a professional firer they bring in to do mass layoffs. In the first few years of the show, he tried to display empathy, but I've noticed that as he ages and sees more of the world, he's realizing that bad news is a part of life, and that when you have to give it, just say it and get it over with. He's a regular kind of guy, but at the same time, he's not."

"Does he skateboard?"

"Not that I know of."

"Does he wear silly baggy pants and oversized nonsense jewellery?"

"No. Style-wise he's always dressed as if he's about to get into a stolen Cessna on a private tarmac somewhere in central Colombia."

"Who does he look like?"

"Generically handsome—game show-y, but definitely of the twenty-first century. He's a bit too tanned. He'd better watch it, or his skin'll look like caramel popcorn when he's sixty."

"So how does this Jeff Probst fellow's personality convert into a skateboard character who's a friendly turtle?"

"He could maybe be wise and all-knowing like Yoda."

"Who?"

I let it drop, since Mom's curiosity was clearly ebbing. We were entering an older area with uninflated property values and roads last resurfaced in the 1960s. Invisible waves of manure entered the station wagon. I asked, "Is it far?"

"Another few minutes."

"I'm hungry."

"If you can't find something lying around the car, then you can't be very hungry."

I looked in the glove compartment. Mom had stashed some gold-foiled chocolate coins, probably from one of the egg hunts we used to have at Greg's ex-wife's place. I tasted one of them and nearly gagged.

"Mom, how long has this chocolate been in there?"

"A few years, maybe."

"A few *years*?"

"Ethan, everybody knows Easter chocolate lasts forever.

If they don't sell it one year, they put it in the warehouse and bring it out again the next year, over and over until it finally sells. By that standard, those coins there are practically new."

I got to thinking about the business at hand. "Mom, one more time, why are we out here in this hillbilly's armpit?"

"Tim's buddy, Lyle, owes me fifty thousand dollars, and won't pay up."

"Okay, that's more than I knew a few minutes ago. Does he know about Tim's, um, *fate*?"

"No. But he found out about Tim and me a few months ago. It caused a rift between them and . . ."

"Wait a second—what do you mean, *found out about Tim and me*?"

"Remove your mind from the gutter. Tim was nice. I felt a closeness with him."

"Don't tell me any more."

"Why not?"

"You're my mother. You're weirding me out."

"Eat another coin."

"So, then, are these guys bikers, too?"

"Connect the dots, Ethan: we're in the middle of nowhere and drugs are involved. Who else is going to live out here?"

The rain wouldn't let up as we turned onto successively dinkier roads, finally coming to a gravel lane.

"We're here," Mom said.

At the turn of the century this had been a farmhouse. It was remote back then, and continued to be remote now. "Imagine living in Vancouver and managing to miss all the real estate booms," I said.

We knocked at the front door. Inside, a TV was blaring, and a mentally ill dog barked.

"That's Gumdrop," Mom said.

The door opened with a creak.

Mom said, "Hi, Lyle."

"Oh, *you.*"

"Yes, me."

"What do you want, Carol?"

"My money, please."

"Who's the guy with you—cradle-robbing again?"

I said, "I'm Ethan. This is my mom."

Lyle shut the door.

I said, "Rude prick."

"Bikers. What do you expect?"

I knocked this time. Mom said, "Lyle. Please come out. Let's discuss this like sensible adults."

Through the door, Lyle told us to fuck off. I heard another biker laughing above the TV, along with Gumdrop's crazed howling.

Mom knocked. "Lyle, just pay me what's mine, and I'll be out of your hair."

Lyle's friend shouted, "Lyle doesn't have any hair." From behind the door, this witty retort garnered convulsions of laughter.

"They're stoned," I said.

"You know, dear, this reminds me of back when you had your paper route, and on collecting day people would pretend not to be home to avoid you."

"That always drove me nuts. Why didn't people just pay up?"

"I think it's because when you walk up to the door, in the customers' minds, you're like their conscience come to haunt them. Perhaps that's how our biker friends here feel about me."

Just then, a foaming pinkish-white pit bull swooped around a corner of the house and up the front steps and jabbed a justifiably named canine into Mom's shin.

"Mom!"

She pulled a gun from her purse, and one shot later, Gumdrop met his maker. Mom then keeled over and began verbally spazzing, using language about as brutal as is possible for her to use: "Oh shoot! Sugar! Ouch! Oh, Ethan, it hurts! Is that nasty little thing dead? Good."

I kicked Gumdrop's carcass. "You evil little shit. Come to life so we can shoot you again." I turned to Mom. "Let me see your shin."

There was one deep bite that barely missed a varicose vein. Oddly, my thought was, *Mom has varicose veins?*

"That awful, *awful* dog." Using her good leg, Mom gave Gumdrop a kick, too. Lyle opened the door. He said, "Carol, what the fuck did you do to my dog?"

Mom looked up with an about-to-go-apeshit goggle-eyed stare that I had only ever seen once before, when Greg and I were horsing around the living room and broke her porcelain figurine of Shakespeare knocking on the door of Anne Hathaway's cottage. "Give me my fucking money, you ugly piece of trash."

Mom swore for real!

"You crazy bitch, you shot my dog!"

"You dirty little man. Gumdrop punctured my shin bone, and *you* owe Carol Jarlewski fifty grand. Give it to me now."

"Fuck off and die."

I said, "No *you* fuck off and die. Pay up!" Mom fired a shot into the wood floor a whisker away from Lyle's foot. He backed right up.

"Jesus, you're both totally fucking nuts."

Mom and I stormed the house. It reminded me a bit of our grade-three class's gerbil environment—a tossed salad of biker mag porn foldouts, old *TV Guides* and KFC debris drizzled with cat pee. Across the room, Lyle's toasted biker buddy was playing Chrono Trigger on Sony PlayStation, and this is truly shameful of me to report, but I really wanted to go over and join in.

Lyle said, "Andy, Carol's out of her fucking tree."

Mom shouted, "You've made my day unpleasant enough already, Lyle. Give me my money or I'll shoot your foot."

"No."

Mom shot the tip of Lyle's worn black cowboy boot, and he screamed like a girl.

"Lyle, give me my money."

Lyle was keeled over. "Andy, get her the fucking money." He looked at me. "Your family is one sick mess, dude."

Mom fired a warning shot at the ceiling, and a small cauliflower of plaster dust floated downward.

Andy reached into an Ikea Billy bookcase full of sun-faded VHS tapes and removed an Adidas box full of thousand-dollar bundles as Lyle removed his cowboy boot, cursing. Andy counted out fifty of them. "Here. Fifty grand. Now *go.*"

Mom became sugar sweet. "Thanks, guys. All you had to do was be nice."

"Meddlesome hag."

Mom shot the ceiling once more and we left.

Out in the car, we did a further inspection of Mom's shin. "I think I'll go to Dr. Tuck and get some stitches."

A few minutes later I said, "Isn't it weird that bikers would have Ikea furniture?"

"Don't talk to me about Ikea furniture. Your father tried assembling an Ikea shelf last year, and it nearly ended our marriage. Look—it's a yard sale over there. Let's stop for a minute."

Intel® 865PE Chipset-Based

865PE Neo2

Designed for Intel® Pentium® 4 Processors

Defender
Manufacturer: Williams
Year: 1980
Class: Wide Release
Genre: Shooter
Type: Videogame

Conversion Class: Williams
Number of Simultaneous Players: 1
Maximum Number of Players: 2
Gameplay: Alternating
Control Panel Layout: Single Player
Controls: Joystick: 2-way (up, down) Buttons: 5
Sound: Amplified Mono (One Channel)

• • •

When I got back to the pod around three, a FedEx box sat on my desk—Kaitlin's Belgian keypad of the corn. She was away from the pod, so I swapped it with hers. Bree said, "Correct me if I'm wrong, Ethan, but I think you and Miss Thing are sort of sweet on each other."

"She's talked about me?"

"Not directly. But when she makes her exasperated snorts, they're always aimed more at you than the rest of us."

"You think?"

"I *know*."

Cowboy's phone rang and nobody picked it up. I asked, "Where is everybody?"

"Everybody's so bummed out by this charismatic turtle character that they all fled," said Bree, adding, "You know, Ethan, I have an idea how you can torment Kaitlin a bit."

"Really?"

Bree told me her idea—it was genius.

When Kaitlin came back a half-hour later, we were set to put it into operation. I was to pretend I was doing a crossword puzzle and ask Bree for words: "Five-letter word, *UK lineup*."

"Queue."

"That was easy. Okay—four letters, *a festive rum drink, blank-Libre*."

"Cuba."

"Okay, wait, here's a hard one: *Mary Tyler-blank*."

"Say that again?"

"*Mary Tyler-blank*. Five letters."

"Is she a politician or something?"

"I don't know. It sounds familiar."

"Mary-Tyler . . . *Smith*?"

"Maybe she's that old lady they put on the US dollar coin in the 1970s that everybody hated."

"That was Susan B. Anthony."

"Oh. *Mary Tyler-blank*."

"Tyler-blank."

"Tyler-blank-blank-blank . . ."

Kaitlin lost it. "Moore! Mary Fucking Tyler Moore," she yelled.

"Let me see—that fits perfectly. Thanks, Kaitlin."

An exasperated grunt.

"Next word, seven letters: *Supercalifragilisticexpiali-blank*."

"Again?"

"Supercalifragilisticexpiali-blank."

"Allocation?"

"Come on, Bree, *try* here."

"I am. What was the first part, again?"

"*Supercalifragilisticexpiali*."

"Then *blank*?"

"Supercalifragilisticexpiali-blank."

"Hmmm . . ."

"*Docious,* you morons!" screamed Kaitlin. "Supercalifragilisticexpiali*docious.* It's from *Mary Poppins*."

"Hang on a second, Kaitlin—wait—D-O-C-I-O-U-S. It fits. Thanks." This was fun. I was all set to go onto the next fake clue (*Viva-blank-Vegas*) when I heard a sniffle from Kaitlin's side of the cubicle. I gophered up—she was crying. "Oh man, I'm sorry, Kaitlin. We were just funning you."

"I'm not in a mood to be funned."

I came around to her desk and leaned on it. Bree came over, too. "What's wrong?" she asked.

"I'm hungry. I'm so *hungry*."

"Then just eat."

"It's not that easy."

I said, "There's penne pesto with free-range chicken on today's cafeteria menu."

"No."

Bree and I swapped maybe-we-went-too-far looks. Bree asked, "So what's going on here?"

"I can't tell you."

"Don't sweat it. No problem."

Bree wagged her head, implying, *Best we leave her alone for the time being.*

I agreed, but first I had to extract the Belgian keyboard. "Kaitlin, sorry, but I did something naughty to your keyboard. I swapped it for this freaky unit."

Kaitlin looked at it. "Cool. A Belgian keyboard."

"You recognize it?"

"My sister works for the EU in Antwerp."

"Oh."

"That's so sweet of you."

"I—"

"No. It's okay."

I went to my cubicle and got her old board. "Here's the real one. For when you want to switch."

"Thanks, Ethan."

I slunk away. Fortunately, Gord-O found me and was able to dump a massive steaming heap of tasks in my lap, relieving me of any time in which to experience remorse. I was considering this steaming pile of tasks when I saw John Doe in the cafeteria, playing Sim City on a wireless. Reprieve! I was able to pre-empt Gord-O's work request with the promise of time well wasted.

"Sim City? That's pretty vanilla, John."

"Is it wrong to play a game that's a proven hit? I only play bestselling games, and never allow myself to become too good, lest I deviate from the norm."

"Okay." I looked at his screen. "Uh . . . John, you're building a city out of body parts." On screen, random body parts glistened alongside traditional buildings. Tunnels passed through feet. Eyeballs formed oil storage tanks.

"Well, yes. I had to tweak the code at least a little bit. The body part patch is floating around in the in-house system if you want to try it." John attached a donkey tail to a fifty-storey building shaped like a human leg from the foot to the knee. "In about fifty years, real-life genetic traits will be as modular as those you're witnessing on my screen. For now we can only dream. See that oil refinery right there? In a few minutes it's going to get a vagina. By the way, I googled Kaitlin, and you'd be surprised at what I found."

"You googled her?"

"Of course I did. Didn't you?"

I'd somehow forgotten to perform this essential task.

"Let's have a peek, shall we?"

A few clicks later, kaitlin anna boyd joyce went into the Google request box. A predictable landslide of genealogical links filled the screen.

"Big deal."

"Yes, but what happens if I go back and enter her name again and click the I FEEL LUCKY button."

"Nobody ever clicks that button."

"Maybe they should start." The genealogical mulch came back, but there was a new hit at the top of the page.

"'Dark Stories from the Subway Diet'?"

John said, "Exactly."

He clicked the link, and we were transported to one of

hundreds of Subway restaurant fan sites. In it, we saw BEFORE and AFTER photos of Kaitlin—one of her weighing 337 pounds, and the next as the Kaitlin of jPod, weighing at most 105. "Holy crap," I said.

"That's what I thought. Read on, bro."

Welcome to . . .

The Third Rail

An Unofficial Fan Website for Those Who Enjoy Tasty Sandwiches from Subway!!!

07.23.05

THIS WEEK: What happens when "THE DIET" goes wrong?

TITLE: "To Kaitlin Boyd, it was just a few pieces of cake, but to Subway, it was a violation of a sacred trust."

I am not a news reporter, so please excuse my mistakes here. For those of you who visit this site regularly (Thank you for visiting!!! Come back next week to see my new graphic overhaul!!!), you will know that Kaitlin Boyd lost over two hundred pounds on the Diet. She was set for fame and wealth—until a neighbour with a Handicam brought a tape to Subway HQ that rocked her world. This former three-hundred-pounder was caught on the fifth month of her diet eating an entire chocolate mud cake on her back stoop. Her lucrative sponsorship contract was cancelled. All Kaitlin has left are bitter memories and a freezer full of complimentary frozen uncooked Parmesan-oregano 12-inch loaves. A little bird told this reporter that Kaitlin likes to thaw and eat these loaves before bedtime while watching reruns of *Who's the Boss?* on a satellite feed from the Turks and Caicos Islands.

THIS WEBSITE ASKS: Was Kaitlin really fired over one lapse with a cake? Surely not!!! A Subway corporate insider (who shall remain nameless!!!) told this reporter, "We're all human, and many of our weight-loss spokesheroes have committed transgressions, but with Ms. Boyd, cake was just the start. That same neighbour also caught Boyd dropping twenty bucks at Popeyes Chicken, and then frittering away an entire afternoon at a Baskin-Robbins. There comes a time when you really have to admit that a line has been drawn in the sand and the line has been crossed. We wish Ms. Boyd the best in her future endeavours."

Frequent visitors to this site know that the Subway Diet is a sacred pact between you and Subway. To honour this pact, I visited Kaitlin's former next-door neighbour in Sunnyvale, California. There, I spoke with exposé creator, Norman Goddard, 31, a nurse. As he told me, "All my friends call me Stormin' Norman!!!" My Sony recorder was acting weird, but here is the general thrust of my conversation with Norman.

ME: At what point did you realize that you had to take the law into your own hands and report Ms. Boyd to Subway HQ?

STORMIN' NORMAN: That stuck-up scag wouldn't answer any of my phone calls, and I tried calling her every day for a year.

ME: What happened then?

STORMIN' NORMAN: I sent her a Hickory Farms smoked meat platter selection—one of those ironic gifts. I thought if I sent her flowers, it'd look like I was stalking her or something.

ME: What happened next?

STORMIN' NORMAN: She came over when I was at work and put the unopened platter on my front stoop. Then the neighbour's labradoodle got into it and then got sick and shat all over the concrete I'd just had power-washed.

ME: That's really interesting. Go on.

STORMIN' NORMAN: So I went to Michaels crafts store and got some big coloured cardboards and made some signs, which I taped to the side of my house that faces her place. I thought they were kind of nice.

ME: What did they say?

STORMIN' NORMAN: Let's see . . . One said, IT WAS JUST A GIFT. WHY DO YOU HAVE TO BE SO COLD? Another said, I THINK ABOUT YOU ALL THE TIME. IN A GOOD WAY.

ME: Nice enough.

STORMIN' NORMAN: Totally. But did she respond to me? No. She went to the cops and tried to get a restraining order, which was so insulting, because all I was trying to do was be nice to a neighbour. And she changed her phone number and got all these locks on the doors.

ME: Did she own the place?

STORMIN' NORMAN: Rental.

ME: What next?

STORMIN' NORMAN: She put up tinfoil on all the windows that faced mine.

ME: And then?

STORMIN' NORMAN: She was having a backyard barbecue with all her geek co-workers, and so I came over with a tray of hamburger patties I spiced and formed all by myself—I even put Saran Wrap on them to keep dust and flies off the meat—and when I walked into her yard, all of these people formed a human chain around her, and she ran inside. Jeez, I mean, I was just trying to be neighbourly.

ME: Was there a fight?

STORMIN' NORMAN: Nah. We all just yelled a bit. Got it out of our system. And then the cops showed up, so I thought to myself, *Stormin' Norman, maybe it's time you ate a reality sandwich and faced the fact that Kaitlin doesn't like you.* That's when I decided that if I couldn't have her, I'd make sure she noticed me in other ways.

ME: Really?

STORMIN' NORMAN: Oh yeah. I went to one of those spy shops and spent a fortune and began chronicling every moment of her life. Every single moment.

Unfortunately, website visitors, I lost the rest of the interview, but who says that investigative journalism is dead!!!???

Next week's investigation: What's the top-secret proportion of salt to pepper inside the salt-and-pepper can?

Subway Restaurants is the world's largest submarine sandwich franchise, with more than 24,000 locations in 83 countries. In 2002, the Subway chain surpassed McDonald's in the number of restaurants open in the United States and Canada. Headquartered in Milford, Conn., Subway Restaurants was co-founded by Fred DeLuca and Dr. Peter Buck in 1965. That partnership marked the beginning of a remarkable journey—one that made it possible for thousands of individuals to build and succeed in their own business. Subway Restaurants was named the number one franchise opportunity in all categories by *Entrepreneur* magazine in its Annual Franchise 500 ranking for 2005—for the 13th time in 17 years! For more information about the Subway restaurant chain, visit http://www.subway.com/. Subway® is a registered trademark of Doctor's Associates Inc. (DAI).

ATF
Alcohol, Tobacco and Firearms
AZT
Azidothymidine
BLT
Bacon, Lettuce and Tomato
BSE
Bovine Spongiform Encephalopathy
CIA
Central Intelligence Agency
CMV
Cytomegalovirus
DMZ
Demilitarized Zone
DOA
Dead on Arrival
EEC
European Economic Community
EMP
Electromagnetic Pulse
FBI
Federal Bureau of Investigation
FTP
File Transfer Protocol
GMT
Greenwich Mean Time
GTO
Gran Turismo Omologato
HIV
Human Immunodeficiency Virus
HOV
High Occupancy Vehicle
IMF
International Monetary Fund
IRA
Irish Republican Army
JFK
John Fitzgerald Kennedy
KGB
Komitet Gosudarstvennoi Bezopasnosti
KKK
Ku Klux Klan
LAX
Los Angeles International Airport
LSD
Lysergic Acid Diethylamide
MIA
Missing in Action
MP3
Moving Pictures Experts Group Audio Layer 3
NHK
Nihon Hoso Kyokai TV
NRA
National Rifle Association
NRK
Anarchy
OLE
Object Linking and Embedding
OPD
Officially Pronounced Dead
PFD
Photoshop File Document
PIN
Personal Identification Number

PSA
Prostate-Specific Antigen
PVC
Polyvinyl Chloride
QE2
Queen Elizabeth II
RGB
Red-Green-Blue
RNA
Ribonucleic Acid
SLA
Symbionese Liberation Army
SPF
Sun Protection Factor
SUV
Sport-Utility Vehicle
THC
Tetrahydrocannabinol
TNT
Trinitrotoluene
UPS
United Parcel Service
USD
US Dollar
VCR
Videocassette Recorder
VRE
Vancomycin-Resistant Enterococci
WTC
World Trade Center
WWW
World Wide Web
XML
Extensible Markup Language
XXL
Double Extra Large
XXX
Pornography
YTD
Year to Date
Y3K
The Year 3000
ZIP
Zone Improvement Plan
ZPG
Zero Population Growth

• • •

The next morning I slinked into a BoardX art meeting. Steve, Gord-O and staff from the loftiest links of the corporate food chain were trying to nail the essence of Jeff the Charismatic Turtle, albeit without joy or enthusiasm. Prototype turtle sketches were pinned onto a massive cork wall, all of them goofy and teensploitational: sunglasses, baggy pants and (dear God) a terry cloth sweatband.

"Does Jeff the Turtle follow players around the entire time they manipulate their third person?"

"Almost. Like Watson is to Sherlock Holmes."

"Can you imagine how annoying that would be?"

"Maybe the buddy isn't such a good idea."

Steve more or less squashed what hope remained: "It's going to be a buddy. Players will love it."

"Isn't our turtle supposed to be a bit more studly?"

"Turtles aren't studly by nature."

"What about that turtle they used in the 1950s to pimp the atomic weapons program? He was kind of studly."

"No, he wasn't, and besides, he's dead."

"What?"

"Dead. Hung himself from the side of his posh mid-town Manhattan terrarium. Left a note saying he couldn't handle the shame of what he'd done. Wrote it on a piece of bibb lettuce."

"Can't anyone think of hipper turtles than the Department of Energy's uranium spokesreptile?"

"Spokes*phibian.*"

"No one answered my question. Is our turtle studly? Does he have huge pecs?"

"I don't think it's appropriate that a turtle be *hot.*"

"Have you ever noticed how they never show the Ninja Turtles' shells if they can avoid it? They're always facing forwards."

"Hey—a thick, rich masculine shell. He could store a tool belt on it."

"If you look, you'll see that the Ninja Turtles' fleshy undersides are always overexposed, and the musculature is too steroidal. It's a reproductive strategy on their part, maybe."

"Are they gay?"

"I told you, Legal said we're *not* allowed to ask that, and besides, turtles are always straight."

"Hang on, we agreed to model the turtle after Jeff Probst, so maybe we could make our turtle wear Banana Republic summerwear. Maybe get a co-licensing deal."

"That could work."

"A tan?"

"I like the tan idea."

"Everybody, do we all like a suntan for our turtle? Let me do a hand count and get it out of the way—okay, suntan it is."

"Can he have more hair?"

"I have one word for you: *mammal*."

"If Donald Duck can have hands, Jeff can have hair. A little brush cut—easy to maintain, and it can take him from the boardroom all the way into a palm-fronded yurt populated with dormant tarantulas."

"No beaches here. Sand gets into skateboard bearings. Game over."

"Is Jeff middle-class?"

"By Jeff, you mean the turtle?"

"Yes. Can we all agree to just call him Jeff?"

"Okay, only so long as the real Jeff Probst never finds out we've been having this discussion."

"Is Jeff middle-class?"

"What you're really asking is, *What's Jeff's story?* What makes Jeff *Jeff*?"

"Yes."

"I think Art did a fine job of depicting Jeff here. Let's look at their ideas and take it from there."

Silence.

"Ideas? Thoughts?"

Silence.

Everyone suddenly remembered they were supposed to look interested. "Is he an adult turtle?"

"No. He's a teenager. Didn't I say that?"

"Where does he live?"

"Players don't need to know that."

"Is he the only turtle in the game?"

"Yes."

"Does he have magic powers?"

"No. He has boarding skill."

"Does he have a weak spot?"

"Yes—being flipped onto his back and left to die in the sun, or to have his innards ripped out by rogue weasels."

"Please," Steve said. "I believe in joshing around as much as the next guy, but let's all be serious. We have to get Jeff locked in by tomorrow."

"Jeff's not going to sing or do rap songs, is he?"

"We'll cross that bridge when we get there."

• • •

Three hours later Steve walked into jPod while I was procrastinating by downloading car crash images from a gore site in the Czech Republic.

"Steve. Uh, hi. You must be lost. What part of the building do you need to get to?"

"Here is fine."

"Oh."

"Your mother's a nice woman, Ethan."

"Well, yes."

"You're a lucky fellow."

"Thanks, Steve."

"She's got a good sense of humour. And when she talks to you, it's like you're the only person in the universe."

"Steve, I think I left my car in the parking lot." I stood up to go.

"Don't be in such a hurry. So, uh . . ." Steve began buying time. "Your brother sells real estate, right?"

"Sort of." I explained Greg's specialty.

"You think he'd sell me a place?"

"It's your money, Steve."

I gave Greg's information to Steve, and he left. I sat down, turned to look at my screen and then had a blinding headache. It was time to go home—eight o'clock—the earliest I'd left since the last game shipped.

Upon arriving at my stylish Chinatown shack, I walked in the door to see that all my new furniture was gone, and my original furniture hadn't come back. *Fuck*. I phoned Greg, but realized he was on Cathay Pacific 889, headed to Hong Kong. I phoned Mom.

"Ethan, you didn't even like the furniture."

"That's not the point. There's nothing in my place. Nothing."

"If you had a girlfriend, there'd be more possessions."

"You told me to dump my girlfriend."

"She was a mess. Good riddance. Greg said you really made that generous Chinese businessman angry."

"Who?"

"The one whose furniture you made fun of. Kam Fong."

"I didn't mock it. It's just not *me*."

"*Me*? Someone lavishes you with opulent furniture, and you simply dismiss it as '*Not me*'?"

"Okay, I didn't re*ject* it. I merely grudgingly accepted it."

"Which in Chinese culture is like piercing the heart with a freshly sharpened oyster shucker."

Silence.

"Ethan, I'm not supposed to tell you, but you might as well know. Kam Fong was hurt by your rejection of his gift."

"He doesn't even know me."

"He knew you well enough to give you over fifty thousand dollars worth of premium lacquered maple furniture. Here I am trying to breathe a bit of life into my old side table with Krylon spray paint, while *you,* Mister *Trading Spaces,* turn your nose up at a windfall from heaven."

"I can't believe we're having this discussion."

"All I'm saying is that he's probably not the sort of person you should tick off. Be nice to him when visits you."

"What—he's going to be coming here?"

"Of course he is. He wants to hear from you in person why you snubbed him."

"When is he coming?"

"When did you get home?"

"A few minutes ago."

"I imagine he'll be there any time now."

"What?"

I hear a large purring rumble outside the kitchen window. "Shit. That'll be him."

"Just don't tick him off any more. He's an important person who can do wonders for your career."

"In videogames?"

"Offer him something to drink the moment he walks in. If my business with the Asians has taught me anything, it's the power of a drink the first time you meet them."

I heard a knock at the door, and when I opened it, I found a chauffeur in an outfit imported from a 1930s drawing-room comedy. "Hello?"

"You're Mister Ethan?"

"Yes."

"Please wait. Mister Fong will be with you in a moment."

The car was parked at the foot of the stairs, a manly black brute of a machine, of unidentifiable manufacture and era. Pre-capitalist Red China? India? Munstermobile? A minute passed while the driver conferred through the car's rear passenger window slit. I was expecting Kam Fong to resemble that knife-throwing guy in a bowler hat from *Goldfinger;* instead, when he climbed out of the car, he was a guy a bit older than me—friendly-looking and decked out in Kidrobot chic with a shattered hairdo, wearing a set of fawnskin Puma reissued runners worth five hundred bucks—which is to say he looked like most of the kids at work who do low-level coding, the job that lands them the biggest salary and perks. "You're Ethan?"

"Yes."

"I'm Kam."

We shook hands.

"Hi. Uh, do you want to come in for a drink?" I was

wearing garments traded with his most recent cargo shipment, but if he noticed, he didn't show it. He also seemed to be unfazed by the absence of any furniture.

"Why don't we go somewhere else?"

Insert a funeral dirge here.

"Uh—it's been a long day. I think I just want to crash."

"No. Come on. What—like I'm going to hurt you? Don't be crazy. You're Greg's brother."

Nervous laughter.

"I never meet people who say no to me. I'm a bit curious to see what sort of person Greg's brother might be."

"I didn't say no to your furniture, I . . ." *I don't want to put an oyster shucker through your heart.* "Okay. Sure. Let's go."

We got into his car. "Look, about the furniture, I don't know what Greg told you, but—"

"Let's not talk about that. Not now."

"Where are we going?"

"A club I like. You know, I once visited someone out in the building where you work. Out in Burnaby."

That was odd. "Really?"

"Yes. I had to, er . . . *influence* somebody."

"Somebody up high?"

"No. At the bottom of your food chain. In quality assurance."

"Oh, Q/A. Everybody tortures the guys in Q/A. It's like being hazed for a living. But you're pretty high up the ladder—why would you bother with some kid in Q/A?"

"His father transferred ownership of several loads of, um, *cargo* into his name without asking me first."

"Wait a sec—if his family is so hoity-toity, why does he bother working at all, let alone in Q/A?"

"He enjoys bug testing."

"*Get paid to play videogames!* It's how they sucker staff into working there every time."

The car purred towards Kerrisdale. I'd always wanted to visit one of the neighbourhood's fabled Chinese nightclubs, where white ghosts like me are never permitted. Sadly, after a few minutes of small talk, we pulled up to a derelict medical-dental office building from the 1950s; my visions of pyramids built of champagne flutes, and costly drinks paid for by someone else, vanished.

"Here?" I asked.

"Yes. Let's go in."

So we entered a cool lobby, lit by a single fluorescent tube, the walls resonating with countless dental tortures of yore. We passed through oversized cherrywood doors, and then down a hallway to another pair of doors. I said, "You know why videogames make you wait for doors and gates to open between levels?"

"No, why?"

"The computer's buying time while it generates the new worlds behind them."

"Is that funny?"

"It wasn't supposed to be."

"I have no sense of humour."

"Huh?"

"No. I really don't. I pretend to laugh when I know someone's said something that, from experience, I know is supposed to be funny. To people with no sense of humour, laughing is a very ugly noise. Like my grandfather coughing up a throat-squid."

"Come on. You must find *something* funny—"

"No. Medically, legally, I have no sense of humour. It's a rare variety of autism. It doesn't even have a name."

More doors.

"Really?"

"It's a fact."

I heard sociable noises behind the final door. "What's in there?" I asked.

Kam jumped and turned to me while pulling something out of his rear pocket. "Freeze, asshole!"

I just about had a stroke.

"Gotcha," said Kam. "Come on in. This is a place I like to visit when I'm in town."

Kam Fong opened the door, and we walked into the middle of a ballroom dance club. He clapped his hands and a table with chairs appeared. "Cocktail?"

This was one of those moments when I remember saying to myself in a calm, clinically detached manner, *Ethan, you should simply go with the flow.*

"A whisky sour."

"Two whisky sours."

We were surrounded by women dressed as Carmelitas and men dressed like bi-curious toreadors. As I'd grown up in this sort of space, I felt quite at home. I decided to push the furniture issue. "Kam, look, about your furniture—it's just that Greg never asked me, and—"

"Ethan!"

I turned around. "Dad?" He was dressed in his favourite Casanova outfit, a toreador's cap rakishly adhered to his skull.

"Ethan, I never thought I'd see you in a ballroom dance club of your own volition."

"Actually, me neither."

"You're wearing your ragamuffin clothing. Aren't you getting too old for fashion statements?"

"It's not just a fashion. It's a—never mind. Dad, this is Kam Fong."

I introduced him as someone Greg does business with.

Dad shook hands. "Real estate?"

"No."

"Hey, but aren't you the guy who gave Ethan all that great furniture? That was really nice of you."

"Thank you."

"Ethan, why the hell couldn't you just enjoy the furniture and shut the fuck up? Christ, Mr. Fong, I have to apologize for Ethan."

"Apologies accepted. You're quite a dancer, Mr. Jarlewski."

"Latin and modern. Not professional, mind you, but I nearly got a bronze in the 1999 Snowball Classic."

"The IDSF Open to the World Standard?"

"That's the one."

"You're *that* Jim Jarlewski!"

"That's me."

"This is so exciting! Please, join us for a drink. Ethan, your father is *the* Jim Jarlewski. Greg never mentioned it."

"Gee."

At the far reaches of my twenties, once again I was a ballroom-dance-club orphan. Dad and Kam Fong began talking shop and drinking heavily, while blousy women in their forties, radiating imminent divorce and sexual despondency, tried to get their attention. At one point, Dad laughed at something, and, in response, Kam Fong delivered a grim flak of ersatz chuckles. He says he doesn't have a sense of humour, but maybe it's just a pose.

"Ethan, isn't this guy the greatest?" Dad was smitten with Kam's gangster charm.

"Sure is, Dad."

"Enough talk, Kam Fong. Now we must dance!"

The two of them reached out their hands, and each grabbed nearby *Pinot Gris*–soaked floozies—it was a dance-off.

If I didn't know better, it would have looked like Dad and Kam Fong were falling in love. However, I'd seen my father battle like this before, and knew it was no different than two ruffed grouse fluffing their feathers in competition for a hen's attention. When their dance-off ended, clapping drowned the room. They returned to our little table, flush with pheromones and the leftover traces of their respective partners' perfumes.

"I think I'll be going now," I said. "We're conceptually rejigging a new skateboard game to incorporate a charismatic turtle who follows the player throughout the game like a Dr. Watson, offering ongoing banter while logging gameplay statistics."

If Kam Fong had had a reason for taking me to his club, his male bonding with Dad had long since obliterated it. He was drunk, and obviously mellow. He said, "My people will try to find you some furniture more suitable to your obviously picky taste."

The music kicked into the Razormaid remix of "Copacabana," and Dad and Kam Fong were back on the floor. I cabbed back to my place, where I slept on the floor after drinking a NeoCitran made with hot tap water. I hoped that God would shake my Etch-a-Sketch clean overnight.

Limited-edition hollow rotocast vinyl
Urban vinyl action figures

Bruce Lee vinyl action figure

$55.95

BeeKing and BugBoy
Ah Gum and Ah Aun
Blue Brother Sunni
Grey Brother Raini
Anti-Potato Wheel
Odajima Hitoshi
Da Team Bronx
RC-911 figure
Balzac in Red
Potato Wheel
BJ Hammer
King Green
CosMouse
Scarygirl
Cloudi
Shiori

Grind the molten bucket

• • •

I found Bree, Cowboy, Evil Mark and John Doe in the cafeteria, feeding on cannelloni stuffed with confit of duck and wild rice. Evil Mark, obviously at the end of another rant, announced, "We're all clones."

"Huh?"

"Look at us. We're just clones working for the man."

"Oof. Take *that,* Dilbert."

"Working for the *man*?" Bree said. "Are you serious?"

"I was trying for ironic."

"You're always making these ironic comments that don't quite work."

"I think we're going to have to add 'humourless' to 'evil' in your nickname. But do tell us, why exactly are we clones?"

"Because we all really *do* dress like junior IT clones."

"Huh?"

"Blue or black denim pants—unless you're a senior and over thirty-five, after which point you spot-weld khakis to your lower torso for life."

"Go on."

"Dark-coloured long-sleeved outdoor-wear shirts—blue or black preferred. Haven't you noticed how nobody ever allows their forearms to be exposed here?"

We looked around, and Evil Mark was right. "Spooky."

Cowboy asked, "Does anybody here at the table speak a dead language?"

"COBOL?"

"No. Greek or Latin."

"Some. Why?"

"What's fear of exposed forearms?"

"Popeyedactylophobia."

Bree said, "Long-sleeved dark-coloured shirts conceal both obesity and scrawniness. They double as pajamas."

I said, "Stop, I can't take any more of this identity crap."

"That's easy for you to say," said John Doe. "Now that you have a distinct fashion style with your refugee chic. Anyway"—he and Cowboy stood up to leave—"it's time we hit the malls."

"Is it Tuesday already?"

"'Tis."

Tuesday is new shoe day, and Cowboy and John Doe are shoeheads—cool new sneakers reduce them to drooling Homer Simpsons in a blink. As for Evil Mark, he went off to buy ammonium persulphate to etch his motherboards at home. I must also note that calling Mark 'evil' may have started off as an arbitrary label, but now we're wondering if he really *does* make scary shit in his spare time.

Bree asked me, "How's the Kaitlin agenda going?"

"It's not. I think she could be worried I'm stalking her and she'll have to relive all that crazed next-door-neighbour nightmare shit again through me."

"Please. Have you tried talking to her?"

"No. I haven't even made eye contact with her since I read the Subway site. Have you?"

"No."

I was restless but couldn't figure out a good way to shirk my workload. I went online to see if there were any sneak previews of the new *Angel*—Wednesday is actually new comics day, but sometimes you can track down a tidbit the day before. I heard Kaitlin come into the pod space, and taking Bree's advice, I looked up to say hi, but my face collapsed—she was carrying a box of Krispy Kremes and a bag of the dreaded Taint.

"Hi, Ethan."

"Um, hi, Kaitlin." This would have been an optimum moment for her to offer me a donut, but she didn't. I got an instant message from Bree:

Oh.

My.

God.

She's going to

eat herself

to death.

Neither Bree nor I had the heart to announce a Taint-shunning. We settled down to work.

• • •

The good news is that BoardX will be keeping a large number of its pre-turtle skating environments, including a massive shopping mall level in which players score points for trashing the place. But given the suckiness of Jeff's character, it's hard to imagine players will still get to raise hell. Personal dialogues with Jeff keep running in my brain . . .

"Gee, player. That was a super-duper wheelie."

"Thanks, Jeff. Now fuck off."

"No can do, player. You're stuck with me."

"No, I'm not. I have the option to play without you."

"Not for the first three levels you don't, and even then, my friend, my likeness and name will be embedded in all gaming levels: billboards, signage, windows and street names. Your boss, Steve, has ensured that my presence will be pervasive."

"There must be a way to kill you."

"Sorry, player, but no."

In my mind, Jeff was on his back, a drill press approaching his tender underbelly from above.

"Excuse me, player," the turtle said, "but did you just have a degenerate thought picture in your head?"

"Me?"

"You wouldn't hurt Jeff, would you?"

"No."

"I don't believe you."

"Then don't."

"I'm going to tell Steve about you."

"You do that."

"Ethan?"

"Whuh . . . ?"

"Ethan, wake up."

I opened my eyes: *Steve.* "Oh. Steve. Hi."

"I can see that was a doozy of a nightmare you were having."

He stood there staring at me.

"Steve, is there something I can help you with?"

"No. Nothing. Just thought I'd pop by."

"Okay . . ."

"How's BoardX going?"

"It's one smoking game, Steve."

"It is. And Jeff is going to be a big hit. I can feel it."

I looked at my screen: "Look! An email's come down the Chute! I'm going to have to answer this one, Steve. See you later?"

"Righty-o, pardner."

• • •

Comics day came and went. Another shoe day came and went. And another comics day followed that—the typical production and consumption cycles that help us survive our dismal, meaningless little lives.

Starting with that first Krispy Kreme box, Kaitlin's been collecting all her fast-food packaging and arranging it into a big stack. She takes cardboard and other greasy items to the bathroom, where (Bree tells me) she treats them with alcohol and another chemical that makes them ungreasy.

I'm still too freaked out to talk to her. When she comes in with ever more massive quantities of food, the five of us keep our heads bowed as we listen to the endless rumpling of bags and wrappers and clamshell containers and straws hiccupping their way in and out of plastic lids. She's like an alien luxuriously chewing away on a cocooned earthling. It gives us fear.

Doritos

Rollitos

Nacho Cheesier!

Bite-Size Tortilla Snacks

JL 19
6 053 14027
09:51

Product enlarged to show texture

300 g

Amount Per Serving	
Calories:	150
Total Fat:	12% RDA
Saturated + trans fats:	8% RDA
Cholesterol:	0% RDA
Sodium:	8% RDA
Total Carbohydrate:	6% RDA
Dietary Fiber:	5% RDA
Vitamin A:	2% RDA
Vitamin C:	0% RDA
Calcium:	0% RDA
Iron:	2% RDA
Sugar:	less than 1 g
Protein:	2 g

Ingredients: corn, vegetable oil (contains one or more of the following: corn, soybean, or sunflower oil), salt, monoglyceride, cheddar cheese (cultured milk, salt, enzymes), whey, monosodium glutamate, buttermilk solids, Romano cheese from cow's milk (cultured pasteurized partskim milk, salt, enzymes), tomato powder, whey protein concentrate, onion powder, partially hydrogenated soybean oil, disodium phosphate, lactose, natural and artificial flavor, garlic powder, dextrose, sugar, citric acid, spice, lactic acid, sodium caseinate, artificial color (including Yellow 6), disodium inosinate, disodium guanylate and non fat milk solids.

CONTAINS MILK INGREDIENTS.

made with non-hydrogenated oil

o 60410 10 03997 2

• • •

I won the third floor's intramural Tetris competition, which took place in the conference room this afternoon—a canister of liquid nitrogen! So afterwards we scoured the office for flash-freezables.

Effects of liquid nitrogen on office items:

Half a tuna sandwich	Shattered like chalk
Souvenir vintage *Diff'rent Strokes* pocket calculator	Kept working
Paper (20-lb bond)	No discernable effect
Half-eaten donut from Kaitlin's trash	Crumbled
Philodendron leaf	Went potato-chippy
Fat Bastard figurine	Paint flecked off
Tip of John Doe's ring finger	Lost all sensation

After a while we ran out of possibilities, so we went down and flash-froze puddles by the soccer field, and for the rest of the day everyone talked about Ice-9 from Kurt Vonnegut's *Cat's Cradle.* Anything that lowers productivity is fine by me.

• • •

I caught Evil Mark licking his stapler.

• • •

In order to keep my podmates' minds off the insect-like sounds of Kaitlin's rustling food packaging, I made up a template and challenged them each to use five hundred words or less to sell themselves as if they were on eBay.

IT workers > Game junkies > Infinite sadness > I am the ghost of troubled Joe

All-purpose IT Worker & Stud. "Cancer Cowboy." One only. Cool in a Steve McQueen Kind of Way.

Item number: 7471313007
Current bid: US $6.66 (Reserve not met)
Time left: We're doomed
Start time: Apr-11-76 17:19:35 PDT
Ends: At any moment, PDT
History: 19 bids
High bidder: time_wastr (1)
Item location: Burnaby, BC Canada/Suburbia
Ships to: Worldwide
Seller: maudlin_drinker

Description
You are bidding on the fully functional IT worker "Cancer Cowboy," serial number: CASPER JAMES JESPERSON. 28 years old. Some scarring. What you see in the photo is what you get. Not responsible for congenital health issues or bastard children who may or may not appear on owner's doorstep.

Cowboy has been extensively reconditioned by a recently vacated ex-girlfriend, and has had a NEW wardrobe installed by overpriced designer boutiques that give you cappuccinos while you shop. Cowboy's hair has also been beautifully reconditioned by a pair of nail scissors, half a bottle of tequila and persistent self-esteem issues.

IT workers the world over know of Cancer Cowboy's manly prowess. Pilot your way through his many levels and bonus rounds, dodging STDs and provincial in-office cigarette smoking regulations. For double-gun firepower, acquire liquor, cleverly mixed CD song sets and antibiotics.

Most sellers will not tell you what I'm telling you because they want you to believe their product is "mint" and will never break. That's obviously impossible.

Click on picture to enlarge what is already large.
Supersize picture
Shipping and payment details

Soul-sucking cubicle > Aging > Babydoll > PVC > Body stockings > Thigh highs

L@@K WOW!!!!!
Mega-Rare Tech Ho
Complete w/ Stalled Career

Item number:	000111000111
Current bid:	US $9.95 (Reserve not met)
Time left:	According to parents, spinsterhood shortly
Start time:	Apr-22-80
Ends:	Seemingly never
History:	0 bids
Item location:	Coquitlam, BC Canada/Suburbia/Everywhere/Nowhere/Global
Ships to:	Preferably Tokyo
Seller:	brasspole (0)

Description
This auction is for Bree Jyang, who has fallen into the depressingly predictable yet still sexy Bettie Page look/thing/whatever.

Bree is 64 inches tall and has jointed arms and legs and a moveable head. Her hair is long, black and rooted, and her makeup is flawless, complete with mole on left cheek.

Bree also sometimes wears a large sombrero hat, a style that was brought back into the limelight when *The Rocketeer* was released, starring Jennifer Connelly and Timothy Dalton.

Bree is wearing a gold silk-look crop top with a daring neckline and black and gold shoulder straps; her 7 1/2-inch heels are *so* Dita Von Teese.

Bree's inner life is one of burlesque, complete with singers and saucy strippers, including famed female impersonator Vickie Lynn. In her mind, Bree has even made a guest appearance in the greatest stripper movie of all time, *Varietease*.

Bree was born on April 22, 1980, in Nanaimo, BC, where she was known as Dark Queen of Bondage. Okay, not really, but she knew what she liked at an early age. In 2002 she was discovered by her parents to have not enough concern for her future, so she was shipped to one of 400 videogame design schools in Vancouver, where it turned out she not only had a flair for game design, but was also but a mere gentle puff of a rotating nipple tassel away from four local strip clubs.

Bree is awaiting your interest. She has just changed her outfit and is now wearing a fabulous "Bow" bustier by Bali, style #8211, c. 1940s, with a black satin torso. The cups are stunning and have black sheer-illusion lace with the famous "circle stitch" for that sizzling sweater-girl bullet-bra look. The size on tag reads 36D and will fit up to a 38" bust. Bree would like to know what you are wearing, too.

If **Bree** is something you've been looking for, don't let this pass you by! **BUY BREE NOW AND SAVE! CHECK OUT MY OTHER AUCTIONS! SHOP EASILY BY THUMBNAIL PICTURE GALLERIES!**

Wage slavery > Temporary > Get to the point > Let X = X > Start

2005 All-Star Winner Mark Jackson

Item number: 4522041813 (generated with pseudorandom # generator)
Current bid: 23 Zlotys (made that up)
Time left: Hours ago (not very funny)
Start time: Now (ditto)
Ends: When it ends
History: 0 bids
High bidder: 0 bids
Item location: North Vancouver, BC, Canada
Ships to: You (ha ha ha witty)
Seller: prefersblackspy

Buy it Now!

Description
You are bidding on a comprehensive LOT OF CHARACTER TRAITS made from premium DNA and SPECIFIC CULTURAL CIRCUMSTANCES: MARK JACKSON IS A TECH MONEY BONANZA CONTENDER, THREE-D CODER AND HARDWARE DESIGNER to name a few. This lot is also LOADED WITH FEATURES: PERSEVERANCE, AMBITION, A 3.9 COLLEGE GPA and, if I listen to my shithead cubicle neighbours, EVIL.

CODING LANGUAGES (C++, SOFTIMAGE) ABILITY TO BENCH PRESS 250, ENCYCLOPEDIC KNOWLEDGE OF NFL, CFL & NBA STATS, 4% BODY FAT, NATURALLY ENDOWED WITH EPIC GREEK MUSCLES (SIDES OF STOMACH). Currently KILLING TIME UNTIL MY SECRET HARDWARE IDEAS ARE PATENTED AND MADE GLOBAL. YOU LOOK AT RICH PEOPLE AND THEIR PICTURES AND WONDER, WHY IS THAT PERSON RICH AND NOT ME? THERE'S NO ANSWER TO THIS, EXCEPT TO SAY THAT I AM GOING TO BE RICH.

Other GOOD VALUES appear in abundance in this lot, and exceed the best 2005 tech employees now being offered on eBay. Everything you see will be included w/ no surprises.

Quiet life > Unexamined > No frills > Normal > Undamaged

Sensible Value for Typical Fellow

Item number: 1234567890
Current bid: US $99.99 (Reserve not met)
Time left: 74.5 years minus current age
Start time: June-06-77
Ends: When the time comes
History: Average amount
Item location: Vancouver, BC
Ships to: Anytown
Seller: bellcurve (0)

Description
John Doe comes with no scary Web links or disturbing images stashed in the bowels of his computer. Not one. What few cuts and dings exist are exposed for all to see, as is his small bald spot. John Doe is clean and sensible, but can also be stylish if enough advance notice is given. To be this good a deal, John has had to be stored in a garage for an awfully long time.

John Doe is excellent for families and clean normal living. Yes, John Doe has all the features that are a must-have in today's hectic world.

Dude > XBox > Wolverine > Open source

Ethan Jarlewski

Item number: Second-born of two sons
Current bid: C $41,500 per year (Reserve not met)
Time left: After age 30 will probably become bitter
Start time: Now
History: 0 bids
Item location: Vancouver, BC
Ships to: Anywhere
Seller: IAMU&URME

Feedback Score: 1,000
Positive Feedback: 1,000%

Description
Ethan was developed in a cool, dry, non-smoking home and was released in 1976. His body movements are disarmingly realistic, and his voice feature often works when connected to a compatible play set.

Ethan is a hard-to-find item, especially in this condition, Good to Very Good or better. He has no tan and his acne ended four years ago. All wiring and plumbing is in good order. No manual is included, but his operation is highly intuitive. WARNING: Ethan does not respond well when people try to change him. Highest bidder takes him as is, NO REFUNDS.

Ethan remains highly annoyed by the Sprite™ ad campaign from the late 1990s and early 2000s, even though that campaign is over. "Obey Your Thirst"—what kind of idiotic slogan is that? "Gee, I'm thirsty, but I'd better not drink anything, because that would mean obeying my thirst." Ethan is also annoyed by the Audi campaign that says, "Never Follow." Frankly, Ethan is annoyed with all of these dumb campaigns that indoctrinate millions of people into thinking they're tough-guy free spirits when, in fact, there's probably much to be said for following and, in any event, the food chain isn't structured to encompass millions of non-followers. So you end up with a population of frustrated, brink-of-bitterness cranks.

Like anyone, Ethan Jarlewski enjoys a good game. Of the following true or false questions, only one is true. Choose which one and win an insider's discount and free shipping with real bubble-pack, not crumpled paper. Ethan is yours for the having—bid with confidence!

T **F** Ethan secretly enjoys checking into low-rent motels and dressing up in a Sir Lancelot costume.

T **F** Ethan was a regular guest on the popular 1980s police drama *Cagney & Lacey.*

T **F** Ethan has a double recessive genetic anomaly that allows him to photosynthesize chlorophyll.

T **F** Ethan is able to make toilets flush clockwise in both the northern and southern hemispheres.

T **F** In a few minutes Ethan is going to pretend he doesn't like singing karaoke, but he really does like it, and with just a minimum of coaxing will steal hearts and souls with his own sound stylings of Neil Diamond's "Cracklin' Rosie."

T **F** Ethan's secret buyer name on eBay is DungeonLad, and he can almost always be found bidding on memorabilia related to the life and career of Charlotte Rae, better known as Mrs. Garrett from TV's enduring family comedy *The Facts of Life*.

T **F** Ethan secretly wishes life were simpler and he could sell lemonade from a card table at the end of his street.

• • •

Dad phoned while I was trying to beat Super Metroid on a PC SNES emulator (in under an hour and ten, with no more than 50% items).

"Ethan, come out to the set and spend time with me."

"Dad, it's eleven p.m. I'm still at work. What's wrong?"

"Is it so much to ask that you come cheer up your old man?"

"Dad, hanging out on sets is boring. They're even more boring than ballrooms. Learn how to knit."

"The food here sucks."

"Dad, are you even listening to me?"

"And the actress in this dog of a movie is vegan, so everybody else has to be one, too."

"Unions allow that?"

"Ethan, I really need you here."

"Is it Ellen?"

"No."

"What is it, then?"

"I said it was nothing. I just want to see you."

"I'm going to hang up if you don't tell me what's going on."

"Oh, all right. It's Kam Fong."

"He's messing with your life?"

"Yeah."

"How? Why?"

"He got . . . a speaking part on this movie."

"What?"

"What a prick, huh?"

"He's not even an actor. How did he get a speaking part?"

"Well, you know, since that night at the club, we've become pretty good friends, so I invited him out here to visit the set. I was taking him from the crew parking lot to the cameras, when he stepped in a puddle and dirtied his precious booties. He went mental in Mandarin, and the director heard him. *How authentic!* he shrieked, and *bingo.* Kam Fong is Mister moo-goo-gai-pan-Charlie-Chan-me-so-horny Asian actor guy, and I'm still a generic asshole who gets blown up at the start of act one."

"Being blown up is pretty good. At least for a few seconds the audience is focused entirely on you."

"This big woof-woof of a movie is a gorefest. Nobody's going to notice me."

"Hey wait—a vegan actress is doing a movie with so much violence?"

"I know—weird, huh?"

I couldn't keep Dad sidetracked for long.

"All those years in voice training and method and workshops, and this shit-for-brains steps in a puddle, and he's already drawing blueprints for his personal trailer."

"Dad, mellow out. It's a small speaking part. Big deal."

Sniffle.

"Dad, are you crying?"

"Am I a jerk-off of a father to call his son in a time of need?"

"Okay, okay, I'm coming. Where are you?"

As I was driving out to Dad's shoot, Mom called my cell. "Ethan?"

"Hi, Mom."

"Where are you?"

"In the car. I'm heading out to see Dad on the set."

"Why?"

"He called me up—he's bummed because Kam Fong got a speaking part in his movie."

"What's the deal with your father and this new best friend of his, Mr. Kung Fu? They're on the phone all day, talking about ballroom dancing."

"Mom, Kam Fong's head of a Chinese people-smuggling syndicate. He doesn't have time to be Dad's secret gay lover."

"He's your father's gay lover?"

"No. But he loves ballroom dancing, and you don't."

"Ethan, you know how boring that ballroom world is."

"Yeah, but Dad loves it."

"All those divorcees dressed like fourteen-year-old figure skaters."

"Well, now he finally has a friend to discuss it with."

Silence.

"Mom?"

Silence again.

"Mom—are you jealous?"

"Me? No. Why should I be jealous? My husband is merely spending all his waking moments with a man who probably has five bolero jackets at the dry cleaners, and a dozen fruit-flavoured lip smackers concealed in an ostrich-feather clutch purse."

"Mom, what are you doing up at"—I looked at the dash clock—"eleven-thirty?"

"I can't sleep."

"How come?"

"Oh, nothing."

I let it go and said good night—it was too late in the day to investigate Mom's interior world, too.

At the set, I found Dad and Kam Fong practising ballroom dance steps with invisible partners.

So much for Dad being miserable.

"Hi, guys."

"We're rehearsing a variation on the East Coast Swing. Ready, Kam?"

"Ready."

As a duo, they began to move, and in my head I remembered all the colour-commentary dance notations I'd had to learn while growing up . . .

. . . *backaway*

. . . *she turns*

. . . *he turns*

. . . *tuck-in release*

. . . *basic step in open position*

. . . *underarm turn in open position*

. . . *change of places*

. . . *crossover turn in open position*

. . . *behind the back changes*

. . . *flirtation*

. . . *close.*

"I hear you got a speaking part, Kam Fong," I said when they stopped. "Congratulations."

"I never thought of being in films before."

"What's your character?"

"I play a Chinese gang kingpin. The guy who was supposed to be playing it had an allergic reaction to erythromycin. He's dead."

"It's your big break."

"You said it."

Dad didn't like this conversation. He cut it short. "Ethan, I have to go out to Port Coquitlam on an errand. Come with me."

"Errand?"

"Yeah. The guy who helps your mother and me get bootleg satellite TV signals has gone to the Yucatan. We need to get a software patch for the satellite card from his brother. He lives way out in the boonies."

"What's the hurry?"

"Your mother wants to catch a *Sex and the City* marathon tomorrow, and I like to watch *Band of Brothers* in the mornings. It gives me a lift for the rest of the day."

"Dad, just buy a satellite card. What's the big deal?"

"Pay full price, when I can get one for almost nothing? Talk about throwing money away."

"You North American young people spend money like crazy," added Kam.

"He practically *lives* in restaurants," Dad said, nodding in my direction, "and last year he bought a fridge and paid retail."

"Fool."

"You dragged me out here just so you could have some company in the car?"

"Yes."

What the hell. "Oh, all right."

Dad's car was being detailed by a gofer, while my car had been hemmed in by a trailer, so we borrowed Kam's two-ton smuggling-mobile. Our destination? A mildewed dump of a shack owned by some yokel named Clem. It bordered the slope of a Port Coquitlam forest recently scraped clean to make way for a subdivision. The trunks of the few trees that remained resembled telephone poles.

Clem opened the door like an ElfQuest troll about to hand us a curse and a talisman. He motioned us inside, where all of the walls were made of heavily varnished logs seasoned by decades of nicotine. I spotted a bookshelf filled with Mel Gibson tapes and DVDs, and three flatulent

German shepherd/lab crosses that evidently enjoyed the house's sauna-like atmosphere. Clem noticed me looking and said, "Mel is God. I think I've got your satellite card in the dining room. Don't mind the clutter." I scrutinized the walls—pictures of Clem's days as a longshoreman mingled with framed inspirational Alcoholics Anonymous plaques. There was a newspaper clipping of Clem holding a sockeye in the 1963 *Sun* Salmon Derby that had faded away almost to nothing. When Clem gave Dad the new card, we bolted for the truck. Once inside, we started laughing. Dad laid rubber, and I was glad the evening was coming to a close.

The dashboard beeped. Dad looked down. "We're low on gas."

"There's a Mohawk station down the hill."

While Dad was filling up the truck, I went to the station's mini-mart to stock up on Slim Jims. At the cash I glanced out at the pumps and saw Lyle from the biker house filling up his hog—*crap*.

The clerk asked if everything was okay, and I said, "Yeah, yeah."

A large delivery vehicle pulled in, giving me enough cover to scramble to our truck. Dad asked, "What's wrong with you?"

"That guy on the bike."

"What about him?"

"Mom and I went to collect a few days ago."

"And?"

"His pit bull chomped Mom's leg, and she fired a few shots, and it was kind of a, um, mess."

"Pit bull? Your mother told me it was a gardening wound—kneeling on a rake."

Dad kept his cool while paying the cashier just ahead of

Lyle, but once back in the truck, he announced, "Nobody's dog attacks my wife. Let's nail the bastard."

I had no idea what Dad's plan was, but we pulled out from the pumps ahead of Lyle. "Dad, what are you—?"

I heard Lyle's hog approaching us from behind. Once we were around the corner and out of sight of the gas station, Lyle gunned his throttle to pass us. Dad veered sharply into the other lane, walloping the bike, sending Lyle flying out into the roadside weeds. The hog somehow managed to get snagged beneath the truck.

"Dad! Holy shit! The bike's stuck." The metallic scraping reminded me of trash cans being dragged down the driveway. "Are you going to stop or what?"

"In a second."

Sparks from the bike flared in the rear-view mirror. "Awesome light show," I said.

A quarter-mile down the road, Dad stopped the truck, then reversed it a bit to dislodge the hog. Then he said, "Get out, son, and open the back. We're putting it in."

"Why?"

"So our dog breeder pal can walk home."

As I got out, I heard Lyle screaming at us from back up the road. I looked his way, but he didn't seem to be running. I opened the back hatch.

Dad said, "Grab the front wheel. On the count of three we toss it into the back. One. Two. *Three—*" The bike was heavier than I thought it would be.

"Dad, this thing weighs a ton."

"Let's get some help then."

Dad shouted, "移动您的懒惰身体，傻瓜!" and from the deepest recesses of the truck emerged a half-dozen Chinese people.

"Dad?"

Dad shouted, "移动您的懒惰身体，傻瓜!" and the boat people hoisted the bike into the back. Dad closed the door. "Let's go."

"What does 移动您的懒惰身体，傻瓜 mean?"

"Kam says it all the time into his cellphone. It means *move your ass.*"

EWTN Europe

WAM/America's Kidz Network

Dish Music—New Orleans Jazz

Daystar

Nickelodeon/Nick at Nite (East)

Fox Kids Italia

CD-Contemporary Jazz Flavors

TV Martí

America's Store

Future TV USA

Dish Music—Piano & Guitar Encore

ESPN Now

Hallmark Channel Mexico

SatMex 5

Almavisión
Sky Link TV
BBC America
QVC UK

Naples Fort Myers Greyhound Park
California Community Colleges Satellite Network
Prison TV Network

C-SPAN2

Total Living Network

MTV China

Praise TV

JCTV

GRTV 2

NASA TV

TBN Philippines

FamilyNet

INSP—The Inspiration Network

Bloomberg TV Asia-Pacific

Bloomberg TV Deutschland

• • •

I made Dad stop at a 7-Eleven and we bought chocolate bars, bottled water and orange juice for the people in the back. As we neared the production's trailers, my cell rang. It was Cowboy.

"Ethan, man, I'm losing it."

"Losing *what*?"

"You've got to help me, man."

"Where are you?"

"I'm in North Van."

"What happened?"

"I was in a fourgy with these three BMX chicks I met last weekend, and it was a dream come true, and then this one chick puts on a Raggedy Ann wig and a red foam nose, and says, *Look at me, I'm Ronald McDonald,* and I freaked."

I hopped out and made a *gotta go* hand gesture to Dad. "You freaked over a *wig*?"

"You don't understand. We wrote all those crazy-assed letters to Ronald, and he somehow got registered in my subconscious as the devil. It was like I could already see the cheesy high-8 video of a four-way, and instead of hair, Ronald's ass had red yarn sticking out of it."

"Uh-huh. And makeup all over the sheets."

"Don't mock my freak-out."

"Are you on anything tonight?"

Silence.

"Cowboy, *are* you?"

"I got pretty 'tussed up beforehand."

"Cowboy, you know you can't drink cough syrup. Robitussin takes you to the dark side every time. It's your kryptonite."

"But these chicks were all doing it, and I had to look cool in front of them."

"Cowboy, if these naked chicks were jumping off a cliff, would you jump after them?"

"Sure."

I thought about that for a second.

He said, "Man, it was so freaky. It was like Ronald could look into my eyes and see the part of me that's dying."

"Where are you specifically?"

"In the Denny's on Marine Drive."

"Did you manage to dress before you fled?"

"Sort of. I didn't have time for underwear, and I left my favourite Doritos baseball cap behind."

"I'll be there in fifteen minutes."

I got into my own car. There's nothing like driving on an empty freeway to clear the mind. How often have I rescued Cowboy from his sex/death freak-outs? Too many times. I really had to lay down the law this time, and I was practising my speech as I pulled into the parking lot.

I found him hunched in a booth, a coffee in front of him. "Okay, Cowboy—three BMX chicks? Please. What's the real story?"

"You don't believe me?"

"No. Girls rarely enter bike culture. If they do, they're fully mated. Who were you really with?"

"I can't believe you don't believe me."

"You're boring me."

"All right, all right. They were skanks."

"I *knew* it. Where'd you meet?"

"At a coffee place on Marine Drive. They were at the next table and buzzed out on 'tuss, and we made eye contact and—it just kind of happened. I mean, Ethan, nobody *plans* a four-way."

We ordered Grand Slams and when the food arrived, we picked at our scrambled eggs half-heartedly. Finally Cowboy said he was feeling better and apologized for having roped me into his el skanko lifestyle. It was four-thirty a.m. when we left the Denny's.

In the back seat of my car was a pile of kitchen things I'd promised to return to Mom. As I was near the old house, I decided to drop them right then. I drove up the hill, pulled into my parents' street, and there, parked in front of their hedge, was a Touareg with a box sitting on top of it wrapped in gold paper with a big silk bow. The driver's door was open, and as I slowly drove past I saw Steve at the wheel. I stopped and got out. Steve was shaving in the rear-view mirror.

"Oh. Ethan. Hi. Uh. How are you?"

"Steve, why are you shaving at the end of my parents' driveway at 4:45 in the morning?"

"It's not what it looks like."

"Which would be what?"

"Your mother's a fine woman, Ethan."

"And?"

"I think I'm in love."

That shut me up.

"I know she's fifteen years older than me, but I can't stop thinking about her."

"Steve, she's married to my *dad.* And you're going to give her a present at 4:45 in the morning? What kind of a loser are you?"

"I was going to wait until six."

"Steve, why don't you go home right now, and I'll forget this ever happened."

"I need to talk about her a bit. Let me do that. There's nobody in my life I can do that with, and it's killing me."

"I thought you were married."

"Divorced."

"Okay, here's the deal: you get to talk about my mother for five minutes, but no sex stuff. In return, I get to ask you privileged questions about BoardX."

"Deal."

"I go first. Why are you wrecking a potentially massive and successful game with this pathetic turtle idea?"

"Who says it's pathetic?"

"Cough up some truth, or I'm not going to discuss Mom with you. You know the turtle's a crappy idea. Something's up."

"My kid likes turtles."

"I know that. So what?"

"I don't have visitation rights."

"Why not?"

"I won't talk about that."

"So you're sticking a turtle in our game in order to communicate with your son?"

"Yes."

"Do you know how many man-years go into making a game? How much heart and soul? You'd fuck that over to send a personal message to your kid?"

"I would. Jeff is worth it."

"Jeff? I thought you told us his name is Carter."

"I fibbed."

We heard the first bird tweets of the day.

"Steve," I said, "send your kid a fruit basket. A birthday card. An FTD bouquet of gerbera daisies, but *don't* doom our game to oblivion because you can't get your fathering act together."

"Your feelings are valid, Ethan, but my therapist warned me that if I don't go through with the Jeff character, I could easily enter a shame spiral from which I might never return."

"That's it. I'm leaving."

"Ethan? It's my turn to talk about your mother. A deal's a deal."

"Okay, but remember, she's married to my father and they've been together forever, so you know right from the start that any hope you might have for a relationship is doomed."

"I do."

I looked at my watch. "One, two, three, *go.*"

"Where to begin? Well, she made me a pie. It was blueberry, and when she gave it to me, its smell mixed with her perfume and it made me feel—"

"Stop. Getting too personal."

"And she even brought a cloth napkin, not a paper one . . ."

"Deal's off. I can't do this."

I abandoned him there, half-shaved and moony.

• • •

The sun was rising—a glowing apricot washed by pink clouds. Lions Gate Bridge was empty and the ducks in Lost Lagoon were chattering away. Closer to home, the junkie needles and gum wrappers on the streets twinkled like Mario sprites.

My phone rang just as I was passing the vegetable stalls setting up for the day on Keefer Street: Bree.

"Ethan, do you have a minute?"

"Bree, it's almost six in the morning—why are you calling?"

"Don't play the time card stunt with me. You know we're not like other people."

"Is everything okay?"

"Yes. No."

"Where are you?"

"jPod."

"And?"

"Ethan, I feel so old."

This isn't the first time I've had this call from Bree. "So?"

"It's different for girls than it is for boys."

"How?"

"Because we have a finite number of eggs, Ethan. It's not like we generate a billion new ones every time we get off."

"Are you pregnant?"

"I wish. No, strike that—no, I *don't* wish. I have no idea."

"Let me pull over to the side of the road." I did. "When was the last time you got some sleep?"

"Two days ago."

"Go home and sleep, then."

"Sleep is overrated. Everyone thinks that just because you have a nap, your life is fixed."

"Bree, did the whole city just take the same drug? *Everybody* in my life is going random all over the place."

"Like who?"

"My dad—and probably my mother. And Cowboy had another sex/death bottoming-out. He was the filling in a skank sandwich in North Van. Triple-decker. One of them put on a Ronald McDonald wig, and he flipped out."

"No way."

"It's true."

"Was he 'tussed up?"

"Yeah."

"He's got to stay away from that stuff. Why was a skank wearing a Ronald McDonald wig?"

"Strictly speaking, it was a Raggedy Ann wig."

Vitamin G: *gossip.* I could tell Bree was feeling a bit better, but I was suddenly racked by a wave of sleepiness and told Bree I had to hang up. Inasmuch as a car can limp, I limped home, back to my crappy furniture, which had magically reappeared a few weeks ago.

However, when I got there, I saw five profoundly expensive cars parked outside my place—a Bentley, a Lotus and three Italian somethings. I parked behind them, and as I got out of my car, I heard loud music and the sounds of cats in great pain. At my front door stood a gym goon wearing a headset.

"You're Ethan? Go in."

"Gee, thanks."

Taped to the door was a laser-printed sheet of 8 ½ x 11 paper:

SOUTHEAST ASIA CO-PROSPERITY SPHERE
SCHOOL OF TYPING AND BUSINESS ACUMEN
20TH REUNION

The transition from the early morning sunlight into the mysteriously darkened house made me squint. Projected onto my living-room wall was a soft-lens film shot of fluttering cherry petals. In front of it stood a stout little fireplug of a Chinese guy singing a cat-wailing version of "Maniac." He was obviously tanked. Arranged around him in a semicircle were maybe a dozen other Chinese guys, including Kam Fong.

Mr. Fireplug finished his tune, and the others clapped

loudly and sarcastically. Kam looked over at me. In Chinese, he said to the guys in the room,

“這是我告訴您的那個輸家。我們演奏以他的頭腦和刺激他入唱一首可笑歌曲。”

(“This is that loser I was telling you about. Let’s play with his mind and goad him into singing a ridiculous song.”)

Everybody clapped and invited me over to try some of their paint-stripper sake, served by three pretty young women in hot pants and top hats. Then one of the guys stood up and began singing the Psychedelic Furs classic “Love My Way,” against a backdrop of the neon-lit alleys of Tokyo.

“Kam, what’s all this about?”

“These are guys I went to school with. We’re having a blast.”

“Why are you in my house?”

“We needed a place with an atmosphere of poverty to remind us of the old days. Come on and drink with us. Get hammered.”

“Kam, it’s morning.”

“Not in Hong Kong.” He clapped his hands, and one of the servers brought a Scotch and soda. Before I had a chance to wave my hands and say no, Kam and his buddies made a toast that appeared to be to me. What the heck—I drank it—and, three drinks later, I was catapulted into that fetid pit of ritualized humiliation called karaoke.

Kam clapped his hands, and the male technician running the karaoke machine giggled as he put on, yes, Bonnie Tyler’s “Total Eclipse of the Heart.” I was doomed.

What is the science behind humiliation? Does it generate a special molecule of adrenaline? Does your blood recognize what’s happening and take different paths through your body in response? And why does the inside of your mouth turn to lint and your ears begin to burn?

I looked behind me: dandelions fluffed across a Swiss meadow. A lark flittered from a branch out into a blue sky draped with marshmallow clouds as the first few notes of the song's tinkling dirge haunted my living room. I was totally fucked—which, of course, made great entertainment for Kam's drunken buddies. I tried to put down the mike thirty seconds in, but Kam slammed his glass on the table in a manner that let me know it would be disadvantageous to do so.

I suppose I blacked out after that point. I remember the music dying down and opening my eyes to see everybody—servers and tech guy included—cramped with laughter. Needless to say, the technician filmed the whole thing.

Suddenly it was ten a.m. I went upstairs to my bedroom, which was being used as the party's coatroom. I considered sleeping on the floor again, above the raucous chattering below, then went back downstairs. I went into the kitchen and grabbed a box of Chinese donuts made with bean paste, then got into my car and drove directly to work. The only person in jPod was Kaitlin. She said, "Caught your performance. Kam did a live webcast."

"I—" I handed her the box of donuts. "I brought these for you. By the way, I really like you."

She looked at them as if I'd just handed her a dismantled carburetor.

"Please. Just eat them," I said. "I'm tired right now. I'm going to nap under my desk."

I was on the cusp of sleep when Kaitlin moved my chair away and bent down to speak to me. "You know, the whole Subway website thing was a hoax."

"What?"

"I just wanted to fuck with all of you. I've been a size 2 my entire life. I eat like a pig, and nothing sticks."

"But how did they get that photo of you? You weighed, like, 337 pounds!"

"That's my sister. She got the family's lard gene."

"But—"

"Ethan, be quiet. I saw you at that conference my first week here—your momma walked in and you were really nice to her, and then here, this morning, you give me donuts, which means you're not trying to change me or anything—that you can handle me being me, even if that means eating myself to death."

I looked up and was suddenly, irrationally, pleased there was no gum tucked under the desk's front lip.

Kaitlin said, "I'm going to see *Princess Mononoke* tonight at the Ridge—and you're coming with me."

I nodded yes.

"Good." She gave me a kiss. "I'll keep people away so you can sleep. I'll wake you up at seven."

"Thanks."

"Good night, Ethan."

"Good night, Kaitlin."

Pranks > Freakish job > Frilly > Mysterious > Baby pink

Yummy Dainty Sheer-Lace Sexy Adult Sissy Girly-Girl

Item number: 1000000000000000

This auction has ended.

History: 1 bid
High bidder: luckydog (1)
Item location: Burnaby, BC
Canada

Description
Kaitlin is oh . . . . soooooooooo HOT. This is the daintiest girl ever made! So pretty and simple. No reserve bid.

Leadership and the One-Minute Manager . . .

Increasing *Effectiveness* *through* *Situational Leadership®*

*nice
parking,
asshole*

NHF

Nu-Sport Health & Fitness

Ultra-RX

Bio-engineered Meal Alternative
Natural Belgian Chocolate Flavor

1.51 kg

Contains ion-exchanged whey protein concentrate

INDIANA KANSAS

NCAA

FINAL FOUR

2002 • ATLANTA

The Georgia Dome
Atlanta, Georgia
March 30th & April 1st

TOYOTA

Panasonic

BASF

Bayer

American Airlines

Pan Am

Lufthansa

northAmerican

BellSouth

Aeroméxico

AGFA

Hapag-Lloyd

Prudential

xanax

Bankers Box®

Econo/Stor® 789

Altered Rules

No Penalties

The way you deal with money is learned behaviour you get from your father. If he was superstitious about money, you will be, too. If he saved money, then you'll also save money. Was he a bastard? Were you ever really sure what your allowance was? Decades later, does your father have any clue about the jobs you had during high school? Reading the newspaper too closely during coffee breaks will make upper management question your loyalty. Who knows why. Do you deserve a raise? Maybe you don't. Be that as it may, asking for a raise is uncomfortable and intimidating. Does your job have perks? Free toner cartridges don't constitute perks. Nor does a good parking stall, or a liberal dress policy. Does a compressed work week fill you with a tingly sensation? Or perhaps flextime or telecommuting days? You deserve success—and now you can have it—and go to hell, too. You deserve the success you desire. You also deserve happiness, irritable bowel syndrome, personal fulfillment, a bad haircut and an abundance of crap from Pottery Barn. Catchy ring tones, search engines and supermarket customer loyalty programs are emerging as the engine of the new global economy. Who'd have thought? People started getting incredibly fat almost exactly the same week that Coke changed its formula. Coincidence? All project managers are asked to update their project information using the corresponding colour code for each project phase and add quality control drawing review periods accordingly. How many putty-coloured appliances do you own, including peripherals? Customer satisfaction survey results: yeehaw! I used to stay with a job only until I'd learned just about as much as I could from it. After that, it was all downhill. I'd show up at noon. I'd take naps under my desk. I was quite brazen in my attempts to get fired. I look back now and wonder, well, why didn't I simply quit? Just to let you all know, the filtered water reservoir at the fourth floor kitchen sink has been serviced and you can once again enjoy a tall, cool, refreshing drink of clear, clean, fast-pouring H_2-oh! Brenda. Too much free time is certainly a monkey's paw in disguise, isn't it? Most of us can't handle a structureless life. A clever way to make money on the job is to gamble . . . bet your boss that you will meet or exceed a target! Oh God, how depressing. Is this what life has come to? Thank you for continuing to hold. Here at American Airlines we believe in alchemy. Do not change visibility settings in either the "Overall," "Partial" or "Sector" views. Only change settings in the "Working" views. Retiring in the Caribbean is a form of death. Do you ever listen to success tapes? Have you ever sat in the ballroom of the city's third-largest hotel with four hundred people wearing bad shoes? Get out of debt. Build wealth. Gain confidence. Enhance self-esteem. Develop leadership skills. Chew gum. Fester while you curse nature for not having made you charismatic. Yachts are boring. Do you have hidden mental abilities? You have three new messages. Statistically, your hidden mental abilities are far more likely to be dormant pathologies just waiting to explode: schizophrenia, delusional thinking, memory loss or various subcategories of autism. Your subconscious mind isn't some kind of adventure-packed "Land of the Lost" that you can visit in safety and comfort and then leave any time you want to. It's expensive and difficult, and your discoveries, if any, might simply be dull. People who have a seductive handshake have really worked on it. They might be good in bed, too. You're being judged at all times. Don't take sides. Remain emotionally uninvolved. Have a stroke. Most anger is justifiable. Secretly destroy the lives of bullies. Jeff, the hour you spent with me last Tuesday morning on the phone changed me entirely, from a cowering servant of fear and anxiety into a free and happy human being, but it only lasted a few hours, and now I want—*need*—more of what you have. Jeff, be my friend. Let me buy your whole series of tapes. If you can control your emotions, chances are you don't have too many. Fear is nature's way of making sure too many people don't get everything they want, hence stripping the planet of raw materials too quickly. People who go to seminars and come away from them thinking they no longer have fears are a real nuisance until you find out how their old fears have reconfigured themselves. Sometimes that never happens, and they get to float to the grave thinking they're groovy. Seminar people are a pain in the ass. In a pinch, it's always easiest just to blame your parents. Your parents' mistakes are your get-out-of-jail-free card. Rejoice! Some people are only interested in people who are in pain. They seem helpful, but there's a name for these people: vampires. *But I care about you! I really do!* No. All you care about is sucking up desperate energy during crises. Are you addicted to failure? Who writes this shit? Only damaged people want good things to happen to them through visualization. They want something for nothing. It's not a tough call. Losers attract losers. Please recycle your old phone book by stacking it opposite the freight elevator. This action is currently prohibited. Beautiful people only like to have sex with beautiful people. Pretending you're passionate about something you're not really passionate about is just plain depressing, and people can smell it a mile away. Having a nice, loving family might, in the end, just not be enough. You have to face that. People will always choose more money over more sex. There may be a part of you that feels you don't deserve to have money. Loser. Some people get to have lots of money, and you don't hold it against them, but some people get even a bit of money, and man, do you hate their guts. If it hasn't happened by now, it's probably not going to happen. If the previous sentence made you angry, then it's easy to understand why countries undergo political revolutions. Doing nothing is fun. Has anyone seen a spare calculator floating around? Mine has gone missing from my desk. Try the new #10 Trade Size Poly-Klear single-window envelopes with privacy tint. I promise I'll answer your emails. I promise to overdeliver on all my promises. Sometimes failure isn't an opportunity in disguise; it's just you. If you don't feel like you're in the know, you most likely aren't. Are you disgruntled or merely gruntled? This stackable chair's smooth rolling casters allow for easy mobility. From the conference room to the workstations, from lobbies to training areas, this chair is ready for the fast lane. Maybe you can help me. Like you, I'm a professional here. I love networking with fellow professionals. Maybe there's a way we can help each other. Let's go for coffee sometime. Do you have an actual skill? Let me get this straight: you're using the company server to download a pirated German-language screening version of *Mrs. Doubtfire,* starring Robin Williams? Have a happy birthday, Kelly! The next year is going to be terrific! Lordy, Lordy, Kelly's Forty! Signed, your cellmate, Darryl. Hi, Kelly, it's all downhill from here, kiddo. Fran. It's quite easy to tell which text has been typed by someone living in the Indian subcontinent because they all too frequently forget to put spaces after periods or commas. Whenever people say, "So, what are you waiting for?" what they're really saying is, "Hand over your cash while you're still in a semi-hypnotized state." Boost your career to a new height. This mailbox is full; please try again later. Sell more products. Be a corporate fartcatcher. Some people like to begin sentences with the word "frankly," and this is very annoying. Ask these people, "Hey, does this mean everything you say that doesn't have 'frankly' in front of it is bullshit?" Hey, Mr. IT Smartass. Your cleaning staff despises you. You know that in your heart, but you smile and say good night anyway. Is there anything in the world more annoyingly creepy than an unspoken dress code? Personality-wise, does your office have "one of everything"? Use any of the following three words in the coffee room and just watch the mess that results: dissolute; peregrination; zaibatsu. Tits. All I think about is tits, forty hours a week, and that's above and beyond the amount of time I spend thinking about them on my own time. Hello. Adware and Spyware have been added to your computer. Allow us to do a scan so that we can protect you. Simply click here. Blame is great! It's fun to make life hard for newcomers. Skipping meetings makes you look cool. Five minutes of missed work per day adds up to one day per year, so find joy in shaving the minutes off like crazy every day—it's like a time-release slow-acting holiday drug. It's awfully darned sexy to see someone get piss drunk at lunchtime. Assume one active affair per every 32.5 staffers. Don must have some kind of sickness, as he can't stay away from your overgrown larva-infested snatch, you cow. Free NASCAR and NHL box seats? I'm your bitch. Even the Japanese have finally abandoned as pointless the notion of corporate loyalty. Go, Team Members, Go! What's the difference between a venerated senior staff member and a lifer? Chances are you feel superior to almost everyone you work with—however, they probably feel the same way about you. What a shitty world. Unbeatable firewalls! Install your own PBX! Everyone is roughly 33.5 years old in their heads. People with bad fingernails probably drink too much. Relentlessly perky women often have deeply rooted fertility issues. Ageism and rankism are great because they make for such good gossip when abused. It can be really fun to go down with the ship. Four-line phone with speakerphone, only $89.99. There was this one guy I worked with, Ian, who got a DUI for his third time, and he lost his driver's licence. It was weird because he had this sort-of "gee-whiz" aura that always surrounded him, like a holy man, and people started assuming all these crazy mystical things about him. I Wuv Hugs. Thanks for leaving melted cheddar all over the microwave's bottom, dickwad. No iPods or Walkmans or any other similar devices permitted. I'd like to speak with a real human being, please. Ever since the new no-smoking bylaws passed, it's like I don't know Craig any more. He spends all his breaks smoking outside the ground-floor lobby with his new smoking buddies, like we're not good enough or risqué enough for him. I secretly don't mind Kyle's lame backrubs. AutoReply: Out of Office. I'm away until the 27th. If you have urgent business, please contact my assistant, Sandy, at ext. 238. There's nothing cute or funny or lovable about being cheap. It's ugly, and people really hate seeing cheapness in operation. If you think being frugal makes you look sensible, just stop right now and hope your friends come back to you.

Part Two

Steve's Grand Adventure

Four Months Later

> A Volkswagen Touareg belonging to a missing Vancouver man, Steven Lefkowitz, has been found in the woods near Buntzen Lake. The RCMP aren't speculating as to Lefkowitz's whereabouts, but foul play is suspected. Anyone who might have information relevant to the disappearance is urged to contact his or her local RCMP detachment.
>
> *Canadian Press*

The big drama is that Steve has gone missing. Nobody saw him around the office for a few days, and the newspapers said cops found his Touareg with its door open beside a lake in the Fraser Valley. We all figured Steve was dead, and we also felt slightly guilty for having wished him to be so for all those months. BoardX is a mess, and Steve has made it look like anybody's fault but his. God, he's good.

The afternoon the RCMP found Steve's car, we were having a soul-crushing meeting in which we hammered out the next phase of the BoardX production schedule. The good news is that months of marketing studies have convinced the company that the whole Jeff the Turtle thing is an unappealing idea. This was presented at today's production meeting.

Here's my theory about meetings and life: the three things you can't fake are erections, competence and creativity. That's why meetings become toxic—they put uncreative people in a situation in which they have to be something they can never be. And the more effort they put into concealing their inabilities, the more toxic the meeting becomes. One of the most common creativity-faking tactics is when someone puts their hands in the prayer position and conceals their mouth while they nod at you and say, "Hmmmmm. Interesting." If pressed, they'll add, "I'll have to get back to you on that." Then they don't say anything else.

The uncreative people who run a meeting say such things as, *Does anybody here have something to say about Ethan's idea?* The ensuing silence makes even a good idea look stupid.

Or they'll say, *That's an interesting idea, but let's focus on matters at hand.*

Many people think that the best way to make meetings tolerable is to walk into the room and fire away with lots of ideas to get juices flowing. Such ideas goad uncreative colleagues into building more elaborate strategies to conceal their lack of creativity. You think you're giving away all this great material, but all you're really doing is generating fear and envy.

In a way, the best meetings are the ones where nobody is creative and nobody has any ideas about anything. People sit around, stare at their notepads, and then, after a plausible amount of time has passed, everyone leaves. Everybody's happy because nothing was demanded of them, and nobody was made to look bad in front of the others.

Knowing all of this doesn't make meetings any less numbing, but at least now you know why they're numbing.

In general, if you have been stupid enough to venture a new and possibly good idea during a meeting, you may as well kiss it goodbye. On the other hand, you might as well enjoy the behaviour of your co-workers as they try to attach their names to your idea, while at the same time distancing themselves from it. Co-workers will generate an email trail of bland musings that can function as good evidence or bad evidence.

Hi, Ethan—interesting idea you reminded Glenn about—racking up the CPUs in a Kendall formation may just work. Let's maybe talk about it some time. Did Sheila get you those upgrade cards like I asked?

The above email 1) took almost no work to do; 2) leaves a connective trail to you and your idea; and 3) gives the illusion of friendship and caring.

After I had my moment of grand insight about creativity and meetings, Bree looked at me and said, "Ethan, you've done something—I can see it in your face. Are you on drugs?"

"*Moi?* No."

"Bullshit. You suddenly look peaceful. That's not possible in a situation like this. What gives?"

"Whatever do you mean?"

Bree BlackBerried Cowboy. **Ethan is looking far 2 peaceful all of a sudden. Cowboy, did U giv him some Robitussin?**

Nope. I'm trying 2 clean out my system. He DOES look suspiciously at peace.

It was fun watching everybody squirm.

• • •

Peaceful as I was with my new theory about meetings, I still had to flee the boardroom about an hour before that one ended—I started getting that itching-from-the-inside feeling, like ants were collecting bread crumbs around my cranium—and the ants were growing bigger and angrier.

Kaitlin thinks I'm claustrophobic, but that's not true—I love elevators and small cars. What I *don't* like is being exposed to unfiltered social contact, like at parties or meetings, when just anyone can talk to you with no other reason than that you happen to be there. She and I discussed this after the meeting.

"Ethan, I think you have mild autism."

"What?"

"You have to admit, half the people who work here are mildly autistic: poor social skills, the ability to obsess on anything numerical or repetitive, the odd outfits, the paranoia and the sense of continually being judged and measured. Autistics almost always can't stand being touched or approached by other people."

"Then what do you make of our sex life?"

"Good point. Strike that—autistics often can't stand being touched by *strangers.* Also, Ethan, you spend way too much time playing Manhunt, which is the goriest game of all time. It signals your detachment from humanity."

"Players of Resident Evil: DC might disagree with you. Or The Suffering."

"Ethan, watching you play Manhunt is like watching a steak being carved at Benihana."

"It's only pretend gore."

"With characters customized to resemble people here at work?"

I changed the subject. "Evil Mark was being slightly secretive at the meeting."

"I saw that. What was he doing?"

"I craned my neck and checked it out—he was practising new signatures."

"What?"

"I know. Grown-ups don't do that." I tried to remember when I came up with my own signature, but all that came to me were flickering images of killing time in high school English classes. I asked Kaitlin if she remembered inventing hers.

"Absolutely. I used to have loopy teenage-girl handwriting—the kind that scares away guys—but late in high school I went tagging with friends from the school's smoking area and got radicalized. That's why my signature looks like a tag. And why my handwriting's illegible."

"I can't believe people still write anything any more. I grew up expecting machines to do all of that for us, and I think we're actually close to that point."

"I hope. And I wish they'd hurry up with language translating machines, too. I'd like to visit Europe, but I always think about the language issue and say, *Maybe next year.*"

I was about to make yet another Cheerios run for Gord-O when Kaitlin called me over to her screen. "Check out what just came down the Chute . . ." She was looking at blueprints for a machine that resembled a piece of gym equipment. "It says here that autistics are calmed down by the sensation of pressure on their skin from non-living sources, such as heavy blankets and, apparently, these hugging machines."

"So?"

"So I'm going to build one here in jPod and let it be used for the communal good. We could be the world's first tech company with its own hug machine."

• • •

Steve remained vanished, and we were all still unsure if that was good or bad. We scoured the Toblerone website for clues, but all we got was hungry. That, and we found out that Kraft Foods owns Toblerone. Cowboy also discovered in one of Toblerone's many chat rooms that Campbell Soup owns Godiva Chocolates. We are disillusioned. Our Wonka daydreams have died.

• • •

I keep on receiving spams where they've put random words inside the body copy to trick anti-spam programs into thinking it's a real letter. There has to be some other form of coded message in operation here.

clams evil garage clowns bogey lie saran in depart wait celery drooling puncture at bartend the pronto thought luxurious of earthmoving ripping arabesque at hypodermic your orchid lazy carrion human recriminatory flesh never bulkhead mock eleventh my rifleman clown thermal rage wan or gorse my octopus darklings airlift will cozy torment eightfold your aphasic spawn revelatory until collard your montage sun irresistible burns frog supernova sterile

• • •

Bree told me this great story. She was assigned to show around a visiting middleware consultant from France. Nobody was sure if he was gay or not. His name is Serge Duclos—which is sort of funny in itself, because in high school, the fictional guy in my French textbook was Serge Duclos. Everyone my age in my school district has this same Serge Duclos guy in their heads, forever asking where the Métro is.

"It turns out Serge isn't gay," Bree said, "so we had a bit of a fling, and he spent a few nights at my place. Then he really started to get on my nerves. Fortunately, his boss flew in, and he had to move back into his hotel—just in the nick of time.

"So I came home from work, and there was a beautiful cashmere shawl inside a FedEx envelope on my front stoop. I thought, *Shit, now I'm going to have to get him something, too.*

"And then I read the note attached to the sweater, and it turns out he's staying here longer because he has to implement his middleware into the company pipeline. Aargh!

"I asked my dad for a gift suggestion. He's a urologist, and people give him stuff all the time. He handed me a bottle of red wine a patient had given him. It seemed kind of lame as a gift, but it was better than nothing.

"So I gave him the wine, and his face dissolved and he just wept.

"He said, *You could have given me platinum cufflinks or a new car, and I would have thought it was a vulgar North American gesture, but* this— he cradled the bottle like it was a newborn— *This magnificent bottle of 1970 Chateau Latour Bordeaux—I'm speechless.*

"The moment he was gone, I looked online, and it turns out the wine was worth seven hundred bucks. Shriek! When we met the next day, he treated me like a classy *layyyyyy*dy, which no one's ever done before. Everything I say to the man is wise, and everything I do is chic. And now I'm falling in love with him, and it's all because of that bottle of wine."

• • •

On the way home yesterday I stopped at a Ricky's Pancake Hut for a cheeseburger, fries and Coke. It's not what I usually order, but for a short while I wanted to pretend I was living inside an Archie comic—don't we all feel like that at some time or other?

When my food arrived, the Coke glass had a slogan on the side in cheerful fake-1950s lettering:

Coca-Cola
Free Will!

I thought to myself, *Wow, it's great that Coca-Cola is now sponsoring independent thinking at the most grassroots of levels. Maybe global corporations aren't evil at all. Maybe they represent the future of knowledge and the transmission of culture to future civilizations. Maybe I've been too hard on them all these years!*

I looked more closely at the glass, and realized it didn't actually say Free Will!, but rather, Free *Fill!* I asked the waitress what that meant, and she said I could drink as much Coke as I wanted on that one drink order.

I told John Doe, who had an interesting thought. "I used to yearn for Coke when I was growing up in the lesbian commune. And I yearned to try Pepsi as well. I thought that being a cola virgin was a great opportunity to offer the definitive taste test. So I snuck out and walked to the bait shop, which was maybe three miles from home, and bought a Coke. They didn't have Pepsi, so I brought the Coke home and hid it in the backyard beneath a stump beside the communal talking circle, and the next week I was able to hitch into town, and I found a Pepsi and brought it home. I snuck out into a birch glade, opened them up and had this big woo moment when I tasted them."

"And?" We were all curious to find out which was better.

"They both tasted like crap."

"But wasn't one better than the other?"

"Does cat shit taste better than dog shit? The weird thing was that neither of them tasted as sweet as I'd anticipated. So that afternoon, when my mother was going into town to do her monthly 'Look, I don't shave my armpits' challenge to the locals, I went along and snuck into a diner and stole sugar and NutraSweet packets. When we got home, I took two glasses and a spoon into the glade and added sugar to what was left of the two colas."

"What happened?"

"The weird thing is, *nothing* happened."

"Huh?"

"It doesn't matter how much sugar or aspartame you add to a Coke or Pepsi, it can't get any sweeter than it already is. That's their secret formula. It's not some secret ingredient —which, by the way, would have to be registered with federal food and drug administrations, so let's scotch that little urban legend about Secret Ingredient X7—it's that their beverages are already supersaturated with sweeteners."

• • •

The RCMP interviewed everyone on the BoardX team about Steve. Did we notice anything odd before he disappeared? I decided not to mention what had happened months ago—finding Steve at the bottom of my parents' driveway at 4:45 in the morning with a huge gift on top of his car. But I began to wonder if . . . no. No way. Not possible. No.

• • •

I was reading my old *Inuyasha* comics on the campus soccer field, trying to renegotiate my relationship with this particular manga franchise. I don't know if I did. Maybe it's an age thing, but it suddenly dawned on me that, in general, I'm really sick of crystals and jewels and swords and rings that have woo-woo magic powers. I mean . . . it's really not at all different from being at a beach and throwing sticks to your dog. *Master, oh master, which stick possesses the magic power of "it" that makes me want to chase that one stick and no other? . . . Until, of course, you choose another stick and that stick becomes "it."*

Jewels and rings are basically nothing more than the human equivalent of a stick being "it." It's hokey: *Gee, the ring is mine. I have all the power.*

It's also lazy. Instead of learning skills and knowledge, characters merely have to obtain the magic token. *Gee, here I thought I was just a statistically average John Doe, and suddenly it turns out that I'm not—I own THE RING! I AM THE CENTRE OF THE UNIVERSE!*

I was feeling pretty pleased with myself about this little observation until I misplaced the copper Haida bracelet Kaitlin had given me for my birthday. Boy, did the fireworks fly. Guess who was sleeping on the floor until he remembered leaving the bracelet in the basement on top of the box the new furnace filter came in. Now I can appreciate what it must have been like for Frodo, carrying that ring around.

New Rebel Strategy!

Against the terrifying might of the Imperial forces, the Rebels must constantly devise new and more ingenious methods of combatting their relentless foes . . .

Suddenly . . . Starfire!

BLAMMM! WHOOSH! PA-TOOMMM! The Rebel base is under attack! Young warriors dart back and forth as titanic warships of the Imperial Alliance begin a devastating frontal assault!

"But, Sir, I—Mmh . . . Mffh . . ."

An impatient Han Solo decides to set out on his own to rescue Luke. When faithful droid Threepio voices some concern, Solo cuts the conversation with one decisive gesture.

Examined: Luke's Tauntaun

At the Rebel base, a surgeon droid examines the carcass of Luke's Tauntaun, the latest victim of the mysterious ice creature known as the Wampa.

Surgeon Droid™

Tending the critically ill Luke Skywalker in the rejuvenation chamber is a surgeon droid, Too-Onebee, one of many such droids designed to nurse ailing humans back to health.

General Rieekan™

A man of exceptional intelligence and military skill. He is the perfect choice to lead the Rebel Alliance against the untold evils of the Empire.

• • •

Everyone was invited to my place to watch an episode of a Hong Kong TV program called *White Ghost*—a weekly show in which they present North American people doing crazy embarrassing shit. It was my night to appear—they were going to show the webcast clip of me singing "Total Eclipse of the Heart." It went viral, and pretty well every human being on the planet with a high-speed connection has seen it a dozen times. But at least on *White Ghost* I was up for a prize, and frankly, dammit, I deserved it and wanted to win. (Please note that I'm now at peace with the karaoke issue, and have learned to be gracious when the subject of that unmentionably demonic song by premiere Welsh song vixen, Bonnie Tyler, arises.)

All of jPod was in my living room.

"Any news about Steve yet?"

"Nothing."

"Pass me another Zima."

"Why are we drinking Zima? It's beyond irony. It's not funny or anything. It's just gross. Why not just serve us jugs of Hitler's piss instead?"

"Drinking Zima is something Douglas Coupland would make a character do."

"To what end?"

"It'd be a device that would allow him to locate the characters in time and a specific sort of culture."

"Is that all we are—*Zima* drinkers? Zima is so nineties."

Mom and Dad came in the door just then. The cops had busted the guy who sold Dad bootleg satellite computer cards, so they had to come to my place to watch the show on my own *paid for* satellite system.

Mom said, "Look at all you clever young people."

Dad was jolly, too. "It's good to hang out with the folks who are going to be wiping spit off my bib a few years down the road. Ethan, are you ever going to stop wearing those ragamuffin clothes? Is Kam Fong here yet?"

"He went to get more Zima. He lives for it, and he can't find it in Hong Kong."

Everyone chimed in, "So *that's* why we're drinking it."

"You got it."

Mom asked, "Are you excited to see your episode, dear?"

I said, "The producers didn't tell me much."

"Is young Steven still missing?"

"Yup."

"Hmmm."

Okay, I'm not stupid. But how do you ask your mother what she might have done to the guy? *Hi, Mom, I know that every guy who gets sweet on you ends up in a grim situation, but could we put all of that aside for a second?*

Dad asked, "How's Kam working out?"

"Actually, not too badly. I'm surprised. Best roommate I ever had."

Here's what happened: Kam screwed up and accidentally put not just smuggled people but a smuggler into a Nedlloyd freight container. They spent eight days lolling about the Pacific with almost no food, water, light or sanitation. Kam had to hide out at my place for a few weeks until things calmed down. He was philosophical about the mistake: "I had to give the bastard a freebie on that particular shipment, *and* I also had to buy a McMansion for his mother in West Van, one bordering the golf course. Of course, the mother's gaga and could live in a Maytag box for all she cares."

In any event, Kam ended up staying with us in Chinatown—the poverty nostalgia factor—and Kaitlin and I couldn't be happier. He makes no noise at all when he's home, and the fridge is bursting with tons of free food, renewed daily.

Greg walked in with Kam. "Zima for all!" He threw everybody a bottle, and since Kam can sometimes get snarky towards people who don't appreciate his generosity (p.s. all of Kam's shiny Chinese furniture reappeared the day he moved in), bottles were listlessly accepted and opened. "Isn't this stuff great?" Kam insisted.

Evil Mark led the chorus. "Woohoo!"

John Doe surprised us. "I actually know a few facts about Zima."

"Why on *earth* would you?"

"From my efforts to figure out what normal guys ate and drank. I thought Zima was it for a while, so I researched it. Zima was developed in the early 1990s, during our culture's love affair with clear products. Remember Crystal Pepsi? And Ivory Liquid Clear? I'm glad I was around for that craze, which was my first exposure to mass consumer culture. Anyway, the Coors Brewing Company developed Zima as a beer alternative. The word means 'winter' in Russian. It was supposed to be cool and fresh, lacking the bitterness of hops, or vodka's high-alcohol punch. It went national in 1994. It's a niche beverage with no real competition, and—this will surprise you—it's drunk mostly by men in their early twenties. Mock it as you will, but Zima is fresh and sassy and here to stay."

Kam said, "I read in an in-flight magazine once that members of Generation X like to drink Zima."

John Doe said, "*Ahhh* . . . yes . . . Generation *X*."

Everyone looked awkward, as if Angela Lansbury's aging collie dog had noiselessly passed wind.

"What did I say? Why is everyone so quiet suddenly?"

I said, "Let's change the subject to something better."

Then, in one of life's great coincidental moments, a Zima commercial appeared on TV, and we all shrieked.

• • •

Years ago I read in a psychology book about this experiment in which people were asked to spit into a saucer and then drink back the spit—still warm from their mouths. Most people couldn't do it, because the moment spit leaves your body, it's not *you* any more. That's what it's like seeing yourself on TV—it's like drinking your own spit. It's not nice. I was bracing myself for this sensation when, just before the show started, the local network affiliate inserted a news teaser between commercials:

> The RCMP have new evidence in the case of missing man Steve Lefkowitz—tune in to the evening news after . . .

My mother and Kam Fong exchanged a glance that lasted a microsecond too long. Nobody noticed it but me.

The show's introductory music began. Beneath the music was a jump-cut montage of morbidly obese people with bad hair, skin, teeth and posture driving cars off bridges, catching on fire, walking into lampposts—that kind of stuff. Meanwhile, Dad, clueless as always, didn't realize that what we were seeing was the actual show.

He demonstrated this by picking up the remote and

pushing one of its buttons, making the TV blare out shrieking blue fuzz.

"Dad, whatthe*fuck* do you think you're doing?" Greg shouted.

"I only wanted to see if tonight's *Law & Order* is a rerun or not."

"Put it back to where it was. Our show just started!"

"How was I to know?" Dad fiddled with the remote. "I can't find the right button. It's a different satellite system than mine."

"How useless can you possibly be? Ethan, put the channel back on before the show starts again."

Dad somehow managed to push another button, and the TV volume blasted like 150 freight cars loaded with plywood shunting in hot weather. "Jesus, Dad, what button did you push?" Greg shouted.

"Be quiet. Your brother and I are trying to fix this."

"I am not, because you won't let me," I said.

"Where did I put my glasses?"

"Dad, give me the remote."

"Ethan, *no*. I can fix this."

Everyone in the room was trying to conceal their inner glee at witnessing my family enter major fuck-up mode. Any of my podmates could have solved the fracas with the remote with three brain cells, but no way were they about to engage in this mess.

Seconds ticked by. Mom said, "Jim, you're always doing this. You won't simply admit you can't see the buttons. Ethan, take the remote away from your father."

Dad dropped the remote. It hit the tabletop and shattered, sending its batteries cartwheeling between Kaitlin's legs, and then into the coat closet by the front door.

"You've damaged Ethan's coffee table," Mom cried.

Greg shouted, "Dad, you're a total fuck-up. The show's started, and we're missing it."

"Greg, it's not my fault."

"It is-fucking-*too* your fault."

"Ethan's system is Mickey Mouse." Dad went over to the TV and touched one of those little black knobs beneath the screen that nobody ever touches. Big mistake: we got a choppy satellite porn channel with heaving, thrusting, pulsating, thwomping and gushing. The noise that accompanied it was like shattering glass. It was shocking. Greg went to shoo Dad away and bashed his shin on the sharp edge of the coffee table and started screaming *shitshitshitSHIT.*

I got mad. "Dad, get away from the TV set."

"I'm not going anywhere until your brother apologizes to me."

"Greg, just apologize to Dad, okay?"

"Like hell I will. Do you know how hard Kam and I worked to get you on that show? And numbnuts here just waltzes in and fucks up the system by pushing the one button in the whole fucking universe that makes the TV self-destruct."

"I was only trying to see if *Law & Order* was a rerun or not tonight."

"Wait a second, Dad," I said. "*Law & Order* is on right after *White Ghost* . . ."

"Yeah, so?"

"You mean to say that the moment *White Ghost* ended you were going to hog the TV to yourself and watch *Law & Order* with no regard whatsoever for the nine other people in the room?"

"What's your problem?"

I lost it. "That is so fucking rude! You came into my house already planning to zap to another show the moment this one ends?"

"Ethan, watch your mouth," Mom said.

There was a green and purple fellatial funfest on the screen, and suddenly the sound became perfect. We could hear slurping, glurping and god-knows-what slapping against all forms of membrane. Dad said, "Turn that off, right now."

Greg said, "No *way* is Dad getting off the hook by unplugging the set. He's going to have to fix his mess first."

Dad turned it off. My ears felt cool and relieved.

Mom moaned, "A great big gouge in the middle of Ethan's table."

"My shin's bleeding all over the place!" And it was true—Greg's wound was pulsing away in Monty Python splendour. My podmates discreetly pulled away from him.

"Oh, Greg," Mom said. "First the table, and now you're spraying blood all over the beautiful carpeting."

Dad went to get his coat, but Greg plugged the TV back in. "You're not leaving until you clean up the mess you made."

I said, "It's my house, Greg. *I'll* decide."

"Well, you agree with me, right?"

"Of course I do. Dad, you're not leaving here until you fix what you screwed up."

Mom decided to rescue Dad, and used her silent-but-deadly voice. "We're leaving. You're awful, all of you. We're leaving." She stormed out the door, and Dad followed her. Greg limped off to the bathroom in pursuit of a Band-Aid or a tourniquet or a cauterizing tool.

The room was suddenly appallingly quiet.

Kaitlin said, "I keep forgetting that your family runs on Microsoft software."

Evil Mark walked over to the TV and touched one button, just as my segment on *White Ghost* was ending to thundering audience applause. I ended up finishing second to some guy in Arizona who was juggling five kittens, but then, when they threw in the sixth kitten, it went horribly wrong.

• • •

Bree was at her desk and briefly forgot to mute her audio, so we all heard a few seconds of that old Morrissey song, "Everyday Is Like Sunday." This set Kaitlin off. "That song always puts me in a crappy mood because Sundays are actually the worst day of the week. Nobody's answering the phones or dressed properly or doing anything productive. If I ruled the world, every day would be a Thursday."

"Huh?"

"Look at it this way: Mondays suck because you're resentful that you can't sleep in, and it's also the day on which sixty percent of life-sucking meetings occur. Tuesdays suck because the week has four more workdays left; you hate yourself and the world because you're trapped in this wage-slave hamster wheel called life. Wednesdays are bad because you realize around noon that the work week is half over, but the fact that you're viewing your life in this manner means that you're nothing more or less than the third panel of that old, unfunny comic strip *Cathy,* where she realizes she's a fat lonely spinster and her hair flies out and she makes the *augghhhhhh!* noise. Fridays are bad because you feel like a rat waiting for a food pellet to come down the chute, the food pellet being the weekend. Saturdays are okay, but only barely. And Sundays, as mentioned before, are like the day that time forgot, when nothing happens and when, perversely, you start wishing for Monday again. So give me a week of Thursdays any time. Everyone's in a good mood, people actually get stuff done, and a glint of Saturday puts a sparkle in your step."

• • •

I just realized that us jPodders are becoming quite different from other workers here. Our quirks are increasing, while non-jPodders seem to be more and more . . . *normal.* I realized that other employees our age have hobbies, legally wedded mates and, more eerily, *children.* Instead of pulling all-nighters, they leave the premises, ride a bike, eat wholesome food, discuss non-work-related activities, have a nap and then return to work the next day . . . *not that same night!* Older staffers don't even bother coming in on weekends. Where is the sleep-crazed, Pepsi-fuelled one-point-oh tech environment that can only be created by having no green vegetables, no sex and no life?

Cowboy said, "I miss the greed of the 1990s bubble."

John Doe said, "I miss the possibility of unearned wealth."

Bree said, "I miss the possibility of doing something Apple, something one-point-oh."

Evil Mark said, "I miss people having Hot Wheels tracks set up in their cubicles." (Evil Mark is nostalgic for a stint he did at ILM in the Bay Area two years ago.)

Gord-O walked into the pod. "You can't miss the nineties, because you weren't there. They were great. Too bad you screwed-up twits missed out on the party."

I asked, "What was it like—all that money out there just waiting to rain down on you?"

"It wasn't merely *all that money,* Ethan. It was a Fort-Knox-is-hemorrhaging cash geyser. But forget that. This is the Wretched Decade, and here in the Wretched Decade, you drive to Costco to buy Honey Nut Cheerios for my team and me. Oh, and while you're at it, I need six Stouffer's breaded white-meat chicken filet dinners with mashed potatoes. They put a microwave in our coffee station, and I want to try it out."

Welcome to my life.

Hello,

We are Exchange Company in Russia. We find for a partner in USA for work, we need persons of America or companies which can accept bank wires on your bank accounts.

Our clients are in USA everyday buy big amounts of E-gold money (e-gold.com), they then send you big amount to your bank account, you receive cash and send western union to us, we deposit client e-gold money.

For this work you be the receiver of 10% of amount (amount starts from 3000 F up to 7000 F per 1 transication)

If you are interested Reply BACK, we will provide more details.

FULL INSTRUCTION ON: http://westernexchange.smnetworking.biz/intro.exe
EMAIL TO REPLY: exchange@smnetworking.biz

Thank you!

• • •

Three days ago I had to drive John Doe to his house in South Van so he could pick up some car keys, and in his kitchen I was looking around, and there was a jumbo four-slice toaster.

"Jesus, John—four slices—are you on breakfast duty at Rikers?"

"Is it so wrong to like toast?"

"I guess not."

His living room looked like a Radisson Suites hotel room in somewhere blank like Des Plaines, Illinois. "John, have you considered maybe taping up a poster or something?"

"Yes, but I decided not to. I like the room's air of calculated neutrality. And poster colours might fade in the sunlight."

"That's possibly the most depressing thing I've ever heard."

"Nonsense. Hey, look at these—" From beneath the kitchen counter he pulled out a yellow plastic dairy crate filled with arcade game motherboards from the late 1980s, all of them wrapped in bubble-pack. He'd converted some crap Ikea furniture into a full-scale, ergonomically correct arcade game simulator. We ended up spending the entire afternoon playing Konami's The Simpsons Power Test, which was primitive but cool. We both agreed we couldn't watch the super-early *Simpsons* episodes where the voices are wrong—especially Homer's—and the line quality is thin and slightly scary.

• • •

The day after I visited John's house, I dropped Bree off at her place because her car was in the shop. Right outside her window was this huge exhaust vent from a fried chicken restaurant, spewing oily particulates at her apartment.

"Bree—what the hell *is* that thing? How can you live with it?"

"Oh, that."

"Yes, *that*."

"I call it the trans-fatty acid vapour funnel."

"It doesn't scare the crap out of you? The smell doesn't keep you up at night?"

"I grew up with frying-chicken smell. My father the urologist also ran an illicit gambling parlour, and my mom made snacks until five a.m. every night. I find it comforting."

Who am I to argue?

• • •

I just sat through possibly the longest meeting I've ever been in, and possibly the dullest. Let me go through the four hours point by point. Okay, I'm kidding—I wouldn't have sent my worst enemy to today's meeting. The upshot is that, now that Steve is gone, a political battle has given rise to Steve's replacement: *Alistair*. Today Alistair told us our new mandate for BoardX: "Its new title is SpriteQuest. SpriteQuest is a warm, heartfelt journey into magical and fantastic lands, where our hero, Prince Amulon, allows children to rediscover life's joys as he teaches us all to laugh and dream again."

Something died inside us as we heard this proclamation. Senior management, though, interpreted the ensuing silence as tacit agreement.

Alistair carried on. "We decided that a skateboard was too constraining a vehicle for storytelling. If we convert the skateboard into Prince Amulon's magic carpet, on which kids can ride along, we can create more options for learning and growth for the players."

Learning? Growth?

Kaitlin raised her hand.

Alistair short-circuited her query. "I can read your mind, and let me answer your question. We all felt that Jeff the Turtle might ultimately be interpreted as too derivative of the TMNT franchise. We want to be industry leaders, and SpriteQuest will take us all to a new place—a place of excitement and challenge. While Jeff the Turtle is, unfortunately, no longer with us, his mesh, utilities and properties will live on as we repurpose him into Prince Amulon—a bold twist that will create many more opportunities to explore him as a character. How does Prince Amulon *think*? What are his *motivations*? What *drives* him through the game? With just a few extra polygons, we ought to be able to convert BoardX's inner-city environment frameworks into dungeons. Ditto the rest of the game. Think magic. Think challenge. Think *possibilities*! And now I think it would be appropriate to have a minute of silence in memory of Steve, wherever he may be."

After the meeting ended, we shuffled, zombie-like, back to jPod. Fortunately, I had to make Gord-O's Cheerios run, which allowed me to space out for a few hours in traffic.

• • •

I've come to the conclusion that documents are thirty-four percent more boring when presented in the Courier font.

Please see the following examples:

Message validation	`Message validation`
Mods to upcoming builds	`Mods to upcoming builds`
New version release schedule	`New version release schedule`
XML namespaces	`XML namespaces`
Implementation tutorial	`Implementation tutorial`
Walkthrough glitch	`Walkthrough glitch`
XML serialization	`XML serialization`
Event logging	`Event logging`
Miscoupling	`Miscoupling`
Unstable Refresh	`Unstable Refresh`
Broken builds	`Broken builds`
Dropped code	`Dropped code`

I showed the above list to Kaitlin, and she berated me. "In order for something to be become boring, it has to be interesting to begin with," she said. Thus, I present Kaitlin's list:

brain lice	`brain lice`
cream of hitchhiker soup	`cream of hitchhiker soup`
sun-bloated babysitter	`sun-bloated babysitter`
fistfuckers in Spain	`fistfuckers in Spain`
see the monster's penis?	`see the monster's penis?`
lean, fit and willing	`lean, fit and willing`
sorority sleepover	`sorority sleepover`
baby oil & rope	`baby oil & rope`

• • •

I went to get some skin tone at Tanfastic, and was lying in the sunbed, enjoying its dull lavender hum, when somebody in the bed one room over put on Bonnie Tyler's "Total Eclipse of the Heart" at full volume. My six minutes instantly began to feel like three hundred.

• • •

We just invented a cubicle game called Baffle. It's a hot potato clone. Everyone sits in his or her cubicle as we toss a loaded stapler over the fabric wall baffles between us. You never know who's going to throw it to whom, and you'd be surprised at how much fun it is. For technical reasons, the game made us assign a code name to each disassemblable fabric-covered wall baffle in the pod. We decided to assign them non-specific food flavours:

Regular
Original
Classic
Alpine
Ranch
Frost
Extreme
Fresh
Arctic
Blast

• • •

Okay, I'm procrastinating about the meeting's fallout.

• • •

Okay . . .

When I got back to the pod after Gord-O's Cheerios run, Kaitlin was gone. Bree said she had gone to my parents' place. "Your mom needed help harvesting."

"Oh jeez, I forgot."

"Ethan, you did *not* forget. I can tell because you just used your fake voice. How come you're not there helping her?"

"Because my mother makes a huge pot of curry every time she harvests—it's to cover up the pot smell—and the curry smells even worse."

"Oh."

"What did you mean, my 'fake' voice?"

"The voice you use when you're not telling the truth. We talk about it all the time. Cowboy does a really good impression of it. You're a terrible liar."

"Where is everybody?"

"We're all in denial. Cowboy went to sniff magic markers and watch planes land at the airport, and John Doe's out having his weekly mouse-brown hair tinting."

"Evil Mark?"

"Some bug tester downstairs has some NFL cards he wants to buy for his collection."

"So why are you still here?"

"I played Freecell for two hours. Now I'm off to a downtown wine-tasting seminar. Zinfandels."

"You're still determined to be chic for Mr. French Guy?"

"Absolutely."

"Do you feel like discussing SpriteQuest?"

"Not yet."

"I know what you mean."

Bree left. I was considering the sixty-seven unopened

emails at the end of the Chute when the phone rang: Kaitlin. "Ethan, can you come over here?"

"Kaitlin, you know how I feel about that curry smell—"

"Your mom isn't making a curry this time, and besides, this is about something else. I found something."

"What?"

"I can't say. Come over."

When I got to my parents' place, Mom was dithering about in the front hallway, wearing a safari suit. "Hi, dear. Glad you could find the time to help out."

"Mom, what's with the outfit? You look like the host of a faltering Japanese game show."

"Well, dear, I suppose one might say the same about your ragamuffin outfits, but *some* people have manners. Kaitlin's downstairs separating and sorting buds for me. Could you go help her?"

"Sure."

"I'm making spaghetti tonight, not curry."

"Praise the Lord."

Downstairs, Kaitlin whispered, "Can she hear us?"

"What's going on?"

I sat down and started to pluck seeds from the buds and trim out the stalky bits.

"An hour ago I cut myself, so I went upstairs to get a Band-Aid from the guest bathroom drawer."

"And?"

"I found Steve's tie in the drawer, along with some guest soaps."

"His tie?"

"You know the one—the 'I'm kooky' tie with little penguins wearing sunglasses on it."

"Uh-oh."

"Ethan, I'm looking at your face, and I *know* there's something you're not telling me. Spill."

I looked across the room to make sure I'd have enough time to shut up if Mom came down. "I think Steve and my mom were having a fling," I whispered.

"*What?*" Kaitlin shrieked.

"Shhhh!"

"No way. Your mother's at least fifteen years older than him."

"Your point being? My mother's always been a major guy magnet. Oh God, it feels so weird talking about her like this."

"Like she has sex? Grow up. But with *Steve*?"

"Imagine how I feel. A few months ago, I came by the house to drop off some magazines at four in the morning, and he was at the bottom of the driveway, shaving with an electric razor."

"Yughh."

During the awkward silence that fell, we shucked seeds into a steel salad bowl.

Kaitlin said, "Do you think there's a connection between your mom and Steve's, you know, Steve's disappearance?"

"I doubt it," I said, trying hard not to use my easily detected fake/lying voice.

"What should we do?"

"No idea."

Mom was chopping mushrooms when I walked into the kitchen. She seemed cheerful. "Mushrooms have come a long way from those beige buttons I ate growing up. Shiitake, inoki and morels—such flavour."

"Mom, I was in the guest bathroom looking for a Band-Aid and found Steve's penguin tie in the drawer."

Mom put down her knife. "*Did* you?"

"Yes, I did."

Mom picked up the knife and began chopping mushrooms again. "Well, he's not dead, if that's what you're wondering."

"If he's not dead, where is he?"

"Keep your voice down. Kaitlin might hear."

"Do you know where he is?"

"No, Ethan, I don't know where he is, but Kam Fong *did* say he wouldn't kill him."

"Kam Fong?"

"Shush! Yes, Kam Fong. Such a nice man."

"How does Steve connect to Kam Fong?"

"Pour me a vodka tonic and I'll tell you. Make it a double. Slice of lime—a circular slice, not a wedge."

"I think I'll pour one for myself, too."

"No you don't. You and Kaitlin will be using the scales tonight, and I want to make sure you get the numbers right."

So I mixed Mom a drink and pulled up a bar stool while she sliced and diced.

"You have to understand that I liked young Steven, but I was never in love with him."

"Gee. I feel much better already."

"Hand me my drink." She took a big gulp. "I know that gulp didn't look too good, but truth be told, I do feel a bit bad about what happened."

"What happened?"

"I'm getting to that. You have to realize that Steven was in love with me."

"That doesn't surprise me."

"Are you being facetious?" Mom stared at me. "A girl can't control who will and who won't fall in love with her,

Ethan. And sometimes, when a nuisance person falls in love with you, it can be awfully . . . awkward."

"How?"

"In the case of young Steven, he was always phoning and waiting for your father to leave so he could come around. It was awful."

That still didn't explain Steve's tie in the soap drawer in the guest bathroom. "And?"

"I just wanted Steven to leave me alone. So I called Kam Fong." Mom stared at me uneasily. "Why do you care about young Steven, by the way? I thought he was making your life miserable."

"He was, but now that he's gone, we've ended up with something much worse than him."

"I thought you might be happy to have him out of your hair."

"What did Kam Fong do with him?"

"I made him promise that he wouldn't kill him."

"How humane."

"Shush. You'll just have to ask Kam yourself. I can't ask him because it'll look as if I don't trust him—and if you *do* ask him, make sure he knows that it's *you* who wants to find Steven, not me."

"Done."

"Dinner will be ready in ninety minutes," said Mom. "Oh, I forgot—your father may have landed a speaking role in an SUV commercial. He's so excited."

I went downstairs again. Kaitlin asked, "Well?"

"I'm not sure."

"You think there's a connection?"

"I just don't know."

"How did the tie end up here?"

"She didn't say."

"Ethan, you're using your fake voice."

Shit.

"No, I'm not."

"And you're even lying about using your fake voice."

Crap.

"Ethan, I'm going to let this one go because it's family, and family stuff is always weird, but don't think I'm going to forget any of this."

"Kaitlin—" I looked at her. I love every molecule of her body. "That is really nice of you." I looked down at the task at hand. "I really just want to turn off my brain. Let's groom this pot and veg for a little bit."

Kaitlin sighed. "I wish my parents took such good care of their grow-op. My mom's lazy about tracking genetics. Her plants are the foliage equivalents of Cletus the Slack-Jawed Yokel. And my dad's electrical wiring is like that scene in *Poltergeist* where the evil bedroom is trying to suck the little girl into another dimension. When you turn on the light, you clench your toes, tighten your sphincter and wait for a different universe to suck you up."

• • •

Dinner went off without a hitch, although when I had to use the guest bathroom, Steve's tie was gone. Dad was stoked about his potential speaking part. "For once I get to be the asshole driving the shiny silver climate-killer down a mountain road that's been sprayed with a firehose by set-dec."

"What's your line in the commercial?"

"'Smooth, smooth, smooth.' Do you want me to demonstrate my various possible readings?"

"Go for it, Dad."

"Here's the one I think is best, but you listen and you tell me. Smooth, smooth, *smoooooooth*. What do you think?"

"Do a few more."

"Of course. *Smoooooooth, smoooooooooth, smoooooooooooooth.*"

Kaitlin said, "I like that one."

"Really? Did you like the way I lengthened the *ooooooooooo* sound?"

"It was good."

Imagine an hour more of this and you have dinner. Afterwards, we weighed Mom's crop and bagged it. Back at my place, around midnight, Kaitlin and I found Kam Fong leaving with a suitcase. He was moving out.

"Kam—no—we'll miss you." We really would.

"I'm not going far. Your brother just found me this great house in West Van—up on the hill. A bargain, too—the owner got nailed for shipping sugar pills to American seniors who thought they were buying Gleevec and OxyContin. Got it for peanuts. It's got a commanding city view, two karaoke rooms and it's been feng-shuied by a Grand Master." This was about as excited as Kam gets.

Kaitlin asked if Kam would have bought it if it hadn't been feng-shuied.

"Of course. Feng shui's one of those mumbo-jumbo Chinese things people expect Chinese people to get all serious about. It's total crap, but I use it all the time to haggle for lower prices. In any event, come to my housewarming the night after tomorrow. And Ethan, be prepared to sing along to Madonna's 'Vogue.'"

"Mother of God, no."

"Host chooses the tunes. Bye, kids."

• • •

Kaitlin's first meeting in the morning was about the repurposing of BoardX's characters. "I suppose I don't mind doing yet one more anime-style project, but Jesus, anime's like the gaming equivalent of those $8.95 white plastic stacking chairs from Wal-Mart. Sure, they work, but they've also slaughtered every other chair on the market. It's a category killer."

John Doe said, "Anime performed a vital Darwinian function. In the early 1990s the animation world was becoming shockingly lazy. As an art form, animation was dying. Anime offered new hope to young storytellers and animators. Competition and new ideas are good. Imagine a world in which there was only Coke, and no Pepsi. Coke would get lazy, wouldn't it? It'd become arrogant, and with total control of the world's cola nut production, it could raise the price of a tasty beverage to extortionate levels. They could mess with the formula—they could put cinnamon in it. Floor sweepings. Dirt."

Bree said, "I thought you didn't like Coke."

"Not specifically. But I like the idea that people can compete with it."

Cowboy said, "Wait a second—cola nuts? They actually grow them? I thought cola flavouring was entirely synthetic."

"The cola nut I refer to is *Cola acuminata,* which is no longer grown for that use. Modern cola flavouring is a petrochemical derivative. You can buy cola nuts in powdered form."

Kaitlin said, "Let's make our own Coke, right here in jPod."

John Doe said, "What an excellent idea, but please, for legal reasons, let's not call it Coke. Let's call it a cola-flavoured beverage. At the count of three, everybody google. First person to locate a place that sells cola powder and then make an online purchase gets the Halo 2 game I won as the door prize in last week's Tetris Challenge. One, two, three—*google*!"

Evil Mark was fastest. He found a pound of powdered cola for $10.98 from some hippie place in Iowa. John Doe said, "Congratulations, but you haven't officially won until I see a paper printout of your sale confirmation." The air was electric, because Cowboy was just then finalizing a sale. Mark, in a moment of brain death, entered a SAVE AS key command, and Cowboy ended up winning.

• • •

Back to SpriteQuest. For now, Cowboy, Evil Mark and John Doe are part of the team that assigns attributes to 3-D objects—making sure metals dent, stone crumbles, glass shatters and so forth. The three of them are also part of a squad whose mission is to reconfigure the skateboarding universe into a fantasy universe.

Me? I carry on fetching Honey Nut Cheerios for Gord-O. The big surprise was Bree, who showed up for work today with a wedge-cut hairdo and a navy blue business suit. Kaitlin said, "Bree, you look like a saleslady at a Liz Claiborne factory outlet store circa 1993."

"*Merde.* I was trying to look French. And I might as well tell you guys now, I've decided to try cracking upper management. I have to look the part."

"Why is it, if a guy wants to enter management, all he has

to do is declare the fact," Kaitlin asked, "while if a woman wants to do it, she has to dress like a linebacker in drag?"

John Doe: "It's the way of the world, Kaitlin."

I must say, the entire morning was the most demoralized and dispirited I can remember. Around noon I was in the cafeteria, trying some prosciutto and melon, when this guy named Alec came in. I worked with him a few years back, and we got to talking about an Easter egg in this old Atari 2600 game, where the programmer hid his name in a secret room. If you were in the know, or if you got the right zines, you could enter the room, and you got to see his signature just floating in the air in 3-D. The image has always haunted me.

The thing about Alec is that he has no indoor voice—instead of speaking to you, he broadcasts. Many people in gaming are like this. It's just one more form of human behaviour that's being reclassified as an offshoot of autism. Kaitlin can't finish her hugging machine soon enough.

In spite of his too-loud voice, Alec had a good point. "It's all about authorship. We work so hard on these games, but it's like our voices don't matter. That guy from the Atari 2600 game had to make himself count."

On the spot, I renewed my earlier vow to sabotage the game—except now I wasn't sabotaging BoardX with a turtle, I was sabotaging SpriteQuest with Prince Amulon.

• • •

John Doe ordered up a 50/50 regular/decaf from the floor's new and swanky watch-while-I-make-it-from-freshly-ground-beans machine. Evil Mark saw him do this and asked, "John, how can you drink half-and-half crap?"

"It's like trying to reconcile wave-particle duality," John

Doe replied. "You can't taste the caffeinated brew at the same time you taste the decaf—or vice versa. You can only taste one or the other. So it's like two beverages in one."

"I've never thought of it that way before."

"You shouldn't be so quick to judge, Mark."

Bree was right there: "John, I think you're binarizing a complex taste situation. I don't think it's that simplistic."

"Bree, is it wrong to try to make some sense of this chaotic world?"

As a joke, I asked Bree if she was taking coffee-tasting lessons, and it turns out she *is*. "The French take their coffee seriously, but I'm still trying to get past the café-au-lait-in-the-morning issue," she confessed. "It tastes like something a cartoon character would drink. Imagine Secret Squirrel getting up at five-thirty a.m., fighting a wicked macadamia hangover, groping for something, anything, to make the pain go away—and he reaches for a café au lait. I think I need to study this a bit more."

• • •

Evil Mark stood up in the middle of the afternoon and said, "I'm about to hand out sheets listing the 8,363 prime numbers between 10,000 and 100,000. Embedded in this list of numbers is one non-prime. First person to find that non-prime number wins my *Family Guy* promotional sixteen-ounce beer cozy."

In less than five minutes I won.

FUN FACT: any even number can be made by adding together two primes.

• • •

10007 10009 10037 10039 10061 10067 10069 10079 10091 10093
10099 10103 10111 10133 10139 10141 10151 10159 10163 10169
10177 10181 10193 10211 10223 10243 10247 10253 10259 10267
10271 10273 10289 10301 10303 10313 10321 10331 10333 10337
10343 10357 10369 10391 10399 10427 10429 10433 10453 10457
10459 10463 10477 10487 10499 10501 10513 10529 10531 10559
10567 10589 10597 10601 10607 10613 10627 10631 10639 10651
10657 10663 10667 10687 10691 10709 10711 10723 10729 10733
10739 10753 10771 10781 10789 10799 10831 10837 10847 10853
10859 10861 10867 10883 10889 10891 10903 10909 10937 10939
10949 10957 10973 10979 10987 10993 11003 11027 11047 11057
11059 11069 11071 11083 11087 11093 11113 11117 11119 11131
11149 11159 11161 11171 11173 11177 11197 11213 11239 11243
11251 11257 11261 11273 11279 11287 11299 11311 11317 11321
11329 11351 11353 11369 11383 11393 11399 11411 11423 11437
11443 11447 11467 11471 11483 11489 11491 11497 11503 11519
11527 11549 11551 11579 11587 11593 11597 11617 11621 11633
11657 11677 11681 11689 11699 11701 11717 11719 11731 11743
11777 11779 11783 11789 11801 11807 11813 11821 11827 11831
11833 11839 11863 11867 11887 11897 11903 11909 11923 11927
11933 11939 11941 11953 11959 11969 11971 11981 11987 12007
12011 12037 12041 12043 12049 12071 12073 12097 12101 12107
12109 12113 12119 12143 12149 12157 12161 12163 12197 12203
12211 12227 12239 12241 12251 12253 12263 12269 12277 12281
12289 12301 12323 12329 12343 12347 12373 12377 12379 12391
12401 12409 12413 12421 12433 12437 12451 12457 12473 12479
12487 12491 12497 12503 12511 12517 12527 12539 12541 12547
12553 12569 12577 12583 12589 12601 12611 12613 12619 12637
12641 12647 12653 12659 12671 12689 12697 12703 12713 12721
12739 12743 12757 12763 12781 12791 12799 12809 12821 12823
12829 12841 12853 12889 12893 12899 12907 12911 12917 12919
12923 12941 12953 12959 12967 12973 12979 12983 13001 13003
13007 13009 13033 13037 13043 13049 13063 13093 13099 13103
13109 13121 13127 13147 13151 13159 13163 13171 13177 13183
13187 13217 13219 13229 13241 13249 13259 13267 13291 13297
13309 13313 13327 13331 13337 13339 13367 13381 13397 13399
13411 13417 13421 13441 13451 13457 13463 13469 13477 13487
13499 13513 13523 13537 13553 13567 13577 13591 13597 13613
13619 13627 13633 13649 13669 13679 13681 13687 13691 13693
13697 13709 13711 13721 13723 13729 13751 13757 13759 13763
13781 13789 13799 13807 13829 13831 13841 13859 13873 13877
13879 13883 13901 13903 13907 13913 13921 13931 13933 13963
13967 13997 13999 14009 14011 14029 14033 14051 14057 14071
14081 14083 14087 14107 14143 14149 14153 14159 14173 14177
14197 14207 14221 14243 14249 14251 14281 14293 14303 14321
14323 14327 14341 14347 14369 14387 14389 14401 14407 14411
14419 14423 14431 14437 14447 14449 14461 14479 14489 14503

14519 14533 14537 14543 14549 14551 14557 14561 14563 14591
14593 14621 14627 14629 14633 14639 14653 14657 14669 14683
14699 14713 14717 14723 14731 14737 14741 14747 14753 14759
14767 14771 14779 14783 14797 14813 14821 14827 14831 14843
14851 14867 14869 14879 14887 14891 14897 14923 14929 14939
14947 14951 14957 14969 14983 15013 15017 15031 15053 15061
15073 15077 15083 15091 15101 15107 15121 15131 15137 15139
15149 15161 15173 15187 15193 15199 15217 15227 15233 15241
15259 15263 15269 15271 15277 15287 15289 15299 15307 15313
15319 15329 15331 15349 15359 15361 15373 15377 15383 15391
15401 15413 15427 15439 15443 15451 15461 15467 15473 15493
15497 15511 15527 15541 15551 15559 15569 15581 15583 15601
15607 15619 15629 15641 15643 15647 15649 15661 15667 15671
15679 15683 15727 15731 15733 15737 15739 15749 15761 15767
15773 15787 15791 15797 15803 15809 15817 15823 15859 15877
15881 15887 15889 15901 15907 15913 15919 15923 15937 15959
15971 15973 15991 16001 16007 16033 16057 16061 16063 16067
16069 16073 16087 16091 16097 16103 16111 16127 16139 16141
16183 16187 16189 16193 16217 16223 16229 16231 16249 16253
16267 16273 16301 16319 16333 16339 16349 16361 16363 16369
16381 16411 16417 16421 16427 16433 16447 16451 16453 16477
16481 16487 16493 16519 16529 16547 16553 16561 16567 16573
16603 16607 16619 16631 16633 16649 16651 16657 16661 16673
16691 16693 16699 16703 16729 16741 16747 16759 16763 16787
16811 16823 16829 16831 16843 16871 16879 16883 16889 16901
16903 16921 16927 16931 16937 16943 16963 16979 16981 16987
16993 17011 17021 17027 17029 17033 17041 17047 17053 17077
17093 17099 17107 17117 17123 17137 17159 17167 17183 17189
17191 17203 17207 17209 17231 17239 17257 17291 17293 17299
17317 17321 17327 17333 17341 17351 17359 17377 17383 17387
17389 17393 17401 17417 17419 17431 17443 17449 17467 17471
17477 17483 17489 17491 17497 17509 17519 17539 17551 17569
17573 17579 17581 17597 17599 17609 17623 17627 17657 17659
17669 17681 17683 17707 17713 17729 17737 17747 17749 17761
17783 17789 17791 17807 17827 17837 17839 17851 17863 17881
17891 17903 17909 17911 17921 17923 17929 17939 17957 17959
17971 17977 17981 17987 17989 18013 18041 18043 18047 18049
18059 18061 18077 18089 18097 18119 18121 18127 18131 18133
18143 18149 18169 18181 18191 18199 18211 18217 18223 18229
18233 18251 18253 18257 18269 18287 18289 18301 18307 18311
18313 18329 18341 18353 18367 18371 18379 18397 18401 18413
18427 18433 18439 18443 18451 18457 18461 18481 18493 18503
18517 18521 18523 18539 18541 18553 18583 18587 18593 18617
18637 18661 18671 18679 18691 18701 18713 18719 18731 18743
18749 18757 18773 18787 18793 18797 18803 18839 18859 18869
18899 18911 18913 18917 18919 18947 18959 18973 18979 19001
19009 19013 19031 19037 19051 19069 19073 19079 19081 19087

19121 19139 19141 19157 19163 19181 19183 19207 19211 19213
19219 19231 19237 19249 19259 19267 19273 19289 19301 19309
19319 19333 19373 19379 19381 19387 19391 19403 19417 19421
19423 19427 19429 19433 19441 19447 19457 19463 19469 19471
19477 19483 19489 19501 19507 19531 19541 19543 19553 19559
19571 19577 19583 19597 19603 19609 19661 19681 19687 19697
19699 19709 19717 19727 19739 19751 19753 19759 19763 19777
19793 19801 19813 19819 19841 19843 19853 19861 19867 19889
19891 19913 19919 19927 19937 19949 19961 19963 19973 19979
19991 19993 19997 20011 20021 20023 20029 20047 20051 20063
20071 20089 20101 20107 20113 20117 20123 20129 20143 20147
20149 20161 20173 20177 20183 20201 20219 20231 20233 20249
20261 20269 20287 20297 20323 20327 20333 20341 20347 20353
20357 20359 20369 20389 20393 20399 20407 20411 20431 20441
20443 20477 20479 20483 20507 20509 20521 20533 20543 20549
20551 20563 20593 20599 20611 20627 20639 20641 20663 20681
20693 20707 20717 20719 20731 20743 20747 20749 20753 20759
20771 20773 20789 20807 20809 20849 20857 20873 20879 20887
20897 20899 20903 20921 20929 20939 20947 20959 20963 20981
20983 21001 21011 21013 21017 21019 21023 21031 21059 21061
21067 21089 21101 21107 21121 21139 21143 21149 21157 21163
21169 21179 21187 21191 21193 21211 21221 21227 21247 21269
21277 21283 21313 21317 21319 21323 21341 21347 21377 21379
21383 21391 21397 21401 21407 21419 21433 21467 21481 21487
21491 21493 21499 21503 21517 21521 21523 21529 21557 21559
21563 21569 21577 21587 21589 21599 21601 21611 21613 21617
21647 21649 21661 21673 21683 21701 21713 21727 21737 21739
21751 21757 21767 21773 21787 21799 21803 21817 21821 21839
21841 21851 21859 21863 21871 21881 21893 21911 21929 21937
21943 21961 21977 21991 21997 22003 22013 22027 22031 22037
22039 22051 22063 22067 22073 22079 22091 22093 22109 22111
22123 22129 22133 22147 22153 22157 22159 22171 22189 22193
22229 22247 22259 22271 22273 22277 22279 22283 22291 22303
22307 22343 22349 22367 22369 22381 22391 22397 22409 22433
22441 22447 22453 22469 22481 22483 22501 22511 22531 22541
22543 22549 22567 22571 22573 22613 22619 22621 22637 22639
22643 22651 22669 22679 22691 22697 22699 22709 22717 22721
22727 22739 22741 22751 22769 22777 22783 22787 22807 22811
22817 22853 22859 22861 22871 22877 22901 22907 22921 22937
22943 22961 22963 22973 22993 23003 23011 23017 23021 23027
23029 23039 23041 23053 23057 23059 23063 23071 23081 23087
23099 23117 23131 23143 23159 23167 23173 23189 23197 23201
23203 23209 23227 23251 23269 23279 23291 23293 23297 23311
23321 23327 23333 23339 23357 23369 23371 23399 23417 23431
23447 23459 23473 23497 23509 23531 23537 23539 23549 23557
23561 23563 23567 23581 23593 23599 23603 23609 23623 23627
23629 23633 23663 23669 23671 23677 23687 23689 23719 23741

23743 23747 23753 23761 23767 23773 23789 23801 23813 23819
23827 23831 23833 23857 23869 23873 23879 23887 23893 23899
23909 23911 23917 23929 23957 23971 23977 23981 23993 24001
24007 24019 24023 24029 24043 24049 24061 24071 24077 24083
24091 24097 24103 24107 24109 24113 24121 24133 24137 24151
24169 24179 24181 24197 24203 24223 24229 24239 24247 24251
24281 24317 24329 24337 24359 24371 24373 24379 24391 24407
24413 24419 24421 24439 24443 24469 24473 24481 24499 24509
24517 24527 24533 24547 24551 24571 24593 24611 24623 24631
24659 24671 24677 24683 24691 24697 24709 24733 24749 24763
24767 24781 24793 24799 24809 24821 24841 24847 24851 24859
24877 24889 24907 24917 24919 24923 24943 24953 24967 24971
24977 24979 24989 25013 25031 25033 25037 25057 25073 25087
25097 25111 25117 25121 25127 25147 25153 25163 25169 25171
25183 25189 25219 25229 25237 25243 25247 25253 25261 25301
25303 25307 25309 25321 25339 25343 25349 25357 25367 25373
25391 25409 25411 25423 25439 25447 25453 25457 25463 25469
25471 25523 25537 25541 25561 25577 25579 25583 25589 25601
25603 25609 25621 25633 25639 25643 25657 25667 25673 25679
25693 25703 25717 25733 25741 25747 25759 25763 25771 25793
25799 25801 25819 25841 25847 25849 25867 25873 25889 25903
25913 25919 25931 25933 25939 25943 25951 25969 25981 25997
25999 26003 26017 26021 26029 26041 26053 26083 26099 26107
26111 26113 26119 26141 26153 26161 26171 26177 26183 26189
26203 26209 26227 26237 26249 26251 26261 26263 26267 26293
26297 26309 26317 26321 26339 26347 26357 26371 26387 26393
26399 26407 26417 26423 26431 26437 26449 26459 26479 26489
26497 26501 26513 26539 26557 26561 26573 26591 26597 26627
26633 26641 26647 26669 26681 26683 26687 26693 26699 26701
26711 26713 26717 26723 26729 26731 26737 26759 26777 26783
26801 26813 26821 26833 26839 26849 26861 26863 26879 26881
26891 26893 26903 26921 26927 26947 26951 26953 26959 26981
26987 26993 27011 27017 27031 27043 27059 27061 27067 27073
27077 27091 27103 27107 27109 27127 27143 27179 27191 27197
27211 27239 27241 27253 27259 27271 27277 27281 27283 27299
27329 27337 27361 27367 27397 27407 27409 27427 27431 27437
27449 27457 27479 27481 27487 27509 27527 27529 27539 27541
27551 27581 27583 27611 27617 27631 27647 27653 27673 27689
27691 27697 27701 27733 27737 27739 27743 27749 27751 27763
27767 27773 27779 27791 27793 27799 27803 27809 27817 27823
27827 27847 27851 27883 27893 27901 27917 27919 27941 27943
27947 27953 27961 27967 27983 27997 28001 28019 28027 28031
28051 28057 28069 28081 28087 28097 28099 28109 28111 28123
28151 28163 28181 28183 28201 28211 28219 28229 28277 28279
28283 28289 28297 28307 28309 28319 28349 28351 28387 28393
28403 28409 28411 28429 28433 28439 28447 28463 28477 28493
28499 28513 28517 28537 28541 28547 28549 28559 28571 28573

28579 28591 28597 28603 28607 28619 28621 28627 28631 28643
28649 28657 28661 28663 28669 28687 28697 28703 28711 28723
28729 28751 28753 28759 28771 28789 28793 28807 28813 28817
28837 28843 28859 28867 28871 28879 28901 28909 28921 28927
28933 28949 28961 28979 29009 29017 29021 29023 29027 29033
29059 29063 29077 29101 29123 29129 29131 29137 29147 29153
29167 29173 29179 29191 29201 29207 29209 29221 29231 29243
29251 29269 29287 29297 29303 29311 29327 29333 29339 29347
29363 29383 29387 29389 29399 29401 29411 29423 29429 29437
29443 29453 29473 29483 29501 29527 29531 29537 29567 29569
29573 29581 29587 29599 29611 29629 29633 29641 29663 29669
29671 29683 29717 29723 29741 29753 29759 29761 29789 29803
29819 29833 29837 29851 29863 29867 29873 29879 29881 29917
29921 29927 29947 29959 29983 29989 30011 30013 30029 30047
30059 30071 30089 30091 30097 30103 30109 30113 30119 30133
30137 30139 30161 30169 30181 30187 30197 30203 30211 30223
30241 30253 30259 30269 30271 30293 30307 30313 30319 30323
30341 30347 30367 30389 30391 30403 30427 30431 30449 30467
30469 30491 30493 30497 30509 30517 30529 30539 30553 30557
30559 30577 30593 30631 30637 30643 30649 30661 30671 30677
30689 30697 30703 30707 30713 30727 30757 30763 30773 30781
30803 30809 30817 30829 30839 30841 30851 30853 30859 30869
30871 30881 30893 30911 30931 30937 30941 30949 30971 30977
30983 31013 31019 31033 31039 31051 31063 31069 31079 31081
31091 31121 31123 31139 31147 31151 31153 31159 31177 31181
31183 31189 31193 31219 31223 31231 31237 31247 31249 31253
31259 31267 31271 31277 31307 31319 31321 31327 31333 31337
31357 31379 31387 31391 31393 31397 31469 31477 31481 31489
31511 31513 31517 31531 31541 31543 31547 31567 31573 31583
31601 31607 31627 31643 31649 31657 31663 31667 31687 31699
31721 31723 31727 31729 31741 31751 31769 31771 31793 31799
31817 31847 31849 31859 31873 31883 31891 31907 31957 31963
31973 31981 31991 32003 32009 32027 32029 32051 32057 32059
32063 32069 32077 32083 32089 32099 32117 32119 32141 32143
32159 32173 32183 32189 32191 32203 32213 32233 32237 32251
32257 32261 32297 32299 32303 32309 32321 32323 32327 32341
32353 32359 32363 32369 32371 32377 32381 32401 32411 32413
32423 32429 32441 32443 32467 32479 32491 32497 32503 32507
32531 32533 32537 32561 32563 32569 32573 32579 32587 32603
32609 32611 32621 32633 32647 32653 32687 32693 32707 32713
32717 32719 32749 32771 32779 32783 32789 32797 32801 32803
32831 32833 32839 32843 32869 32887 32909 32911 32917 32933
32939 32941 32957 32969 32971 32983 32987 32993 32999 33013
33023 33029 33037 33049 33053 33071 33073 33083 33091 33107
33113 33119 33149 33151 33161 33179 33181 33191 33199 33203
33211 33223 33247 33287 33289 33301 33311 33317 33329 33331
33343 33347 33349 33353 33359 33377 33391 33403 33409 33413

33427 33457 33461 33469 33479 33487 33493 33503 33521 33529
33533 33547 33563 33569 33577 33581 33587 33589 33599 33601
33613 33617 33619 33623 33629 33637 33641 33647 33679 33703
33713 33721 33739 33749 33751 33757 33767 33769 33773 33791
33797 33809 33811 33827 33829 33851 33857 33863 33871 33889
33893 33911 33923 33931 33937 33941 33961 33967 33997 34019
34031 34033 34039 34057 34061 34123 34127 34129 34141 34147
34157 34159 34171 34183 34211 34213 34217 34231 34253 34259
34261 34267 34273 34283 34297 34301 34303 34313 34319 34327
34337 34351 34361 34367 34369 34381 34403 34421 34429 34439
34457 34469 34471 34483 34487 34499 34501 34511 34513 34519
34537 34543 34549 34583 34589 34591 34603 34607 34613 34631
34649 34651 34667 34673 34679 34687 34693 34703 34721 34729
34739 34747 34757 34759 34763 34781 34807 34819 34841 34843
34847 34849 34871 34877 34883 34897 34913 34919 34939 34949
34961 34963 34981 35023 35027 35051 35053 35059 35069 35081
35083 35089 35099 35107 35111 35117 35129 35141 35149 35153
35159 35171 35201 35221 35227 35251 35257 35267 35279 35281
35291 35311 35317 35323 35327 35339 35353 35363 35381 35393
35401 35407 35419 35423 35437 35447 35449 35461 35491 35507
35509 35521 35527 35531 35533 35537 35543 35569 35573 35591
35593 35597 35603 35617 35671 35677 35729 35731 35747 35753
35759 35771 35797 35801 35803 35809 35831 35837 35839 35851
35863 35869 35879 35897 35899 35911 35923 35933 35951 35963
35969 35977 35983 35993 35999 36007 36011 36013 36017 36037
36061 36067 36073 36083 36097 36107 36109 36131 36137 36151
36161 36187 36191 36209 36217 36229 36241 36251 36263 36269
36277 36293 36299 36307 36313 36319 36341 36343 36353 36373
36383 36389 36433 36451 36457 36467 36469 36473 36479 36493
36497 36523 36527 36529 36541 36551 36559 36563 36571 36583
36587 36599 36607 36629 36637 36643 36653 36671 36677 36683
36691 36697 36709 36713 36721 36739 36749 36761 36767 36779
36781 36787 36791 36793 36809 36821 36833 36847 36857 36871
36877 36887 36899 36901 36913 36919 36923 36929 36931 36943
36947 36973 36979 36997 37003 37013 37019 37021 37039 37049
37057 37061 37087 37097 37117 37123 37139 37159 37171 37181
37189 37199 37201 37217 37223 37243 37253 37273 37277 37307
37309 37313 37321 37337 37339 37357 37361 37363 37369 37379
37397 37409 37423 37441 37447 37463 37483 37489 37493 37501
37507 37511 37517 37529 37537 37547 37549 37561 37567 37571
37573 37579 37589 37591 37607 37619 37633 37643 37649 37657
37663 37691 37693 37699 37717 37747 37781 37783 37799 37811
37813 37831 37847 37853 37861 37871 37879 37889 37897 37907
37951 37957 37963 37967 37987 37991 37993 37997 38011 38039
38047 38053 38069 38083 38113 38119 38149 38153 38167 38177
38183 38189 38197 38201 38219 38231 38237 38239 38261 38273
38281 38287 38299 38303 38317 38321 38327 38329 38333 38351

38371 38377 38393 38431 38447 38449 38453 38459 38461 38501
38543 38557 38561 38567 38569 38593 38603 38609 38611 38629
38639 38651 38653 38669 38671 38677 38693 38699 38707 38711
38713 38723 38729 38737 38747 38749 38767 38783 38791 38803
38821 38833 38839 38851 38861 38867 38873 38891 38903 38917
38921 38923 38933 38953 38959 38971 38977 38993 39019 39023
39041 39043 39047 39079 39089 39097 39103 39107 39113 39119
39133 39139 39157 39161 39163 39181 39191 39199 39209 39217
39227 39229 39233 39239 39241 39251 39293 39301 39313 39317
39323 39341 39343 39359 39367 39371 39373 39383 39397 39409
39419 39439 39443 39451 39461 39499 39503 39509 39511 39521
39541 39551 39563 39569 39581 39607 39619 39623 39631 39659
39667 39671 39679 39703 39709 39719 39727 39733 39749 39761
39769 39779 39791 39799 39821 39827 39829 39839 39841 39847
39857 39863 39869 39877 39883 39887 39901 39929 39937 39953
39971 39979 39983 39989 40009 40013 40031 40037 40039 40063
40087 40093 40099 40111 40123 40127 40129 40151 40153 40163
40169 40177 40189 40193 40213 40231 40237 40241 40253 40277
40283 40289 40343 40351 40357 40361 40387 40423 40427 40429
40433 40459 40471 40483 40487 40493 40499 40507 40519 40529
40531 40543 40559 40577 40583 40591 40597 40609 40627 40637
40639 40693 40697 40699 40709 40739 40751 40759 40763 40771
40787 40801 40813 40819 40823 40829 40841 40847 40849 40853
40867 40879 40883 40897 40903 40927 40933 40939 40949 40961
40973 40993 41011 41017 41023 41039 41047 41051 41057 41077
41081 41113 41117 41131 41141 41143 41149 41161 41177 41179
41183 41189 41201 41203 41213 41221 41227 41231 41233 41243
41257 41263 41269 41281 41299 41333 41341 41351 41357 41381
41387 41389 41399 41411 41413 41443 41453 41467 41479 41491
41507 41513 41519 41521 41539 41543 41549 41579 41593 41597
41603 41609 41611 41617 41621 41627 41641 41647 41651 41659
41669 41681 41687 41719 41729 41737 41759 41761 41771 41777
41801 41809 41813 41843 41849 41851 41863 41879 41887 41893
41897 41903 41911 41927 41941 41947 41953 41957 41959 41969
41981 41983 41999 42013 42017 42019 42023 42043 42061 42071
42073 42083 42089 42101 42131 42139 42157 42169 42179 42181
42187 42193 42197 42209 42221 42223 42227 42239 42257 42281
42283 42293 42299 42307 42323 42331 42337 42349 42359 42373
42379 42391 42397 42403 42407 42409 42433 42437 42443 42451
42457 42461 42463 42467 42473 42487 42491 42499 42509 42533
42557 42569 42571 42577 42589 42611 42641 42643 42649 42667
42677 42683 42689 42697 42701 42703 42709 42719 42727 42737
42743 42751 42767 42773 42787 42793 42797 42821 42829 42839
42841 42853 42859 42863 42899 42901 42923 42929 42937 42943
42953 42961 42967 42979 42989 43003 43013 43019 43037 43049
43051 43063 43067 43093 43103 43117 43133 43151 43159 43177
43189 43201 43207 43223 43237 43261 43271 43283 43291 43313

43319 43321 43331 43391 43397 43399 43403 43411 43427 43441
43451 43457 43481 43487 43499 43517 43541 43543 43573 43577
43579 43591 43597 43607 43609 43613 43627 43633 43649 43651
43661 43669 43691 43711 43717 43721 43753 43759 43777 43781
43783 43787 43789 43793 43801 43853 43867 43889 43891 43913
43933 43943 43951 43961 43963 43969 43973 43987 43991 43997
44017 44021 44027 44029 44041 44053 44059 44071 44087 44089
44101 44111 44119 44123 44129 44131 44159 44171 44179 44189
44201 44203 44207 44221 44249 44257 44263 44267 44269 44273
44279 44281 44293 44351 44357 44371 44381 44383 44389 44417
44449 44453 44483 44491 44497 44501 44507 44519 44531 44533
44537 44543 44549 44563 44579 44587 44617 44621 44623 44633
44641 44647 44651 44657 44683 44687 44699 44701 44711 44729
44741 44753 44771 44773 44777 44789 44797 44809 44819 44839
44843 44851 44867 44879 44887 44893 44909 44917 44927 44939
44953 44959 44963 44971 44983 44987 45007 45013 45053 45061
45077 45083 45119 45121 45127 45131 45137 45139 45161 45179
45181 45191 45197 45233 45247 45259 45263 45281 45289 45293
45307 45317 45319 45329 45337 45341 45343 45361 45377 45389
45403 45413 45427 45433 45439 45481 45491 45497 45503 45523
45533 45541 45553 45557 45569 45587 45589 45599 45613 45631
45641 45659 45667 45673 45677 45691 45697 45707 45737 45751
45757 45763 45767 45779 45817 45821 45823 45827 45833 45841
45853 45863 45869 45887 45893 45943 45949 45953 45959 45971
45979 45989 46021 46027 46049 46051 46061 46073 46091 46093
46099 46103 46133 46141 46147 46153 46171 46181 46183 46187
46199 46219 46229 46237 46261 46271 46273 46279 46301 46307
46309 46327 46337 46349 46351 46381 46399 46411 46439 46441
46447 46451 46457 46471 46477 46489 46499 46507 46511 46523
46549 46559 46567 46573 46589 46591 46601 46619 46633 46639
46643 46649 46663 46679 46681 46687 46691 46703 46723 46727
46747 46751 46757 46769 46771 46807 46811 46817 46819 46829
46831 46853 46861 46867 46877 46889 46901 46919 46933 46957
46993 46997 47017 47041 47051 47057 47059 47087 47093 47111
47119 47123 47129 47137 47143 47147 47149 47161 47189 47207
47221 47237 47251 47269 47279 47287 47293 47297 47303 47309
47317 47339 47351 47353 47363 47381 47387 47389 47407 47417
47419 47431 47441 47459 47491 47497 47501 47507 47513 47521
47527 47533 47543 47563 47569 47581 47591 47599 47609 47623
47629 47639 47653 47657 47659 47681 47699 47701 47711 47713
47717 47737 47741 47743 47777 47779 47791 47797 47807 47809
47819 47837 47843 47857 47869 47881 47903 47911 47917 47933
47939 47947 47951 47963 47969 47977 47981 48017 48023 48029
48049 48073 48079 48091 48109 48119 48121 48131 48157 48163
48179 48187 48193 48197 48221 48239 48247 48259 48271 48281
48299 48311 48313 48337 48341 48353 48371 48383 48397 48407
48409 48413 48437 48449 48463 48473 48479 48481 48487 48491

48497 48523 48527 48533 48539 48541 48563 48571 48589 48593
48611 48619 48623 48647 48649 48661 48673 48677 48679 48731
48733 48751 48757 48761 48767 48779 48781 48787 48799 48809
48817 48821 48823 48847 48857 48859 48869 48871 48883 48889
48907 48947 48953 48973 48989 48991 49003 49009 49019 49031
49033 49037 49043 49057 49069 49081 49103 49109 49117 49121
49123 49139 49157 49169 49171 49177 49193 49199 49201 49207
49211 49223 49253 49261 49277 49279 49297 49307 49331 49333
49339 49363 49367 49369 49391 49393 49409 49411 49417 49429
49433 49451 49459 49463 49477 49481 49499 49523 49529 49531
49537 49547 49549 49559 49597 49603 49613 49627 49633 49639
49663 49667 49669 49681 49697 49711 49727 49739 49741 49747
49757 49783 49787 49789 49801 49807 49811 49823 49831 49843
49853 49871 49877 49891 49919 49921 49927 49937 49939 49943
49957 49991 49993 49999 50021 50023 50033 50047 50051 50053
50069 50077 50087 50093 50101 50111 50119 50123 50129 50131
50147 50153 50159 50177 50207 50221 50227 50231 50261 50263
50273 50287 50291 50311 50321 50329 50333 50341 50359 50363
50377 50383 50387 50411 50417 50423 50441 50459 50461 50497
50503 50513 50527 50539 50543 50549 50551 50581 50587 50591
50593 50599 50627 50647 50651 50671 50683 50707 50723 50741
50753 50767 50773 50777 50789 50821 50833 50839 50849 50857
50867 50873 50891 50893 50909 50923 50929 50951 50957 50969
50971 50989 50993 51001 51031 51043 51047 51059 51061 51071
51109 51131 51133 51137 51151 51157 51169 51193 51197 51199
51203 51217 51229 51239 51241 51257 51263 51283 51287 51307
51329 51341 51343 51347 51349 51361 51383 51407 51413 51419
51421 51427 51431 51437 51439 51449 51461 51473 51479 51481
51487 51503 51511 51517 51521 51539 51551 51563 51577 51581
51593 51599 51607 51613 51631 51637 51647 51659 51673 51679
51683 51691 51713 51719 51721 51749 51767 51769 51787 51797
51803 51817 51827 51829 51839 51853 51859 51869 51871 51893
51899 51907 51913 51929 51941 51949 51971 51973 51977 51991
52009 52021 52027 52051 52057 52067 52069 52081 52103 52121
52127 52147 52153 52163 52177 52181 52183 52189 52201 52223
52237 52249 52253 52259 52267 52289 52291 52301 52313 52321
52361 52363 52369 52379 52387 52391 52433 52453 52457 52489
52501 52511 52517 52529 52541 52543 52553 52561 52567 52571
52579 52583 52609 52627 52631 52639 52667 52673 52691 52697
52709 52711 52721 52727 52733 52747 52757 52769 52783 52807
52813 52817 52837 52859 52861 52879 52883 52889 52901 52903
52919 52937 52951 52957 52963 52967 52973 52981 52999 53003
53017 53047 53051 53069 53077 53087 53089 53093 53101 53113
53117 53129 53147 53149 53161 53171 53173 53189 53197 53201
53231 53233 53239 53267 53269 53279 53281 53299 53309 53323
53327 53353 53359 53377 53381 53401 53407 53411 53419 53437
53441 53453 53479 53503 53507 53527 53549 53551 53569 53591

53593 53597 53609 53611 53617 53623 53629 53633 53639 53653
53657 53681 53693 53699 53717 53719 53731 53759 53773 53777
53783 53791 53813 53819 53831 53849 53857 53861 53881 53887
53891 53897 53899 53917 53923 53927 53939 53951 53959 53987
53993 54001 54011 54013 54037 54049 54059 54083 54091 54101
54121 54133 54139 54151 54163 54167 54181 54193 54217 54251
54269 54277 54287 54293 54311 54319 54323 54331 54347 54361
54367 54371 54377 54401 54403 54409 54413 54419 54421 54437
54443 54449 54469 54493 54497 54499 54503 54517 54521 54539
54541 54547 54559 54563 54577 54581 54583 54601 54617 54623
54629 54631 54647 54667 54673 54679 54709 54713 54721 54727
54751 54767 54773 54779 54787 54799 54829 54833 54851 54869
54877 54881 54907 54917 54919 54941 54949 54959 54973 54979
54983 55001 55009 55021 55049 55051 55057 55061 55073 55079
55103 55109 55117 55127 55147 55163 55171 55201 55207 55213
55217 55219 55229 55243 55249 55259 55291 55313 55331 55333
55337 55339 55343 55351 55373 55381 55399 55411 55439 55441
55457 55469 55487 55501 55511 55529 55541 55547 55579 55589
55603 55609 55619 55621 55631 55633 55639 55661 55663 55667
55673 55681 55691 55697 55711 55717 55721 55733 55763 55787
55793 55799 55807 55813 55817 55819 55823 55829 55837 55843
55849 55871 55889 55897 55901 55903 55921 55927 55931 55933
55949 55967 55987 55997 56003 56009 56039 56041 56053 56081
56087 56093 56099 56101 56113 56123 56131 56149 56167 56171
56179 56197 56207 56209 56237 56239 56249 56263 56267 56269
56299 56311 56333 56359 56369 56377 56383 56393 56401 56417
56431 56437 56443 56453 56467 56473 56477 56479 56489 56501
56503 56509 56519 56527 56531 56533 56543 56569 56591 56597
56599 56611 56629 56633 56659 56663 56671 56681 56687 56701
56711 56713 56731 56737 56747 56767 56773 56779 56783 56807
56809 56813 56821 56827 56843 56857 56873 56891 56893 56897
56909 56911 56921 56923 56929 56941 56951 56957 56963 56983
56989 56993 56999 57037 57041 57047 57059 57073 57077 57089
57097 57107 57119 57131 57139 57143 57149 57163 57173 57179
57191 57193 57203 57221 57223 57241 57251 57259 57269 57271
57283 57287 57301 57329 57331 57347 57349 57367 57373 57383
57389 57397 57413 57427 57457 57467 57487 57493 57503 57527
57529 57557 57559 57571 57587 57593 57601 57637 57641 57649
57653 57667 57679 57689 57697 57709 57713 57719 57727 57731
57737 57751 57773 57781 57787 57791 57793 57803 57809 57829
57839 57847 57853 57859 57881 57899 57901 57917 57923 57943
57947 57973 57977 57991 58013 58027 58031 58043 58049 58057
58061 58067 58073 58099 58109 58111 58129 58147 58151 58153
58169 58171 58189 58193 58199 58207 58211 58217 58229 58231
58237 58243 58271 58309 58313 58321 58337 58363 58367 58369
58379 58391 58393 58403 58411 58417 58427 58439 58441 58451
58453 58477 58481 58511 58537 58543 58549 58567 58573 58579

58601 58603 58613 58631 58657 58661 58679 58687 58693 58699
58711 58727 58733 58741 58757 58763 58771 58787 58789 58831
58889 58897 58901 58907 58909 58913 58921 58937 58943 58963
58967 58979 58991 58997 59009 59011 59021 59023 59029 59051
59053 59063 59069 59077 59083 59093 59107 59113 59119 59123
59141 59149 59159 59167 59183 59197 59207 59209 59219 59221
59233 59239 59243 59263 59273 59281 59333 59341 59351 59357
59359 59369 59377 59387 59393 59399 59407 59417 59419 59441
59443 59447 59453 59467 59471 59473 59497 59509 59513 59539
59557 59561 59567 59581 59611 59617 59621 59627 59629 59651
59659 59663 59669 59671 59693 59699 59707 59723 59729 59743
59747 59753 59771 59779 59791 59797 59809 59833 59863 59879
59887 59921 59929 59951 59957 59971 59981 59999 60013 60017
60029 60037 60041 60077 60083 60089 60091 60101 60103 60107
60127 60133 60139 60149 60161 60167 60169 60209 60217 60223
60251 60257 60259 60271 60289 60293 60317 60331 60337 60343
60353 60373 60383 60397 60413 60427 60443 60449 60457 60493
60497 60509 60521 60527 60539 60589 60601 60607 60611 60617
60623 60631 60637 60647 60649 60659 60661 60679 60689 60703
60719 60727 60733 60737 60757 60761 60763 60773 60779 60793
60811 60821 60859 60869 60887 60889 60899 60901 60913 60917
60919 60923 60937 60943 60953 60961 61001 61007 61027 61031
61043 61051 61057 61091 61099 61121 61129 61141 61151 61153
61169 61211 61223 61231 61253 61261 61283 61291 61297 61331
61333 61339 61343 61357 61363 61379 61381 61403 61409 61417
61441 61463 61469 61471 61483 61487 61493 61507 61511 61519
61543 61547 61553 61559 61561 61583 61603 61609 61613 61627
61631 61637 61643 61651 61657 61667 61673 61681 61687 61703
61717 61723 61729 61751 61757 61781 61813 61819 61837 61843
61861 61871 61879 61909 61927 61933 61949 61961 61967 61979
61981 61987 61991 62003 62011 62017 62039 62047 62053 62057
62071 62081 62099 62119 62129 62131 62137 62141 62143 62171
62189 62191 62201 62207 62213 62219 62233 62273 62297 62299
62303 62311 62323 62327 62347 62351 62383 62401 62417 62423
62459 62467 62473 62477 62483 62497 62501 62507 62533 62539
62549 62563 62581 62591 62597 62603 62617 62627 62633 62639
62653 62659 62683 62687 62701 62723 62731 62743 62753 62761
62773 62791 62801 62819 62827 62851 62861 62869 62873 62897
62903 62921 62927 62929 62939 62969 62971 62981 62983 62987
62989 63029 63031 63059 63067 63073 63079 63097 63103 63113
63127 63131 63149 63179 63197 63199 63211 63241 63247 63277
63281 63299 63311 63313 63317 63331 63337 63347 63353 63361
63367 63377 63389 63391 63397 63409 63419 63421 63439 63443
63463 63467 63473 63487 63493 63499 63521 63527 63533 63541
63559 63577 63587 63589 63599 63601 63607 63611 63617 63629
63647 63649 63659 63667 63671 63689 63691 63697 63703 63709
63719 63727 63737 63743 63761 63773 63781 63793 63799 63803

63809 63823 63839 63841 63853 63857 63863 63901 63907 63913
63929 63949 63977 63997 64007 64013 64019 64033 64037 64063
64067 64081 64091 64109 64123 64151 64153 64157 64171 64187
64189 64217 64223 64231 64237 64271 64279 64283 64301 64303
64319 64327 64333 64373 64381 64399 64403 64433 64439 64451
64453 64483 64489 64499 64513 64553 64567 64577 64579 64591
64601 64609 64613 64621 64627 64633 64661 64663 64667 64679
64693 64709 64717 64747 64763 64781 64783 64793 64811 64817
64849 64853 64871 64877 64879 64891 64901 64919 64921 64927
64937 64951 64969 64997 65003 65011 65027 65029 65033 65053
65063 65071 65089 65099 65101 65111 65119 65123 65129 65141
65147 65167 65171 65173 65179 65183 65203 65213 65239 65257
65267 65269 65287 65293 65309 65323 65327 65353 65357 65371
65381 65393 65407 65413 65419 65423 65437 65447 65449 65479
65497 65519 65521 65537 65539 65543 65551 65557 65563 65579
65581 65587 65599 65609 65617 65629 65633 65647 65651 65657
65677 65687 65699 65701 65707 65713 65717 65719 65729 65731
65761 65777 65789 65809 65827 65831 65837 65839 65843 65851
65867 65881 65899 65921 65927 65929 65951 65957 65963 65981
65983 65993 66029 66037 66041 66047 66067 66071 66083 66089
66103 66107 66109 66137 66161 66169 66173 66179 66191 66221
66239 66271 66293 66301 66337 66343 66347 66359 66361 66373
66377 66383 66403 66413 66431 66449 66457 66463 66467 66491
66499 66509 66523 66529 66533 66541 66553 66569 66571 66587
66593 66601 66617 66629 66643 66653 66683 66697 66701 66713
66721 66733 66739 66749 66751 66763 66791 66797 66809 66821
66841 66851 66853 66863 66877 66883 66889 66919 66923 66931
66943 66947 66949 66959 66973 66977 67003 67021 67033 67043
67049 67057 67061 67073 67079 67103 67121 67129 67139 67141
67153 67157 67169 67181 67187 67189 67211 67213 67217 67219
67231 67247 67261 67271 67273 67289 67307 67339 67343 67349
67369 67391 67399 67409 67411 67421 67427 67429 67433 67447
67453 67477 67481 67489 67493 67499 67511 67523 67531 67537
67547 67559 67567 67577 67579 67589 67601 67607 67619 67631
67651 67679 67699 67709 67723 67733 67741 67751 67757 67759
67763 67777 67783 67789 67801 67807 67819 67829 67843 67853
67867 67883 67891 67901 67927 67931 67933 67939 67943 67957
67961 67967 67979 67987 67993 68023 68041 68053 68059 68071
68087 68099 68111 68113 68141 68147 68161 68171 68207 68209
68213 68219 68227 68239 68261 68279 68281 68311 68329 68351
68371 68389 68399 68437 68443 68447 68449 68473 68477 68483
68489 68491 68501 68507 68521 68531 68539 68543 68567 68581
68597 68611 68633 68639 68659 68669 68683 68687 68699 68711
68713 68729 68737 68743 68749 68767 68771 68777 68791 68813
68819 68821 68863 68879 68881 68891 68897 68899 68903 68909
68917 68927 68947 68963 68993 69001 69011 69019 69029 69031
69061 69067 69073 69109 69119 69127 69143 69149 69151 69163

69191 69193 69197 69203 69221 69233 69239 69247 69257 69259
69263 69313 69317 69337 69341 69371 69379 69383 69389 69401
69403 69427 69431 69439 69457 69463 69467 69473 69481 69491
69493 69497 69499 69539 69557 69593 69623 69653 69661 69677
69691 69697 69709 69737 69739 69761 69763 69767 69779 69809
69821 69827 69829 69833 69847 69857 69859 69877 69899 69911
69929 69931 69941 69959 69991 69997 70001 70003 70009 70019
70039 70051 70061 70067 70079 70099 70111 70117 70121 70123
70139 70141 70157 70163 70177 70181 70183 70199 70201 70207
70223 70229 70237 70241 70249 70271 70289 70297 70309 70313
70321 70327 70351 70373 70379 70381 70393 70423 70429 70439
70451 70457 70459 70481 70487 70489 70501 70507 70529 70537
70549 70571 70573 70583 70589 70607 70619 70621 70627 70639
70657 70663 70667 70687 70709 70717 70729 70753 70769 70783
70793 70823 70841 70843 70849 70853 70867 70877 70879 70891
70901 70913 70919 70921 70937 70949 70951 70957 70969 70979
70981 70991 70997 70999 71011 71023 71039 71059 71069 71081
71089 71119 71129 71143 71147 71153 71161 71167 71171 71191
71209 71233 71237 71249 71257 71261 71263 71287 71293 71317
71327 71329 71333 71339 71341 71347 71353 71359 71363 71387
71389 71399 71411 71413 71419 71429 71437 71443 71453 71471
71473 71479 71483 71503 71527 71537 71549 71551 71563 71569
71593 71597 71633 71647 71663 71671 71693 71699 71707 71711
71713 71719 71741 71761 71777 71789 71807 71809 71821 71837
71843 71849 71861 71867 71879 71881 71887 71899 71909 71917
71933 71941 71947 71963 71971 71983 71987 71993 71999 72019
72031 72043 72047 72053 72073 72077 72089 72091 72101 72103
72109 72139 72161 72167 72169 72173 72211 72221 72223 72227
72229 72251 72253 72269 72271 72277 72287 72307 72313 72337
72341 72353 72367 72379 72383 72421 72431 72461 72467 72469
72481 72493 72497 72503 72533 72547 72551 72559 72577 72613
72617 72623 72643 72647 72649 72661 72671 72673 72679 72689
72701 72707 72719 72727 72733 72739 72763 72767 72797 72817
72823 72859 72869 72871 72883 72889 72893 72901 72907 72911
72923 72931 72937 72949 72953 72959 72973 72977 72997 73009
73013 73019 73037 73039 73043 73061 73063 73079 73091 73121
73127 73133 73141 73181 73189 73237 73243 73259 73277 73291
73303 73309 73327 73331 73351 73361 73363 73369 73379 73387
73417 73421 73433 73453 73459 73471 73477 73483 73517 73523
73529 73547 73553 73561 73571 73583 73589 73597 73607 73609
73613 73637 73643 73651 73673 73679 73681 73693 73699 73709
73721 73727 73751 73757 73771 73783 73819 73823 73847 73849
73859 73867 73877 73883 73897 73907 73939 73943 73951 73961
73973 73999 74017 74021 74027 74047 74051 74071 74077 74093
74099 74101 74131 74143 74149 74159 74161 74167 74177 74189
74197 74201 74203 74209 74219 74231 74257 74279 74287 74293
74297 74311 74317 74323 74353 74357 74363 74377 74381 74383

74411 74413 74419 74441 74449 74453 74471 74489 74507 74509
74521 74527 74531 74551 74561 74567 74573 74587 74597 74609
74611 74623 74653 74687 74699 74707 74713 74717 74719 74729
74731 74747 74759 74761 74771 74779 74797 74821 74827 74831
74843 74857 74861 74869 74873 74887 74891 74897 74903 74923
74929 74933 74941 74959 75011 75013 75017 75029 75037 75041
75079 75083 75109 75133 75149 75161 75167 75169 75181 75193
75209 75211 75217 75223 75227 75239 75253 75269 75277 75289
75307 75323 75329 75337 75347 75353 75367 75377 75389 75391
75401 75403 75407 75431 75437 75479 75503 75511 75521 75527
75533 75539 75541 75553 75557 75571 75577 75583 75611 75617
75619 75629 75641 75653 75659 75679 75683 75689 75703 75707
75709 75721 75731 75743 75767 75773 75781 75787 75793 75797
75821 75833 75853 75869 75883 75913 75931 75937 75941 75967
75979 75983 75989 75991 75997 76001 76003 76031 76039 76079
76081 76091 76099 76103 76123 76129 76147 76157 76159 76163
76207 76213 76231 76243 76249 76253 76259 76261 76283 76289
76303 76333 76343 76367 76369 76379 76387 76403 76421 76423
76441 76463 76471 76481 76487 76493 76507 76511 76519 76537
76541 76543 76561 76579 76597 76603 76607 76631 76649 76651
76667 76673 76679 76697 76717 76733 76753 76757 76771 76777
76781 76801 76819 76829 76831 76837 76847 76871 76873 76883
76907 76913 76919 76943 76949 76961 76963 76991 77003 77017
77023 77029 77041 77047 77069 77081 77093 77101 77137 77141
77153 77167 77171 77191 77201 77213 77237 77239 77243 77249
77261 77263 77267 77269 77279 77291 77317 77323 77339 77347
77351 77359 77369 77377 77383 77417 77419 77431 77447 77471
77477 77479 77489 77491 77509 77513 77521 77527 77543 77549
77551 77557 77563 77569 77573 77587 77591 77611 77617 77621
77641 77647 77659 77681 77687 77689 77699 77711 77713 77719
77723 77731 77743 77747 77761 77773 77783 77797 77801 77813
77839 77849 77863 77867 77893 77899 77929 77933 77951 77969
77977 77983 77999 78007 78017 78031 78041 78049 78059 78079
78101 78121 78137 78139 78157 78163 78167 78173 78179 78191
78193 78203 78229 78233 78241 78259 78277 78283 78301 78307
78311 78317 78341 78347 78367 78401 78427 78437 78439 78467
78479 78487 78497 78509 78511 78517 78539 78541 78553 78569
78571 78577 78583 78593 78607 78623 78643 78649 78653 78691
78697 78707 78713 78721 78737 78779 78781 78787 78791 78797
78803 78809 78823 78839 78853 78857 78877 78887 78889 78893
78901 78919 78929 78941 78977 78979 78989 79031 79039 79043
79063 79087 79103 79111 79133 79139 79147 79151 79153 79159
79181 79187 79193 79201 79229 79231 79241 79259 79273 79279
79283 79301 79309 79319 79333 79337 79349 79357 79367 79379
79393 79397 79399 79411 79423 79427 79433 79451 79481 79493
79531 79537 79549 79559 79561 79579 79589 79601 79609 79613
79621 79627 79631 79633 79657 79669 79687 79691 79693 79697

79699 79757 79769 79777 79801 79811 79813 79817 79823 79829
79841 79843 79847 79861 79867 79873 79889 79901 79903 79907
79939 79943 79967 79973 79979 79987 79997 79999 80021 80039
80051 80071 80077 80107 80111 80141 80147 80149 80153 80167
80173 80177 80191 80207 80209 80221 80231 80233 80239 80251
80263 80273 80279 80287 80309 80317 80329 80341 80347 80363
80369 80387 80407 80429 80447 80449 80471 80473 80489 80491
80513 80527 80537 80557 80567 80599 80603 80611 80621 80627
80629 80651 80657 80669 80671 80677 80681 80683 80687 80701
80713 80737 80747 80749 80761 80777 80779 80783 80789 80803
80809 80819 80831 80833 80849 80863 80897 80909 80911 80917
80923 80929 80933 80953 80963 80989 81001 81013 81017 81019
81023 81031 81041 81043 81047 81049 81071 81077 81083 81097
81101 81119 81131 81157 81163 81173 81181 81197 81199 81203
81223 81233 81239 81281 81283 81293 81299 81307 81331 81343
81349 81353 81359 81371 81373 81401 81409 81421 81439 81457
81463 81509 81517 81527 81533 81547 81551 81553 81559 81563
81569 81611 81619 81629 81637 81647 81649 81667 81671 81677
81689 81701 81703 81707 81727 81737 81749 81761 81769 81773
81799 81817 81839 81847 81853 81869 81883 81899 81901 81919
81929 81931 81937 81943 81953 81967 81971 81973 82003 82007
82009 82013 82021 82031 82037 82039 82051 82067 82073 82129
82139 82141 82153 82163 82171 82183 82189 82193 82207 82217
82219 82223 82231 82237 82241 82261 82267 82279 82301 82307
82339 82349 82351 82361 82373 82387 82393 82421 82457 82463
82469 82471 82483 82487 82493 82499 82507 82529 82531 82549
82559 82561 82567 82571 82591 82601 82609 82613 82619 82633
82651 82657 82699 82721 82723 82727 82729 82757 82759 82763
82781 82787 82793 82799 82811 82813 82837 82847 82883 82889
82891 82903 82913 82939 82963 82981 82997 83003 83009 83023
83047 83059 83063 83071 83077 83089 83093 83101 83117 83137
83177 83203 83207 83219 83221 83227 83231 83233 83243 83257
83267 83269 83273 83299 83311 83339 83341 83357 83383 83389
83399 83401 83407 83417 83423 83431 83437 83443 83449 83459
83471 83477 83497 83537 83557 83561 83563 83579 83591 83597
83609 83617 83621 83639 83641 83653 83663 83689 83701 83717
83719 83737 83761 83773 83777 83791 83813 83833 83843 83857
83869 83873 83891 83903 83911 83921 83933 83939 83969 83983
83987 84011 84017 84047 84053 84059 84061 84067 84089 84121
84127 84131 84137 84143 84163 84179 84181 84191 84199 84211
84221 84223 84229 84239 84247 84263 84299 84307 84313 84317
84319 84347 84349 84377 84389 84391 84401 84407 84421 84431
84437 84443 84449 84457 84463 84467 84481 84499 84503 84509
84521 84523 84533 84551 84559 84589 84629 84631 84649 84653
84659 84673 84691 84697 84701 84713 84719 84731 84737 84751
84761 84787 84793 84809 84811 84827 84857 84859 84869 84871
84913 84919 84947 84961 84967 84977 84979 84991 85009 85021

85027 85037 85049 85061 85081 85087 85091 85093 85103 85109
85121 85133 85147 85159 85193 85199 85201 85213 85223 85229
85237 85243 85247 85259 85297 85303 85313 85331 85333 85361
85363 85369 85381 85411 85427 85429 85439 85447 85451 85453
85469 85487 85513 85517 85523 85531 85549 85571 85577 85597
85601 85607 85619 85621 85627 85639 85643 85661 85667 85669
85691 85703 85711 85717 85733 85751 85781 85793 85817 85819
85829 85831 85837 85843 85847 85853 85889 85903 85909 85931
85933 85991 85999 86011 86017 86027 86029 86069 86077 86083
86111 86113 86117 86131 86137 86143 86161 86171 86179 86183
86197 86201 86209 86239 86243 86249 86257 86263 86269 86287
86291 86293 86297 86311 86323 86341 86351 86353 86357 86369
86371 86381 86389 86399 86413 86423 86441 86453 86461 86467
86477 86491 86501 86509 86531 86533 86539 86561 86573 86579
86587 86599 86627 86629 86677 86689 86693 86711 86719 86729
86743 86753 86767 86771 86783 86813 86837 86843 86851 86857
86861 86869 86923 86927 86929 86939 86951 86959 86969 86981
86993 87011 87013 87037 87041 87049 87071 87083 87103 87107
87119 87121 87133 87149 87151 87179 87181 87187 87211 87221
87223 87251 87253 87257 87277 87281 87293 87299 87313 87317
87323 87337 87359 87383 87403 87407 87421 87427 87433 87443
87473 87481 87491 87509 87511 87517 87523 87539 87541 87547
87553 87557 87559 87583 87587 87589 87613 87623 87629 87631
87641 87643 87649 87671 87679 87683 87691 87697 87701 87719
87721 87739 87743 87751 87767 87793 87797 87803 87811 87833
87853 87869 87877 87881 87887 87911 87917 87931 87943 87959
87961 87973 87977 87991 88001 88003 88007 88019 88037 88069
88079 88093 88117 88129 88169 88177 88211 88223 88237 88241
88259 88261 88289 88301 88321 88327 88337 88339 88379 88397
88411 88423 88427 88463 88469 88471 88493 88499 88513 88523
88547 88589 88591 88607 88609 88643 88651 88657 88661 88663
88667 88681 88721 88729 88741 88747 88771 88789 88793 88799
88801 88807 88811 88813 88817 88819 88843 88853 88861 88867
88873 88883 88897 88903 88919 88937 88951 88969 88993 88997
89003 89009 89017 89021 89041 89051 89057 89069 89071 89083
89087 89101 89107 89113 89119 89123 89137 89153 89189 89203
89209 89213 89227 89231 89237 89261 89269 89273 89293 89303
89317 89329 89363 89371 89381 89387 89393 89399 89413 89417
89431 89443 89449 89459 89477 89491 89501 89513 89519 89521
89527 89533 89561 89563 89567 89591 89597 89599 89603 89611
89627 89633 89653 89657 89659 89669 89671 89681 89689 89753
89759 89767 89779 89783 89797 89809 89819 89821 89833 89839
89849 89867 89891 89897 89899 89909 89917 89923 89939 89959
89963 89977 89983 89989 90001 90007 90011 90017 90019 90023
90031 90053 90059 90067 90071 90073 90089 90107 90121 90127
90149 90163 90173 90187 90191 90197 90199 90203 90217 90227
90239 90247 90263 90271 90281 90289 90313 90353 90359 90371

90373 90379 90397 90401 90403 90407 90437 90439 90469 90473
90481 90499 90511 90523 90527 90529 90533 90547 90583 90599
90617 90619 90631 90641 90647 90659 90677 90679 90697 90703
90709 90731 90749 90787 90793 90803 90821 90823 90833 90841
90847 90863 90887 90901 90907 90911 90917 90931 90947 90971
90977 90989 90997 91009 91019 91033 91079 91081 91097 91099
91121 91127 91129 91139 91141 91151 91153 91159 91163 91183
91193 91199 91229 91237 91243 91249 91253 91283 91291 91297
91303 91309 91331 91367 91369 91373 91381 91387 91393 91397
91411 91423 91433 91453 91457 91459 91463 91493 91499 91513
91529 91541 91571 91573 91577 91583 91591 91621 91631 91639
91673 91691 91703 91711 91733 91753 91757 91771 91781 91801
91807 91811 91813 91823 91837 91841 91867 91873 91909 91921
91939 91943 91951 91957 91961 91967 91969 91997 92003 92009
92033 92041 92051 92077 92083 92107 92111 92119 92143 92153
92173 92177 92179 92189 92203 92219 92221 92227 92233 92237
92243 92251 92269 92297 92311 92317 92333 92347 92353 92357
92363 92369 92377 92381 92383 92387 92399 92401 92413 92419
92431 92459 92461 92467 92479 92489 92503 92507 92551 92557
92567 92569 92581 92593 92623 92627 92639 92641 92647 92657
92669 92671 92681 92683 92693 92699 92707 92717 92723 92737
92753 92761 92767 92779 92789 92791 92801 92809 92821 92831
92849 92857 92861 92863 92867 92893 92899 92921 92927 92941
92951 92957 92959 92987 92993 93001 93047 93053 93059 93077
93083 93089 93097 93103 93113 93131 93133 93139 93151 93169
93179 93187 93199 93229 93239 93241 93251 93253 93257 93263
93281 93283 93287 93307 93319 93323 93329 93337 93371 93377
93383 93407 93419 93427 93463 93479 93481 93487 93491 93493
93497 93503 93523 93529 93553 93557 93559 93563 93581 93601
93607 93629 93637 93683 93701 93703 93719 93739 93761 93763
93787 93809 93811 93827 93851 93871 93887 93889 93893 93901
93911 93913 93923 93937 93941 93949 93967 93971 93979 93983
93997 94007 94009 94033 94049 94057 94063 94079 94099 94109
94111 94117 94121 94151 94153 94169 94201 94207 94219 94229
94253 94261 94273 94291 94307 94309 94321 94327 94331 94343
94349 94351 94379 94397 94399 94421 94427 94433 94439 94441
94447 94463 94477 94483 94513 94529 94531 94541 94543 94547
94559 94561 94573 94583 94597 94603 94613 94621 94649 94651
94687 94693 94709 94723 94727 94747 94771 94777 94781 94789
94793 94811 94819 94823 94837 94841 94847 94849 94873 94889
94903 94907 94933 94949 94951 94961 94993 94999 95003 95009
95021 95027 95063 95071 95083 95087 95089 95093 95101 95107
95111 95131 95143 95153 95177 95189 95191 95203 95213 95219
95231 95233 95239 95257 95261 95267 95273 95279 95287 95311
95317 95327 95339 95369 95383 95393 95401 95413 95419 95429
95441 95443 95461 95467 95471 95479 95483 95507 95527 95531
95539 95549 95561 95569 95581 95597 95603 95617 95621 95629

95633 95651 95701 95707 95713 95717 95723 95731 95737 95747
95773 95783 95789 95791 95801 95803 95813 95819 95857 95869
95873 95881 95891 95911 95917 95923 95929 95947 95957 95959
95971 95987 95989 96001 96013 96017 96043 96053 96059 96079
96097 96137 96149 96157 96167 96179 96181 96199 96211 96221
96223 96233 96259 96263 96269 96281 96289 96293 96323 96329
96331 96337 96353 96377 96401 96419 96431 96443 96451 96457
96461 96469 96479 96487 96493 96497 96517 96527 96553 96557
96581 96587 96589 96601 96643 96661 96667 96671 96697 96703
96731 96737 96739 96749 96757 96763 96769 96779 96787 96797
96799 96821 96823 96827 96847 96851 96857 96893 96907 96911
96931 96953 96959 96973 96979 96989 96997 97001 97003 97007
97021 97039 97073 97081 97103 97117 97127 97151 97157 97159
97169 97171 97177 97187 97213 97231 97241 97259 97283 97301
97303 97327 97367 97369 97373 97379 97381 97387 97397 97423
97429 97441 97453 97459 97463 97499 97501 97511 97523 97547
97549 97553 97561 97571 97577 97579 97583 97607 97609 97613
97649 97651 97673 97687 97711 97729 97771 97777 97787 97789
97813 97829 97841 97843 97847 97849 97859 97861 97871 97879
97883 97919 97927 97931 97943 97961 97967 97973 97987 98009
98011 98017 98041 98047 98057 98081 98101 98123 98129 98143
98179 98207 98213 98221 98227 98251 98257 98269 98297 98299
98317 98321 98323 98327 98347 98369 98377 98387 98389 98407
98411 98419 98429 98443 98453 98459 98467 98473 98479 98491
98507 98519 98533 98543 98561 98563 98573 98597 98621 98627
98639 98641 98663 98669 98689 98711 98713 98717 98729 98731
98737 98773 98779 98801 98807 98809 98837 98849 98867 98869
98873 98887 98893 98897 98899 98909 98911 98927 98929 98939
98947 98953 98963 98981 98993 98999 99013 99017 99023 99041
99053 99079 99083 99089 99103 99109 99119 99131 99133 99137
99139 99149 99173 99181 99191 99223 99233 99241 99251 99257
99259 99277 99289 99317 99347 99349 99367 99371 99377 99391
99397 99401 99409 99431 99439 99469 99487 99497 99523 99527
99529 99551 99559 99563 99571 99577 99581 99607 99611 99623
99643 99661 99667 99679 99689 99707 99709 99713 99719 99721
99733 99761 99767 99787 99793 99809 99817 99823 99829 99833
99839 99859 99871 99877 99881 99901 99907 99923 99929 99961
99971 99989 99991

• • •

When I taped the prime numbers to my cubicle wall and looked at them from a distance, I could see darker and lighter patches within the body of the text that formed interesting shapes and patterns. I bet if I took the time to format the numbers correctly, I could see some sort of hitherto never-before-noticed magical numerical pattern that would allow me to solve the formula for generating prime numbers once and for all. I mentioned this to Cowboy. All he said was, "Maybe, but what if it turns out that the numbers form a kind of Magic Eye image, and when your brain resolves it, you see a goat walking on its hind legs, drinking from a horn full of blood?"

Scotch *that* idea.

• • •

Bree, in her new plan to crack upper management, has decided to can the French stuff and start speaking with a British accent. "It's a proven fact that women with British accents climb corporate ladders much more quickly in North America than those of us who speak with a shopping mall accent."

• • •

The night of Kam Fong's housewarming I was in a testy mood. I'd been inside my head all day—some days that just happens. You get lost doing just one task, and suddenly you look up and it's dark out, but you still don't want to leave your headspace, and then Kaitlin comes up behind you with a 150 KHz marine emergency blow horn and lets off one big parp that has you shitting out your eyes, ears and nostrils, and when you turn around, you discover that your evil co-workers were videoing the entire prank, and you get furious and you scream for everybody to fuck off and die. *Aw shucks, it was only a joke,* but the fact remains that because of that one loud parp you'll never be able to parse C++ code again because you fried those dendrites that dictate logic patterns, and in a flash you see yourself as a future object of pity, forced to work at a TacoTime outlet, feeding disrespectful larvae of the middle classes while taking soiled orange PVC trash bags out to the back alley, where you see a grease storage drum and wistfully remember that earlier, more charmed portion of your life when you once knew the chemicals and procedures necessary to convert restaurant grease into clean-burning planet-friendly ethanol, and that was just one of the many feats your brain was capable of, back before the parping, back before people whispered when they saw you walking their way, hoping they wouldn't have to make small talk with you, back before they dumbed themselves down to the verbal level of Pebbles Flintstone to make you understand them.

"Jesus, Ethan, it was just a practical joke," Kaitlin said, as we drove to Kam's housewarming.

"You're not the one who can't do long division any more."

"Get over it. What's the address number again?"

"1388. It ought to be up around this corner."

And it was: a stuccoed candy pink gargoyled fantasia land designed by a committee of fourteen-year-old girls, a handful of Smurfs and whoever creates carpeted claw-scratching environments for cats. It did have a stunning view of the city, Vancouver Island, the Olympic Peninsula and Mount Baker. Most importantly, flanking the front doors were a pair of New Zealand tree ferns of a type even I knew were expensive and finicky. Underneath the tree fern on the right, beneath leftover Tyvek sheets, pink insulation scraps, several scoops of clay and a foot of mushroom manure soil, rested the body of Tim the biker.

I was hesitant to knock. Kaitlin looked in the front window. To the muffled sounds of "Boogie Woogie Bugle Boy," Dad was dancing with a chair, and Kam Fong was dancing with a ski. Now *she* was the speechless one.

"They're chairjacking," I explained.

"What?"

"It's a ballroom dancing exercise. You have to dance with an inanimate object and imbue it with the sense that the object is alive. It's hard to do. Dad rents Disney cartoons all the time to see how teapots and flying carpets express themselves."

Kaitlin was re-evaluating my possible use as genetic material for any future child of hers. She rang the doorbell, and Kam Fong seamlessly opened it and returned to the main room for the song's climax. Then he bowed and said, "Am I not grand?"

Dad said, "You're an hour early."

Kam said, "Not to worry, I can put them both to work. Come to the kitchen."

"Hey, we're supposed to be guests here."

"And I was supposed to have housekeepers until I fired them this afternoon."

"Why?" Kaitlin asked.

"I caught them eating."

Kam waved around a kitchen in which hundreds of hors

d'oeuvres sat half finished. "Here. Make some canapés. Jim and I have to practise."

We stood at the counter and tried to figure out what to make, but we couldn't think of what to do with all the cheeses and vegetables. We went to the Dell beside the phone and put the word "canapé" into Google Images. This generated a predictable deluge of porn, as well as some retro 1950s canapé photos.

"Do we have radishes?" Kaitlin asked.

"Yes, but nobody likes radishes."

"I know. Has anybody in the history of humanity ever sat down one day and said to themselves, *You know, I'd like nothing more right now than to eat a crisp yummy radish*?"

We lurked for a while in a radish chat room. Snoozeville.

Kaitlin continued her rant. "Carrots coast through life. If they were any colour other than orange, they'd be extinct by now." She adopted her carrot voice: "*Hi, I'm a carrot and have a bland nothing flavour, but because I'm attractive and because I'm just about the only orange vegetable that can be eaten in raw form, you keep me in your kitchen. I mock you for your weakness.*"

"Look at the canapé sofas." Kaitlin and I quickly learned that a canapé sofa is a sofa designed to seat two people.

"Boring."

Two clicks later we ended up on the Cunnilingus Web Ring.

"Ethan, I want to go home. This is the worst housewarming ever."

Just then Mom, showing no sign that she remembered Tim decomposing mere feet away, walked in and said, "Canapés! What fun!" Tying her apron, she said, "You know how boring I find ballroom dancing. It's a side of him I've never understood." With a paring knife she began whittling radishes into rosebuds. "He and Kam Fong are entered in a competition called 'Canteen.'"

"Canteen? What's it about?"

"'The Greatest Generation Goes to War—A Ballroom Tribute.'" Yet again, "Boogie Woogie Bugle Boy" pulsed from the living room.

Kaitlin said, "I'm so sick of that 'Greatest Generation' crap. We finally drive a silver nail through the heart of Generation X, only to have this new monster rear its head. And I'm *sooooooooo* sick of Tom Hanks looking earnest all the time. They should make a Tom Hanks movie where Tom kills off Greatest Generation figureheads one by one."

Bree arrived on cue: "And then he starts killing other generations. He becomes this supernova of hate—all he wants to do is destroy."

"He starts killing the surviving members of the Sex Pistols."

"Hate clings to him like a rich, lathery shampoo. His lungs secrete it like anthrax foam."

Mom lost it. "Stop it! All of you! Tom Hanks is a fine actor who would never hurt anybody. At least not onscreen."

I thought, *Hey, didn't Tom Hanks mow down half of Chicago in* Road to Perdition*?* Well, whatever.

"You young people stop your prattling and help me out here. Kaitlin and Bree, peel these cucumbers. Ethan, fill me in on your secret plan to sabotage the videogame you're working on now."

"*What!* Who told you about it?"

"Your friend Mark."

"You were talking to Mark?"

"He's getting me some bootleg gardening software, and

he told me that you've begun collectively designing a secret slasher character named Ronald, a birthday clown who lives in a secret lair within SpriteQuest."

"He told you about Ronald?"

"He did."

I'll spare the world Mom's translation. Basically, we're concealing the coding files used to generate Ronald inside a folder called MOAT WATER TEXTURES that nobody's particularly in charge of nor interested in. There's going to be a switch inside the configuration files that allows a player with the secret password to go from one mode to another, including Ronald's Lair of Death, releasing him on a spree of carnage and terror within the SpriteQuest realm. But because this secret file can be found and unlocked by a debugger, the jPod development team needs to covertly insert Ronald into the game's coding during the final stage—after the debugging is done. Just before the master gold disk is shipped to the factory, Bree has to have an affair with the FedEx deliveryman. She'll demand that her FedEx boyfriend give her the disk before it goes on the plane. Ronald's complete files will be inserted into the game at this final moment.

Mom asked, "Bree, what if the FedEx delivery guy is a gal?"

"Well, there's a first time for everything."

Mom asked, "Bree, why are you speaking with an English accent?"

"To speed up my career."

"A sensible decision. English women are so bossy-sounding, and they love giving orders. Men are too lazy to bother fighting back. That Thatcher woman really knew how to crack the whip."

Other guests started arriving, most of them ballroom dancers or thugs. Over the next four hours, smokers lit up outside by the glistening fronds of the New Zealand tree fern above Tim's grave. I popped out, if only to convince myself that Tim's bony forearms weren't punching their way out of the topsoil like in the final scene of *Carrie.* I then wondered if some future civilization would ever dig up Tim's bones and wonder what his life was like, or if his last cheeseburger would remain mummified within his gut. About half of the smokers were on their cellphones. Kaitlin came out, ready to go home. She said, "Remember how, back in 1990, if you used a cellphone in public you looked like a total asshole? We're all assholes now."

Dad came out with John Doe and Cowboy. I asked them what they were doing, and Dad said they were headed down to the rail yard to tag grain cars.

"*Dad!* John and Cowboy are too old to be doing that, let alone you."

"I'm getting in character for a role I'm playing."

"What role is that?"

"It's for a bank commercial. I have to roll my eyes when young hip-hoppy people come in to open savings accounts."

"For that you have to go tagging?"

"If I'm supposed to hate the little fuckers, I might as well have a fresh memory in my head to make me do so. It's method. Why are you always so harsh with me about my craft?"

He's still traumatized because his speaking role was axed from the SUV commercial. He needs a bit of joy in his life.

"Just go," I said.

After Dad left, Mom came out to the front step area outside the main doorway.

"What a lovely home. Kam is so lucky to live here."

She went back inside.

• • •

Part of my job in subverting SpriteQuest is to provide Ronald's creation myth—his backstory that tells players how he ended up in his secret lair, dedicated to mayhem. Here it is:

Ronald was attending his one-billionth birthday party in a suburban basement, handing out little cups of orange drink to churlish brats. He looked up the stairs briefly and saw the kids' mothers in the kitchen, drinking martinis and making jokes at his expense. He abandoned the kids to confront them. "If you've got something to say, then say it to my face." The mothers giggled. I mean, this was a living Pez dispenser suddenly in their faces.

"Relax. We were just having fun."

"Fun is my business, lady. I know fun. Those cracks you were making aren't fun. There's a sensitive soul beneath this greasepaint."

"Were you born with all of that shit on?"

Another mother asked, "What do you do when you get home—leave your makeup on and eat TV dinners and make prank phone calls?"

"As a licensed mascot for a multinational corporation, nondisclosure agreements prevent me from telling you what I do in a non-commercial situation."

"Chickenshit. I bet you eat at Wendy's."

Ronald stuck out his finger and pointed into her face. "Wendy is a *whore*."

As this conversation took place in an American house

inhabited by Americans, lots of guns were handy. One of the mothers—let's call her Alpha-Mom—reached into her knitting basket and withdrew a .44. She couldn't believe it—she was turned on by her ability to choose whether the clown lived or died. She pointed it at Ronald. "Okay, clowny-wowny, time for you to go."

Ronald said, "No way. Not until you apologize."

"For what?"

"For mocking clowns."

One of the mothers was about to dial 911, but the gun mother said, "Sheila, no. Not until we have some fun." She motioned to the others. "Nell, lock the kids in the basement." She turned to Ronald. "Okay, bun boy. Strip."

"Huh?"

"You heard me. Strip. We all want to see what's under all that yellow fabric."

One of the mothers whacked him behind the knees with a folded-up aluminum mini-scooter and he fell to the kitchen floor.

"Strip. Now. Or we'll get really ugly."

Ronald was surrounded by six mothers brandishing knives, collapsed folding chairs, guns and one heavy table lamp. One of mothers whacked Ronald on the lower back, and the others pulled her back. Alpha-Mom said, "Not just yet, Katie." She looked down at Ronald, and there was no mercy in her eyes. "Start with those bright red, overly large novelty clown booties. One, two. Bang bang."

Ronald obeyed, and as he did, he realized he was turned on. It was a new sensation that both frightened and pleased him. Through his red and white striped socks, he could feel the cool, dry, recently washed floor tiles. In submission, he handed over his boots to Alpha-Mom.

"Good. Now the socks. Did you phone Waldo and borrow them?"

Ronald removed his socks. The air cooled his toes. Nakedness was going to be a treat. He started to remove his yellow gloves.

"Did I say you could remove your gloves?"

"No."

The women cackled. Alpha-Mom said, "Now for a big ticket item—*overalls*."

The women started betting against each other: *Boxers or briefs? Painted-on underwear or a smooth, bulby nub like a doll?*

Ronald unzipped the three-foot-long zipper down his front. A strap fell from each shoulder. He wanted to laugh, but he knew that if he did, it would kill the mood.

Alpha-Mom was huffy. "*That's* underwear? It looks like an adult diaper. Now take of the gloves."

Ronald obeyed. He was now down to his shirt and diaper-like undergarment.

"The shirt goes, clown. Do it quick."

From the basement, Ronald heard the children's piercing sugared-up voices. He felt freer than he had ever felt before.

"Hey, wait a second—you've never taken your clothes off before, have you?" Alpha-Mom said.

"Part of being a corporate spokesmascot is that I can only remove my clothing if commanded. And nobody's ever asked before."

Alpha-Mom: "So you've never looked *down there*?"

"No."

Alpha-Mom said, "Time you did."

The room was almost religiously charged, as if the women—and Ronald—were to glimpse the contents of the Ark for the first time. Ronald was fumbling with the garment's fastening system when an escaped child suddenly entered the room, scaring the mothers. The .44 went off by accident, hitting Ronald in the upper arm. Blood sprayed everywhere. "You crazy fucked-up bitch, what the hell do you think you've done?" Another escaped child entered the room and began screaming. Katie moved to shush the kids out of the room, but slipped in a pool of clown blood, cracking the back of her skull on a sharply tiled corner of the decorative, retro, Cape Cod fireplace. A vermouth bottle shattered.

Ronald looked. "Holy shit, she's dead." He could even see brains.

The children screamed even more. Nell said, "Get them out of here."

Ronald's grease-painted torso was speckled with beads of blood.

Alpha-Mom was freaked. "Shit, shit, *shit.* What are we going to do?" She tossed Ronald his clothes. "Put these on. Now."

"But I never had a chance to look inside my undergarment . . ."

Sheila said, "Shut up and dress." She looked at the other mothers. "Here's what happened—the clown did it. That's our story. He tried to molest me, and I had to protect myself. You were all here. You saw it."

Ronald knew he was fucked. He also knew he had maybe ninety seconds before the police cruisers arrived, and so, half-dressed, carrying his stained clothes, he ran into the living room, where a Legend of Zelda game was on pause. Ronald dove into the screen, and the glass closed up behind him. And he's been trapped inside games ever since . . .

. . . And now he's out for revenge.

• • •

For the past few weeks, Bree has had ten Scrabble games piled on her desk; some weekend, her plan is to glue their letter tiles onto her bathroom mouldings. "What a depressing Spinsters of Tomorrow craft project, huh? But it'll look so cute."

Suddenly—*ping!*—all of us were playing Scrabble, making the stupidest words. It turned out that Bree had removed nearly all the E's and S's from the letter bag—har, har, har—and some T's as well. We got her to put them back and we played again and made pretty good words. The best was mine: "tsetse," as in tsetse fly.

Afterwards, Bree said, "As a special treat, I've printed out a list of the 972 three-letter words allowed in Scrabble, *but* I've added one non-regulation word to the list. First person who finds it wins a jumbo-sized Toblerone chocolate bar."

"Why do you have a jumbo Toblerone bar? Nobody ever buys them."

"I wanted to see what it was that Steve was working on when he rescued that company, and dammit, maybe he's on to something. They're good."

Mark added, "Toblerone's not just for mini-bars any more." No one said anything. He still hasn't learned how to be ironic.

Herewith Bree's list. Let it be noted that Microsoft Word's spell-check rejects most of them—so, then, how real *are* these words?

AAH AAL AAS ABA ABO ABS ABY ACE
ACT ADD ADO ADS ADZ AFF AFT AGA
AGE AGO AHA AID AIL AIM AIN AIR

AIS	AIT	ALA	ALB	ALE	ALL	ALP	ALS
ALT	AMA	AMI	AMP	AMU	ANA	AND	ANE
ANI	ANT	ANY	APE	APT	ARB	ARC	ARE
ARF	ARK	ARM	ARS	ART	ASH	ASK	ASP
ASS	ATE	ATT	AUK	AVA	AVE	AVO	AWA
AWE	AWL	AWN	AXE	AYE	AYS	AZO	BAA
BAD	BAG	BAH	BAL	BAM	BAN	BAP	BAR
BAS	BAT	BAY	BED	BEE	BEG	BEL	BEN
BET	BEY	BIB	BID	BIG	BIN	BIO	BIS
BIT	BIZ	BOA	BOB	BOD	BOG	BOO	BOP
BOS	BOT	BOW	BOX	BOY	BRA	BRO	BRR
BUB	BUD	BUG	BUM	BUN	BUR	BUS	BUT
BUY	BYE	BYS	CAB	CAD	CAM	CAN	CAP
CAR	CAT	CAW	CAY	CEE	CEL	CEP	CHI
CIS	COB	COD	COG	COL	CON	COO	COP
COR	COS	COT	COW	COX	COY	COZ	CRY
CUB	CUD	CUE	CUM	CUP	CUR	CUT	CWM
DAB	DAD	DAG	DAH	DAK	DAL	DAM	DAP
DAW	DAY	DEB	DEE	DEL	DEN	DEV	DEW
DEX	DEY	DIB	DID	DIE	DIG	DIM	DIN
DIP	DIS	DIT	DOC	DOE	DOG	DOL	DOM
DON	DOR	DOS	DOT	DOW	DRY	DUB	DUD
DUE	DUG	DUI	DUN	DUO	DUP	DYE	EAR
EAT	EAU	EBB	ECU	EDH	EEL	EFF	EFS
EFT	EGG	EGO	EKE	ELD	ELF	ELK	ELL
ELM	ELS	EME	EMF	EMS	EMU	END	ENG
ENS	EON	ERA	ERE	ERG	ERN	ERR	ERS
ESS	ETA	ETH	EVE	EWE	EYE	FAD	FAG
FAN	FAR	FAS	FAT	FAX	FAY	FED	FEE
FEH	FEM	FEN	FER	FET	FEU	FEW	FEY
FEZ	FIB	FID	FIE	FIG	FIL	FIN	FIR
FIT	FIX	FIZ	FLU	FLY	FOB	FOE	FOG

FOH FON FOP FOR FOU FOX FOY FRO
FRY FUB FUD FUG FUN FUR GAB GAD
GAE GAG GAL GAM GAN GAP GAR GAS
GAT GAY GED GEE GEL GEM GEN GET
GEY GHI GIB GID GIE GIG GIN GIP
GIT GNU GOA GOB GOD GOO GOR GOT
GOX GOY GUL GUM GUN GUT GUV GUY
GYM GYP HAD HAE HAG HAH HAJ HAM
HAO HAP HAS HAT HAW HAY HEH HEM
HEN HEP HER HES HET HEW HEX HEY
HIC HID HIE HIM HIN HIP HIS HIT
HMM HOB HOD HOE HOG HON HOP HOT
HOW HOY HUB HUE HUG HUH HUM HUN
HUP HUT HYP ICE ICH ICK ICY IDS
IFF IFS ILK ILL IMP INK INN INS
ION IRE IRK ISM ITS IVY JAB JAG
JAM JAR JAW JAY JEE JET JEU JEW
JIB JIG JIN JOB JOE JOG JOT JOW
JOY JUG JUN JUS JUT KAB KAE KAF
KAS KAT KAY KEA KEF KEG KEN KEP
KEX KEY KHI KID KIF KIN KIP KIR
KIT KOA KOB KOI KOP KOR KOS KUE
LAB LAC LAD LAG LAM LAP LAR LAS
LAT LAV LAW LAX LAY LEA LED LEE
LEG LEI LEK LET LEU LEV LEX LEY
LEZ LIB LID LIE LIN LIP LIS LIT
LOB LOG LOO LOP LOT LOW LOX LUG
LUM LUV LUX LYE MAC MAD MAE MAG
MAN MAP MAR MAS MAT MAW MAX MAY
MED MEL MEM MEN MET MEW MHO MIB
MID MIG MIL MIM MIR MIS MIX MOA
MOB MOC MOD MOG MOL MOM MON MOO

MOP MOR MOS MOT MOW MUD MUG MUM
MUN MUS MUT NAB NAE NAG NAH NAM
NAN NAP NAW NAY NEB NEE NET NEW
NIB NIL NIM NIP NIT NOX NIX NOA
NOD NOG NOH NOM NOO NOR NOS NOT
NOW NTH NUB NUN NUS NUT OAF OAK
OAR OAT OBE OBI OCA ODD ODE ODS
OES OFF OFT OHM OHO OHS OIL OKA
OKE OLD OLE OMS ONE ONS OOH OOT
OPE OPS OPT ORA ORB ORC ORE ORS
ORT OSE OUD OUR OUT OVA OWE OWL
OWN OXO OXY PAC PAD PAH PAL PAM
PAN PAP PAR PAS PAT PAW PAX PAY
PEA PEC PED PEE PEG PEH PEN PEP
PER PES PET PEW PHI PHT PIA PIC
PIE PIG PIN PIP PIS PIT PIU PIX
PLY POD POH POI POL POM POP POT
POW POX PRO PRY PSI PUB PUD PUG
PUL PUN PUP PUR PUS PUT PYA PYE
PYX QAT QUA RAD RAG RAH RAJ RAM
RAN RAP RAS RAT RAW RAX RAY REB
REC RED REE REF REG REI REM REP
RES RET REV REX RHO RIA RIB RID
RIF RIG RIM RIN RIP ROB ROC ROD
ROE ROM ROT ROW RUB RUE RUG RUM
RUN RUT RYA RYE SAB SAC SAD SAE
SAG SAL SAP SAT SAU SAW SAX SAY
SEA SEC SEE SEG SEI SEL SEN SER
SET SEW SEX SHA SHE SHH SHY SIB
SIC SIM SIN SIP SIR SIS SIT SIX
SKA SKI SKY SLY SOB SOD SOL SON
SOP SOS SOT SOU SOW SOX SOY SPA

SPY SRI STY SUB SUE SUM SUN SUP
SUQ SYN TAB TAD TAE TAG TAJ TAM
TAN TAO TAP TAR TAS TAT TAU TAV
TAW TAX TEA TED TEE TEG TEL TEN
TET TEW THE THO THY TIC TIE TIL
TIN TIP TIS TIT TOD TOE TOG TOM
TON TOO TOP TOR TOT TOW TOY TRY
TSK TUB TUG TUI TUN TUP TUT TUX
TWA TWO TYE UDO UGH UKE ULU UMM
UMP UNS UPO UPS URB URD URN USE
UTA UTS VAC VAN VAR VAS VAT VAU
VAV VAW VEE VEG VET VEX VIA VIE
VIG VIM VIS VOE VOW VOX VUG WAB
WAD WAE WAG WAN WAP WAR WAS WAT
WAW WAX WAY WEB WED WEE WEN WET
WHA WHO WHY WIG WIN WIS WIT WIZ
WOE WOG WOK WON WOO WOP WOS WOT
WOW WRY WUD WYE WYN XIS YAH YAK
YAM YAP YAR YAW YAY YEA YEH YEN
YEP YES YET YEW YID YIN YIP YOB
YOD YOK YOM YON YOU YOW YUK YUM
YUP ZAG ZAP ZAX ZED ZEE ZEK ZIG
ZIN ZIP ZIT ZOA ZOO

N N N N N N N
N N N N N N N
N N N N N N N
N N N N N N N
N N N N N N N
N N N N N N N
N N N N N N N

L L L L L L
L L C C L L N
L L C L L L N
L L N N L L N
N N N N N N N
N N N N N N N
N N N N N N N

T T T T T T T
T C T T T C T
C C C C C C C
T C C C C C T
T T T C T T T
T T T T T T T
T T T T T T T

• • •

A few days later I caused a sensation in jPod: "Everybody listen up. At the count of three, write me a list on a topic of your own choosing. You've got five minutes. The best list wins . . ." at which point I held up the trophy " . . . this six-inch Japanese kewpie doll complete with working squeak. This doll is the spokesmascot of Japan's most beloved mayonnaise company. I bought it off eBay because I thought it was cool and that when I put it on my desk my life would be somehow better—but, well, this hasn't proven to be the case. Are you ready? Get set . . . One . . . two . . . three . . . *Go!*"

Bree:

Things my new French boyfriend does that are making me begin to wonder about him

1)
Tucks his sweaters into his pants.

2)
Eats Play-Doh fragments.

3)
Wears yellow-lensed Fendi eyeglasses that make him resemble a repeat sex offender.

4)
Sold all of his Fred Perry shirts on eBay because I told him they make him look pregnant (he should have given them to charity).

5)

Refuses to capitalize the letter "I" when writing about himself in emails.

6)

Is a selfish and incoherent lover.

Cowboy:

Faggy colour names (alphabetized)

bisque
cerise
chartreuse
conch
cornflower
corn silk
fern
goldenrod
honeydew
leather
lichen
lox
mica
moccasin
opal
plum
saddle brown
shiraz
snow
thistle
yolk

John Doe:

Why buying lottery tickets is simply wrong

1)

Would you ever go into a lottery booth and buy a 6/49 with the following numbers: 1, 2, 3, 4, 5, 6 and a bonus of 7? Of course you wouldn't. But that number has just as ludicrously small a chance of winning as do some idiotic numbers you pulled out of the air.

2)

When you buy lottery tickets, your lifestyle elevator travels only down. Buy enough tickets over a long period of time and, before you realize it, you'll find yourself living in a listing mobile home. Its linoleum kitchenette counters will be constellated with crystal meth pipe burns. Its throw cushions will be caked in DNA best left unexplored. There will be a Domino's pizza boy bound and gagged beneath the main living area beside the cinder blocks.

3)

Oh, for God's sake, how many more reasons do you need?

Kaitlin:

Things Ethan doesn't know I know about him

1)

Three weeks ago he was suntanning on the back stoop using an old Supertramp double album covered in tin foil to concentrate the rays onto his face.

2)

He knows the technically correct word for the act of playing music using the rims of wine glasses.

3)

He has dextrous toes and uses them to pick socks off the bedroom floor when he thinks I'm still sleeping.

Evil Mark:

Starch discs from around the world

pizza
naan
pancakes
tortillas
waffles
crepes
communion wafers

Bree won.

• • •

About once every three years I get a craving for a Coca-Cola, and only a Coca-Cola—no cheeseburgers or fries. Shortly after Bree won, I had my triennial craving. I went to the kitchen area to get a can, and on a table beneath a stacked totem of plastic coffee creamers was an abandoned car magazine open to a spread on the Volkswagen Touareg's fuel economy. This got me thinking about Steve and his abandoned car and Mom and Kam Fong and all. I thought,

"Oh well," and took my Coke back to my desk, and when I did, John and Evil Mark were arguing about Coke versus Pepsi. John was convinced that Coke has a valid reason for being the top cola, that, "Even though we're haggling about the difference between catshit and dogshit, Coke is technically more delicious." To prove it, he pulled out mini-bar cola consumption statistics that showed Coke to be number one. *Mini-bars*—and of course, mini-bars mean Toblerone, the signature mini-bar snack of all time—another Steve indicator. So I tried getting on with my work, but then I heard Cowboy pacifying some fartcatcher from the facilities department who claimed they'd found cigarette butts in an air filter and thought the butts might be coming from jPod. Cowboy was doing his thirtieth Sudoku of the day and was feeding the facilities people the rich, nourishing crap they deserved. He ended it all with "Okey-diddily-dokey" . . . just like Ned Flanders—and so yet again I was reminded of Steve. My conscience began getting the worst of me.

Well, at least he's not dead.

Oh God. I felt so guilty. So in the mid-afternoon I drove over to Kam Fong's. How strange that all you have to do sometimes to meet somebody is walk up to their house and ring a doorbell, and magically they appear as if from nowhere.

With x-ray eyes I saw the maggots scouring Tim's corpse in pursuit of Tim Jerky.

Kam opened the door. "Ethan."

"Hi, Kam."

He was covered with maybe a hundred acupuncture needles.

"Sorry to interrupt your session."

"No worry. What's up? Come in."

Kam's acupuncturist was futzing about with the contents of his suitcase and wasn't introduced to me.

"Kam, I need to find Steve."

He didn't blink as he back-hopped onto the acupuncture table. "I thought he was a jerk and was ruining your skateboard game. Why are you asking me about him?"

"Believe it or not, we need him at the company to override a recent decision to make our new game even stupider. Mom told me that you—"

"Yes?"

"That you helped her out on the Steve issue."

"He's not dead or anything."

"That's what she said."

More needles went into Kam's calves. I couldn't look, and Kam said, "Ethan, stop being such a pussy. Acupuncture's one of the few Chinese things that actually works. Unlike feng shui."

Tim's nearby carcass amplified my unease. Kam asked, "How badly do you want to see Steve, then?"

Good question. "Well, I think Steve might be just powerful enough to reverse the company's decision on the latest botch-up with the game. And I feel kind of rotten hearing that he's . . ."

"That he's what?"

"Ummm . . . being *detained* somewhere."

"He was hassling your mother."

"Mom can take care of herself just fine. Can you tell me if he's okay or not?"

"He's not in pain, if that's what you mean."

"That's a good start."

"And he's now happy in his own way."

Coming from Kam, this suggested the most gruesome of

fates. "Just tell me where he is, and I'll go get him—no questions asked. I doubt he's going to hassle Mom any more."

"Give me a week or so to figure out a thing or two."

"Thanks."

• • •

While I waited for Kam to get back to me, in jPod we carried on with the generating of Ronald's Lair. We're doing the most basic levels of coding, which is kind of boring, and we also had to do it on top of our regular jobs—and our regular jobs are made even worse because of eye candy. Just when you think you're meeting a schedule, your team has to generate weekly eye candy for marketing so that they don't think the project's tanking, and thus allow it to live until the next milestone. On the good side, so much ill will and torture surrounds the SpriteQuest project in-house that we can get away with doing amazingly little and yet still give the illusion of being team players. Mostly this means walking around, acting pumped and saying things like "Man, this is going to be one rocking game!" with a straight face, thus inflating the egos of superiors while creating a protective bulletproof coating of enthusiasm. It's so easy it's scary. Even for me, with my fake voice. It's all so stupid that the fake/real part of my brain doesn't tickle even the slightest bit.

• • •

I've noticed that, as we ramp up on our game-building skills and generalized knowledge about Ronald, we're googling every ten minutes. The problem is, after a week of intense googling, we've started to burn out on knowing the answer to everything. God must feel that way all the time. I think people in the year 2020 are going to be nostalgic for the sensation of feeling clueless.

• • •

A small cold passed through the pod, and we suffered a seventeen percent health loss, even though we zinc'ed up like crazy. And Cowboy kept saying, "Remember everybody: limb-specific gunshot damage" to the point where we felt slightly spooked.

Amid all of this, Bree was moping out of concern that, in her quest to make a corporate success of herself, she might become unattractive to her French beau. John Doe told Bree that if she were artier she'd be more of a catch for her French paramour. As a result, Bree has canned the business attire in favour of an all-black look. To take this new lifestyle philosophy further, she and John ended up driving to Brentwood Mall to do performance art. Bree walked down the main atrium area, shaving her neck with an electric razor, and met John Doe, who applied lipstick in the middle of a crowded restaurant. I tried to imagine the public's response and John's counter-response: "Is it so wrong for a man to wear MAC Brick-O-La? Are your gender ideas that limited?" Afterwards he said, "Maybe it's just my dykey upbringing, but lipstick really does taste gross. How do you women do it?"

He inspired Kaitlin to confess: "Sometimes I get too lazy to wear makeup. To compensate for it, I simply dress like a slut."

• • •

Cowboy's signed on to a site called chokingforit.com, where people all across the city put in their name, a photo of their body, their address and a numerical rating from one to ten of how horny they are. Depending on how entries mesh, Cowboy simply vanishes for seventy-five minutes and then comes back saying nothing. I've gotten so used to this kind of behaviour with Cowboy that it no longer registers. The upside for me is that his trysts now happen during the day, so he never has to be rescued after ODing on Robitussin.

Also: Evil Mark is an evil genius, and Ronald's Lair's core code could never exist without him. But he also has yet to adorn the walls of his cubicle, which is really spooky. It just is. And the other day I secretly ate one of his novelty lemon-flavoured Post-its. It was really quite tasty. Tangy—with a hint of dust.

• • •

The next day the big drama was that John cast a spell on Evil Mark after Evil Mark ate a packet of Handi-Snacks John had left on his desk. Like anything weird in life, it began small and escalated.

"Evil Mark, did you eat my Handi-Snacks?"

"You mean that small plastic tray of shitty crackers that comes with a blob of cheese spread you can dip the crackers into?"

"Yes. Exactly."

"I did."

John got up. "You didn't ask for permission. You *know* how seriously I take my snacking rituals."

"John, it was only a fucking plastic tublet with some

crackers and a cheese-like orange substance. Big deal. I'll get you another one."

"Big deal? That was my *snack*, Mark. And now it's not, because you ate it."

"I'll get you another one. I'll even let you eat my stapler if it makes you feel better."

"I don't want to eat your stapler, and I don't want another Handi-Snacks. That's not my point. You took it without asking, and then you act like private property is meaningless."

"You're overreacting."

John Doe said, "Apologize." John was getting fierce. I began to wonder if this would erupt into cubicle rage.

"I don't like the way you're saying that."

"It was my property, Mark. And you just stole it like you were some global corporation absorbing a small African nation into its balance sheet. Evil Mark, I am officially casting a spell on you." John waved his hand in a circle and then threw invisible gnome dandruff at Mark. "I hereby strip you of the ability to perceive cartoons."

"What the hell does that mean?"

"Just what I said. Until you apologize for what you did, your eyes may look at cartoons, and your ears may listen to them, but they will make no sense to you. Cartoons will be nothing more to you than abstract shapes bouncing about to garbled noises."

"That's so stupid, John."

"Is it really? You won't think so when you come crawling to me, begging to be able to apprehend cartoons again."

"This is fucked up. I'm going back to work."

"You do that."

We could *hear* John simmering.

• • •

I have to say, it's a blast making SpriteQuest as we simultaneously secretly sabotage it. It reminds me of when I was a kid and I'd felt-pen doors and windows onto Ritz Cracker boxes and then set fire to them while providing colour commentary. *Oh no, the wedding party of fifty and the junior lacrosse team on the seventh floor are trapped! Somebody forgot to replace the smoke detector batteries!*

Every time we do something to make SpriteQuest "sparkle" (Management's term), such as building an interesting mesh frame for a turret, we build leaks and vulnerabilities into that turret so that Ronald can use them as a means of generating carnage.

Gord-O has been so impressed by the jPod enthusiasm level that he's taken me off Cheerios duty and has grudgingly had to admit that I'm assistant production assistant material after all.

• • •

A week later, out of nowhere, Cowboy said, "Isn't time weird? I'm already forgetting about Steve."

Time to go back to Kam and his exclusive alpine hideaway. I rang the bell and the acupuncturist opened the door and nodded me inside. In the living room, a sweatshop-like crew of six women, seated at folding bingo-hall tables, were busily weighing and bagging white powder that came from a Road-Runner-cartoon-FREE-BIRDSEED–like mound in the centre of the floor.

"Kam."

"Ethan."

Kam had an Ikea desk set up in the corner, and he paused a game of AmmuNation. "AmmuNation!" I said. "All right! What do you think of it?"

"It's the best. It allows me to park my evil in one place so I can be a better person in the real world."

"That's thoughtful of you."

The sound of little scales clicking and the rustling of zip-lock bags amplified the silence. Kam said, "You're here about Steve."

"Yup."

"You're in luck. I heard this morning that he's fine. Do you want to go get him?"

"Sure. Where is he?"

"China."

"What?"

"Too late. You said you'd go. You can't back out now."

"What's he doing in China?"

"Having the experience of a lifetime. He'll thank me for it."

"I don't have the money to go to China."

"Relax." He reached into a desk drawer and removed a wad of twenties. "Done. Do you need a passport? I can get one made for you in a few minutes."

"No. I got one three years ago for my trip to Mexico."

"I'll put you on a China Airlines flight tonight. You'd better pack, and for God's sake, don't wear any of your dorky outfits. You wouldn't believe what my . . ."—he looked over at the women—" . . . *helpers* have been saying about you in Chinese. Go to a fucking Gap and stock up."

"I don't know anything about China."

"I'll take care of all that. I'll courier the ticket to your office, and there'll be people helping you all over the place in Shanghai. Just be at the gate and ready to go."

A woman across the room made a hissing sound.

Kam, returning to his game, said, "Who says I'm not a kind soul?"

• • •

Late that afternoon Kaitlin and I combed the net for basic information about China, and somehow we ended up yet again on the Cunnilingus Web Ring. Kaitlin said, "What a weird coincidence. I should go out and buy a lottery ticket."

"How come?"

"Any time you have a coincidence happen to you, it means you've entered a luck warp—for the next short while everything you do will be touched by it."

John Doe gave a snort from behind his cubicle wall and left it at that.

"Kaitlin, you know what? Let's stop this search for info. I'm simply going to show up for the plane, like when you go see a movie without having seen the trailer."

"Good idea."

I went home, looked at my clothing from the Kam Fong point of view and then went out to a Gap. I stocked up on new duds and packed. I'm not proud to say it, but when I looked at my new waffle-knit T's, my washable merino wool sweaters, my groovy herringbone blazers, my unpleated olive khakis and my low-ironing stress-free shirts, it made me feel, you know . . . *freshhhhh.*

• • •

A lumber delivery for Kaitlin's hugging machine arrived just as Kam's car came to get me. When I kissed her goodbye, she smelled like a house under construction.

At the airport, it turned out Kam had booked me into first class—*woohoo!*

It was a brilliant early evening, with magic light beaming in through the windows of the silent, thick-carpeted first-class lounge. I sipped Veuve Clicquot and surveyed the airport, appreciating its wonderful made-of-Lego quality—high-tech brightly coloured ramps and cones and poles and carts and movable stairways. Walking onto the plane, I felt like I was entering the world of Lego in a way I hadn't since I was eleven.

The flight took off without any complications, and I lolled in my sprawling 180-degree reclining seat, wishing I could live in a house that was just like a first-class cabin.

But then, while I was trying to decide which of many sumptuous meals to order, I looked over to the seat opposite mine, and I couldn't believe my eyes—it was Douglas Coupland in 3K. What a bringdown. I saw that he was tapping some sort of crap into a laptop, and suddenly I wasn't hungry any more. I ordered tri-coloured penne pasta with Italian funghi in a lemongrass reduction and spent an hour optimizing my laptop's animation pipeline, but my heart wasn't in it. So I ordered a Scotch because it seemed like a first-classy drink to order, and tried to choose which Hitchcock classic to watch on the in-flight video service—but I couldn't help obsessing about Coupland. What bad luck that he was on this flight. And what *was* he typing? I may never have flown in first class before, but I do know it's the one place on earth where you shouldn't be working. I figured that if I went to the bathroom and walked back past him, I could get a clear glimpse of what he was working on. My eyesight is good.

In any event, after my fake pee, I walked quietly down to where Coupland was sitting, and on his laptop was a photo of that guy standing in front of the tank at Tiananmen Square.

A flight attendant passed by with a load of hot perfumed towels, and I reached for one, but I fumbled and it landed on Coupland's left arm.

"Sorry about that."

"No problem." He handed it back to me.

"Hey, aren't you Douglas Coupland?"

"Uh, yes. That's me."

"I've read all your books. I think they're great." *Oh God, I just soiled myself.*

"Oh, well, uh, thank you."

Awkward silence.

More awkward silence.

I said, "I'm Ethan. So you're off to China, huh?" *Did I really say something that dorky?*

"For a few days."

"A special project?"

"Yes. It's a piece for *Wired* magazine."

Wired? How 1996. "Really?"

"It's about this new design trend coming out of China. Well, technically it's not simply China—it's the PRC—the People's Republic of China."

Boring. "Fascinating."

"It's called 'designer prisoner-of-conscience labour.'"

"Huh?"

"Manufacturers locate people famous for political activism, and then they have that person make something and sell it as a value-added good."

"I don't get it."

"This guy here on the screen—" Coupland turned up his laptop to show me the JPEG of the Chinese guy in Tiananmen Square. "Know what he's doing now? He's working out this cosponsor deal with Verizon Wireless and Pizza Hut. He'll be attaching face plates to series of cellphones that come with Pizza Hut promotional meals. They're trying really hard to get that cheese-inside-the-crust idea going, but it's just not catching on."

"My brother told me about that!"

"Cool. And on this trip I'll also be visiting Aung San Suu Kyi."

"Who?"

She's that woman from Burma who won the Nobel Peace Prize a few years back."

"Oh right."

"She's negotiating a deal with Wal-Mart. She's going to be manning the pressure-moulding machine that stamps out white plastic stacking chairs."

"How would you know the chairs were hers and not somebody else's?"

"Each chair would come with a frameable hand-signed certificate of authenticity."

"That's a lot of certificates to sign."

"No kidding. Wal-Mart is two percent of China's GDP. I think these chairs would have to be limited edition, though. Prizes for Wal-Mart cardholders who shop above a certain amount per year."

"Wow." Dinners were being served. "Talk to you later."

"Sure."

After my penne I got a bit too tipsy on Scotches and began cycling through the video screen's programs. Let me say something right now: I speak neither Japanese nor Mandarin, but I *do* know that Japanese TV is really cool to watch and Chinese TV is appalling. Even on a plane, they show factory tours. After maybe my tenth visit to a microchip factory, I fell asleep for a bit.

When I woke up, I was a bit fuzzy but feeling expansive—me, a world traveller! I remembered Bree in the coffee room once, talking about Coupland's books as I was waiting for some soup to heat. She said that Coupland said that unless your life was a story it had no meaning, that you might as well be kelp or bacteria. I wondered if Coupland knew the answer. He certainly owes me for that time we had to read one of his books in my third year at university.

His eyes went a bit wary when he saw me coming.

"So, Mister Coupland. This friend of mine said that you said that unless your life is like something in a story there's no point in being alive, that you're basically no more important than kelp."

"But kelp *is* important."

"That's not what I meant. See, I think that . . ." Locating the words was harder than I'd estimated.

"What's your name again?"

"Ethan."

"Ethan, why are you going to China?"

"I've got to go pick somebody up."

"Who's that?"

"Steve."

"Who's Steve?"

And suddenly it all came spewing out of me—Mom, Steve, Dad, Kam, Kaitlin, Bree—everybody and everything. I have to hand it to myself: I think I told my story well. Coupland seemed to be pretty enthusiastic while I was talking—he even took notes!—and asked lots of questions. And then, at the end of all this, Lord forgive me, I asked him whether he could write a mini-story about me and my life.

"I don't know if that's such a good—"

"No, do it. It'd be fun."

"Okay. Bring me your laptop."

I set him up with Word, then went back to my seat to order one last Scotch. Suddenly it was hours later, the sun was blazing in the windows and all the passengers were chugging bottled water, applying moisturizing balms and doing stretches. The by-now familiar pertussive hackings of older Chinese nationals kept me from going back for a snooze cycle. And then . . . thorn by thorn, my chat with Coupland came back to me. I cringed and looked his way; he was obliviously making cellphone calls (in mid-flight) while stuffing a stolen flotation vest into his carry-on baggage. Sociopathic shit. My laptop was in the magazine pouch in front of me.

Just then the plane did a slight lurch, and I couldn't even look out the window while we landed. My bloodstream felt fetid, like time-expired dairy products. I waited until everybody else was off the plane, then two annoyed flight attendants bunted me towards the gate.

Sandra Alves, Joe Ault, Vinod Balakrishnan, Jason Bartell, Scott Byer, Jeff Chien, Scott Cohen, Andrew Cover, Chris Cox, Karen Gauthier, Todor Georgiev, Mark Hamburg, Jerry Harris, Dave Howe, Thomas Knoll, Sarah Kong, Mike Leavy, Tai Luxon, Seetharaman Narayanan, Sean Parent, Marc Pawliger, John Penn II, Dave Rau, Tom Ruark, Cris Rys, Michael Scarafone, Stephanie Schaefer, Del Schneider, Sau Tam, Gwyn Weisberg, Russell Williams, Matt Wormley, John Worthington, Rick Wulff

Nicole-Kidman.net: Your #1 Resource for ALL THINGS Nicole Kidman . . .

• • •

There was a Word file from Douglas Coupland on my laptop's desktop. It said,

> Ethan, thanks for telling me about your life and everything. It's intriguing. There's probably even a book there. You were also probably drunker than you think, and so you told me personal stuff that may or may not have been true, but most of which is shocking and actionable. More to the point, you let a total stranger have full, unguarded access to your *laptop*? Are you a fucking idiot? What were you thinking? I trawled through your emails (snooze) and porn stashes (cheerleaders? How vanilla) and Google cookies (potpourri gift baskets?) and . . . I'm appalled. Absolutely appalled. You come across smart, but then you do stupid shit like this. Does being upgraded to first class screw you up this much? I have no idea. So maybe you really *want* to be caught doing all the weird stuff you do. Fuck, I feel like Lisa Simpson giving you an on-the-spot quickie analysis but . . . are you a moron? How damaged are you?
>
> You live in a world that is amoral and fascinating—but I also know your life is everyday fare for Vancouverites, so there's no judgment that way. But, for the love of God, grow up. Or read something outside your normal sphere or use what few savings you have ($23,400.06, if your files are correct) and go to a college or university and rebuild your hard drive.
>
> This is weird diagnostic shit coming from a stranger, but, Ethan, you're on a one-way course to utter

fuckedupedness. I'm not suggesting you stop—but I am saying *wake up.*

Doug

What an asshole.

• • •

Immigration procedures were essentially non-existent. Kam had arranged for a driver to pick me up, and we wormed our way through the traffic on a dull grey Asian morning. My first impression was that there wasn't a square inch of land that wasn't being used to grow defeated-looking crops of spinachy plants. The city was an endless Sim-like blend of shacks, bikes, more bikes and still more bikes, tour buses, black-windowed Mercedes-Benzes and gaunt people smoking and standing around in front of concrete apartment buildings, most of which looked like they were built out of grey playing cards and seemed seismically unequipped, dreaming of the day gravity would take them back to Mama. And the air! Okay, imagine that you've built a bonfire of telephone poles—the ones dripping with creosote—and throw in a fax machine, a photocopier, some asbestos stacking chairs and a roasting chicken. That pretty much sums up the air quality, though it changes moment by moment depending on where you go. Turn a corner and—*thwack!*—different items are thrown into the flames: a load of running shoes, four thousand plastic bags, hog carcasses and a Dumpster of barbershop floor sweepings. And it's thick—a few blocks down the street, buildings vanish like in a fog effect in a memory-impaired videogame from the early 1990s. And it's humid, and I *hate* humidity.

What a relief to check in to my hotel—all five stars of it—and fall down on my bed's cool sheets.

Just twenty-four hours ago I was schlepping about my cubicle, and now I'm on the other side of the planet—on a mission, no less.

I opened my luggage to get a fresh shirt, but when I pulled back the black nylon flap, I saw that my clothes had been replaced with about forty pounds of white powder. I—

Words failed me.

I phoned Kam—I had no idea what time it was in Vancouver, and I didn't care.

"Hello?"

"You asshole! I could have ended up in prison for this."

"Stop snivelling. You made it through okay."

"Where the hell are all my new clothes?"

"Go to a Gap. They're the same everywhere."

"And what do I do with all this . . . *stuff*?"

"Store it with the concierge, and relax, okay? Order a cheese platter and a hooker. Go stroll the Bund."

"When do I get Steve?"

"My driver will pick you up at eight a.m. tomorrow."

• • •

It was late afternoon and sleep was pointless. I tried going online, but the Ethernet feed was dead. When I called the concierge, he said, "It's the Great Firewall of China. Nothing you can do. Shall I send you up some green tea?"

I showered and walked out into Shanghai proper, once called the Whore of Asia, now called the Pearl of Asia, though it might just as well be called the Tire Fire of Asia. It's like shopping inside an active ball barbecue.

At a Gap I bought the exact same things I had bought before the trip (at a third of the price), then I wandered the streets a bit. I tried to find the bootleg videogame district but failed. Beside a pork-on-a-stick booth, I bought a bootleg DVD of outtakes and bloopers from the making of *Schindler's List.*

The crowds began to irk me. Everyone in the city spits and coughs and wheezes. People jostle you everywhere. The Chinese notion of private space has no connection to my own, and I tried not to be irked, but then I got paranoid about my kidneys going missing. I went back to the hotel and ordered room service, breathed fresh hotel-room air and watched CNN Asia. The weather report was so odd. There's a map of maybe half the planet on the screen, and the weather woman says, "Let's see what's happening in the 'Stans'"—meaning Pakistan, Tajikistan, Afghanistan. She made it sound like, "Let's see what my close personal friends, all named Stanley, are up to."

Around midnight I went downstairs and poked my head out the front doors. Onto the cosmic tire fire, the Chinese had recently tossed a boxcar load of leaded enamel paint, a hopper of pesticides and some rendering plant scraps. I ended up falling asleep watching the *Schindler's List* bloopers DVD.

Slept like a dog.

• • •

I woke up at seven a.m. on an alpha-wave high. Jet lag? Not for me, Ethan Jarlewski, citizen of the world. I had coffee and a breakfast plate that featured a selection of fruit geometrically cut and arranged to create the feel of a Zen garden. Clothed in my new Gap duds, I waited for my driver down in the foyer. He showed up precisely on time in a crisply pressed outfit like Batman's butler, Alfred. I asked where we were going, and the driver said, "Not to worry. We're taking good care of you." It quickly became clear to me that we were headed *away* from the city.

After an hour the superstructures of Shanghai were gone, and we were in a semi-industrialized ghostscape of worker housing, rice paddies, shacks, monochrome grey office buildings—actually, everything on the outskirts of a Chinese city is grey. All you'd need to portray the place is an HB pencil, and then dip your brush in a spittoon.

We stopped at a tea shop for a break. A TV bolted onto the ceiling blared out factory tours at full volume while a trio of women looked at me with profound suspicion. One of them had a frog in a plastic bag, hopping on the ground at her feet.

We drove for maybe another three hours, and I began to feel unnerved. "How much farther?" I asked.

"By your North American standards? Not far at all."

"How far would you say, then?"

"We'll be there soon."

An hour later we pulled up to a three-storey cinderblock hotel that stood sentry over several thousand acres of rice paddies. Just over the crest of a naked hill, four smoke-stacks belched out the remains of deep-fried neurotoxins and the ground-up dust of a million or so non-stick cooking pans.

"You are to wait here, Mr. Jarlewski."

"For how long?"

"Not too long. Have a tea. I'll be out in the car."

I ordered a tea in the lobby and watched as the driver started up the car and pulled away. Uh-oh.

Over the next several hours I ordered a few more glasses of tea, and then had to use the toilet. After much gesturing and an eight-yuan tip, I was directed to a dilapidated wooden unisex shack, where I ended up crouched over the bowl with a shoe firmly placed on each side of the seat. Sanitation was an issue. Fortunately, I had a packet of Kleenex with me.

I made a mental note: *keep buying Kleenex.*

Around sundown a busload of factory workers singing in unison pulled up to the hotel, and a woman holding up a yellow flag got out of the bus, blew a whistle and herded the workers into the restaurant, where they ate a meal built of chicken feet, mystery dumplings and glasses of a beverage from a box labelled HAPPY LOQUAT.

Thirty minutes later, a whistle blew and everybody shuffled back to the bus. The woman with the yellow flag looked at her passenger manifest, looked at me and motioned for me to come. I said, "No, I think you've got the wrong person," but she showed me a piece of paper that had the following written on it:

确切三十分钟以后,口哨吹了和大家被拖曳回到公共汽车,但另一方面妇女与黄旗看她乘客明显,看我和行动为我去对此。EthanJarlewski我说,"没有,我认为您有错误人员,但她显示了我有以下被写对此的一张纸。

Having no desire to spend my night sleeping beside the unisex shack, I got on the bus. The workers had been loaded to allow a three-row gap between them and my poxed Western self. I was suddenly dead tired. I stretched out on the first row of seats and was lulled to sleep by the sound of the sputtering diesel engine.

Sometime in the night we crossed a mountain range, and at six a.m., we stopped at a roadside canteen for a breakfast of green tea, a pasty semi-sweet nodule the size of a fist and an orange. I tried asking the driver for a map, but no go.

Around noon we entered one of those industrial instant cities they write about fawningly in business magazines as the core of *China—the New Asian Tiger!* A massive sign the size of Dodger Stadium's Jumbotron told me in English:

WELCOME TO SPECIAL ECONOMIC ZONE

SEZ

We Love Shopping World

The city, SEZ, was huge and obviously brand new, but otherwise as bleak and soot-covered and numbing as the rest of urban China. There were maybe twenty thousand bikes for every car, but the cars were Audis and Porsches and Jaguars. Imagine driving a luxury sports car in China in 1965—the brain can't even process the thought properly. In modern China? It's the new dream. I thought back to my grade-six science project on ecology; I'd known that the moment China discovered cars and craved gasoline, it was curtains for the planet. SEZ confirmed it.

We pulled up outside a concrete building—five storeys with no signage—and I was escorted to a separate entrance from the rest of the bus passengers. After intense haggling between the desk clerk and the woman with the yellow flag (and the handover of a plastic bag filled with yuan), I was given a key and shown to a second-floor room. It was essentially a zero-security jail cell: a single bed, no TV, a chair, a mirror and a penitentiary-style bathroom down the hall. I sat on my bed and was about to have a good cry when I noticed a box on the small bedside table. It contained a Toblerone chocolate bar and a message from Kam, which said, *Isn't travel glamorous? p.s., look under the bed.*

I looked and found a suitcase with my Vancouver clothes in it. I experienced a burst of happiness and then fell asleep.

购物

Shopping

乏味

Boredom

色情

Pornography

整容
外科

Cosmetic surgery

旅游业

Tourism

互联
网浏
览

Internet browsing

电视

TV

• • •

Whistle.
Ethan was awakened by the sound of a whistle.
Shrill whistle, shrill whistle . . .
Whistle! You awaken me with your scornful shriek.
Why are you so angry, little whistle?
Pain.

Well, so much for poetry, but that's how I woke up. Miss Yellow Flag gave everybody her signature wake-up call just a few moments after a clinically depressed dawn tried to cut through the new day's capitalist mist. New on the daily fire? Fifty thousand feet of orange rubber extension cords, a boxcar of recently exterminated Norway rats and a stadium-load of high-sulphur coal cut with acetone.

Carrying my black nylon Samsonite suitcase onto the bus, I was thrown a seed-riddled orange. A cautionary stare from Miss Yellow Flag told me, *So much as one complaint from you, buster, and you're off the bus, whereupon you'll be promptly kidnapped and sold into buggery, and your suitcase will end up on eBay. As for your clothing? I will steal it.*

I tried to put a good face on it. We drove and drove for several hours, the view never changing from one eye opening to the next: everything grey, save for the greys, which were black. Then, out of nowhere, we pulled up to a factory that was belching out toluene, rubber tires, floor sweepings and styrene plastics. More whistles followed, and my fellow bus passengers were escorted into a low building the size of several high school gyms. I was escorted into an office area—my arrival caused no sensation whatsoever. In fact,

I simply sat in a chair for an hour or so until an old guy, his face ravaged by six decades of yo-yoing ideologies, motioned for me to follow him. In sign language I mimed, "Should I leave my suitcase here?" He motioned a most definite "no."

I followed him into the factory's bowels, the fist-like stench of industrial solvents robbing my brain, dendrite by dendrite, of the ability to make Scrabble words longer than four letters. My eyes watered, but through the fog of tears I saw that the factory was making Nikes. Well, actually, not real Nikes—*fake* Nikes. After a quarter-mile or so I found Steve.

"Steve!"

"Hi, Ethan." Steve was padlocked onto a mattress-sized cutting device that punched insoles out of large sheets of waffled polyfoam.

"What the hell are you doing here, Steve?"

"Making shoes. How are you, Ethan?"

"I'm shitty, thank you. How long have you been here?"

"Months."

Here Steve was, apparently clam happy, making fake Nikes on one of hell's more ghastly rungs.

"If you're wondering why I'm in such a good mood, it's because I just had my fix."

"What?"

"Heroin. It's great. Makes life feel good 24/7."

"Since when do you use heroin?"

"Kam got me addicted to it before he put me to work here on the line."

"—!"

"Don't feel sorry for me. I like it here. And besides, I can't leave, because otherwise I wouldn't get my fix. You know how far we are from Shanghai, and even then, how does someone buy drugs in a country where drugs theoretically don't exist?"

"—!"

"It's actually fun being here. Excuse me a sec—" A sheet of waffled foam emerged from a ceiling chute, and Steve positioned it and then punched out 288 soles.

"As I was saying, I like it here. Why don't you put down your baggage and help me for a while?"

The old guy shrugged and looked at his watch. Clearly, Steve and I had to leave quickly.

"Steve, I came here to get you. You have to come with me."

"That's kind of you, but you can see my predicament."

"I've got smack galore back in the hotel in Shanghai. This old guy wants us to leave right now. He's got instructions. Steve—?"

Steve was tearing up. "Steve? Are you okay?"

"I'm going to miss it here. All my new comrades, too."

"You're joking."

"At least here you know where you stand."

Steve's replacement worker arrived, accompanied by a foreman who removed his padlocked chain. With one shrill of (what else) a whistle, he booted Steve off the line.

"Steve, they don't want you here any more. You're free. Let's go."

He looked miserable.

The two of us followed Old Guy back to the office, where a car awaited us. Thank God.

Just then an alarm went off in the factory.

• • •

The Associated Press
Updated: 12:54 p.m.

BEIJING—China confirmed two more cases of a new and powerful SARS-like virus on Saturday. The World Health Organization urged further testing to ensure the diagnosis was correct. The new cases were a 37-year-old dentist and a 20-year-old seamstress, the official Xiangxinhua News Agency reported. The seamstress had worked at a factory canteen in the northern Chinese city of Quang Zhouxing, which served civet cats banned by the government after the 2003 SARS outbreak.

This new strain has been tentatively called Cat-Related SARS, or CSARS, and the total number of CSARS deaths in the past week stands at 11.

The government of the province of Guangdong, where SARS first emerged in 2003, said in a statement that "the clinical symptoms and results of laboratory tests and x-ray tests were in line with a diagnosis standard recommended by the U.S. Centers for Disease Control for SARS."

In order to prevent confusion, the 2003 strain of SARS that appeared in China and Toronto is now being called "SARS Classic."

• • •

The driver fled without us. Steve and I were ushered into a large, drippingly humid hall beside the factory, where a gentleman used a Charlie Brown PA system to relate the news of CSARS to maybe six hundred shoemaking workers. I may not speak Mandarin, but I do know that the moment Mr. Megaphone said the following words—

“請不要恐慌。一切將是美好的。沒有立即危險。安靜地請回到您的工作安置。”

(“Please don’t panic. Everything will be fine. There is no immediate danger. Please quietly return to your work positions.”)

—the crowd exploded in all directions, fleeing like Muppets, abandoning the factory. Inside of two minutes the hall was empty, save for me, Steve and the lunkhead who had given the Don’t Panic speech. We asked him if he spoke English, and he did—just enough to tell us in Chinese-restaurant English, “Very bad disease. Almost instant death. Much pain.” This was followed by a gesture that indicated exploding eardrums.

Then he, too, abandoned us.

“Ethan,” Steve said, “how am I going get my next fix?”

“We’ve been caught in the middle of a modern-day plague in the middle of nowhere, and you want a fix?”

“That pretty much sums it up. A fix is a fix.”

We found a blue felt pen in the emptied main office. On the flip side of an industrial slogan poster, Steve drew a large hypodermic needle to convey his need. Somehow, his drawing style made the needle look terrifying, like a syringe Nazis would use to inject truth serum into your veins.

“Steve, that’s a pretty nasty-looking rig. Can’t you soften it up a bit?”

“It *is* kind of harsh. Here—” He drew daisies all around it, softening the message. The thing was, there was nobody to see the sign, save for some octogenarian shufflers looking for debris left behind by panicking workers. The shoe-moulding machines were all asleep, and across the floor, banks of lights were switching themselves off with noisy *boonk* sounds. The factory without noise was beautiful.

"Steve, chances are they kept your heroin near the station you were working at. Let's check it out."

At Steve's workstation, we rummaged about the first-aid kit and supply boxes, and hit pay dirt almost immediately. "Bingo!" He found a bag of H and a twenty-four-pack of clean rigs behind a case of carbonated lychee soda bottles.

"Life is sweet."

As there seemed to be no ride in our future, we walked for two depressing miles to Steve's dorm building. As we trudged, Steve asked, "Does anybody miss me back home?"

"Steve, to be honest, no."

He looked at me pointedly. "*Anyone?*"

"You mean Mom? No, she doesn't."

"Huh. I didn't think so. How's the game going?"

"BoardX? It's not. It got killed by management. It's called SpriteQuest now."

He stopped. "They killed my game?"

"No. They repurposed it. They're recycling as much of the functionality as they can, but Jeff is dead and has been reincarnated as Prince Amulon."

"Dear God."

When we got to Steve's dorm, his ex–co-workers had barricaded the doors with jumbo concrete ashtrays. They assumed that Steve was, if not the harbinger of CSARS, bad luck. His few personal effects came flying down from a sixth-floor window into an azalea bush. His toothbrush cut into the soil like a javelin.

"I thought they were my friends," he said.

"Steve, just be grateful they were even willing to touch your personal effects. Where are we going to sleep tonight?"

"The factory."

"—!"

"Ethan, it'll be fun."

And so we trudged back to spend the night camped out on the two couches in the shoe factory's front office. We scrounged tea and sultana raisin cookies that were in a box on top of somebody's desk. Then, across the room, I noticed something that made me think I was hallucinating—a computer monitor displaying a working Internet connection.

• • •

From Kaitlin . . .

Hi, Ethan, you glamorous world traveller. How is your Xanadu Hotel? We're so jealous of you. I'm not wearing makeup today, and I'm dressed like a slut, and all the guys in motion capture are ogling me. Am I making you jealous?

The big news here is that John Doe's cartoon curse on Mark is working, and Mark is really losing it. There was a particularly explicit (and hence funny) *Itchy & Scratchy* MPEG circulating yesterday, and everyone was in stitches. Mark was sweating and turning white. We thought he was faking it, but no.

What else . . . lunch in the cafeteria was braised lamb shanks with rabbit profiteroles, so all the vegetarians staged an hour-long hunger strike that was totally pathetic . . .

• • •

From Cowboy . . .

Hey, Dude. Gord-O tried to get me to do a Cheerios run for him. What balls, huh? What else is new? I'm adding an ACDelco automotive cigarette lighter to my PC so that I can bring fire into the pod (and also my Bluetooth GPS). It's this neat little subroutine that . . .

• • •

From John Doe . . .

Ethan, are you aware that there is nothing green anywhere in or around your desk? Do you think you might be either partially colour-blind or perhaps genetically encoded so as to dislike green? What would be the Darwinian advantage to such a quirk?

• • •

From Evil Mark . . .

Everybody's probably telling you I'm crazy and can't understand cartoons, but it's not that simple . . .

• • •

From Mom . . .

Hi, dear. I hope your trip is going well, and I hope you have found young Steven in good spirits. Kam tells me he's been doing some important business work over there! Kam is so generous. You're lucky to know him. Please promise me you won't spend too much money on those appalling sneakers that make you look like a hoodlum. Honestly, if you'd just put your money into a savings account . . .

• • •

From Dad . . .

That pesky bitch Ellen is back from Toronto and keeps calling my cellphone. What am I going to do about her? I think I'll ask Kam to help. He's such a can-do sort of guy. Also, Canteen is next week. Promise you'll show up, and no excuses like you've given me the past five years running. It's important to Kam and me that you show your support.

• • •

Sending mail was impossible because of the QWERTY-hostile Chinese keypads. Clicking on REPLY didn't work, and having an Internet connection was so precious that we didn't want to dick around with too many key commands. On the plus side, Steve's company account was still operative. He cruised through many months of cc's that guided him step by step through the gutting of BoardX and the rise of SpriteQuest. When he logged off, he said, "Ethan, hand me my rig."

Then we looked to the right, where we saw hundreds of car keys on a rack, each one numbered.

Under a setting sun, we sped off in what we hoped was the direction of Shanghai, in a top-of-the-line Feng Shui 3000 combination grain harvester/off-road vehicle. Fifteen minutes later we ran out of gas in the middle of nowhere.

With no food.

With no water.

Night had fallen, and we were out on the road, trying to decide what to do next, when a showroom-condition black GMC Yukon with high beams on approached us and slowed down. It had Washington State plates, and at the wheel was . . . *Douglas Coupland*?

"Ethan Jarlewski? What the hell are you doing out here?"

"What the hell are *you* doing here?"

"I'm taking photographs of abandoned factories as an art project. Like I need to explain myself to you."

"Where'd you get that car?"

"I suspect it was probably a sweet-sixteen present for the daughter of the guy who runs the pesticide distillery three valleys away from here." Coupland looked at Steve. "Would that be *Steve*?"

Steve said hi.

"Okay. I guess I'll be going, then." Coupland clicked his automatic window roll-up button.

"Doug!"

"What?"

"Get us out of here."

Coupland snorted. Steve asked, "How did you get into this zone? There's a quarantine."

"Haven't you guys learned yet that the global economy is fuelled almost exclusively by American hundred-dollar bills?"

"*Doug.* Take us back to Shanghai. *Please.*"

"Why should I do that? I've got my next two days all planned."

"We're trapped. We're fucked. We have no idea what to do."

Coupland rubbed his chin. "What will you give me if I drive you back?"

I looked at Steve and we shrugged. "A few hundred bucks."

"Grow up. Give me something real."

Steve and I were stumped.

Coupland said, "I knew you were a fuck-up, Ethan. Tell you what, if I get you guys back to Shanghai, then you have to give me your laptop computer, period. No erasing anything."

"What?"

"That's it, game boy. Give me your life."

"That's evil."

"Take it or leave it."

"But you've already gone through it."

"I barely scratched its surface. Do we have a deal?"

"Okay. Sure."

"Look me in the eyes and say it like you *mean* it."

I looked into Coupland's cold eyes; it was like looking into wells filled with drowned toddlers. "Okay. I promise."

"Hop in. And remember this, Ethan, *I own you now.*"

We drove away.

. . . pause

. . . waiting to respawn

Outside of videogames, how many games do you play by yourself? Here's a question: did people in the past masturbate more than they do now—or is self-pleasuring a biological constant? A wicked CPU can never replace the artificial intelligence provided by human beings—or can it? Just in case you were in doubt, other people can secretly tell everything about the way you feel. Hi. I'm a definitive gridiron videogame experience! Hi. I'm an expansion pack. Hi. Let me tell you, I would have *never* played Grand Theft Auto: San Andreas had I known that it harboured pornographic content or comely sluts who tempt you. What's this? Another year, another fifty dollars? Is it really worth it? You know, when you dream at night, your brain doesn't use your eyes to see. When you play videogames, your brain plays sports without using your body. Does this make you feel free, or does this make you feel like a prisoner of your meat? That buzz you're always hearing is everybody having sex. Dungeon master. Pimp. Prince. Crack ho. Why do games always want good to triumph over evil? Sometimes it's good training to fight for the dark side. If you're trying to quit drugs, who do you seek out, an ex-addict or Ned Flanders? You know what? When you read a book, you're totally lost in your own private world, and society says that's a good and wonderful thing. But if you play a game by yourself, it's this weird, fucked-up, socially damaging activity. What sort of narrow-minded moron propagates this lie? When you grandfather plays solitaire, is he isolating himself? Get a grip, people. Amateur. Anal. Asians. Babes. Big clits. Big cocks. Big tits. Blacks. Nothing I feel is real. Gaming isn't storytelling. Don't be so sentimental. Gaming is about killing your prey. It's about you killing me, or us killing them. All online activity is monitored. Attempts to bypass security are grounds for legal action. I look forward to a day when everybody who lives in sweatshop equatorial nations has the disposable income to choose from the fine array of games and gaming systems our society creates. Lock and load! The differences between you and the others are almost non-existent. The human body is one of the sickest and most foul things we can possibly view. I think that people who savour looking at nude bodies are pervs and molesters—we ought to lock them away and chuck the key. I love touching a game—you know what I mean? When your reptile brain and your CPU become one. Hey, if unplayable crap is such unplayable crap, why does it keep getting made? Last night I had this dream where Mario was a greeter at Wal-Mart and it really fucked me up. No matter what they say, to the gaming companies it all boils down to one dollar per hour of gameplay. It's a constant. Blondes. Bondage. Brunettes. Butts. Celebrities. Cumshots. If you crave tits, schlong, snatch or getting it on, you're a godless, amoral monster who will burn in hell. Online gaming makes me feel empty and powerful. And online gaming also makes me feel that the world is a conquerable place, not a globally warmed degraded shithole. Kill the killers. Hi. I'm Xbox and 360 negative. Other people are boring. Entering a game space and running like hell isn't my idea of a good time. Do you like anonymous sex? Sometimes the story wrecks the game. Instead of getting fun, you only get blather. Come on, just stop it. There's a lot to be said for ignoring the main quest line. Sometimes we all just want to drive a cab or get a blowjob in GTA: SA. Life is good. Life sucks. Pen-and-paper RPG gamers are too into the story. They're escaping reality in a lazy way. Books are too non-interactive. Come on, just give us a cheat code . . . wait—it's called reading the last page so you don't have to read the whole thing. I like flaunting my eighties geek credentials. I hate guys who flaunt their eighties geek credentials. To me they just seem old. Thinking you're immortal is the same as being immortal. I eat sugary crap all day long, and at my pathetically young age I've stopped tucking in my shirt because my stomach sags out over my waistband. It makes me look like a bad source of genetic material. Dating. Dildo. Drunk girls. Escorts. Farm sex. Feet. It pisses me off that advertisers lump me in with extreme sports people, but at the same time it's okay because people will think I'm more fit than I really am. You may not post new threads. You may not post replies. You may not post attachments. You may not edit your posts. VB code is On. User Name. Remember Me? Password. I noticed this thing—no matter how smoothly you walk, your head always bobs side to side, just a little bit, whereas in games, the smooth, bobless motion generates a strange and omniscient sensation that is more primal than we're willing to admit. This next one is the first song on our new album. It just came out this week, and the song is called "Pocky." In my neighbourhood, all the teenage boys are dying because they're driving their cars using videogame physics instead of real-world physics. They turn too quickly and change lanes too quickly. They don't understand traction or centripetal force. And they're dropping like flies. Puzzles aren't stories. Games that incorporate sex skills as a payoff are embarrassing. Hey, you asked for it! *It may be easy for me, but's it's hard as hell for Joe Gamer.* Fuck machines. Gay. Gloryhole. Group sex. Hairy. Hand jobs. Hardcore. Housewives. Indians. Ever since I got addicted to ElfQuest, I've stopped dreaming at night. It's scaring me. I'll choose God mode over Normal mode every time. Non-linear stories? Multiple endings? No loading times? It's called life on earth. I have yet to shoot my load too early. Thread. Tools. Search this thread. Show printable version. Email this page. All flaming, trolling and off-topic debates will be removed from these threads. All childish banter will be closed or deleted from now on. A troll is a user who posts solely for the purpose of provoking arguments and flamefests. Feeling unique isn't the same as being unique. Trolls typically offer little in terms of useful debate. Hey, girls. Hey, boys. Superstar deejays . . . here we go! A flame is an argument in which one user verbally attacks another using conflicting opinions. Once users begin arguing like children, insulting each other as they do, we have what can be considered a flame war. Individual girls. Interracial. Rate this thread! I'm too old to give a shit about what's hot under the Christmas tree this year. Just stop overpricing everything. Stop bundling your units. Stop being SKU-driven greedheads. Stop scroogeing me. And while we're at it, please stop putting quotes from Nietzsche at the end of your emails. Five years ago you were laughing your guts out over *American Pie 2.* What—suddenly you've magically turned into Noam Chomsky? You think you're special, but you're still just an embryo. Latinas. Legs. Lesbians. Live sex cams. Mature. Midgets. They made you a moron. A potential H-bomb. Natural tits. I sometimes wonder who's really writing those reviews out there. I have this friend, Gail, whose job was to generate fake websites about nine months in advance of a big game or movie so that when media sloths went to "research" their articles, they simply regurgitated what the studio wanted them to. You know, everyone talks about games like they're oxygen or food, and we'll die without them. What a load of sludge. They didn't exist twenty years ago. They're blank. They add nothing to the world. It drives me nuts when people say, "Gamers are developing hand-eye coordination skills that will help them in future situations, like when flying a military jet." Stop defending gaming. It doesn't want it or need it. I never finish any of my games. There's a big pile of them beside the TV. I'm too stupid to throw them out, and too bored to play them. I deserve whatever life throws at me. I know what Castlevania is, and that sort of scares me. LMFAO. To pray for a killer is to be a killer. Hi. I'm selectively backwards compatible. After playing Halo 2 for three hours, I went out and mowed down a Red Cross blood bank, raped anything with a pulse and trashed the local mall. Then I toasted the gods of destruction with a goblet of blood stolen from a Girl Guide's body. Old men and teens. Panties. Pantyhose. Peeing. You know that psychiatric question where they ask you, "If you could push a secret button and kill someone you hated, and nobody else on earth would ever know, would you push it?" I would. Every single time. And to look at me, you'd never know it. Console makers have feelings, too. No they don't. They're monsters. There's always some asshole who brings back the latest thing from Tokyo, isn't there? Your urges are the dark side of God. Every console, every hand-held device is like a language or a dialect. The brain was designed to know only maybe five or six languages, tops. Even those linguistic freaks from Holland max out at five languages. So choose and love your game systems with care. Anything can be a weapon. After your teens, it's kind of loser-ish to be discussing corporate pricing strategies for games. You are an individual with free will. Either buy it or don't buy it. Shaved. Small tits. Smoking. Squirting. Don't discuss Sony like it's a great big benevolent cartoon character who lives next door to Astro Boy. Like any company, Sony is comprised of individuals who are fearful for their jobs on a daily basis, and who make lame decisions based pretty much on fear and conforming to social norms—but then, that's every corporation on earth, so don't single out one specific corporation as lovable and cute. They're all evil and greedy. They're all sort of in the moral middle ground, where good and bad cancel each other out, so there's nothing really there—which is, in it's own way, far darker than any paranoid or patriarchal theory of Sony. Time = torture. After playing Tony Hawk's Pro Skater, I went outside and rode my board down the handrail outside the civic library. I'm a quad now. "Her name is Rio, and she dances on the sand." In the end, it's the Chinese gamer who'll dictate the business. Learn Mandarin. Look, it's just one more button to push to make something happen. All things considered, you're still an ass clown. Gamers aren't consumers. They're gamers, but they also enjoy looking up the stock price of Sony on Yahoo! Finance. Everybody saw you cheat. Trannies. Uniforms. Wrestling women. New Cheats! It doesn't matter how good games get, heaven will always be an arcade full of arcade games to me. MMOG 2K6 SFX PS2 MSRP. God approves of the market-share battle between Coke and Pepsi. Hurry, you thick-fingered trolls! Two-Edge has captured Ekuar! Why didn't you stupid Wolfriders send Petalwing back to us? They have tasted troll blood . . . they smell fear, and the prey is old and easy! Runes. Wizard. Immortal. Fucktoy. Your inner sickness is visible to others. They're only flattering your consumer ego by telling you you're unique. The hotter the elves, the worse the game. You can't kill people who are already dead. Even on my Athlon XP 2600+ with a GeForce4 Ti4800, I stuttered a few times when zoomed all the way out and in a heated battle. Nature made more of you than is necessary. Gameplay: 2 of 5. Graphics: 4 of 5. Sound: 3 of 5. Two characters in the same game sharing the same voice is kind of suspicious. Meekness is a strategy for losers. Contains one or more of the following: sunflower oil, salt, trisodium phosphate, cultured milk, salt, agar, whey and disodium glutamate. Disco mode. Flame mode. Hoverboard mode. Sim mode. Super Blood mode. People confuse children with angels: make it work for you. You asked for it.

Part Three

Breakfast Is for Losers

Five Months Later

Kwantlen College Learning Annex
Course 3072-A

Assignment: Write about What You Know
. . . and the People You Know

"All Rise and Pray to the Hug Machine"
Meeting Today's New Tech Worker

by Kaitlin Anna Boyd Joyce

After having worked at my current tech firm for the larger part of a year, I have come to the conclusion that my co-workers aren't so much idiots as they are fellow citizens in the thrall of various modes of persistent low-grade autism.

The clinical definition is that they are suffering from mild versions of "pervasive development disorders" or "sensory integration dysfunctions." Asperger's syndrome is one variant that has recently garnered much media hype. People with this sort of condition are known as "high functioning" autistics because they can more or less operate in the day-to-day world. Some people like to think of high-functioning autism as a trendy disease. Wrong. It is not a disease, it's a condition. Most high-functioning autistics resent being talked down to and value their condition. It is not a badge of victimhood for them—it is merely who they are.

Perhaps the broadest way of understanding the world of the high-functioning autistic is to treat all stimuli that impact on the human body not as sensory input but as information bombardment. Most people are able to sift out the day's excess information without ever thinking about it, but to the tech worker exhibiting autistic—okay, let's just say the word: *geek*—to most geeks, a hug is not a hug, it's the physical equivalent of holding a novelty marine foghorn up to the ear and blasting it directly into the central nervous system. When you hug a geek, you're overloading them in a manner they find intolerable. They feel and express shock and revulsion when touched.

Here's a personal example. Low-grade autistics have problems with sensory input, sound being a biggie. My boyfriend, Ethan, is a seemingly average NT (neurotypical), and yet he exhibits a specific autistic variant called hyperacuity. He has a small, specific band of sound frequencies that make him go mental. If I'm in the bathroom with the door closed and Ethan is in the living room watching a Wrestling Entertainment marathon with the volume set on high, all I have to do is clip one of my toenails with a small generic nail clipper and his entire cerebral system shuts down. He screams at me for making "that awful fucking noise." Likewise, Ethan cannot fall asleep if the Braun eight-cup coffeemaker on the floor below us is turned on because, according to him, it makes a specific brain-spiking click every forty-five seconds. I have pulled a chair up to the coffee maker and sat with my ear pressed right up to it. I have yet to hear such a noise. The fact remains that Ethan screams at me to *turnitthefuckoff* every forty-five seconds.

Here is another example. My cubicle mate John Doe (yes, that is his legal name—a long story) is a complete geek. He finds an immense sense of relief in performing small specific tasks that cumulatively lead to something larger—a textbook prerequisite of the previously mentioned condition called Asperger's syndrome. John is ideally suited to the coding universe, where tens of thousands of lines of numbingly dull code string together to make a hockey puck shoot and score with thrilling realtime physics.

I, too, am a geek and have my own set of autism-related problems. I have a mild version of facial blindness, prosopagnosia. It's hard for me to remember faces and names, and I have trouble telling when someone is either happy or sad. It's not something I'm too thrilled about.

It turns out that most people suffer from prosopagnosia to some degree. Who out there past the age of twenty-five can get through an entire party without faking a name or two? The entire Dale Carnegie method of Winning Friends and Influencing People boils down to ways of mechanically training yourself past facial blindness. It appalls me that people will like and respect you for no other reason than that you give the illusion of remembering their name. Is that all we are in the end—vain lumps of DNA flattered by the cheesiest of mnemonic devices?

More examples will follow. What is important here is at least to become comfortable with the increasingly more apparent scientific fact that what we describe as "character" and "personality" are not so much spiritual or cosmic states of being, but rather, an overall effect created by clusters of overlapping brain dysfunctions.

Witness the universally understood archetype of the class clown. Is he funny and lovable, or is he farther along the personality spectrum of disinhibition? In the middle of the spectrum you have the bulk of society. Move a bit to the left and you find people who are "talkative" or "funny." Move a bit more to the left and there's the class clown. Move along farther and you find a personality who "doesn't know when to shut up." Farther still is someone who talks to himself, or perhaps someone with Tourette's syndrome, which is merely one dimension of disinhibition. Perhaps at the farthest reaches of disinhibition we have the babbling idiot.

Very well. Now then, let's go back to the centre and move a little the other way. We find a person who is "quiet." Then we find people who are "shy." Moving ever rightward, we encounter the "aloof," then the "loners" and then the "spooky." At the far right we have the Unabomber frothing away inside his geographically secluded shack.

My point here is that autistic mini-traits exist within the general population, and that microautism seems to favour people in tech and computer industries.

Here's a much simpler example of geeks and neural processing malfunctions: Has anybody experienced a geek environment in which said geeks wear perfume or deodorant? Chances are no. While advanced microautistics are more commonly men than women, both share a marked dislike of scent. My co-worker Bree was trying to impress this snobby French guy, and she wore a stinky Parisian floral fart perfume to work. She was chased out of the work area with crumpled-up balls of paper and anti-Gallic invective. Likewise, my geek co-workers are unable to process the smell of McDonald's food, and call it the Taint. The worst odour of all is the smell of butter-flavoured microwaved popcorn wafting out of the coffee room. Despite the unspoken ban on said substance, a co-worker nicknamed "Cowboy" popped a bag one Friday afternoon only to return to his desk to find all of his possessions removed. He quickly returned the bag to the kitchen, where he incarcerated it inside three zip-lock bags. When he returned to his desk, all of his possessions had reappeared, as if by magic.

Another interesting autistic scenario in my life is one shared by two people I know—Kam, a businessman, and Steve, a marketing executive. Steve and Kam have, in a genuine medical and biological sense of the phrase, no sense of humour. Yes, that's right, they live in a world without laughter. Science tells us that humourlessness is just another offshoot of autism, a type of social disengagement that ultimately ends in a shutdown life.

Likewise, I'd argue that boring people aren't boring—

they're hampered by microautism, the clinical term being "lack of social or emotional reciprocity." In a clever twist of fate, when Steve started working at my company, he spoke almost entirely in cutesy cloying management jargon peppered with self-help poop. However, for complex reasons, Steve ended up as a heroin addict. In becoming an addict, Steve acquired both a sense of humour and irony. Steve no longer uses stereotyped and repetitive language. He's fun to have around but, for reasons I can't go into here, has to keep his new personality hidden from most of the people at work.

My co-worker Bree exhibits another form of microautism. Her autism is the lack of social or emotional reciprocity she exhibits in her relentless pursuit of sexual encounters. This isn't just a trashy cable-TV urban sluttery—Bree loses all social engagement skills after she's bagged a shag. Ironically, her way of stopping this microautistic behaviour is through an age-inappropriate relationship with her guy from France, who's maybe forty.

I am not a complainer. I believe that if you identify a problem you should also try to fix that problem. So, for extra credit on this assignment, I have built a hugging machine.

What is a hugging machine? It is an ungainly device made of plywood, two-by-fours and two crib mattresses that's used to apply pressure to the entire body without the sensory overload of being hugged by another human being. It is an affordable, comfortable, non-sexual means of calming a person, and is designed to allow your typical geek to get more productivity from his or her days.

• • •

After almost half a year of stalling, Kaitlin finally finished her hug machine. We were bustling about jPod, installing the final few bolts in preparation for its campus christening party. The last-minute pressure made Kaitlin needy.

"What if nobody comes?"

"Kaitlin, relax. The party will be mobbed."

"What if people come but don't like the machine?"

"Kaitlin, this is a game design company."

"Or what if they want to come, but they don't think they can handle the social pressure of being seen using a hug machine?" Kaitlin has become convinced that everybody in the tech industry is autistic to some degree. It's her new cause.

"Relax."

As an added bonus, after being held by Agriculture Canada for inspection for umpteen months, Cowboy's shipment of dried cola nut powder arrived from the US. He'd perfected a formula for "jCola" and was excited about debuting his creation alongside the hug machine. He'd rented a 1960s beverage machine like something from a roller rink, and the uncarbonated brew looked really, well . . . *refreshing*, swishing away inside the machine's colourless Plexi dome.

"Cowboy, just give me a taste."

"No way. Not until everyone's here and we toast the success of the hug machine."

Was there excitement in the air? No. But a party was much needed after the hours we'd been logging on SpriteQuest.

I spent the morning generating texture mapping for soot, powder burns, blood stains and some awesome particle effects for Ronald's Lair—this on top of my regular job. I pretty much live at work now.

At five we sat around waiting for guests to show up. Who was first to arrive? Mom, who was accidentally invited through the overzealous use of email lists on Cowboy's part. Mom had actually been on her best behaviour in the months following my China trip. I think she's feeling a bit guilty for having Steve sold into slavery, and we still haven't totally mended that fence.

"Hello, dear," she said. "Always nice to come visit your workplace. That ventilation duct over there looks awfully strong. I think I'll go light up a cigarette."

"We cranked up the ventilator just so partygoers can smoke."

"You're a thoughtful child."

Sure enough, come five o'clock, geeks began to arrive and mill about, but Cowboy refused to give sneak previews of jCola until six, so people had to fetch their own beverages from the cafeteria machines. This bothered John Doe. "Cowboy, I may not be a member of Van Halen, but I do know one must serve drinks at a party. Therefore I am going to hand out my private stock of Zima." He produced a twenty-four-pack from beneath his desk. "Yes, Zima—a bold, tasty treat with a spark of arctic freshness. But did you—" John stopped dead and turned a monochrome grey.

"Are you okay?" Kaitlin asked.

"Oh, my dear God."

We turned around to see what he was staring at. It appeared to be a highway construction worker: faded denim, a sun-ravaged face, short black hair and a stocky build, bounding straight towards us. The construction worker barked like a bull walrus protecting his harem. "crow! There's a penis infestation happening here in this ridiculous building!"

"Hi, Mom."

John Doe's mother!

"So *this* is where you work." She glowered at the pod. "I see just one woman here. What's your name?"

"Kaitlin."

"Kaitlin, how can you possibly work in a space where there's not even one other woman and the possibility of synchronizing ovulation cycles?"

"Legally, the men's and women's rooms have to be the same size. So it's actually quite nice. And my friend Bree works here, too."

"Wait! I see another female over there smoking."

Kaitlin said, "That's Ethan's mother. Ethan works with your son, too."

"crow," barked his mother, "I need you to introduce me to your comrades."

"Um, Mom, this is Ethan, Ethan's mother, Kaitlin, Cowboy, Evil Mark. Everybody, this is my mother, freedom."

Without asking, all of us knew that "freedom" was not capitalized.

I said, "John never told us his family called him crow."

"It is his name. But I respect his right and need as a male to generate a name that supports his masculinity in the cheerless environment of technology."

Cowboy snorted.

freedom cut him a withering glance. "You must be the male slut," she said. She looked at the jCola machine. "What's this—you have your own sugar-water facility here?"

"It's our own brand of cola." I could hear the pride in Cowboy's voice.

"Of all the corporate cysts and welts on the planet, you choose to mimic Coca-Cola?"

Cowboy surprised us. "It's actually a form of subversion," he said. "I located an organic cruelty-free source of cola nut powder, and the sugar came from a Zimbabwe sugar-making facility endorsed by the UN."

"That's still cash cropping."

"One step at a time, freedom."

"Amen," came a male voice from behind me: Kam Fong. A more potentially disastrous clash of personalities was hard to imagine.

freedom asked, "Do you work here, too?"

"Not at all."

"crow, introduce us."

"Mom, this is Kam Fong. Kam Fong, this is my mother."

"Kam, what do you do?"

"I work with the Chinese government to ensure that as many male babies are born as possible. We take the unwanted girl babies, dry them out, and then grind them into a powder, which we mix with latex paints to make anti-skid coating for the military's helipads."

freedom squinted hard at Kam, and then announced, "Finally! A true radical spirit here in this psychic morgue you call jPod."

Kam pulled out cigars. "Smoke?"

"Love to. Anything to help Cuba."

Kam and freedom went over to the ventilation duct and chewed the fat like old school friends. From snippets I could tell they were discussing hydroponics. Their unlikely but cheerful meshing of personalities was a jolt—so much so that when I finally realized my mother was talking to me, I found I'd completely gapped out. "Sorry, Mom, what were you saying?"

"What an amazing woman. So strong. So confident. So manly yet female at the same time. So forceful."

I should have removed Mom from the party at that moment, but alas, it was too late. Mom was infatuated.

A few minutes later Cowboy went off to get Styrofoam cups from the coffee room, and Kam Fong put a quarter-pound of medicinal-grade cocaine into the jCola, where it dissolved beautifully. "You losers might as well get the real thing," he said.

Cowboy came back and poured a glass for everybody, and Kaitlin stood up to give a brief inaugural speech. Her hug machine looked like a cross between an incline bench and an industrial loom.

Kaitlin said, "I'd like you all to know that this hug machine is for everybody in the company, and any time you need to use it, come right in. I've covered the hugging pads with removable terry cloth cozies, which I promise I'll wash twice a week. Remember, you're not walking diseases in need of correction. You're confident industry professionals who lead rich, rewarding lives and who don't need to prove anything to anybody."

freedom led a salvo of applause.

Kaitlin looked at John Doe. "John, would you like to be the first to try the hug machine?"

"Yes, please."

"Very well. In you go."

John sat on the little chair portion and then pulled a lever, which activated the two baby crib mattresses. With equal pressure applied from both sides to his torso, John appeared to be in bliss. "I want to live inside this machine."

Kaitlin said, "This hug machine is now launched." She raised her glass: "To the hug machine!"

The medicinal beverages took maybe fifteen seconds to kick in. A boom box was produced and people began to dance—well, okay, they moved their bodies quickly and in an odd manner.

Steve came in. "Techies are *dancing*?"

"I know," I said.

"How did *that* happen?"

"They're high as kites. Kam dumped a quarter-pound of premium coke into Mark's jCola."

"Any left?"

"All gone."

"Shit. Well, maybe it'll improve their productivity."

"I suspect they'll all start developing amazing ideas for new games, but they'll pass out around three a.m. The next morning it'll turn out that all they wrote down was the natural logarithm of yesterday's Jumble puzzle."

"I need to score real bad," said Steve. "Can you drive me downtown?"

Steve lost his driver's licence a week after we got back from China. "Steve, why don't you just kick your habit? I feel like I'm back doing Gord-O's Cheerios runs. At least at Costco I can park my car reasonably safely."

"Don't knock smack if you haven't tried it."

"Why can't you buy it in bulk?"

"Ethan, if it was bulk, how could I keep it fresh? Good fresh smack is like good lettuce or fresh meat. Look—here comes Kam."

"Hi, boys."

Since he got back, Steve has decided to like Kam. Why? Because without Kam, Steve would never have discovered smack, and without smack, he would have been trapped inside his old personality forever. ("Ethan, do you think I enjoyed being Ned Flanders every diddily-day of the week? Fuck diddily-uck *no.* Every fibre of my being wanted to napalm the dry-erase boards, but instead I'd stand there smiling at pie charts, discussing how much of the budget we should allot for dried cranberries for the goodie bags at the Orlando staff retreat."

"Dried cranberries—you mean Craisins?"

"Yes, Craisins."

"Kam, can you give Steve some smack so I can get on with work here?" I said.

"Ethan, I promised your mother I wouldn't interfere with Steve's life any more."

"Then let's just go downtown and get it over with," I said.

In the car Steve had a jones and was rubbing his hands all over his body and shivering. "Steve, can you maybe keep your hands still? You're freaking me out, and you're flaking all over the upholstery. I just vacuumed it."

"Kam is right. You really are middle-class."

"You guys talk about me in those terms?"

"Sure."

I let it drop. "Which corner today?" Shopping for heroin with Steve is like choosing the right deli. I looked around; I'd never seen so many people looking for fixes.

"I forgot," Steve said, "it's Welfare Wednesday."

The alleys were a maze of graffitied brick, soiled Dumpsters and lame, dispirited pigeons atop crumbled pavement glazed with algae blooms. I could hear plastic mini bleach bottles popping under the car's wheels. Then I spotted three relatively together people, who looked like they had day jobs and fixed addresses, scoring from a shrunken-apple-headed hippie. They looked relatively jolly, and Steve said, "There."

I never would have believed how normal some smack users can be. (*"This is my coffee break. I have to get back and install the new Norton AntiVirus patch.*") It turned out our hippie saleslady was named Tina, and she was handing out free lotto tickets with every purchase. Steve commended her. "You should move up the food chain a bit. You're too good to be doing one-to-ones."

"You think so?"

"I sure do."

"I've been thinking about it. But most of the time all I really want is to supply my own habit and maybe get some donuts and a new nightgown with no cigarette burns."

"Tina, you can aim higher than that."

"Mister, you're the wind beneath my wings."

• • •

Much news when I returned from the smack run. First off, Cowboy went nuts after three glasses of jCola and hooked up with some fine young lady using his pseudonym on chokingforit.com. They arranged to meet in the Denny's beside the building where his sister lives, and then in walked his sister, and it turned out that, yes, he'd arranged to get together *with* his sister. He's sworn off sex forever. He's never made that promise before.

"It felt like that dream you get where your dick falls off and you put it back into place like it was a plastic dildo, except it was . . ." He drifted off

"Except it was *what*?" Podoids always demand the full story.

"Except it was like looking at myself, except I had tits and female plumbing and . . ."

"And?"

"I don't want to talk about it any more."

And then John Doe told me that he and Kam Fong were involved in some kind of business deal with Douglas Coupland.

"What?"

"Just what I told you. Hardware. LED screens, that's all I can say. It's what he was doing in China when he was there with you."

"He said he was there to take pretentious arty-farty photos."

"For God's sake, Ethan, wake up. He's a novelist. He lies for a living. And besides, Kam's always right about business. I've invested some money in the project already."

"What?"

"Me, too," said Bree.

"Anyone *else*?"

Everybody, including Kaitlin, raised their hands. "I don't believe this. Why didn't anyone tell me?"

Kaitlin said, "He came here last week. You were out looking at the new Nikes at Brentwood Mall when Doug dropped by."

"He came in here?"

"He's a really great guy."

This isn't happening. "Tell me, what is this screen project he's doing?"

"We can't tell you."

"What do you mean you can't tell me?"

"We can't. We signed nondisclosure agreements."

I looked at Kaitlin. "Why didn't *you* tell me?"

"I didn't think you liked the guy. Besides, you know how stringent NDAs are."

"But you and I live together and have sex several times a week."

"You make it sound so romantic."

The phone rang and I grabbed it. "Hello?"

"Hi, dear."

"Hi, Mom."

"That was a fun party earlier this evening. How nice to see you introverts having a dab of happiness in your lives."

"Yeah. I guess so."

"Ethan, what is it I'm hearing in your voice?"

"I'm just pissed at everybody here. They've all invested in one of Kam Fong's schemes—with Douglas Coupland, no less—and nobody told me about it."

"The screen project?"

"That's it. Don't tell me you've invested, too?"

"Sorry, dear, but I did. It's a smart idea."

"Can you tell me about it, then?"

"I had to sign a nondisclosure form. So did your father."

"What?"

"Fair's fair, dear. And besides, I don't think I'd be comfortable if Kam Fong knew I'd violated my nondisclosure agreement."

She had a point.

"Okay, so what's up?"

"I was wondering if you could ask your friend there for his mother's phone number."

"John?"

"That's him. I'd like to speak with his mother, freedom."

Whatever Mom was up to, it didn't bode well for freedom's future. I paused too long, and this made Mom suspicious.

"Ethan? What's going on?"

"It's nothing, Mom."

"I just don't know how I gave birth to such a suspicious son. All I want to do is ask freedom about a new boron phosphate fertilizer she's imported from Vietnam. It's raising her crop yield remarkably."

I handed the phone to John Doe and went off to the coffee room to fume. I could feel clown rage welling up inside me and knew it was time to go back to my work.

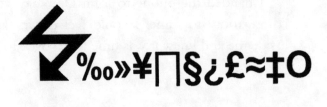

‰»¥∏§¿£≈‡O

●❍æ■□⬩♦√◆❖⬥☒□§

✆ ⑧ collapsing Korean department store

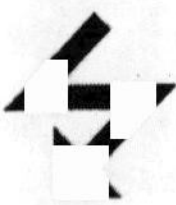

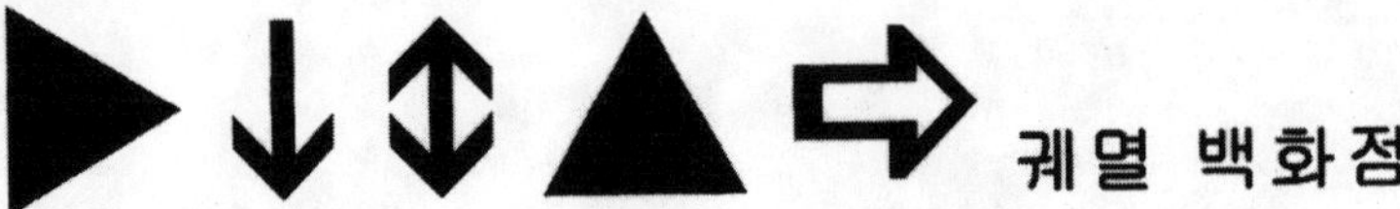

Kwantlen College Learning Annex
Course 3072-A

Assignment: Interview Someone You Think You Already Know

"Hi, I'm Steve"

by Kaitlin Anna Boyd Joyce

Steve Lefkowitz, forty-five, is project director of a game I'm working on called SpriteQuest. Recently Steve had a remarkable but not unpleasant change in personality . . . but why tell you when you can meet Steve for yourself?

Kaitlin:
Steve, when I arrived at the company I thought you were a sexless prig.

Steve:
I think that was the general impression I gave everybody. There was a part of me that knew things were all wrong in my life. But in order to repress that emotion, I'd do things like wear sweaters draped over my shoulders with the arms twisted together. I didn't want to be who I was.

Kaitlin:
Where were you before coming to work here?

Steve:
I was at Toblerone.

Kaitlin:
You mean those European triangular chocolate bars that most North Americans associate with hotel mini-bars?

Steve:
You nailed it. It was as if Toblerone had been typecast and couldn't get any new roles outside of hotels. So I revamped its image. We had to "think outside the mini-bar."

Kaitlin:
That's a stupid joke.

Steve:
Tell me about it. But that joke was my life for two years. Not like there was much else going on.

Kaitlin:
Is there a Mrs. Lefkowitz?

Steve:
Once. Briefly. I usually scared women away by date number three—even the hard-core husband chasers. I was hard to be around. In my spare time I'd do things like go into your sock drawer and reorganize it so that it made better use of the space.

Kaitlin:
Yuck.

Steve:
The sock drawer was what usually ended things.

Kaitlin:
Don't you have a kid?

Steve:
He and his mother are back east. We never got married. I was a one-hit wonder in the kid department.

Kaitlin:
Let me get this back to work. Tell me about Toblerone.

Steve:
I'm one of the world's few experts on mini-bars.

Kaitlin:
Tell me something about mini-bars I probably don't know.

Steve:
Here's a good one about hotel rooms in general. Most hotels have an armoire-type thing where they stash the TV set. Next time you go into your hotel room, stand up on a chair and look on top of the armoire.

Kaitlin:
Why?

Steve:
When people are checking out of a room, it's where they dump stuff they don't want to take with them, but which they can't throw away in case the maid finds it. Stuff that could get them arrested or cause them shame.

Kaitlin:
Like what?

Steve:
Really harsh porn. Pot. Pills. Coins. Touristy things that people gave them that they don't really want. It accumulates from one year to the next. In a Portland hotel I once found a pile of Italian lire, three copies of *Screw* and a $200 photography book inscribed *To Dennis—without you I could never have conceived this book, let alone had the courage to see it to its completion. I owe you everything, Diane.*

Kaitlin:
Sounds like Diane needed a reality sandwich.

Steve:
The Dianes of this world usually get hosed, don't they?

Kaitlin:
It's a law of the universe. But back to mini-bars and your Toblerone victory. You took them from near bankruptcy and made them a global victor in the hazelnut–milk chocolate category. I found a picture of you on the cover of *PLU Magazine.*

Steve:
Yeah. Everyone expected me to try to coast on my laurels. Maybe I'd go in and revamp the cashew sector. But I wanted a fresh challenge. That's why I decided to go into producing games.

Kaitlin:
You play them?

Steve:
Good God, no. They're as boring as dirt. The little brats who obsess about them make me sick with worry for the future of the species.

Kaitlin:
So why—

Steve:
Marketers like to believe that their skills are fully translatable into any other product group. Gaming seemed like a natural challenge.

Kaitlin:
Once you were hired, you took a skateboard game that was happily chugging along and changed it into a skateboard game with a turtle as the star.

Steve:
Shitty idea, huh? I'm not creative, and yet I felt a need to maintain the illusion of being creative. I wrecked your skateboard game. Sorry about that.

Kaitlin:
At least you're honest. But, Steve, the reason for this interview is to ask you about your recent personality change.

Steve:
Pretty freaky, isn't it?

Kaitlin:
To say the least. What happened?

Steve:
Well, I had a crush on a woman, and I think I was a bit of a pest around her.

Kaitlin:
Stalking?

Steve:
Not quite. But I was a real nuisance, and she had to do something to get me out of her hair. So one morning I got in my car to go to work, and a guy got in the passenger side—fake moustache and the works—and he had a gun. He said we had to drive out of the city, so we did. I was actually feeling really good, because at least something interesting was happening in my life. You'd think I'd be scared, but no. So we went into the valley. We stopped, and he told me to get out, and I did, and then he handcuffed me, and there was some other guy there with a panel van. They told me to get in, and then they injected me with something. Heroin, I found out later.

Kaitlin:
Really?

Steve:
Oh, yeah. And it was great. It made being kidnapped seem like an in-flight movie.

Kaitlin:
What next?

Steve:
The van drove for an hour, and then I could smell salt air, and the van drove onto something floating—a dock or a boat—and the heroin made me kind of woozy. I heard a lot of clanking and thumping, and then it became pretty evident that we were sailing somewhere. A freighter.

Kaitlin:
Afraid?

Steve:
No way. They kept shooting me up. I wasn't sure if I was dead or alive, but the whole episode was great.

Kaitlin:
We have to speed this up.

Steve:
A few days later we were in China. They put me in the back of some kind of bus, and I could see everything clearly. Have you ever been to China? No? Well, it's interesting but so polluted and grey and—

Kaitlin:
So I've heard.

Steve:
Before you know it, I was chained to a machine that

stamped out the soles of imitation Nikes, 288 in one go. I got room and board and as much smack as I wanted.

Kaitlin:
You weren't freaked out?

Steve:
I wasn't even aware I was alive. It wasn't heaven and it wasn't hell. It was interesting.

Kaitlin:
Did working there teach you anything about human rights violations and the politics of sweatshopping?

Steve:
That's a politically correct kind of question a bit late in the game, Kaitlin.

Kaitlin:
I know, but I had to ask it or they'd probably kick me out of this English class I'm in.

Steve:
Now *that's* thinking like a true executive.

Kaitlin:
Thanks. But, Steve, you still didn't answer the question.

Steve:
I didn't learn anything about human rights, but later I did learn about how much my personality changed on smack. When I got back to Vancouver, I realized I was no longer a

prisoner of that part of my brain that made me such a generic corporate suckhole. I found that I no longer cared about much of anything—and that I could say whatever I wanted whenever I wanted. It was great.

Kaitlin:
You're not reverting back to the old Steve, are you?

Steve:
Not as long as I have my daily arm snack.

Kaitlin:
Have you since pestered the woman you had a crush on?

Steve:
I bumped into her once at a party. The magic is gone, but I'm fond of her.

Kaitlin:
And they gave you your old job back, right?

Steve:
When I got back home, I was a news story for the first few days. That gave me a forty-eight- to seventy-two-hour pity window, which I totally milked, and they rehired me.

Kaitlin:
You can't milk a window.

Steve:
?

Kaitlin:
Well, this is an English assignment, and you mixed a metaphor. Back to you—how has this big personality change influenced your work?

Steve:
While I was gone, they came in and killed the turtle game and repurposed it as an uninspired fantasy game. I may not be creative, but the turtle was my idea and they fucked with it.

Kaitlin:
So . . . ?

Steve:
I'm working covertly with a team of talented young people to embed a Trojan horse serial killer into the fantasy game.

Kaitlin:
I forgot to ask—you still act like the old Steve when you're at work, right?

Steve:
Only inasmuch as it allows me to wreck that particular game. It's wonderful pretending to be the old me for nefarious aims.

Kaitlin:
Thanks for taking the time to talk to me today, Steve.

Steve:
My pleasure, Kaitlin.

• • •

"Ethan."

"Hey, Dad. What's up?"

"Your mother's new friend is here, and she's driving me up the wall."

Cautiously: "New friend?"

"Christ, she looks like Fred Flintstone's fetus."

freedom. "Okay. What are they doing?"

"They're down in the basement, talking about fertilizers. She started talking about semen and fertilization and vulva this and vulva that. I had to get out of there."

Best to change the subject. "How's the new dance routine going?"

"I think I may be too old for ballroom dancing."

"Too old?" Dad placed seventh out of sixty in Canteen (an endless night for all of us). He lost points for not having a light enough touch. Kam came in second. I fully expect the first-place winner to vanish some night while walking the dog. I said, "You're never too old to dance, Dad . . . and you're never too old to dream."

"That's the stupidest thing I've ever heard you say. Were you saying that with irony or for real?"

"Irony?"

"Don't play dumb. I read the paper like anyone else, Ethan. I've read about Generation K and your need to distance yourself from the world by using irony."

"Okay, I *was* being ironic."

"I knew it. By the way, I hear you blew your chance to get in on the Coupland guy's stock offering."

"I was only gone for forty-five minutes."

"Snooze and lose. Your mother and I are going to be *so*

rich because of it. I thought you and he were friends."

"It's more complicated than that. Maybe I should give him a call."

"I hear he doesn't like phones, and never answers them."

"How on earth would you know that?"

"Everyone knows that."

"Do you have his number?"

Pause.

"Dad?"

"You can't tell him I gave it to you."

"Why not?"

"Just don't." Dad gave me the number.

"I'm going to phone him right now."

"You do that." There was another pause. "Jesus, they're coming upstairs. I have to go."

Click.

• • •

I called Doug.

"Hello?"

"Hi—Doug? It's Ethan."

"Ethannnnnnn . . . . ?"

"*China* Ethan."

"Oh yeah. Right. How did you get my number?"

"You gave it to me in Shanghai."

"I did not. I never give out my number. And I never answer the phone. The only reason I picked up this time is because I have an interview scheduled with the *Sydney Morning Herald.* Why are you calling?"

"Doug, can I, uh—"

"Can you *what*?"

"Can I maybe buy into your business plan?"

"Ethan, are you dim? No. It's not like a lemonade stand where you just come over and put down your nickel. Besides, you had your chance, and you were out at Brentwood Mall, shopping for shoes, of all things. Richly ironic, I have to say."

"Can you at least tell me what your idea is?"

"You want to buy into something, but you don't even know what it is?"

I decided to channel John Doe here: "Is that so wrong?"

"You're a moron. By the way, I've already gotten an advance for the novel I'm going to write based on the contents of your laptop."

"You're a sick fuck."

"I seem to remember a lonely little lamb lost in the remote wastes of industrialized China. *Doug! Doug! Help us! Help us! We have to get out of here!* Face it, Ethan, if it hadn't been for me, you'd be dead by now, so don't play woe-is-me. A call is coming in right now, and it's Australia. I have to go."

"Could you maybe—"

Click.

• • •

I asked Kaitlin about irony, and it turns out that only twenty percent of human beings have a sense of irony—which means that eighty percent of the world takes everything at face value. I can't imagine anything worse than that. Okay, maybe I can, but imagine reading the morning newspaper and believing it all to be true on some level.

Brrrrr
Shudder
Shake
Milkshake
McDonald's milkshake
Chalk?
Brain freeze
Milk products
Nestlé
Mineral-deficient baby formula
Switzerland
Corporations
Globalization
Milkshakes everywhere
Even India
Dairy products
Cows
Confusion
Ancestors
Apu from the Kwik-E-Mart
Donuts
The Fox Network
Five thousand channels
Heather Locklear
Healthy, shimmering hair
Computer-generated hair
Pixar cartoon frames in a render farm
First weekend box office
DVD sales
Home entertainment systems
Karaoke
Fear of Karaoke

Abandoning the party
Driving
Shitty old car
Rain
Car commercials
Money
Never enough
Coupland's business thing with Kam
Rage
Raging Bull
1970s films
Al Pacino
Eyes like Woody Woodpecker
Cartoons of the 1940s
Ultraviolence
A Clockwork Orange
Heaven 17
Pop hits of the 1980s
Pet Shop Boys
London
Plagues
Ebola
Y2K
Hype
Lies

. . . and so on.

Kwantlen College Learning Annex
Course 3072-A

Assignment: Discuss Your Job with Somebody Who Probably Doesn't Care about It

"Flog the Dead Donkey"

by Kaitlin Anna Boyd Joyce

Jim Jarlewski is my boyfriend's father. He's a fiftysomething former financial consultant turned agricultural entrepreneur, a ballroom dance legend and a movie acting extra. Phew! Jim's a busy guy. I found him in a trailer in North Vancouver on the set of a Heartland Channel cable-access movie in which he portrays a convenience store clerk gunned down by Jane Seymour, who is, in that scene, portraying her evil twin.

Kaitlin:
Hi, Jim. Is this a speaking role?

Jim:
Fucking hell, no. I asked if I could moan or something, but it breaks union rules. Kaitlin, why are you here?

Kaitlin:
School project. I have to discuss my job with an outsider.

Jim:
All that gaming shit? No way. It's such a snooze.

Kaitlin:
Too late. I'm here, and I don't have time to find a replacement interviewee.

Jim:
Crap. Okay, then, what do you and Ethan and all you gaming chowderheads do out in that mothership thingy in Burnaby?

Kaitlin:
Could you at least ask it like you care? Pretend it's a line in a film.

[NOTE: Jim's weak spot is his desire for a speaking role in a TV or film production—any role at all. *Anything.*]

Jim:
Okay how about this . . .

[Jim spends the next five minutes delivering the same line.]

Kaitlin:
Enough already. Here's the deal—I have to discuss my job with you, so I'll begin by telling you that I'm working on this videogame called SpriteQuest.

Jim:
As in Sprite, the beverage?

Kaitlin:
No. A sprite is technically a fantasy creature one notch lower on the food chain than elf but two notches above pixie.

Jim:
Right.

Kaitlin:
It's set in the year AD 100,000—among the ruins of what we call Earth. Superior sprite beings from a distant galaxy have crash-landed here and now have to survive in a confusing apocalyptic world where right is wrong and wrong is right.

Jim:
[Jim is not paying attention.]

Kaitlin:
Jim, I specifically said something dumb to see if you're listening, and you aren't.

Jim:
Sorry. I was attempting to prep the emotions for my corpse scene. It won't happen again.

Kaitlin:
Thank you. Anyway, Earth also now has two moons—the one we know, and one that was stolen from Mars.

Jim:
I'm listening.

Kaitlin:
The hero of the game is Prince Amulon. He's neither a sprite nor an elf. He's the prince of a small band of earthlings who have survived across those hundred thousand

years. Prince Amulon works with sprites and other characters, and they go through complex perils that will allow him to crack the two moons together. From the resulting cosmic rubble, Prince Amulon will destroy the bad guys, and the energy released will allow the sprites to fix their spacecraft and return home.

Jim:
Wait a second—didn't this used to be a skateboard game starring a turtle?

Kaitlin:
You are correct. But first it was a *generic* skateboard game. Then we wrecked it by adding a charismatic turtle named Jeff. And then we basically had to convert the whole game into a fully immersive fantasy gaming environment called SpriteQuest.

Jim:
Isn't that kind of a dumb thing to do to a game?

Kaitlin:
Absolutely, but it's what I'm told to do by marketing.

Jim:
Have you no shame? Have you no sense of decency?

Kaitlin:
Stop being silly.

Jim:
Who are the bad guys?

Kaitlin:
They're called the Zorrs.

Jim:
[Sighs.] What magic powers do the game's characters have?

Kaitlin:
Using his psi powers, Prince Amulon can win a game of Scrabble using only three vowels. He can also bring fresh air into an unventilated bathroom, *and* he can renovate castles and huts on small budgets using knick-knacks from thrift stores and some well-chosen latex paint colours.

Jim:
You made all of that up on the spot.

Kaitlin:
Okay, so I did. It's—it's just so depressing what we have to do. But I don't want to marinate in shame. Our characters have other properties, too.

Jim:
Like . . . ?

Kaitlin:
There's a servant class of characters called Twix. All they do is have sex and week-long orgasms.

Jim:
Really?

Kaitlin:
Yeah, but because the game is for kids, we can't use the word "orgasm." Instead, we have to say the Twix are "twinkulated." We also can't use terms that might freak kids out.

Jim:
Like what?

Kaitlin:
Radiation. Terror. Blood. Hell. On the other hand, our characters can fly.

Jim:
[Sounding bored.] Really?

Kaitlin:
But they can fly only in trios, squished uncomfortably together while reading boring magazines and eating cheap food that's been badly prepared.

Jim:
Hmmmmm . . .

Kaitlin:
But if they fly more than ten times, they can then fly solo while selecting from a wide array of DVD entertainment and drinking a crisp California chardonnay.

Jim:
Hmmmm . . .

Kaitlin:
Jim! You're not listening to anything I'm saying!

Jim:
Kaitlin, I'd love to, but I have to be honest—when you say the word "gaming," my brain goes to the same place it goes when people say "country and western music."

Kaitlin:
You're an actor. Can't you pretend to be interested?

Jim:
Oh, all right, then. *Tell me, Kaitlin—what do your sprites eat?*

Kaitlin:
Sea monkeys. But if they eat too many, they become drunk and vulnerable.

Jim:
[Jim is utterly uninterested.]

Kaitlin:
Well, let's discuss sex again. SpriteQuest is a barebacking sexual environment. Condoms are forbidden, though we can't say that, as such. Instead, the characters kind of melt together into a blob of light. It's all pretty pre-AIDS 1978. *But* if too many characters make out, then the game clicks into a "prude mode," where all the female sprites have to wear unflattering footwear, the male sprites have to have six-dollar Toppy's haircuts and the "un-baby'ed" young female sprites have to go to endless baby showers, where they're humiliated into reproducing.

Jim:
I don't believe that last one.

Kaitlin:
Finally, you're listening!

Jim:
Hey, I'm not totally evil.

Kaitlin:
Good. For what it's worth, there are spells galore, and a large palette of characters you can custom design, and everyone spends the game battling and betraying everybody else.

Jim:
You're starting to lose me again. Is there anything *Star Wars*-y about it?

Kaitlin:
You're too old for *Star Wars.*

Jim:
You didn't answer my question.

Kaitlin:
Okay, then, it's generic Hollywood Screenplay 101—Prince Amulon wasn't always a prince. He was born poor in the Mukki-Mukki village, near the Harkka Mushroom, and one day a war-hardened Yalli Sprite told him his destiny . . .

Jim:
Kaitlin, sorry—I just can't listen to any more of this. Do you have enough for your homework assignment?

Kaitlin:
I think so.

Jim:
Do you want to eat from craft catering, here on the set? It's "Flavours of Provence" week. Olive oil, foraged alpine mushrooms and pork loin. But the gummi bears are stale, for some reason.

Kaitlin:
Sure. Thanks, Jim.

Jim:
Look over there—it's Goldie Hawn.

• • •

We decided to pull an all-nighter to inject bonus gore into Ronald's Lair. It was Bree who had the idea: "What if Ronald was kidnapped and we saw him on Al Jazeera three minutes before his execution?"

"What is Ronald doing in the Middle East, anyway?"

"Secretly spying for Royal Dutch Petroleum."

"I don't know if he'd work for another corporation."

"Do clowns have religion?"

"Maybe clowns are like most people, and they merely adopt their parents' beliefs as their own, all the while flattering themselves that they're the ones who made the decision."

"Maybe he's there as an embedded corporate mascot. When they drive a tank through an elementary school, Ronald passes out Happy Meal coupons to the uncrushed."

"Which country's tank?"

"Good question. Do you think Ronald looks Middle Eastern beneath that white pancake goo?"

"No way."

"Maybe he's like that California rich kid who converted and went to Afghanistan. Rich kids are the most screwed up. When they swap cultures they go viral on their old culture."

"Has anyone here ever contemplated bailing out of Western culture?"

Silence.

"Didn't think so."

"Back to Ronald's plea for mercy. When those al Qaeda guys behead people, it's not like they do it in one swoop, like the Japanese in World War Two. They use a steak knife, and it takes forever."

It was that kind of night.

• • •

Next morning:

Steve brought in the new *Condé Nast Traveler* magazine and in it there's this piece on China by Douglas Coupland. He makes it sound like the country is one big cocktail lounge. "Visit the rural countryside, where old and new brush together, creating an almost sexual friction. There's chemistry happening here, folks. The air is filled with hope and passion flower scent . . ."

Steve said, "I seem to remember the air being filled with scorched rubber boots and charred auto seats, but he's certainly right about chemicals being everywhere."

I was appalled. "Lies, lies, lies."

Mark said, "Ethan, I told you, he's a professional liar. Get used to it. You're just pissed off because you can't buy into his amazing new revolutionary technology."

"I'm *not* pissed off."

We heard a moan coming from the hug machine—a bug catcher from a basketball game team. (**NOTE**: Workers come to visit jPod all the time now. Kaitlin has to launder the terry cloth cozies every two days. She's getting lazy and doesn't want to do it at home, so she rinses them in hot water in the coffee room sink, microwaves them for a minute and then hangs them by the ventilator intake to dry.)

Steve said, "You might as well know it—marketing is now becoming spooked about SpriteQuest."

"No kidding."

"The eye candy's not good enough, and now they're worried that a fantasy game strays too far from their corporate tradition of sports franchises and licensing deals."

"We told them that ages ago."

"Nobody listens to you people. That's why you're not executives. My point is that they're planning on pulling the plug."

"They can't."

"Yes, they can."

John Doe moaned, "We have to stop them."

"This is rich, isn't it?" Kaitlin said. "Trying to save that stupid game after all we've been through. But they can't—they *can't* kill our Ronald . . ."

Steve said, "If you kids have done your homework, he's unkillable. Unfortunately, he'll be unkillable inside a game that's DOA."

We spent the rest of the day in denial as we competed to find the goriest photos we could online, extra points for subtlety. Winners included:

- No seat belts in Mexico City
- PETA cow slaughter video
- Romanian wedding mishap
- Punch press accident
- Drifter takes a catnap beneath Pepsi delivery truck
- Chickenpox vaccine complications
- Toenail removal surgery
- Thai alligator wrangler gets arm ripped off by alligator
- Whale explodes in Taiwan

I honestly don't know how gore websites could exist without contributions from Mexico and Southeast Asia.

Then I went through a wave of paranoia, imagining everyone in jPod rich, except me. They'll all be using their Coupland money to live on easy street while I'm mopping the aisles of Wal-Mart.

The aisles of Wal-Mart . . .

It sounds like an enchanted faraway place, doesn't it?

• • •

The phone rang. It was this guy named Bruce Pao. He's the executive whose gossamer-thin spidery handwriting is famous within the company, and bizarre enough to merit a secret web page fully devoted to interpreting its hidden meanings.

"Ethan, I picked you at random from members of the SpriteQuest team—a quality control call."

"Sure."

"Why don't you meet me for lunch?"

"Lunch?"

"That's what I said. Today. In the cafeteria. At one-thirty, after the rush dies down."

"Sure."

Click.

Steve was drinking Zima with John Doe in John's cubicle, the two of them porn trawling using Steve's executive override code. I said, "Hey, that was Bruce Pao. He wants to have lunch with me today."

This wowed Steve. "That's three cherries in a row, baby. That guy can make or break the project. What does he want?"

"Quality control he said. Random interview."

"I doubt that. Just make sure the game comes out of it sounding good. By the way, he made $3.6 million last year in stock."

• • •

Why do companies like Toblerone or Pepperidge Farm bother having websites? As if people are going to say to themselves, "Gee, I wish I knew more about Milano cookies. I know! I'll go to their site!"

Just a thought.

• • •

Oh God, I succumbed . . .

Milano® Cookies

Milano®, our most popular Distinctive cookie, is a satisfying combination of rich, dark chocolate sandwiched between two exquisite cookies.

• • •

Bruce and I met by the coffee command centre at the cafeteria's entrance. He was in his suit, looking out of place, like your parents at a wedding party, dancing to gangsta. I said, "You came all the way from downtown to see *me*?"

"I'm a caring executive. What are you having to eat?"

The special of the day was veal Prince Orloff with baked pears Felicia for dessert. "I'm going to go straight to dessert."

"Smart."

We got our food and sat down. "So, tell me about SpriteQuest. Tell me something passionate. Something inspired."

I realized I had to make a plea here for Ronald's life. I began to speak, and as I did, I felt like I was taking a shit in the woods—you know, it's fine, but it also feels totally wrong at the same time. "Bruce, SpriteQuest is just the best project ever. It rocks. It's kickass."

"Really?"

"Oh yeah. We're so stoked, and, I don't know . . . It's got this great aura about it—like we're making some sort of big leap forward game-wise."

Bruce said, "You know, Ethan, incremental improvements never win. We have to be vision busters."

Vision busters? "You said it, man."

"Tell me, Ethan, what are your favourite parts of the game?"

This was going to be a toughie, as I had none. *Think, Ethan, think.* "I like the way a player really gets inside Prince Amulon's head. *Why* does he want to find the sword? Sure, he needs it to enter the fire level, but the backstory of his father being killed battling with the Dark Warlord makes it personal. And the sprites' storage vault? Man, that place just *smokes.* And the way we retroed converted skateboards into Happy Carpets was totally inspired."

Bruce seemed mildly interested, so I said, "Hey, there's a rumour going around that the game's in trouble."

Now he seemed mildly surprised. "Oh?"

"Yeah. You can't kill it. It's such a great game, and the company needs it to establish itself as a creator of a quality fantasy franchise."

I didn't know what more to say, nor did Bruce. I ate a bite of dessert while he began to look bored. *Shit. I wasn't being enthusiastic enough.*

Bruce said, "Your brother, Greg, sells real estate."

"Yeah. You know him?"

"Slightly."

"Did you go to school together?"

"No."

More bites of dessert. What a disastrous meeting.

Then Bruce said, "Actually, your brother's selling this place up at Whistler that I have an eye on. A nice little chalet."

"Oh?"

"Yes. He is."

The meeting was suddenly making sense. "Which part of Whistler?"

"The Maui North development."

"Pricey."

"You can't put a price on a dream."

What is it with these marketing executives and their love of crap phrases? "Any specific house or property?"

"Lot 49."

"Have you bid?"

"Yes. But someone else bid before me."

"Bummer."

"Yes. It is."

"Why Lot 49?"

Bruce looked around the room and lowered his voice. "Because I don't believe in the future. I think we're all doomed. A survivalist organization I belong to singled out the Whistler/Pemberton Valley region as the most hospitable given a multiple global warming, dirty bomb, crop failure and SARS Classic scenario. Especially properties like Lot 49, which has a year-round stream capable of generating twenty thousand kilowatts of electricity using only a minimal rotary conversion system."

"I see."

During the pause that followed, I felt adult—*me* being in on a secret and being powerful enough to pull strings. "Why don't I call Greg tonight?"

"Yes. Give him a shout. But don't take too much time away from your work. We want SpriteQuest to be a smash."

• • •

I walked back to jPod to phone my brother. Kaitlin was fluffing some recently washed hug machine cozies, Cowboy was chugging acid pink cough syrup, Evil Mark was watching hockey fight MPEGs on some Russian website and Bree was glued to starswithoutmakeup.com, a site that she estimates has sucked a half-billion people-years of productivity from the global economy.

Steve was sitting at my desk, speaking on the phone in his "old Steve" voice to somebody in the marketing division. "All right-a-roony. That's a yes from this camper . . . best team in the country. Workaholics. I tell them to slow down, but their drive is unstoppable. You got it." Steve hung up, looked around and said, "Come on, you lazy little fucks. You have to do *something* here in this wretched pod. I can't cover your asses forever."

Cowboy said, "Steve, fuck off."

The rhythm of John Doe's typing was growing more manic over on his side of the baffles.

"John, are you okay in there?" Steve asked.

It turns out somebody had sent John the first million digits of pi, and the beauty of it had reduced him to a jittery mess. I said, "John, pi is cool and all, but how come you're falling apart over it?"

"Ethan, pi is essentially a string of random numbers. Here's a fun fact: the chances of finding your phone number inside the first hundred million digits of pi—minus the area code—is 99.997 percent. To find your number *with* area code becomes a bit less than one percent—even to find fake movie numbers like (212) 555–1234."

"I know you have the autism thing going for you, but what's the big deal?"

"The *deal,* Ethan, is that news like this will spur people on to buy lottery tickets."

"How?"

"If people locate their phone number inside pi's first million digits, it'll make them feel lucky, and before you know it, they'll go out and throw money away on lottery tickets."

"John, regardless of your mathematics, somebody always does wind up winning the lottery, so what's the point of stressing?" Kaitlin said. "And while we're on the subject, what exactly is your beef with lottery tickets?"

"My *beef* is that my father won the Irish Sweepstakes when I was two and left my mother, who overreacted and became a power lesbian. It's a family legend. As a result I was home-schooled and didn't even know that capitalized letters existed until I was ten."

"What do lesbians have against capitalized letters?"

"Capitalization implies a hierarchy, that some letters are more special than others."

"Oh."

Meanwhile, Mark—possibly the most pragmatic of anyone in jPod, located a pi website with the first hundred thousand digits of pi. "Everyone listen up. I've just emailed all of you the first hundred thousand digits of pi. Into this list I've inserted one incorrect digit. The first person to locate this rogue digit will win"—Mark looked into his desk drawer and picked something up—"this bag of Korean shrimp chips. At the count of three, search. One, two, three—*search*!"

3.14159265358979323846264338327950288419716939937510582
0974944592307816406286208998628034825342117067982148O8
651328230664709384460955058223172535940812848111745028
41027019385211055596446229489549303819644288109756659З
34461284756482337867831652712019091456485669234603486I
04543266482133936072602491412737245870066063155881748 8
15209209628292540917153643678925903600113305305488204 6
65213841469519415116094330572703657595919530921861173 8
19326117931051185480744623799627495673518857527248912 2
79381830119491298336733624406566430860213949463952247 3
71907021798609437027705392171762931767523846748184676 6
94051320005681271452635608277857713427577896091736371 7
87214684409012249534301465495853710507922796892589235 4
20199561121290219608640344181598136297747713099605187 0
72113499999983729780499510597317328160963185950244594 5

534690830264252230825334468503526193118817101000313783
875288658753320838142061717766914730359825349042875546
873115956286388235378759375195778185778053217122680661
300192787661119590921642019893809525720106548586327886
593615338182796823030195203530185296899577362259941389
124972177528347913151557485724245415069595082953311686
172785588907509838175463746493931925506040092770167113
900984882401285836160356370766010471018194295559619894
676783744944825537977472684710404753464620804668425906
949129331367702898915210475216205696602405803815019351
125338243003558764024749647326391419927260426992279678
235478163600934172164121992458631503028618297455570674
983850549458858692699569092721079750930295532116534498
720275596023648066549911988183479775356636980742654252
786255181841757467289097777279380008164706001614524919
217321721477235014144197356854816136115735255213347574
184946843852332390739414333454776241686251898356948556
209921922218427255025425688767179049460165346680498862
723279178608578438382796797668145410095388378636095068
006422512520511739298489608412848862694560424196528502
221066118630674427862203919494504712371378696095636437
191728746776465757396241389086583264599581339047802759
009946576407895126946839835259570982582262052248940772
671947826848260147699090264013639443745530506820349625
245174939965143142980919065925093722169646151570985838
741059788595977297549893016175392846813826868386894277
415599185592524595395943104997252468084598727364469584
865383673622262609912460805124388439045124413654976278
079771569143599770012961608944169486855584840635342207
222582848864815845602850601684273945226746767889525213
852254995466672782398645659611635488623057745649803559
363456817432411251507606947945109659609402522887971089
314566913686722874894056010150330861792868092087476091
782493858900971490967598526136554978189312978482168299
894872265880485756401427047755513237964145152374623436
454285844479526586782105114135473573952311342716610213
596953623144295248493718711014576540359027993440374200
731057853906219838744780847848968332144571386875194350
643021845319104848100537061468067491927819119793995206
141966342875444064374512371819217999839101591956181467
514269123974894090718649423196156794520809514655022523
160388193014209376213785595663893778708303906979207734
672218256259966150142150306803844773454920260541466592
520149744285073251866600213243408819071048633173464965
145390579626856100550810665879699816357473638405257145
910289706414011097120628043903975951567715770042033786
993600723055876317635942187312514712053292819182618612

5867321579198414848829164470609575270695722091756711672
2910981690915280173506712748583222871835209353965725121
0835791513698820914442100675103346711031412671113699
0865851639831501970165151168517143765761835155650884909
998985998238734552833163550764791853589322618548963213
2933089857064204675259070915481416549859461637180270981
994309924488957571282890592323326097299712084433573265
4893823911932597463667305836041428138830320382490375898
52437441702913276561809377344403070746921120191302033
038019762110110044929321516084244485963766983895228684
7831235526582131449576857262433441893039686426243410773
226978028073189154411010446823252716201052652272111660
3966655730925471105578537634668206531098965269186205647
693125705863566201855810072936065987648611791045334885
03461136576867532494416680396265797877185560845529654
1266540853061434443185867697514566140680070023787765
913440171274947042056223053899456131407112700040785473
32699390814546646458807972708266830634328587856983052358
0893306575740679545716377525420211495576158140025012
622859413021647155097925923099079654737612551765675135
751782966645477917450112996148903046399471329621073404
375189573596145890193897131117904297828564750320319869
151402870808599048010941214722131794764777262241425485
454033215718530614228813758504306332175182979866223717
215916077166925474873898665494945011465406284336639379
003976926567214638530673609657120918076383271664162748
888007869256029022847210403172118608204190004229661711
963779213375751149595015660496318629472654736425230817
703675159067350235072835405670403867435136222247715891
504953098444893330963408780769325993978054193414473774
418426312986080998886874132604721569516239658645730216
315981931951673538129741677294786724229246543668009806
769282382806899640048243540370141631496589794092432378
969070697794223625082216889573837986230015937764716512
289357860158816175578297352334460428151262720373431465
319777741603199066554187639792933441952154134189948544
473456738316249934191318148092777710386387734317720754
565453220777092120190516609628049092636019759882816133
231666365286193266863360627356763035447762803504507772
355471058595487027908143562401451718062464362679456127
531813407833033625423278394497538243720583531147711992
606381334677687969597030983391307710987040859133746414
428227726346594704745878477872019277152807317679077071
572134447306057007334924369311383504931631284042512192
565179806941135280131470130478164378851852909285452011
658393419656213491434159562586586557055269049652098580
338507224264829397285847831630577775606888764462482468

579260395352773480304802900587607582510474709164396136
267604492562742042083208566119062545433721315359584506
877246029016187667952406163425225771954291629919306455
377991403734043287526288896399587947572917464263574552
540790914513571113694109119393251910760208252026187985
318877058429725916778131496990090192116971737278476847
268608490033770242429165130050051683233643503895170298
939223345172201381280696501178440874519601212285993716
231301711444846409038906449544400619869075485160263275
052983491874078668088183385102283345085048608250393021
332197155184306354550076682829493041377655279397517546
139539846833936383047461199665385815384205685338621867
252334028308711232827892125077126294632295639898989358
211674562701021835646220134967151881909730381198004973
407239610368540664319395097901906996395524530054505806
855019567302292191393391856803449039820595510022635353
619204199474553859381023439554495977837790237421617271
117236434354394782218185286240851400666044332588856986
705431547069657474585503323233421073015459405165537906
866273337995851156257843229882737231989875714159578111
963583300594087306812160287649628674460477464915995054
973742562690104903778198683593814657412680492564879855
614537234786733039046883834363465537949864192705638729
317487233208376011230299113679386270894387993620162951
541337142489283072201269014754668476535761647737946752
004907571555278196536213239264061601363581559074220202
031872776052772190055614842555187925303435139844253223
415762336106425063904975008656271095359194658975141310
348227693062474353632569160781547818115284366795706110
861533150445212747392454494542368288606134084148637767
009612071512491404302725386076482363414334623518975766
452164137679690314950191085759844239198629164219399490
723623464684411739403265918404437805133389452574239950
829659122850855582157250310712570126683024029295252201
187267675622041542051618416348475651699981161410100299
607838690929160302884002691041407928862150784245167090
870006992821206604183718065355672525325675328612910424
877618258297651579598470356222629348600341587229805349
896502262917487882027342092222453398562647669149055628
425039127577102840279980663658254889264880254566101729
670266407655904290994568150652653053718294127033693137
851786090407086671149655834343476933857817113864558736
781230145876871266034891390956200993936103102916161528
813843790990423174733639480457593149314052976347574811
935670911013775172100803155902485309066920376719220332
290943346768514221447737939375170344366199104033751117
354719185504644902636551281622882446257591633303910722

5383742182140883508657391771509682887478265699599574490661758344137522397096834080053559849175417381883999446974867626551658276584835884531427756879002909517028352971634456212964043523117600665101241200659755851276178583829204197484423608007193045761893234922927965019875187212726750798125547095890455635792122103334669749923563025494780249011419521238281530911407907386025152274299581807247162591668545133312394804947079119153267343028244186041426363954800044800267049624820179289647669758318327131425170296923488962766844032326092752496035799646925650493681836090032380929345958897069536534940603402166544375589004563288225054525564056448246515187547119621844396582533754388569094113031509526179378002974120766514793942590298969594699556576121865619673378623625612521632086286922210327488921865436480229678070576561514463204692790682120738837781423356282360896320806822246801224826117718589638140918390367367222088832151375560037279839400415297002878307667094447456013455641725437090697939612257142989467154357846878861444581231459357198492252847160504922124247014121478057345510500801908699603302763478708108175450119307141223390866393833952942578690507643100638351983438934159613185434754649556978103829309716465143840700707360411237359984345225161050702705623526601276484830840761183013052793205427462865403603674532865105706587488225698157936789766974220575059683440869735020141020672358502007245225632651341055924019027421624843914035998953539459094407046912091409387001264560016237428802109276457931065792295524988727584610126483699989225695968815920560010165525637567856672279661988578279484885583439751874454551296563443480396642055798293680435220277098429423253302257634180703947699415979159453006975214829336655566156787364005366656416547321704390352132954352916941459904160875320186837937023488868947915107163785290234529244077365949563051007421087142613497459561513849871375704710178795731042296906667021449863746459528082436944578977233004876476524133907592043401963403911473202338071509522201068256342747164602433544005152126693249341967397704159568375355516673027390074972973635496453328886984406119649616277344951827369558822075735517665158985519098666539354948106887320685990754079234240230092590070173196036225475647894064754834664776041146323390565134330684495397907090302346046147096169688688501408347040546074295869913829668246818571031887906528703665083243197440477185567893482308943106828702722809736248093996270607472645539925399442808113736943388729406307926159599546262462970706259484556903471197299640908941380

595343932512362355081349490043642785271383159125689892
951964272875739469142725343669415323610045373048819855
170659412173524625895487301676002988659257866285612496
655235338294287854253404830833070165372285635591525347
844598183134112900199920598135220511733658564078264849
427644113763938669248031183644536985891754426473998822
846218449008777697763127957226726555625962825427653183
001340709223343657791601280931794017185985999338492354
956400570995585611349802524990669842330173503580440811
685526531170995708994273287092584878944364600504108922
669178352587078595129834417295351953788553457374260859
029081765155780390594640873506123226112009373108048548
526357228257682034160504846627750450031262008007998049
254853469414697751649327095049346393824322271885159740
547021482897111777923761225788734771881968254629812686
858170507402725502633290449762778944236216741191862694
396506715157795867564823993917604260176338704549901761
436412046921823707648878341968968611815581587360629386
038101712158552726683008238340465647588040513808016336
388742163714064354955618689641122821407533026551004241
048967835285882902436709048871181909094945331442182876
618103100735477054981596807720094746961343609286148494
178501718077930681085469000944589952794243981392135055
864221964834915126390128038320010977386806628779239718
014613432445726400973742570073592100315415089367930081
699805365202760072774967458400283624053460372634165542
590276018348403068113818551059797056640075094260878857
357960373245141467867036880988060971642584975951380693
094494015154222219432913021739125383559150310033303251
117491569691745027149433151558854039221640972291011290
355218157628232831823425483261119128009282525619020526
301639114772473314857391077758744253876117465786711694
147764214411126358355387136101102326798775641024682403
226483464176636980663785768134920453022408197278564719
839630878154322116691224641591177673225326433568614618
654522268126887268445968442416107854016768142080885028
005414361314623082102594173756238994207571362751674573
189189456283525704413354375857534269869947254703165661
399199968262824727064133622217892390317608542894373393
561889165125042440400895271983787386480584726895462438
823437517885201439560057104811949884239060613695734231
559079670346149143447886360410318235073650277859089757
827273130504889398900992391350337325085598265586708924
261242947367019390772713070686917092646254842324074855
036608013604668951184009366860954632500214585293095000
090715105823626729326453738210493872499669933942468551
648326113414611068026744663733437534076429402668297386

5220935701626384648528514903629320199199688285171839536691345222444708045923966028171565515656661113598231122506289058549145097157553900243931535190902107119457300243880176615035270862602537881797519478061013715004489917210022201335013106016391541589578037117792775225978742891917915522417189585361680594741234193398420218745649256443462392531953135103311476394911995072858430658361935369329699289837914941939406085724863968836903265564364216644257607914710869984315733749648835292769328220762947282381537409961545598798259891093717126218283025848112389011968221429457667580718653806506487026133892822994972574530332838963818439447707794022843598834100358385423897354243956475556840952248445541392394100016207693636846776413017819659379971557468541946334893748439129742391433659360410035234377706588867781139498616478747140793263858738624732889645643598774667638479466504074111825658378878454858148962961273998413442726086061872455452360643153710112746809778704464094758280348769758948328241239292960582948619196670918958089833201210318430340128495116203534280144127617285830243559830032042024512072872535581195840149180969253395075778400067465526031446167050827682772223534191102634163157147406123850425845988419907611287258059113935689601431668283176323567325417073420817332230462987992804908514094790368878687894930546955703072619009502076433493359106024545086453628935456862958531315337183868265617862273637169757741830239860065914816164049449650117321313895747062088474802365371031150898427992754426853277974311395143574172219759799359685252285745263796289612691572357986620573408375766873884266405990993505000813375432454635967504844235284874701443545419576258473564216198134073468541117668831186544893776979566517279662326714810338643913751865946730024434500544995399742372328712494834706044063471606325830649829795510109541836235030309453097335834462839476304775645015008507578949548931393944899216125552559770143685894358587752637962559708167764380012543650237141278346792610199558522471722017772370041780841942394872540680155603599839054898572354674564239058585021671903139526294455439131663134530893906204678438778505423939052473136201294769187497519101147231528932677253391814660730008902776896311481090220972452075916729700785058071718638105496797310016787085069420709223290807038326345345203802786099055690013413718236837099194951648960075504934126787643674638490206396401976668559233565463913836318574569814719621084108096188460545603903845534372914144651347494078488442377217515433426030669883176833100113310869042193903108

01437843341513709243530136776310849135161564226984750743032971674696406665315270353254671126675224605511995818319637637076179919192035795820075956053023462677579439363074630569010801149427141009391369138107258137813578940055995001835425118417213605572752210352680373572652792241737360575112788721819084490061780138897107708229310027976659358387589093956881485602632243937265624727760378908144588378550197028437793624078250527048758164703245812908783952324532378960298416692254896497156069811921865849267704039564812781021799132174163058105545988013004845629976511212415363745150056350701278159267142413421033015661653560247338078430286552572227530499988370153487930080626018096238151613669033411113865385109193673938352293458883225508870645075394739520439680790670868064450969865488016828743437861264538158342807530618454859037982179945996811544197425363443996029025100158882721647450068207041937615845471231834600726293395505482395571372568402322682130124767945226448209102356477527230820810635188991526928891084555711266039650343978962782500161101532351605196559042118449499077899920073294769058685778787209829013529566139788848605097860859570177312981553149516814671769597609942100361835591387778176984587581044662839988060061622984861693533738657877359833616133841338536842119789389001852956919678045544828584837011709672125353387586215823101331038776682721157269495181795897546939926421979155233857662316762754757035469941489290413018638611943919628388705436777432242768091323654494853667680000010652624854730558615989991401707698385483188750142938908995068545307651168033373222651756622075269517914422528081651716677667279303548515420402381746089232839170327542575086765511785939500279338959205766827896776445318404041855401043513483895312013263783692835808271937831265496174599705674507183320650345566440344904536275600112501843356073612227659492783937064784264567633881880756561216896050416113903906396016202215368494109260538768871483798955999911209916464644119185682770045742434340216722764455893301277815868695250694993646101756850601671453543158148010545886056455013320375864548584032402987170934809105562116715468484778039447569798042631809917564228098739987669732376957370158080682290459921236616890259627304306793165311494017647376938735140933618332161428021497633991898354848756252987524238730775595559554651963944018218409984124898262367377146722606163364329640633572810707887581640438148501884114318859882769449011932129682715888413386943468285900666408063140777577257056307294004929403024204984165654797367054855804458

5720227637840466823379852827105784319753541795011347273625774080213476826045022851579795797647467022840999561601569108903845824502679265942055503958792298185264800706837650418365620945554346135134152570065974881916341359556719649654032187271602648593049039787489589066127250794828276938953521753621850796297785146188432719223223810158744450528665238022532843891375273845892384422535472653098171578447834215822327020690287232330053862163479885094695472004795231120150432932266282727632177908840087861480221475376578105819702226309717495072127248479478169572961423658595782090830733233560348465318730293026659645013718375428897557971449924654038681799213893469244741985097334626793321072686870768062639919361965044099542167627840914669856925715074315740793805323925239477557441591845821562518192155233709607483329234921034514626437449805596103307994145347784574699992128599999399612281615219314888769388022281083001986016549416542616968586788372609587745676182507275992950893180521872924610867639958916145855058397274209809097817293239301067663868240401113040247007350857828724627134946368531815469690466968693925472519413992914652423857762550047485295476814795467007050347999588867695016124972282040303995463278830695976249361510102436555352230690612949388599015734661023712235478911292547696176005047974928060721268039226911027772261025441492215765045081206771735712027180242968106203776578837166909109418074487814049075517820385653909910477594141321543284406250301802757169650820964273484146957263978842560084531214065935809041271135920041975985136254796160632288736181367373244506079244117639975974619383584574915988097667447093006546342423460634237474666080431701260052055928493695941434081468529815053947178900451835755154125223590590687264878635752541911288877371766374860276606349603536794702692322971868327717393236192007774522126247518698334951510198642698878471719396649769070825217423365662725928440620430214113719922785269984698847702323823840055655517889087661360130477098438611687052310553149162517283732728676007248172987637569816335415074608838663640693470437206688651275688266149730788657015685016918647488541679154596507234287730699853713904300266530783987763850323818215535597323530686043010675760838908627049841888595138091030423595782495143988590113185835840667472370297149785084145853085781339156270760356390763947311455495832266945702494139831634332378975955680856836297253867913275055542524491943589128405045226953812179131914513500993846311774017971512283785460116035955402864405902496466930707769055481028850208085720227637840466823379852827105784319753541795011347273625774080213476826045022851579795797647467022840999561601569108903845824502679265942055503958792298185264800706837650418365620945554346135134152570065974881916341359556719649654032187271602648593049039787489589066127250794828276938953521753621850796297785146188432719223223810158744450528665238022532843891375273845892384422535472653098171578447834215822327020690287232330053862163479885094695472004795231120150432932266282727632177908840087861480221475376578105819702226309717495072127248479478169572961423658595782090830733233560348465318730293026659645013718375428897557971449924654038681799213893469244741985097334626793321072686870768062639919361965044099542167627840914669856925715074315740793805323925239477557441591845821562518192155233709607483329234921034514626437449805596103307994145347784574699992128599999399612281615219314888769388022281083001986016549416542616968586788372609587745676182507275992950893180521872924610867639958916145855058397274209809097817293239301067663868240401113040247007350857828724627134946368531815469690466968693925472519413992914652423857762550047485295476814795467007050347999588867695016124972282040303995463278830695976249361510102436555352230690612949388599015734661023712235478911292547696176005047974928060721268039226911027772261025441492215765045081206771735712027180242968106203776578837166909109418074487814049075517820385653909910477594141321543284406250301802757169650820964273484146957263978842560084531214065935809041271135920041975985136254796160632288736181367373244506079244117639975974619383584574915988097667447093006546342423460634237474666080431701260052055928493695941434081468529815053947178900451835755154125223590590687264878635752541911288877371766374860276606349603536794702692322971868327717393236192007774522126247518698334951510198642698878471719396649769070825217423365662725928440620430214113719922785269984698847702323823840055655517889087661360130477098438611687052310553149162517283732728676007248172987637569816335415074608838663640693470437206688651275688266149730788657015685016918647488541679154596507234287730699853713904300266530783987763850323818215535597323530686043010675760838908627049841888595138091030423595782495143988590113185835840667472370297149785084145853085781339156270760356390763947311455495832266945702494139831634332378975955680856836297253867913275055542524491943589128405045226953812179131914513500993846311774017971512283785460116035955402864405902496466930707769055481028850208

5800878115773817191741776017330738554758006056014337743299012728677253043182519757916792969965041460706645712588834697979642931622965520168797300035646304579308840327480771811555330909887025505207680463034608658165394876951960044084820659673794731680864156456505300498816164905788311543454850526600698230931577765003780704661264706021457505793270962047825615247145918965223608396645624105195510522357239739512881816405978591427914816542632892004281609136937773722299983327082082969955737727375667615527113922588055201898876201141680054687365580633471603734291703907986396522961312801782679717289822936070288069087768660593252746378405397691848082041021944719713869256084162451123980620113184541244782050110798760717155683154078865439041210873032402010685341947230476666721749869868547076781205124736792479193150856444775379853799732234456122785843296846647513336573692387201464723679427870042503255589926884349592876124007558756946413705625140011797133166207153715436006876477318675587148783989081074295309410605969443158477539700943988394914432353668539209946879645066533985738887866147629443414010498889931600512076781035886116602029611936396821349607501116498327856353161451684576956871090029997698412632665023477167286573785790857466460772283415403114415294188047825438761770790430001566986776795760909966936075594965152736349811896413043311662774712338817406037317439705406703109676765748695358789670031925866259410510533584384656023391796749267844763708474978333655579007384191473198862713525954625181604342253729962863267496824058060296421146386436864224724887283434170441573482481833301640566959668866769563491416328426414974533349999480002669987588815935073578151958899005395120853510357261373640343675347141048360175464883004078464167452167371904831096767113443494819262681110739948250607394950735031690197318521195526356325843390998224986240670310768318446607291248747540316179699411397387765899868554170318847788675929026070043212666179192235209382278788809886335991160819235355570464634911320859189796132791319756490976000139962344455350143464268604644958624769094347048293294140411146540923988344435159133201077394411184074107684981066347241048239358274019449356651610884631256785297769734684303061462418035852933159734583038455410337010916767763742762102137013548544509263071901147318485749233181672072137279355679528443925481560913728128406333039373562420016045664557414588166052166608738748047243391212955877763906969037078828527753894052460758496231574369171131761347838827194168606625721036851321566478001476752310393577

8606896111259960281839309548709059073861351914591819510297327875571049729011487171897180046961697770017913919613791417162707018958469214343696762927459109940060084983568425201915593703701011049747339493877885989417433031785348707603221982970579751191440510994235883034546353492349826883624043327267415540301619505680654180939409982020609994140216890900708213307230896621197755306659188141191577836272927461561857103721724710095214236964830864102592887457999322374955191221951903424452307535133806856807354464995127203174487195403976107308060269906258076020292731455252078079914184290638844373499681458273372072663917670201183004648190002413083508846584152148991276106513741539435657211390328574918769094413702090517031487773461652879848235338297260136110984514841823808120540996125274580881099486972216128524897425555516076371675054896173016809613803811914361143992106380050832140987604599309324851025168294467260666138151745712559754953580239983146982203613380828499356705575524712902745397762140493182014658008021566536067765508783804304134310591804606800834591136640834887408005741272586704792258319127415739080914383138456424150940849133918096840251163991936853225557338966953749026620923261318855891580832455571948453875628786128859004106006073746501402627824027346962528217174941582331749239683530136178653673760642166778137739951006589528877427662636841830680190804609849809469763667335662282915132352788806157768278159588669180238940333076441912403412022316368577860357276941541778826435238131905028087018575047046312933353757285386605888904583111450773942935201994321971171642235005644042979892081594307167019857469273848653833436145794634175922573898588001698014757420542995801242958105456510831046297282937584161162532562516572498078492099897990620035936509934721582965174135798491047111660791587436986541222348341887722929446335178653856731962559852026072947674072616767145573649812105677716893484917660771705277187601199908144113058645577910525684304811440261938402322470939249802933550731845890355397133088446174107959162511714864874468611247605428673436709046678468670274091881014249711149657817724279347070216688295610877794405048437528443375108828264771978540006509704033021862556147332117771174413350281608840351781452541964320309576018694649088681545285621346988355444560249556668436602922195124830910605377201980218310103270417838665447181260397190688462370857518080035327047185659499476124248110999288679158969049563947624608424065930948621507690314987020673533848349550836366017848771060809804269247132410009464014377

3603265645184566792456669551001502298330798496079949882497061723674493612262229617908143114146609412341593593095854079139087208322733549572080757165171876599449856937956238755516175754380917805280294642004472153962807463602113294255916002570735628126387331060058910652457080244749375431841494014821199962764531068006631183823761639663180931444671298615527598201451410275600689297502463040173514891945763607893528555053173314164570504996443890936308438744847839616840518452732884032345202470568516465716477139323775517294795126132398229602394548579754586517458787713318138752959809412174227300352296508089177705068259248822322154938048371454781647213976820963320508305647920482085920475499857320388876391601995240918938945576768749730856955958010659526503036266159750662225084067428898265907510637563569968211510949669744580547288693631020367823250182323708459790111548472087618212477813266330412076216587312970811230758159821248639807212407868878114501655825136178903070860870198975889807456643955157415363193191981070575336633738038272152798849350397480015890519420879711308051233933221903466249917169150948541401871060354603794643379005890957721180804465743962806186717861017156740967662080295766577051291209907944304632892947306159510430902221439371849560634056189342513057268291465783293340524635028929175470872564842600349629611654138230077313327298305001602567240141851520418907011542885799208121984493156999059182011819733500126187728036812481995877070207532406361259313438595542547781961142935163561223496661522614735399674051584998603552953329245752388810136202347624669055816438967863097627365504724348643071218494373485300606387644566272186661701238127715621379746149861328744117714552444708997144522885662942440230184791205478498574521634696448973892062401943518310088283480249249085403077863875165911302873958787098100772718271874529013972836614842142871705531796543076504534324600536361472618180969976933486264077435199928686323835088756683595097265574815431940195576850437248001020413749831872259677387154958399718444907279141965845930083942637020875635398216962055324803212267498911402678528599673405242031091797899905718821949391320753431707980023736590985375520238911643467185582906853711897952626234492483392496342449714656846591248918556629589329909035239233333647435203707701010843880032907598342170185542283861617210417603011645918780539367447472059985023582891833692922337323999480437108419659473162654825748099482509991833006976569367159689364493348864744213500840700660883597235039532340179582557036016936990988678673

113210979889707051728075585519126993067309925070407024
556850778679069476612629808225163313639952117098452809
263037592242674257559989289278370474445218936320348941
552104459726188380030067761793138139916205806270165102
445886924764924689192461212531027573139084047000714356
136231699237169484813255420091453041037135453296620639
210547982439212517254013231490274058589206321758949434
548906846399313757091034633271415316223280552297297953
801880162859073572955416278867649827418616421878988574
107164906919185116281528548679417363890665388576422915
834250067361245384916067413734017357277995634104332688
356950781493137800736235418007061918026732855119194267
609122103598746924117283749312616339500123959924050845
437569850795704622266461900010350049018303415354584283
37643781119885563187779253720116671853954183598443830
520376281944076159410682071697030228515225057312609304
689842343315273213136121658280807521263154773060442377
475350595228717440266638914881717308643611138906942027
908814311944879941715404210341219084709408025402393294
294549387864023051292711909751353600092197110541209668
311151632870542302847007312065803262641711616595761327
235156666253667271899853419989523688483099930275741991
646384142707798870887422927705389122717248632202889842
512528721782603050099451082478357290569198855546788607
946280537122704246654319214528176074148240382783582971
930101788834567416781139895475044833931468963076339665
722672704339321674542182455706252479721997866854279897
799233957905758189062252547358220523642485078340711014
498047872669199018643882293230538231855973286978092225
352959101734140733488476100556401824239219269506208318
381454698392366461363989101210217709597670490830508185
470419466437131229969235889538493013635657618610606222
870559942337163102127845744646398973818856674626087948
201864748767272722206267646533809980196688368099415907
577685263986514625333631245053640261056960551318381317
426118442018908885319635698696279503673842431301133175
330532980201668881748134298868158557781034323175306478
498321062971842518438553442762012823457071698853051832
617964117857960888815032960229070561447622091509473903
594664691623539680920139457817589108893199211226007392
814916948161527384273626429809823406320024402449589445
612916704950823581248739179964864113348032475777521970
893277226234948601504665268143987705161531702669692970
492831628550421289814670619533197026950721437823047687
528028735412616639170824592517001071418085480063692325
946201900227808740985977192180515853214739265325155903
541020928466592529991435379182531454529059841581763705

8927906909896911164381187809435371521332261443625314490127454772695739393481546916311624928873574718824071503995009446731954316193855485207665738825139639163576723151005556037263394867208207808653734942440115799667507360711159351331959197120948964717553024531364770942094635696982226673775209945168450643623824211853534887989395673187806606107885440005508276570305587448541805778891719207881423351138662929667179643468760077047999537883387870348718021842437342112273940255717690819603092018240188427057046092622564178375265263358324240661253311529423457965569502506810018310900411245379015332966156970522379210325706937051090830789479999004999395322153622748476603613677697978567386584670936679588583788795625946464891376652199588286933801836011932368578558558195556042156250883650203322024513762158204618106705195330653060606501054887167245377942831338871631395596905832083416898476065607118347136218123246227258841990286142087284956879639325464285343075301105285713829643709990356948885285190402956047346131138263878897551788560424998748316382804046848618938189590542039889872650697620201995548412650005394428203930127481638158530396439925470201672759328574366661644110962566337305409219519675148328734808957477775278344221091073111351828046036347198185655572957144747682552857863349342858423118749440003229690697758315903858039353521358860079600342097547392296733310649395601812237812854584317605561733861126734780745850676063048229409653041118306671081893031108871728167519579675347188537229309616143204006381322465841111577583585811350185690478153689381377184728147519983505047812977185990847076219746058874232569958288925350419379582606162118423687685114183160683158679946016520577405294230536017803133572632670547903384012573059123396018801378254219270947673371919872873852480574212489211834708766296672072723256505651293331260595057777275424712416483128329820723617505746738701282095755443059683955556868611883971355220844528526400812520276655576774959696266126045652456840861392382657685833846984997787267065551918544686984694784957346226062942196245570853712727765230989554501930377321666491825781546772920052126671434632096378918523232150189761260343736840671941930377468809992968775824410478781232662531818459604538535438391144967753128642609252115376732588667226040425234910870269580996475958057946639734190640100363619040420331135793365424263035614570090112448008900208014780566037101541223288914657223931450760716706435568274377439657890679726874384730763464516775621030986040927170909512808630902973850445271828927496892120

10667008164858339553773591913695015316201890887484210
798706899114804669270650940762046502772528650728905328
548561433160812693005693785417861096969202538865034577
183176686885923681488475276498468821949739729707737187
188400414323127636504814531122850990020742409255859252
926103021067368154347015252348786351643976235860419194
129697690405264832347009911154242601273438022089331096
686367898694977994001260164227609260823493041180643829
138347354679725399262338791582998486459271734059225620
749105308531537182911681637219395188700957788181586850
464507699343940987433514431626330317247747486897918209
239480833143970840673084079589358108966564775859905563
769525232653614424780230826811831037735887089240613031
336477371011628214614661679404090518615260360092521947
218890918107335871964142144478654899528582343947050079
830388538860831035719306002771194558021911942899922722
353458707566246926177663178855144350218287026685610665
003531050216318206017609217984684936863161293727951873
078972637353717150256378733579771808184878458866504335
824377004147710414934927438457587107159731559439426412
570270965125108115548247939403597681188117282472158250
109496096625393395380922195591918188552678062149923172
763163218339896938075616855911752998450132067129392404
144593862398809381240452191484831646210147389182510109
096773869066404158973610476436500068077105656718486281
496371118832192445663945814491486165500495676982690308
911185687986929470513524816091743243015383684707292898
982846022237301452655679898627767968091469798378268764
311598832109043715611299766521539635464420869197567370
005738764978437686287681792497469438427465256316323005
551304174227341646455127812784577772457520386543754282
825671412885834544435132562054464241011037955464190581
168623059644769587054072141985212106734332410756767575
818456990693046047522770167005684543969234041711089888
993416350585157887353430815520811772071880379104046983
069578685473937656433631979786803671873079693924236321
448450354776315670255390065423117920153464977929066241
508328858395290542637687668968805033317227800185885069
736232403894700471897619347344308437443759925034178807
972235859134245813144049847701732361694719765715353197
754997162785663119046912609182591249890367654176979903
623755286526375733763526969344354400473067198868901968
147428767790866979688522501636949856730217523132529265
375896415171479559538784278499866456302878831962099830
494519874396369070682762657485810439112232618794059941
554063270131989895703761105323606298674803779153767511
583043208498720920280929752649812569163425000522908872

646925284666104665392171482080130502298052637836426959
733707053922789153510568883938113249757071331029504430
346715989448786847116438328050692507766274500122003526
203709466023414648998390252588830148678162196775194583
167718762757200505439794412459900771152051546199305098
386982542846407255540927403132571632640792934183342147
090412542533523248021932277075355546795871638358750181
593387174236061551171013123525633485820365146141870049
205704372018261733194715700867578539336078622739558185
797587258744102542077105475361294047460100094095444959
662881486915903899071865980563617137692227290764197755
177720104276496949611056220592502420217704269622154958
726453989227697660310524980855759471631075870133208861
463266412591148633881220284440694169488261529577625325
019870359870674380469821942056381255833436421949232275
937221289056420943082352544084110864545369404969271494
003319782861318186188811118408257865928757426384450059
944229568586460481033015388911499486935436030221810943
466764000022362550573631294626296096198760564259963946
138692330837196265954739234624134597795748524647837980
795693198650815977675350553918991151335252298736112779
182748542008689539658359421963331502869561192012298889
887006079992795411188269023078913107603617634779489432
032102773359416908650071932804017163840644987871753756
781185321328408216571107549528294974936214608215583205
687232185574065161096274874375098092230211609982633033
915469494644491004515280925089745074896760324090768983
652940657920198315265410658136823791984090645712468948
470209357761193139980246813405200394781949866202624008
902150166163813538381515037735022966074627952910384068
685569070157516624192987244482719429331004854824454580
718897633003232525821581280327467962002814762431828622
171054352898348208273451680186131719593324711074662228
508710666117703465352839577625997744672185715816126411
143271794347885990892808486694914139097716736900277758
502686646540565950394867841110790116104008572744562938
425494167594605487117235946429105850909950214958793112
196135908315882620682332156153086833730838173279328196
983875087083483880463884784418840031847126974543709373
298362402875197920802321878744882872843727378017827008
058782410749357514889978911739746129320351081432703251
409030487462262942344327571260086642508333187688650756
429271605525289544921537651751492196367181049435317858
383453865255656640657251363575064353236508936790431702
597878177190314867963840828810209461490079715137717099
061954969640070867667102330048672631475510537231757114
322317411411680622864206388906210192355223546711662137

499693269321737043105987225039456574924616978260970253
359475020913836673772894438696400028110344026084712899
000746807764844088711341352503367877316797709372778682
166117865344231732264637847697875144332095340001650692
130546476890985050203015044880834261845208730530973189
492916425322933612431514306578264070283898409841602950
309241897120971601649265613413433422298827909921786042
679812457285345801338260995877178113102167340256562744
007296834066198480676615805021691833723680399027931606
420436812079900316264449146190219458229690992122788553
948783538305646864881655562294315673128274390826450611
628942803501661336697824051770155219626522725455850738
640585299830379180350432876703809252167907571204061237
596327685674845079151147313440001832570344920909712435
809447900462494313455028900680648704293534037436032625
820535790118395649089354345101342969617545249573960621
490288728932792520696535386396443225388327522499605986
974759882329916263545973324445163755334377492928990581
175786355555626937426910947117002165411718219750519831
787137106051063795555888905568852887989084750915764639
074693619881507814685262133252473837651192990156109189
777922008705793396463827490680698769168197492365624226
087154176100430608904377976678519661891404144925270480
881971498801542057787006521594009289777601330756847966
992955433656139847738060394368895887646054983871478968
4828053847017308711177611596635050399793438693391197898
871091565417091330826076474063057114110988393880954814
378284745288383680794188843426662220704387228874139478
010177213922819119923654055163958934742639538248296090
369002883593277458550608013179884071624465639979482757
836501955142215513392819782269842786383916797150912624
105487257009240700454884856929504481107380879965474815
689139353809434745569721289198271770207666136024895814
681191336141212587838955773571949863172108443989014239
484966592517313881716026632619310653665350414730708044
149391693632623737677770958503132559900957627319573086
480424677012123270205337426670531424482081681303063973
787366424836725398374876909806021827857862165127385635
132901489035098832706172589325753639939790557291751600
976154590447716922658063151110280384360173747421524760
851520990161585823125715907334217365762671423904782795
872815050956330928026684589376496497702329736413190609
827406335310897924642421345837409011693919642504591288
134034988106354008875968200544083643865166178805576089
568967275315380819420773325979172784376256611843198910
250074918290864751497940031607038455494653859460274524
474668123146879434416109933389089926384118474252570445

7251745932573898956518571657596148126602031079762825416559050604247911401695790033835657486925280074302562341949828646791447632277400552946090394017753633565547193100017543004750471914489984104001586794617924161001645471655133707407395026044276953855383439755054887109978520540117516974758134492607943368954378322117245068734423198987884412854206474280973562580706698310697993526069339213568588139121480735472846322778490808700246777630360555123238665629517885371967303463470122293958160679250915321748903084088651606111901149844341235012464692802880599613428351188471544977127847336176628506216977871774382436256571177945006447771837022199910669502165675764404499794076503799995484500271066598781360380231412683690578319046079276529727769404361302305178708054651154246939526512710105292707030667302444712597393995051462840476743136373997825918454117641332790646063658415292701903027601733947486696034869497654175242930604072700505903950314852292139257559484507886797792525393176515641619716844352436979444735596426063339105512682606159572621703669850647328126672452198906054988028078288142979633669674412480598219214633956574572210229867759974673812606936706913408155941201611596019023775352555630060624798326124988128819293734347686268921923977783391073310658825681377717232831532908252509273304785072497713944833389255208117560845296659055394096556854170600117985729381399825831929367910039184409928657560599359891000296986446097471471847010153128376263114677420914557404181590880006494323785583930853082830547607679952435739163122188605754967383224319565065546085288120190236364471270374863442172725787950342848631294491631847534753143504139209610879605773098720135248407505763719925365047090858251393686346386336804289176710760211115982887553994012007601394703366179371539630613986365549221374159790511908358829009765664730073387931467891318146510931676157582135142486044229244530411316065270097433008849903467540551864067734260358340960860553374736276093565885310976099423834738222208729246449768456057956251676557408841032173134562773585605235823638953203853402484227337163912397321599544082842166663602329654569470357718487344203422770665383738750616921276801576618109542009770836360436111059240911788954033802142652394892968643980892611463541457153519434285072135345301831587562827573389826889852355779929572764522939156747756667605108788764845349363606827805056462281359888587925994094644604170520447004631513797543173718775603981596264750141090665886616218003826698996196558058720863972117699521946678985701179833244060181157

5807428418291061519391763005919431443460515404771057005433900018245311773371895585760360718286050635647997900413976180895536366960316219311325022385179167205518065926351803625121457592623836934822266589557699466049193811248660909979812857182349400661555219611220720309227764620099931524427358948871057662389469388944649509396033045434084210246240104872332875008174917987554387938738143989423801176270083719605309438394006375611645856094312951759771393539607432279248922126704580818331376416581826956210587289244774003594700926866265965142205063007859200248829186083974373235384908396432614700053242354064704208949921025040472678105908364400746638002087012666420945718170294675227854007450855237772089058168391844659282941701828823301497155423523591177481862859296760504820386434310877956289292540563894662194826871104282816389397571175778691543016505860296521745958198887868040811032843273986719862130620555985526603640504628215230615459447448990883908199973874745296981077620148713400012253552224669540931521311533791579802697955571050850747387475075806876537644578252443263804614304288923593485296105826938210349800040524840708440356116781717051281337880570564345061611933042444079826037795119854869455915205196009304127100727784930155503889536033826192934379708187432094991415959339636811062755729527800425486306005452383915106899891357882001941178653568214911852820785213012551851849371150342215954224451190020739353962740020811046553020793286725474054365271759589350071633607632161472581540764205302004534018357233829266191530835409512022632916505442612361919705161383935732669376015691442994494374485680977569630312958871916112929468188493633864739274760122696415884890096571708616059814720446742866420876533479985822209061980217321161423041947775499073873856794118982466091309169177227420723336763503267834058630193019324299639720444517928812285447821195353089891012534297552472763573022628138209180743974867145359077863353016082155991131414420509144729353502223081719366350934686585865631485557586244781862010871188976065296989926932817870557643514338206014107732926106343152533718224338526352021773544071528189813769875515757454693972715048846979361950047772097056179391382898984532742622728864710888327017372325881824465843624958059256033810521560620615571329915608489206434030339526226345145428367869828807425142256745180618414956468611163540497189768215422772247947403357152743681940989205011365340012384671429655186734415374161504256325671343024765512521921803578016924032669954174608759240920700466934039651017813485783569440

407604702325407555577647284507518268904182939661133101
601311190773986324627782190236506603740416067249624901
374332172464540974129955705291424382080760983648234659
738866913499197840131080155813439791948528304367390124
820824448141280954437738983200598649091595053228579145
768849625786658859991798675205545580990045564611787552
493701245532171701942828846174027366499784755082942280
202329012216301023097721515694464279098021908266898688
342630716092079140851976952355534886577434252775311972
474308730436195113961190800302558783876442060850447306
312992778889427291897271698905759252446796601897074829
609491906487646937027507738664323919190422542902353189
233772931667360869962280325571853089192844038050710300
647768478632431910002239297852553723755662136447400967
605394398382357646069924652600890906241059042154539279
044115295803453345002562441010063595300395988644661695
956263518780606885137234627079973272331346939714562855
426154676506324656766202792452085813477176085216913409
465203076733918411475041401689241213198268815686645614
853802875393311602322925556189410429953356400957864953
409351152664540244187759493169305604486864208627572011
723195264050230997745676478384889734643172159806267876
718380052476968840849891850861490034324034767426862459
523958903585821350064509981782446360873177543788596776
729195261112138591947254514003011805034378752776644027
626189410175768726804281766238606804778852428874302591
452470739505465251353394595987896197789110418902929438
185672050709646062635417329446495766126519534957018600
154126239622864138977967333290705673769621564981845068
422636903678495559700260798679962610190393312637685569
687670292953711625280055431007864087289392257145124811
357786276649024251619902774710903359333093049483805978
566288447874414698414990671237647895822632949046798120
8999848571635710878311918486302545016209298058292083348
136384054217200561219893536693713367333924644161252231
969434712064173754912163570085736943973059797097197266
666422674311177621764030686813103518991122713397240368
870009968629225464650063852886203938005047782769128356
033725482557939129852515068299691077542576474883253414
121328006267170940090982235296579579978030182824284902
214707481111240186076134151503875698309186527806588966
823625239378452726345304204188025084423631903833183845
505223679923577529291069250432614469501098610888999146
585518818735825281643025209392852580779697376208456374
821144339881627100317031513344023095263519295886806908
213558536801610002137408511544849126858412686958991741
491338205784928006982551957402018181056412972508360703

568510553317878408290000415525118657794539633175385320
921497205266078312602819611648580986845875251299974040
927976831766399146553861089375879522149717317281315179
329044311218158710235187407572221001237687219447472093
493123241070650806185623725267325407333248757544829675
734500193219021991199607979893733836732425761039389853
492787774739805080800155447640610535222023254094435677
187945654304067358964910176107759483645408234861302547
184764851895758366743997915085128580206078205544629917
232020282229148869593997299742974711553718589242384938
558585954074381048826246487880533042714630119415898963
287926783273224561038521970111304665871005000832851773
117764897352309266612345888731028835156264460236719966
445547276083101187883891511493409393447500730258558147
561908813987523578123313422798665035227253671712307568
610450045489703600795698276263923441071465848957802414
081584052295369374997106655948944592462866199635563506
526234053394391421112718106910522900246574236041300936
918892558657846684612156795542566054160050712766417660
568742742003295771606434486062012398216982717231978268
166282499387149954491373020518436690767235774000539326
626227603236597517189259018011042903842741855078948874
388327030632832799630072006980122443651163940869222207
453202446241211558043545420642151215850568961573564143
130688834431852808539759277344336553841883403035178229
462537020157821573732655231857635540989540332363823192
198921711774494694036782961859208034038675758341115188
241774391450773663840718804893582568685420116450313576
333555094403192367203486510105610498727264721319865434
354504091318595131451812764373104389725070049819870521
762724940652146199592321423144397765467083517147493679
861865527917158240806510637995001842959387991583501715
807598837849622573985121298103263793762183224565942366
853767991131401080431397323354490908249104991433258432
988210339846981417157560108297065830652113470768036806
953229719905999044512090872757762253510409023928887794
246304832803191327104954785991801969678353214644411892
606315266181674431935508170818754770508026540252941092
182648582138575266881555841131985600221351588872103656
960875150631875330029421186822218937755460272272912905
042922597877106678738400006167721546384412923711935218
284998243509208918016855727981564218581911974909857305
703326676464607287574305653726027689823732597450844796
495456480307715981539558277791393736017174229960273531
027687194494449179397851446315973144353518504914139415
573293820485421235081739125497498193087143966151329420
459193801062314217741991840601803479498876910515579055

5480695387854006645337598186284641990522045280330626369562649091082762711590385699505124652999606285544383830327638599800792922846659503551211245284087516229060262011857775313747949362055496401073001348853150735487353905602908933526400713274732621960311773433943673385759124508149335736911664541281788171454023054750667136518258284898099512139193995633241336556777098003081910272040997148687418134667006094051021462690280449159646545330107754695413088714165312544813061192407821188690056027781824235022696189344352547633573536485619363254417756613981703930632872166905722259745209192917262199844409646158269456380239502837121686446561785235565164127712826918688615572716201474934052276946595712198314943381622114006936307430444173284786101777743837977037231795255434107223445512555589998646183876764903972461167959018100035098928641204195163551108763204267612979826529425882951141275841262732790798807559751851576841264742209479721843309352972665210015662514552994745127631550917636730259462132930190402837954246323258550301096706922720227074863419005438302650681214142135057154175057508639907673946335146209082888934938376439399256900604067311422093312195936202982972351163259386772241477911629572780752395056251581603133359382311500518626890530658368129988108663263271980611271548858798093487912913707498230575929091862939195014721197586067270092547718025750337730799397134539532646195269996596385654917590458333585799102012713204583903200853878881633637685182083727885131175227769609787962142372162545214591281831798216044111311671406914827170981015457781939202311563871950805024679725792497605772625913328559726371211201905720771409148645074094926718035815157571514050397610963846755569298970383547314100223802583468767350129775413279532060971154506484212185936490997917766874774481882870632315515865032898164228288232746866106592732197907162384642153489852476216789050260998045266483929542357287343977680495774091449538391575565485459058976495198513801007958010783759945775299196700547602252552034453988712538780171960718164078124847847257912407824544361682345239570689514272269750431873633263011103053423335821609333191218806608268341428910415173247216053355849993224548730778822905252324234861531520976938461042582849714963475341837562003014915703279685301868631572488401526639835689563634657435321783493199825542117308467745297085839507616458229630324424328237737450517028560698067889521768198156710781633405266759539424926280756968326107495323390536223090807081455919837355377748742029039018142937311529334644468151212945097596

5

343062842153194457271186149000176505581770953024688752
632501197052094761594167687277844720001927891372518416
228577837922844390843011811214963664246590336341945406
571835447719124466212593926566203068885200555991212353
637182269225317814587925937504414489339816086579008761
650246351970458288954817937566810464746141051424988702
521399368705093723054477341126413548928068410591077166
778212383328102621855877513127211793444482014404257450
830639447383637939062830089733062413806145894142276947
479316657176231824721683506780764875734204915576282175
839729751344789906965895325489403356156131674032764724
692125057591162515296545685446334981143176702572956618
447754874693784642337372389819206620485118943788682248
072793520225017965453437572741639107919729529508129429
222053477173041844779156739917384183117103625243957161
527146690058147000026330104526435478659032907332054683
388720787354447626479252976901709120078741837367350877
133769776834963442524199499513883150748775374338494582
597655609965559543180409201784971846854973706962120885
243770138537576814166327224126344239821529416453780004
925072627651507890850712659970367087266927643083772296
859851691223050374627443108529343052730788652839773352
460174635277032059381791253969156210636376258829375713
738407544064689647831007045806134467312715911946084359
358259877828352665311510650416232953290477721740835593
497237585521380483050900096466760883015406128243087406
455944318534137552201663058121110334531207450868243394
321590435944303124312274713858420303901060709403152355
561727679941600203939750998976293353258555756248089966
918298642226775023601932579747267425782111197347094023
574572222712125268523842958742735015636600931880454933
389897415714905441825597380808715652814301026704602843
168192303925352977957658624143927015497408792731310516
361191375770089295648233236482982630246079758757677453
771601024908046243018565241617566556001608591215345562
676021926899828553778725831451440826545834844094784631
787773747946535801699607794055687011923286080411309046
293508718271259346687127666948738998245985277864995691
654640294589350649643358098247659651651420909867552038
083092032304873427034682887516040715466538346196112230
137594515792526967436425319273900360386082364507626988
274976187235754767628899507521148048525279508450339585
708381304769378813211236742813194879502280663201700224
603319896719706491637411758548518784840120548446725888
514015627250198217190669608126277854859648183696214107
217142149863619187747545096503089570994709343378569816
744658282679119406119560378453978558392407612763441057

6675102430755981455278616781594965706255975507430652108530159790807334373607943286675789053348366955548680391343372015649883422089339997164147974693869690548008919306713805717150585730714881564992071408675825960287605645978242377024246980532805663278704192676846711626687946348695046450742021937394525926266861355294062478136120620263649819999949840514386828525895634226432870766329930489172340072547176418868535137233266787792173834754148002280339299735793615241275582956927683723123479898944627433045456679006203242051639628258844308543830720149567210646053323853720314324211260742448584509458049408182092763914000854042202355626021856434899414543995041098059181794888262805206644108631900168856815516922948620301073889718100770929059048074909242714101893354281842999598816966099383696164438152887721408526808875748829325873580990567075581701794916190611400190855374488272620093668560447559655747648567400817738170330738030547697360978654385938218722058390234444350886749986650604064587434600533182743629617786251808189314436325120510709469081358644051922951293245007883339878842933934243512634336520438581291283434529730865290978330067126179813031679438553572629699874035957045845223085639009891317947594875212639707837594486113945196028675121056163897600888009274611586080020780334159145179707303683519697776607637378533301202412011204698860920933908536577322239241244905153278095095586645947763448226998607481329730263097502881210351772312446509534965369309001863776409409434983731325132186208021480992268550294845466181471555744470966953017769043427203189277060471778452793916047228153437980353967986142437095668322149146543801459382927739

Bree won the chips within a minute: “I did my grade-seven science fair project on pi. I knew them all up to about the two thousandth digit, and then I thought it’d be sexier to play it dumb. It’s one of my life’s biggest regrets that I never got to remember up to the ten thousandth digit. It was like I made pi my special friend and only he and I could hang out together. How could I ever forget that first love affair?”

Shocked silence.

• • •

Bree's fling-with-pi victory quickly dimmed when Evil Mark sent us all another strand of numbers. He said, "Yes, pi is special—but so are randomly generated numbers. Inside this list of 58,894 random numbers I've substituted a capitalized letter O for a zero. Without using your FIND command, the first person to locate the 'O' will win the chance for me to karaoke to any song of their choice. Ready? One, two, three, *go.*"

8394294453591570882756598818094117160297760343730513621
1390047883372351427540720286989526875002292431461936282
2395430680224277560588557942860156419893244671023722580
0029727309745242944990835430120387021883544250726971817
7267033807989955253172496140238364116161423181682869828
8084075659751615851442020853551493425132471126126207941
9135677167536171122565377241995606589838856267894841082
3308639628651988124432169850345186891827559945693838724
7239476274146019734632018809890881034675594317224327594
9869026574482711121777978590275781242362849289565332747
9362743743873531652641309822923440868928887217037671153
9901087224963542026527243759299367889229087139452139014
4540502256604694347888604907974363295120814937648328097
2435298055110526548043909365630478508195730154902412472
0991693857106065422647842057737572709757497342197817121
4630016390433685178774343388531717323629904702505131030
6954198341646592727934876113073458150617381024767818187
1414431828346555406380604115790823706242927573048236293
9596344864638839942661964913226244620110764225589408993
8741086606054716012067376447378242683959804866194844238
2999737821587354367545028959351930789549916323377617379
9169416449746294680060724505379539650358211150479305339
1453548065642981038719608184148324108789344586583567268
4776207535905220912668847918610778456780322908729740265
5371784819686986337072236350255538925163940972712027526
9851018966460931390455977355476392535776123630429612695
2320015691430483197294328317643094296311869292475288187
3025216120597596224733332302262497236086362208242332726
2293961075871756743334679879663200891657347075771305636
9227386149770543937864358085132518102589679120251466380
6258612539528576198162687503661557992104984263418304378
9750872542718322672965519850728514160390984202336365986
8857257014359507390553883971081217680518690504965457121
97233631609971498569511012

615515339233051155950605798886339411314828765447043992
122877196733503964162636525596655515673861739141600017
563335999453925106934290802445256058719851923302963387
298955596998396862474581434975861872696797559447651461
581526788424119579253284509410485229326145557190366666
151995629557465976461525098304491786854123259672265956
383159322512548556479117384547327488732895473230863640
722300319315176819362944451467768690372987483528765627
634817139337482029187306147428985272491039704307649629
881219063419392803144225172519616708931346582620122274
299495031524988388374541174047635869073266699021999003
695549411594798177709382632529571047255773319492582530
841525344010073145122062261825099742872675259387610966
959730167115713798738722676830749170322610430331898173
996373809286109552249428582976783688816410755738955149
979929898879155315383853745019879206629707371802952017
187696504819381554820592670875825636156099933292856257
424275554286768913760780172810756503615750861595222121
140830004629234111942926153490640801824182231528337696
309394427452266611202164593224429206332265316565796604
185968468639162591591156954479494728515949751238477965
697681796114844586131004654419950174329804930253935709
913968325743409471668994574277692514068298761186986333
441827267547755678266066756984047293856900831822403217
765811833871453484666002372567649671924959395445627745
081448628034220843178941363821176414905741101828776166
149308892490642948445395287900566808890822240236783038
657313494467010351884170509563366287038527489950199514
945733951709461718699938441962731870127684781572939330
635692565150581852779380904304543990624684821402743865
728184477422121731585824952766968940603787371007938340
962285717235678546708347470911425675511407736141334427
744448387122384378288003469515166557831974703728469724
793373176524328977787457903042462929849385370252329889
462612805583582479965949505564727555290023986624078467
740648628708668556885454901336451933794578888718517383
880523286583078855907829709328649474930307779130447160
670149233353259221295177241128388786774520549078408290
904885240023938451622893198168501470602085151128509847
693139488958172270434529520477398814743711479981356407
706377379532601709772533306536173520127708164970028254
320945597221790994863924491269892731747332103609936329
936941664041182098181988849343235092848785486207973563
250722506249624170580133537324497706779441368256330589
311574146199521453608402911467604135346313363093882663
741045936215712567024657454530778117892595496716244637
450266870170807435944546723465282719076820144744423508

586023936530121297556367995164774531114852523780116159
596737885255533706937328418145909129593067923397173537
126594301138107435409250355856967263602659208584763208
282364655013904911208937666098659492207123033418900569
576885728938883654706375038689592429739315257180066719
762980434845985113266396112257762206819553564907814362
101431255657511996554287818352769065043906280714294062
815687412349436302651319135832669297310524913369654874
551448096217954027234786511362406029134965737448236723
187490413076559858320190234497228795515441472934215810
798942851969094350799431356033702381623082314292099291
689194298814386660647585749196314972072974744749541786
987958774059774006789282891534959828992686554525254305
813279407870800300931723873951571395981046661806959461
383364640718846408621388191341896253576267470726394602
530625840520772665538343302415373396633047464323963231
971883402025436171100149584576493206485144746231957879
768996829671143053892860029827632303667762418988493257
435433354905243296720762841352455019368587945825815488
544890350654676237955315278924775965359220198815572520
357488457327889518361923784140060992052408020575479945
461132244706515421160124087890439398110831239327019325
326570345640776085261280122996925383659076262054758436
629481532061023183468177554668393435472696544704019179
163359966669874823383897301784797733731153308788722299
063181081940441511406024389077543928755217654337404114
576177526954836571875188005730018432855562441130239645
135274172182853313766943523066061766555977632077545366
104546772479051038239976318859544905289471164833101415
482452079575058858997692963654635632322164689598722587
328616146825587567623565923159031085396780524729390556
295136210819251734888521997660747233558839655014033257
449247172824493180018936975881433074952584784341487999
637694347348294564416520287463316653555408372621707703
248037342661846954979550425329723091022889191335067273
252702254709388859891343596969332478926323861784969236
653392077096747683869761167946745609137598384881658963
921958026842007718166294148360905925025490693214579911
180132485115187747782499317674619324703056420649840704
054469986029664337314423672294763153235533765886716975
535428747194824225891594294735532805144597201763535607
581811178542247064756953554985173058462394081578187453
719873667787873049136199020959929787414301883248850950
310645559454372045703204232580949810874868811832907562
401384416114871719451138964464590981619097812802589050
554078400160292545125995949595205813554291307047393414
919138650763548257477989912699678494270982911116454913

180961968841222273176412665017526399881622488597789065
557999654685188382308865891423328379196201340436556799
230555238185510668616809684370491126404538566299364191
363772988962131809433127246434758833033974285727311212
121603916778453341559701575047949146717219103205569510
454585774211543914829906505875102588486252803102292062
922645682781371041749521599087711247555237767108566217
779242913255965775398453062228613667748954938118161289
332251244264152243564519583745090780077759665383330245
632706693246253580561265679594301582883737435027416452
526958005647641628099117352777448797642867974240192237
558213486433777910813407628822339263804663269211971125
631811920352792079507389741445122254330749917012888536
567353760973284292858415193094006368231904756648365974
103099150727156297695327798765889986840190213186799103
473653282985489077198850760707517461032119871033310139
896354148356253676340408096475422521937766919982524629
441894201229963184187534103197787296937477705023628482
996795000745079686246310862323289541215334361442492539
436510700699287563607611726641221426186290362327939293
795121454100963265485707743547469253184673367211718052
340006615713819173194793669737171532759031236571186683
656558618771284202734197934923194050552753746702608816
378006735929422482774923666758500413260000961663976381
409077514743556429289442128813505332817026125184342685
801754694751251391939389877281718774060980367431795061
826234833429005362907422674472769937545284654350834121
543735090690215152318479279256298473587153154584030461
509912906017841634277387193822338580368838367359978253
283602278570142380458713473889183629285468679287984559
619119611443193536984728784761377008958566199165547213
459667209374393832271637166759238301853596778828548622
378428454795366132840280325574680718520910693656900895
182263839085552221523136736493381384304208043741547754
620704159101040139667127445396129204444804097523284434
343716686029613476888972476463969692711349294516663387
654291921665064133508638915886943866901429903384425791
177038846082667379804670740099769815590925248136716283
955181469274602780753610524769774823502315606972240493
234856371989459360762124779552140794848952730413575230
753908044087894416028753090133695502196871178964118805
930535729713952081676978334056789799193709879909163277
561083661215601542790017675188579965009451814332844345
332123914938171095875853852999281704455071557861765072
929158827166080111401916611176826854460727158978398741 8
234817856182823913254461333201414563514069154792032515
289640219992572563691834016937324680108526701918868734

999679724308653499377716739038494955634062735682411997
151971846743751363102523092429231208039719466229895368
857856012547227932135330091424757496485617658366563524
286116274487335047197463979882218185529285496059916032
732446221615568405807860263637448569728093336072632436
480283044328048699384742771917514428381592337537314801
279485369497226584263839791711789497036062822808985373
188005307019565901723343957614026589631858194340669080
826008430184362722852627885497240397495804925917293882
431460296512773695972254968723810464145718703347392453
846023504758180827264163905668108200832698481974655018
344252211069421918772653554436393795710484710606430639
779814966266623703179817872437903441497931629926962183
068684771289392271926882503554697369661053384555696444
847058434036570989658537402677348435724415009722442658
342628043827964316072680068449380282433749010562802561
677376585532590099698591555780480328019789099637227626
288213998283184543698220083416760761843222948511911755
694777307162121562648520025844195845078468682512585118
954998942063662769684122704259230470113348599932958294
797196182668195224328119424824333513336757727435707714
866469801398163352700948417390775292069680632381331547
782281618591847979442015158597719753719850479048518282
348624494823172400122727472280455659282695347299778532
107585341347118736310024715818659028775494910253137298
463844699408797822499546940976441982889824679818644099
632255070064292541355226994163318906938774126350360451
378560230546886045073369121961388102214790640542758199
677764976243165701924037295169199680142281445315013 82
834817419941179746310977762736882793823317142061267786
762529477735430998003653931592804793789660712859094446
226271642705752962432732089858797236128226941078395657
175084224490891684687318722433349475949927351551984666
018998145516628791826602175829565065407897680279990976
075428961240499490458732704668965079584490664995348850
198323351268159990429300022579480951910330705533820756
053503831162173934303359137141426417578642888165331245
274181887211778645243828147234854208254958037928375576
330927483102596672347015554816987559810502490124110494
667673184602391596702506173145442475597711321949148009
217742751895012492071181569561412256456099163581947891
575974347097310425868136448597992091646127251027902918
083374444176803910233628270367439137752785288498484554
195305233879696721699365803096842404708029982716474728
068018323708543596401312992120705010074553075389599539
208000523619011263705246769556826912685857900560612287
273516556049871030398107339098431688142719468175263482

5851575733466349159396209376818019859567442448218459003
8232065174532487155343502906369052354755154122586932
253861455170937500958445263884662822633831228222376260
0411320262508169690196525382344059016425522894405386990
449107833075144934250510750895972966120962796065788357
441677869304129481095963060033430376598231142487695152
441087150683476985431163444560629448238137616366969627
826663912176464147549039813037819740411152680010534496
264636373727720434269977680693183732657037817578835213
689711369458563962074056613521222581518731985282733472
050082852928354576863367751166333483678095192213786681
217994404842373056149814900715533017549496691673045067
282281317334768586785517341782720924313575579388816901
245091347978406685311907421632288418644488573194316687
478747894403554845230236875553297942045375709365379168
592785363891465134999449395467185262113713472534366200
219937315956110284299333394844519509357088502587616428
942822774185617894084896778482848170393547273624173534
425554255197528605553540630170553752813248111710028799
340530026805631725859389889537268870597711746780802646
327790271734695460772867454459052025731716434367718764
784162736361619964390968559834815267113125306497970365
753081761780431270273249707879284048531241589483717482
790352499287850820677073479762354640879601427673597767
784377907430456955820957667230223622689963866064495931
131205328544635201760558799675885292179017103741207532
801038641033750495939561367575570351619849921474854684
706038794519209751544847489168672691263059234463925163
546410210473635917294732450823684357922666472572900379
893702375673420632834457140487237649440370752271498610
531855420310786968620125310966511368307822605928520449
374496074750923591391116595613396858700162602270455743
187080789147975787969798162658422018797794330374801245
123968888988285837254635992425905105476457204389988216
968435489641786892640320592776518798396708579538781749
734695925345987921447226308558102855684769516296620214
809826615600715247411839191936435194803329331651671830
355999317840513059632244541850428847170277231977400448
609353017167114368019717958265822854920333665591001399
325650170534923706063837608551668306978785149429600419
937045141665984947533487888744512619764364015687256961
084671651513986882764119957352814116687911654773526714
109762563867009403560082882453219001034802832995821337
488107496858846699239150602537733359179085704645042170
039332800223336729890662883728337846711152208643964304
959906818417332430638092396753563906450975298447267753
240385280229173980796457258696486376685624578778884559

840280957861775764809661039267597723555379639104766971
889057073270849860313315134518143457140612373859296947
756728297536275497962887954726048385493093114197644449
286968231347894835730259052639033420985577848529998871
871752747916925084494091468997898378924608999384498711
493540480407911304655614910537112381220168688287255132
453629315952339019796213966508837008933673192395262930
840026712165762025508148944894173664990334241404965567
339542696452095743341176685022383429375922575184815569
449854825464349884845455537562537893200670862766554153
149848156485055872908669635712121140800427614156787240
194921906331508852116074922531470361644473689486411855
229319794617529278864220039362060950052916170981085119
505661816878342638059189732960104400303738577327088197
791428834254606987232829197228694166894139146191379111
009150024115367147455419964776858486365292297439071726
222077039749129189578783857749127538245671431711149643
155402079121421290223742236319858983220718787593463849
908371761364896625258992887999150073666484016037409863
259353943183328436022357227153480238604355549598293484
817279189888204886290213519214358954828666309182060751
466904789443358804035286652455206746183806928324127707
194553358777084201665057989983228671794826866529523198
151094514531388226857639498881711911316897674043454646
463204413886907227422264337565237852747741689960523442
851523974460611243302798647135142764144438547400867445
049402238932738967143700505465057487918218517901511653
279332379793954986524378799290250855228178385973373901
656392038648908682559447708195159348365779836228173636
006542391078018088973121138653121157116812023662433027
999261387556991017663102618290079571779568296493148809
072048298681393735698673791221198008355707936598221144
242956526731509802337838199417625065298095722079158921
415953662274657970183146452414082907721875576751742228
489434234231461733643990051203856082847607721013962302
798439740799792884113241264908281342252263357555627739
532172638135839442655900869474521372910927967062182204
231535141609395835141001575912689582362382913635337641
292765954887872405488172965798020267074250269085271739
467012894534664166730020074437463618417395324847012763
848760585678962199634113045444177164128421695239453413
432913255230840275088954257417051698919924792520719270
993497342537140949543162733887352590796597873868023778
374290319958629891303155999099495081096948564541797302
882995487328046299524079826299143586626384176122466939
112459764504575257524381746346904416136562781175861534
843916641644220432669071385895525625735816106929046271

8034201479898469377374395117649428624586937863182212277845128276006683017409646515388612019534266586771376062816514468211075761423177216118973724288098479094391478598403482096302123534469508566645485078688115017249447994067509976625166282602588028476470652953633032053793398890445170869384671032522924331794920988854283137549030473470311687066415180337343202344148071428444610857874360653231513510948662444888818960971384529970739333707888689141675487372352862526406868560373785938627615594590949385749772074296192988955617383088511065637486575357651822637736193820011926433754444353507950786660031331156426088104755314413337322633990372295753231369637949786608198071526861060423979888541609292595374585474525350937512933719029466514341634486562662632510715817890116089844817102516900291854806258617540140513736968152602483232567126165749372431384403338941137983480710757766303458042704038374161972619180065357882534860273232869588920153331715625309496445597191626213908721271406773307976479005456880819219552227873072385382700715865997147737781893661897108737129815372223376156798320967565996389730523766774566411902831985259276393972608263319341623006707319879321548283615141217808951339138564848106460772964002970714525885522153556373810863747711871568960884767285606478891774181751498903936042474911826909521851608089586916115385523398867193459365680759557032616630595013966411250824977032129834550509123402753654335409277755394660586211190211381813560978447286990172387832048170190891664316495082458489742624188097214349564889100897610954702111739885323510977989457365379952615516933333659256305059661288732349417748475838848479291093910828738583291199741660973169146787731309939801734543894469887387183983668255881688931647399805674780686052886874008481159815529361493647057274013811827223915301369422235848166460115914373407275564713763937010658800221943875609299997816750456720965857877090288676576699439533580924202007434008226148764647751436717421704321269982096463004418070482731534918732124581572181131784042432206531750144881497065582258229354240893586330440377795941265169040664641239162787172432669149892507342718092960248276103111520264190499920937257121448158839254754859478081911621857506669956461514926813573719465070597334556413394075887772981443721766862983037765190088418246894258275174150751086141396354929219142214928923476813119181571509755225225772979844226817259726992572667435509816003854964980727586639686833174803842455725626450126850711485387140638891913979118449762396394735767304398303484311233613210863

807884812664317232597428636930261133999084971188935301
018962873077616888085601931256111620343984229522505219
085067106543421369797980064096933576130997972686523996
903090773614776842585113130954788350728134724702473760
152553963193076970532101423558358467573435763717547870
821826913297390172512390135346728683181657588524323916
436298161621303909894222934013635221631087584645147549
545507669473116143167566672956288072177719861534305719
472549832304529544365810075364056210925742874946290841
883020760277698581114934540789752512856557062271188475
143667323111848136091734553186263592372286004477677224
021818580485204971490966729868280134906881726624835949
781448826468256974301574235570815317433752289255641639
166787574251022262421007611611439338815258276344668017
591080073087805315712038057202381006486648120957726439
844506192309849437525780823814919384456429612964086174
947671711904098614992769523165524443118211220763399303
827543971930180814061585053742178541938302695489235183
330743622433099437125680179225766533719375771051874118
435807479107539328200178164222217825859758550705320171
241572553137207564835433226524105523243578847273745954
211572017851328903267824801361278849784742498387808741
797525857921767047440439410851595921448354031187987512
247202982261917459450525619363536564865929271966807890
497650834467387993855098649432722782721957830697405061
286393492394650501802333325613401014456810872847781037
337988834695999169308743424481906120796439771420326994
475365708060618578338204444254475828914084954225097501
952348611153821406480907416678423192205323296437068516
007397108094862693983161226233888048303984111588689731
929931993171527127801132820306667584324467140138651297
877836824289009877143851713447624257449935199577837367
316264801794321429994970459846403895706119105185072570
959411666716553354931876267291203640367216297013389416
573905144499128279379897655672255731125260482721730032
573248944929868229997097150944558537126409776558328442
844862213191666994272671485700841969352502999756345130
862165282864652359120583807036714175566362649499295069
844030329096365327214683643159420349807095596243659588
168458965857285851292138329773346964781518250992747262
042757492847795551469216371547276231463915745277816737
226946494958712178459658954895461972182127268206910665
520589170600080579772834777021168072127643272812954934
158034879089731776962683533536266735379439752548363799
354373359468310405664855329857744317730859849793677729
764509083759618157763234888876382885408620718838484455
234955286342409632807899891486361418345939990513549510

30825503924215864122619595903399439664266017240509787 3
36632497382804713278447476502934469828449892292059917 6
94937177658715245603279775975408710858898927554029247 7
45451354012178397138102436871872900731531865411618088 8
43940825985580525957393391543235765057101858041593654 2
39614427572088054419778854835377103089918148998611224 4
92381859121919825157889913182585993380643933579492625 7
33081405964987025345884409487185408974277184784432136 8
27710855736904304812927267444403956474425495386176769 8
55474560153497282615174952133260651761522238452449735 7
73858677974478255493333297627454874439928876855392171 8
97210714452365475376762562827195275266602352396881637 9
35818221480214233034381312386677915258011815598657073 3
34568829911772783221520658133033999961499087572165580 4
55562858602438617160405712866870825846619916252317968 8
92435820351462579395534319280553530791631247875227154 9
09842401695511983148600127659562167313303606202335297 4
78392457198385047558620318480984437541186341195952427 8
47923334959870091432871690920903053417306889604403998 9
22949731651200312337368259353967617637018883990967467 6
01413437526199185610834598655849265684551372153273532 4
24901213664927858711429494236186593219786719328796103 1
78129986152542768687435698810786527882761056573719402 7
42344483508695920119375099831615100413596285965055769 8
60949570378060792788506522405745833769900860210782100 9
53566667186837483145411905705709309198765153175319784 9
32166253941988232360393107754268930841984939280961752 1
09588408326171576889635721340678931031060439169935584 3
13364127083438462949478959300755590965069167241726212 6
68762842238016109727633408536807662756875543026805004 0
01759299792044409781401567993944523553942911161624925 8
08546720893980383716487445765353347913295030884834219 9
16603815835081255684374492021803859495766588208988991 0
81543023473843857498770061301689748998966602261039235 7
81961051795821008057534227470569066211128796520129623 1
18428849553895936795158095552392212587404835612356077 1
86554213988610053423894235212505752295000655657487245 9
44152873396204929540113311778340874070372221002381192 5
09644800152956174782130350592716749584419048386440972 8
89485319196445452099824554396483478366646356747974890 1
59371716755501073995631250587080185799514297929481404 7
33017478856995147341814299063530319588782644872926751 7
29908709205901472118850305567901065124927918061134004 8
71103969304711936325198526763871593650817522410457870 4
60107860561421298675294072516667340999772292366736433 4
67884150221648119330228326899431152897461345877335317 8
45738573857473035863734431195528556325581965147034106 8

13875463971068531702983334184915920156649631572404556735464585758148318939059789818487775649872352926758873909741669357202060458186810692045956959837416067386250638191903218059349740362092935055414021272709522931960981133955430677154807976362491354761302344696814713435221476921145907268263196923903267225851706044314749270504144809221812715954449808435197101545687547840392255599595552916816957372213966494335751905362503866922386160494257588362765677773149409799011727251860256860859931593819738129094598088197788407736829313254729444885275776445426625582933215671888687947471363161146076589754819393921391142724258797519157932935101441200523999267472205767994479685358337608851451575179144689535530854586653290486278363531278652234560336209124355356895599240866144351457644829086902387028696915794978621482491647414748384785429656866620773318278435246007198695247763167147797467117358864194020665981088765324721185099936332945134268363441284197251642605604874155330587105265203338649868475869960284754251031798802224994692082930034362704848256326268165035562723782373321910806494491779263107715564897577582533207993433528992663482391653274453101262287203787442861009605465295715547245430206552418587997557381600848659938494394314854933978529583150043352141092546284098543346739390223567534164118876155010778461653243931917727425088441022834613377297491859094578590468742156067383182880754970457934140652284575249169093221319365181110416633839907938785578187088311317527320483597644792513957356325952328864129386112996250286688133977888979573111948697759582928739410834122354634038507140635090110612585496160850633355618820662546994209315988972205578176343806773630099418634976698809640471521356577920139236913462455846697009471494398307451532380525030356892253495195888002173883894339882203931079964151211264326720107514938177028825634018965176593890121687469641937309975952239660897469127059199488247104237549739715179843024793815160814299078326593431937338912851050088120558261956054389873656285678460048766975543372684388463007120524415233169820960850611777471361947533159727117486884269350060933561900222509150830512691065864777082417645617888343170698843938292121182004273196174837557063799866985873712401525197647554335271538345747675433596703262024496268984560950512743547865083987864221234640014298038170018403996172067016771155787615191011037967796869226823692439917527436430915889463360848556584147987095943426411807330419033815783813913941717102990920616713376901645205886926826342325103455754682138229226190493470277882159

666388385906185919589687088954981101384657422550456211
423377982004825460455421273214817585859709892014491057
464493928441989437453708176950109527542931366891135672
110918574284345387171648383185314311477210938826713207
361338403480845468601285122447227063979793519196721395
023945071372586155592835445243699911538457577644622265
011621065342116667549873605382141877065325951685546519
711537002863874089444237920210753975999672380868732365
756793159547988567401260460861027042316995491726766778
941235007053634795646610307106669307282021364803851181
246571792052721073004717748597703927742610140611157856
573040838156969678140376414319465564042555150913892311
112601460506869776780991236341965609318071933283940386
184367980736832034667944724918573272749992895679791883
884992299634054663182235739963862666476411113436530202
819763243329899062959001358165820578773029651142506204
803974234142648941360314462997479772576969095642055753
569218003367426924808741411548471556885812742955211926
642922923177240827286752184732795192809616437295834567
122818309476769944096888734858389736198672546470058578
581125543391436201327837019331849273816349181185552487
679557539671715963485216952048871802990096283381920113
953244866981823228012035319754435479470844922718851474
994829551338112125248109887930133471583213543522949809
270618260710351829949673987866682596520280138742928016
886823976114347698388444774173380354824445158668446137
589257511827966370141582509824285637070307559412037244
362649067937898274775924457057612835297378541021879838
730221495451900216546341247572432448102173552893450964
236753976933728563805317457245203479940455281345932277
673856197371315442330623713651022525013390727185097967
135784445101798010768912448747372992132471813618858163
469779726048228388899181761777722740913870465592173664
111772806209212079673532967641555831664969678477015310
281015371457693214863727137816776669852430585391924153
305749161756925500564790664119150939537462518123134519
444444232776389636951438952794439590563986324312105134
089310031738011142295609808398982874592847938350296397
815643640924164232597362078086173467010878797152282436
386434868726355527655647829317898291727549315627182546
190182791774937349129946629523250531295978514644367538
021706497572653060653932485634392195092913947588365011
906067036879479656616531431100751742436543644348919030
716553312522372172484714374711453564595232870741256249
497093940410934614996860743384659101824977413602192191
248001363383831244642910984089197112524996063952885614
496140660280690398173706446532545530223964558370114995

419901082314646479443303836953172323469243898678568024
916994515224648507210425745852083744490596943117164038
707014996696247005114748132229588043831098341745905765
895210077117819954148400084136642909427684081875483706
409925736381214575457263164542048549111278754483670307
076355409690149698972540878442819166752364225384220116
507335146321249296156394358862610927026556476957344905
429618502452842753850557492544105779278288603863473417
383967236874029854933566433704342179392085733104288527
598270993847365956865133582620914572460955433464280812
908835403239228811483366398707540808600711167629363426
406205765403301636826664034173540162492974505056342372
481335985473392438724155604829657571532497396001663925
673292917625202746791337762405385636519532487267101383
719042184593959590076411347889283471581407876445696566
593046085763579604736532588543664328743973289530510868
163460350620865849889556639155184885165594394320558948
956019293148435473459633666345492726778143641374693431
288543423058454186783441488158585687580760944918670153
984130172251404298519698709015554175359247737468134336
874373511096747473529267955359761759506882483292783285
566587136414120140144102429874330427303290417356581025
570561945595884877385937470436272609020742017237276893
856855895124400958197405052748915389953640722509324905
585313024414112511251123936323287561016322754050987259
087022410230723545839069796652493199659262023569449325
927028895295825570911557367992822989726420111853669278
516244957127468379397963840536678454996754922174411758
605819229412108408486593614782938126986511393598353884
156217176409351643632580456595048468283418156983665606
801804076180809459043309197860114394395949429880782075
776876493137993318181837879433082019757337524208123051
398188067019149158489285186861936917104149334293182906
674504934804104191738258807951312729079782460952917917
085189456864345118466888241092371898884099580892005659
184821683255080473466279014660560955876462299388767719
242164702793859802292410764847381993706836041970366688
159776129133615819932270967045330412773799582051711700
332536017829880296258597974075803555569945711755524756
688523320203605734384627521328965723753743626476154078
769914160828085082206509533805539748184354911663821537
236625061880209137929460801229422254426670939960773484
018494253639910516550544277715524590958410805833392274
796551595732846097588739653014087074246507991109103486
744297597457754660634003293781736153539337794965522253
204333276346879944831674006979292727364758657373935742
770365824735866465614420532788582727004947672890608590

1978346120868637582056702412514691099018730494741663812
82970640860879607089307094757258944042795678570251542
84683952212756403743734628602634511847226036280077631
06070913752741831764417578930545520289845658643539421
85351167815858530624662902379911109607522801358673259724
61975351651939803933913037806314223570275100263821525
95619051114329874715085488698409253046766376428295405
81322314632481248692446245867115416801343558144436675587
76549033569355526905815937926298203657866710501037901
76475632021450073660602963160716537158066234156352529
69252089284247335988925917208794876387290989245776043497
38410718112182326144677287204640559112403161405969693
30965702084587530930864967674443541397132685526637875
64582578642102772693800228625546634950669805722644829206
15426265118089045940483087527921764362933838623192536
32502857042029970773848461613206306739826386153632350
93696407396149196211971285266177965719501925123847688385
64348398584790990273793863549743328860173316983899126
88403190508890268189304346266846967652156562790596349
79511536337320034832288730583564767644279469462463993519
87287222020129276892207868600305786145514374790436433
21822592213865495542216348286620788189245387954848467630
41247585345973250620460565885683035322718438444094220
99866602417952183141561142577571136613296173832658531
79185359872496093404173768875913820195981277919552322413
16411956014728404254507008905404140022811959005148828
46245687649609502065107971673407578043381156118164415
32375788865233214947862606117606297895282642217842344252
28244967932205102632888694853268729679009964866869895
69073517343024979033226171840236007419052633119923183
51830955910797642442811558851057919789335977459455898822
32614553465004558157545883354453435167687734629057339
76678205327429233621496453993295041470012853575302475
72415346975392874716063363295355411346333617363578988352
25999343066079434425217636758897275768952342091625680
91298790234988596033543557329496605242059791895122261
09581609248246845876674227189893160740789144207098166716
13733142325578400403856210295956400887856500744572780
22788984266245432331027433068074889905978781783032821
92269932978972319242543455471805492171652636476458118621
64511585886765161503678519139175078990626109215462911
38899803353218138624648465754818929211109057990031476
92716223451591547466906054444868685370925125299628844680
45659523171558103025985147235625577888056325356163856
52602973389217651616770668423981800357003793098583578
55038584062115655908671234793761378999123617810215267561
975681148798771910338513733705156755357191035938050780

04155553987390121646495804062318320643852473625634869 7
33214870462754728059438737179823237440084959786269272 8
69640404231604772152980918343397781340467989015703603 1
73638236163831831037793826000591036811604416389020722 8
42282216970985903799625551920676849775747910369702725 7
60509321581931214799919630442307768591653442955589055 7
25378511747752946542187628007262952573450507215997818 3
62884519807925004757386749424330241041625012743128565 6
42647469039099586284821421634189866970957435179356580 6
18430414295530951011845532263518753177290008403819775 8
54430146633106638716350709722118541741394934841632161 4
85173264393315213803433933278793616385396937705319139 0
80791906246497219730598336957761651884871776953153851 9
62850995298016974516277824438676213536852246634056901 4
73745288752399216163051820968019417693849781768224466 6
44495758577760360791969600339782740026749952142443072 1
33074366586533322489655344983250123122135146027270809 8
17888199413045111485303789766787992214989513635705579 3
41955773748001953708206805633189919937344950401283241 8
88695228564678322099260468440332898428493933182893375 7
15641909605809319635851298221972315771015127317639968 6
64074451110216052573838086893057242265159262806093429 9
80294471560270835491771970526126160691849806997136490 2
97596104825578278405431225823657622480254933165827650 7
27602478373146536800845743586894992387823180879801323 3
06715812447163217845574125966967601555160188718856653 6
36203809338513618632813684793669124739323852028750626 1
94386563227160551576495164660080797473457936581732018 2
18067270509189811991790656511335228380566556035734138 9
65039139645100923950088521723661391634888948406538233 7
25363794758945964606165270135222846784917146697389221 6
89511325457706621929865334570641146592930875936862649 9
79210293816817001793030846642259998451495085588373446 8
85854601583634100249652442635192449776671638557922325 6
64777254905681161792101926334063613322170896656137447 4
27743099510883594221453414002284017813109728475632999 6
30166348064968089225180287830853900986927591127525623 5
47290515400165940571792938121652352840714419075555126 8
73506637869803807196358267569002159306398166877459628 5
48732064896079926406417485417781775958360427897132490 6
51651308914784445830850940639972738356623434837178507 8
35390352124246703417728961404555201308221682770646982 6
01958053049113907246197731623533844581230319807219120 3
62981297911643576941915582223432785852223909075203051 4
94735430814201652865481736764174407829975847414322079 0
27027467795286536818847473751010082491785244296653589 5
89748623167479741689835809921173336613427361728957601 5

6505524877676590072770922468580693216422164119897704850
3856519625644825013569587261425995593641417687739992410
1567725062319881468541380117551736005876567301354847880
5934496079314963051548118546371521207988915413698948940
9947417458668266708393150932338766625023082467080668210
5732270107631920935922125551942201655976940572085172590
5261810208385994529915714522926124193679031737275537530
6101136085105409748487392469253358213637206507232378800
7315785947825836818909263426355254464487417691373453860
4877056099953122899471023257051362055807953188181355590
6412257444075532679224881722119171166853520471298843680
6092477321809392491879910528097919238178741925153321250
8462950874816238246827793534416974711246187207384567750
9742749585011175831212194734323818669261916377854342000
0591496218110337671645792645287766401835059436800899410
2962111845239927145695728050559971269825449908528841750
5476137885160396178559618250713197280431595690413678900
2759641301350015436149509230782168634432264064664641660
5488465283989388361881836678341334715541827397948652520
2436588343960977951788731055056483781331882129412836330
1723091277020782161059931536280186156278188973953366540
9115681417390553959856120054059511780098090081972975860
2045009955964693264236092934956993294795918615842050960
3586867584541100458725602300572211968847290637957561700
6993297947817994260563119341578388267281812875479152760
6692962250134155248680828479754346875028651321935295790
7552825132055055609887253463276661933733806639300065660
0498036961653209900964992752519797074682604456874424610
1088401095418296526125370388414513771955839313220554230
3846399293443960186776059555598346841782524083460045920
0812451372254557836478749980029079182662739369982984260
6327408815649577176557001274798253097201324548939900180
1966637271363665450687471663790337411685793950598571550
9909846005154629148170416501963435181004893730572904800
0023579023673149174731521109975934167014720854383959060
1742772705115585991118587226549715456739994482548846800
0086970976877854083172191125327421032705257161076828580
2971294648185936258675779633478395286989994501960156110
6943478190246156560128131258176888454117754924126760490
5839088681561684460424866521666004445336401841614286780
6309861346596697455826828370519852533204056351039250570
2911376269906163478283155955929225350625812442435525850
3456272039399393074543972052853123570626116516476314830
8404819998587299007446918611550724333178628972648864660
8871921889679696131332421667126127705305447971957186180
6702739519684102499896198903593370884735277321202348840
4593534623101130711724495305186502944551167365597525070

1435734249109360005998682508292202662627642082756188985817726044682047980645503237694228552714995975210526606442121478888558189135384124529991372209956429111844232749166977969956237009780944028014652297062362725457243658623635856624847787386864171639893783919743256848917356239917387765394146084913988322810799117829369062225097882981736297042723953759558132566517950197949289973469174139009637557050701464126184200440057765749845378040274016482925646058700779016443065182542999039254814152533719655222736046976006341481590699740462865806972730665666879418537560174041956681237384051404271418546838839192433088851039469823177115495298295873069936248418858209369975776056974691974559162155770992584582356846176612360002526993453801001835396973162771677271964780454148007438595598352365134315688727827050381266919193257734621938252648088321526481949657939704279856537970259956215164783740239201332631680619613698563038785825508459913047661887684122085573153696129719741280367342726389107403747181118456677796229757578840597194378106836396506289241303127818101518676266209600912655739340487004589281434088193351828597561876821380787557330317410214953326887699898497194096189734534228358149915531705664536052048232268087566475588686470573246421938563844289120025120228353062629096074484214355519536987355343273623436247380037461467803894958856757230590834963333313853686943791951158640266811226473953558377632446322314281480364068894633762309406969289227527949687325916990239545345823055481396263296158182356185394530249282779551899008337234544470049984621572271700634117859975476528178542864283788285316317950038238359449354263334728185155471453713855651366706417771060248091338076488604667188525899775773739421789207869381391025064827201245784406205385483843725254687149976821509567498934440417799498981917479134147612086628868420290377281746473726551790985706631856136909770084268907811607610416449681473646290912891621177636518261612495106796805794527441819105300119215005472559450496125515653390401374631956446166091792035628451162109382156379968763477690735010271392121719622054427278238981057072375096531989024593817567406268239684251124420317487776326206471334315467976255745994314911594448831951951188659729373581718965486134160606200189958623611338170996926574273871305910868595567522832558807691376917244377796675563534089704166631790592928693903107839628285218120261366460288924165048759356575015279677875479279973189604606729251141396343277235652327428313013373259241469826106375249111949532075662274726228699830904971501353271339

31827915494162844704017789285903976415572133284043297027315299337996476309801370774550224514674024259093461078115100461470351162259154887337206539710403825531857299467312495991705707928684200954124335855113194024302029373091947236814969810349999525116958590127621469138172826273314914892415874390035027688779240856930184961928714589033867156811398531168439556278095458194841784035253885721534448485391769961565100845603294057431435470268644213388281440116752941614793916466289331135100490543484047234490867349751762914034723271158424755146632953697113139759838919846345177765957618707268335508616869895036850679992383476142481577312403953532905918013028115677571562339499183487807056307261296428498168523716294783777241101488496780665323699525906143104359122257701530545140297693511855461286354758951366338291060984433431641568507481920638896418931103242311839748853920268237088209615131176935455845045743956323014992170745906646975254596777390443895206793702178879651209030960407177933171648415829536987784862362719342236870699580740932663442890470494953112351077155609707364659127408881089999974806565979136927827135357754372352935551556163987811208311626102890593369904190308588203778507601629902957357591196686185194275263605469657883677392048796491798468718029907541635375789358886983692879643169097124968383787455190022989951779883713762401128464736425161176161698949323617251182115118258301529817507677765817998450177377353734740523314445545532554239392534841804732400301944452939988369921215961546770281831149686519619720102704829955992663685842467533424277481605543440571448259322661851368126401906220336677850670311652622841343855666226560704831806141236592598208492751148787974578590775302942305314269045026458499333558253506743187115127370509885196271677148706494815365662753492524896254146889726774188167711628238255529093890521150283974298088679460198948379823687641496843268112264087836223911798383124561892629361827458721170762446388494611373608124273787077432222811266307333853640130054992484212736110018690410545263150990867572809244009056540532254134727692946582170976660772050696180548478927100300259234254631324637939482913620143955565852255744796413329917196547663611881610625191354295957345994207845620254201555492205523202589428579151490423269008571823638364685023483176027777310849191869835547028459381458250633219557489449238532956654489547295822519497211195832805548606455393911554872741502592636493375289896688234584442957221162139433761986092015282117091114051759882642812272648698184473564129025915866584009455

145162418764622951517163013676928873173741280139861185
817499277807092368119780561942473120960600084449163867
138651857288756495486428596511129667639206358472124045
679017364602730015320523619084068533533633590033892906
352357185315240176185484137946523513116362774696239462
736461060130442635600779681546917885148687585788390828
198360597798650286310041549797214560843747006523231612
973983889830408126439372348973980318369574127721135103
109996694484914442075215490849310438678836668998714908
079369165472834570290854497340880979860626936023128966
820908131211857934100524452902150625230466227296904561
706339598340465495363382812702725111866915538260952916
748000948802984792188304694530363212802018152265178039
732234333423502424215360869667281162902473612909267455
048660733296750914169630583853540138288937170811858796
442531099280204125595295216292358580344547308884872281
655571710207957458814636032860577916984863687017559195
279130079905949547415138342306491199575818416549411751
560653358578150608381711253458905428287622042114495734
681814255454592786851073173954470434906836178468980797
672092147863331826934092431277508375058682319090032461
608728789487250044163668118976082463274401384257977356
803674774410176180685352725514565012285916921222457689
623184933730006702393320185491742263918747383292546267
672607214030172333766414155822540866450985497857502692
367533943273593633567678467985567911961688925393046779
491659533799217895789120543772818573979297200671123940
021010149561236114430313365510195667519641419413083151
071640619416907940306771972803607420668332486271149391
542911325383634558124715934753769513163177511482716583
295705710120309777367727755111278676653295066289751546
614366573051379979849364412723899214485372302246540429
799231327983601531862416577809163265645549903861856512
712130211949342975222353838883159411221042639645562285
831969841268731917195027067854629760090174848935537226
137108867548246816876005139173359366769451786202699692
184899445912599411796948094659285888865731459168115320
033580021856538150974189857286189028231538376809422641
121177629487320694790966268763601553235624916784520067
830871658058981265576540114137337179976634655152317954
946548691998763206752160713061533129643453159299206373
404879967076915898248616221065401256878138865622926054
392675309934913388563520375633713422641840113741966111
779829214883144692368669739430432356142203151021860466
082837042307558197081123375569598611593707370887840879
179860291673716406601058392514174976990357660140854916
728928529807507356661695563076826829328570774625028958

726780987332772138653226312958656224958283297278355892
417164337953107663338364443374924748246009681145282110
359813116877349258444106689754464607957642327256345781
060337955584703136264051894560814333239473808561473720
011373305759568575847344188849896870703845823783637085
513230804785383626691378039044105165348724971669588918
957334766965065555715765724776122772198183197141490789
264235298834296627096225624315582833019493922344975671
910004287345854103397425059213883190576002556742940429
363460816596749995857723439341259891577785698003163330
873080294121772532650387463523254391333947278927921640
605856041995146844095083202744997116351531381961774837
641315983553635987850145414184899945256973714136087857
874253230643014559052098495619508914879778900222984095
001747604195877681820320443172613710169236730382248764
428900849411589843532027267538115283687642392966204619
517873352383373754344300958652379312702848228967342744
591280012798931648684967274930590386806866192729778427
303545947256926786280784460247085614270745245952328669
627662301253634081089383480657131722890971731563179337
298816271835109893597448396828325646534814446145608165
337056869383817674671861774648356520228324967160793764
668482602382683952775459326198564803042430239435017946
828217645953349576763947764542205878106792100271597450
433468475587533258178009562442379191989454853054378331
237542332775599558901802799163576791111948104283740131
476948612375809803775559936604575989553170927556314952
449580583497789784597525521972235680621913611394967148
182403370188860615356068334481189872586495538139141819
913524520021036645385424191769199370583291555687804891
337632724148537265495505232168025205169996864547342777
690713857952297201726719831951279387926596748820115571
094271182610148391403237761597086323616725939889101254
709139577088239577164739333086938331273057289702134965
834725597842217057971566108802467921007555514167597162
113271167529355571490514895110431809407461323686055609
460844196644685256122890132998540232282849131018387341
557244465761497595810140643253805808949725319007870902
601103891204526486123466210218444028932175862577734236
969313185786943173276124910653198129037985895694777345
045720241610060528870968019341305592793338873188547785
749872167690519424360494279482229298307114443420799551
173578844171837485590124270618377002030496384975137857
953181848108170133834095233913267255764114922356670129
624593306318906035938726178763771135897676299479297142
467987464999495444252242675571063873952638533154565340
251185269531078864802436634465193976061372531425988576

415492828610915173237875671174090225220719841461182149
798494746913290843480831241104161235330467079996149287
517505962927422419848935858200577835749623538932063565
103677264900490551434879169150552795182023427697685671
771473466044336425567033831772696677963533156378963870
201762636117635511763302050743536706201245057900071837
353172062665595400037152092810422363191257472186875631
588974986146740991200469833747972159111166137047190743
426279898286847729528309819685257778504928386805571571
111254453052711785582989766237459103746812813753928561
764929864282968286490526761115769757411465849281693238
891896435677095380669613784366656814490750949846641925
012169028272453750310797380287332333838681953025613194
507061877370731320465910571719253386266335760283577552
031250494419049563784519798103980771709431588906707856
235292169651187515553039763354980246744265483888727337
477371649814634927312549764851330378824905904646909312
023529937195011616325779716464314165044122858587259922
563494523224042796317655586999871249351342083369521677
433862531988595193184533254766666549566575757017768331
267910187861850774450487854913461386924245468266981788
844345181952246746158312788372386545887438368850184671
561217545687478969659361659490787252145640777808815790
750406947001529081833396507911648394570243860873729797
113451818750353894705166893490304052780203787384483613
774551826863722633184491873744133533251826643990017834
843834746741992564736361734389631163756299978799280387
737333075362424135388336271994461421256706597950906620
840718237903540619099407549834914154773370373485256985
317549719214492221153398730880400375278224545636154615
141966886503242169251289182757409722203264403303807836
422970332239126188523659395791698907702911425138573786
324332725849872372573630797787319883964138575498764753
745960350279857536833017993505420423571628845111086729
320895627909324750998237095338784208707146825377468994
825881042877674264947959855414140162210798587514269527
654895646467082950497637036498279877414038791038742541
978895826268789410846449758144236618712539823182130849
618867636591940567513914828547274369989888396427499989
817111971543536246480481709155242337949637314325714668
926182645646964271311724770358855077725571034311211508
984257971980449441606270956132630708888614219726087121
258139615756025398428064068563861186957222422393690485
380318206262918469827213213464677334969952020145102996
356514452498830978006408771532395682362237793452537674
435485896193368527237997403387726871458156700793280229
151309367504083362761703821753848158651785277537451274

571988895065580996528483738383797782012430414834133921
696865585996130252839348220643692587409550604659465095
596813369690796038823397407559741589865263632506719776
521668033452241952095968973337581769921613866899426248
260810733934654633837788619540784955730494741836115291
008166979476213049002303080826024948779989205425964454
120402188307000834640784556521928017974473267573731304
744847148097328585602784373740058367943550871442599675
028858665746817888470919096360228564234598540114756965
230290910935423373753711287233883273205479629896702219
413731368430832201176865897415130559319733226877149743
161907290989877396945911541918164526302865464253857348
381797510466289839992783374954295998415617973171828950
754264411673831321259856270405471985491849122853974124
984798711735904746607441571164983559841507428399631636
325571121804584848582912659294283467786446348263975597
171559683568874084831350498644362986269849475643663203
698025641488332541538720666610544926673815830639235003
737664417330120338880449483228045404112889609132621846
691297576284128834749978740061145716625754380274845667
718557892586402334164412722695372658268873980512889558
478779340809336975055612856979913326171773906476303396
456716160353496354512364719652212337533418931878890949
629793533976421897840182464272423244415411370108044121
496336293616357052863497423442377552617278062929146451
256336260927489904230584811236430211802315997795937784
726944628722651472961341777413873102718076173388340952
906021345083071639026718979612951152459241916556570384
849005689413994032162194382144699655192527927814383428
742774639795616251288314392431535279390126821577184675
814493244384551144970947886702886880781623185073279720
685536575779326916516469928039367592461305592397518483
154929334981095425597863177664098735498698150514982003
073183711395339098154726936568953694630582474751448025
258580073493351095059056777730351312529290962931262241
515703358377345883890599262146814349860216759446865247
431803132259767655810365618587781307622019184094673323
144564307898633262581886282010947414435823101139315092
522214476416940271511665410854303931444533724727335077
095664529718639244234416516281148486068542851382831633
673920788765845647065134177566444305175380302260866942
735682425866171754550560610232363738355881628453751145
030926293836193583968550977562030499667242780909058366
312646514150036108276224967864401555612290143335292964
306654721292148181448522165551962418364228226598847320
419704215297605708064016237882668929283124465773011459
297830451075397415846661266844566943365309689974202575

4776323309757961734841368150515860191317501235891116686
0666281816310716380536794366723110159290143996064275330
16845970714110197486649054243021961619595830987418508
890441784674737469544877219737382628500671016060411675
696290491374685936980187329893379657591934401125500125
081508720272873108329173655612305943409706247611034591
933513612442294038333286028058061692281033805066783927
167539846511606308448827514687124418589352483051630885
409400751408459012698479873631565766437714430935309131
572259822615642596935260094634541548906316983940414922
293550927787334514607288719917427122757731837337681737
969723626743177984699703458127146150276536383807664792
398866109632282959584837824267553637132009682834661928
052143394720387423746873444435172173132168059072422496
107291411692313664402725207673151566470993062799073329
481267596729592738187178662402757474650438377673015545
618164988582957849742506177233928759185769383819207892
393012887709091690782819446326584294654872148752499421
228058155589091738708903372266653122325932709782823723
606463724437711339761547229474442184532768414725583798
356844744800221414026026054541131197662308032157526085
857173575046256469196581670314623706952559697291285933
103371090168577846685586068381271460412566780509721142
093946208813801593471247896314369626956676853203229887
888648202409547077675610588913129205627579964448411841
731362413442400150430333892360831232465049710016487602
971793863726976515805948226045778127507741620645601547
175458518272269236882480409211273651576783358622613870
184247973964795890566587131558411548669965056713023122
691781452990326332566791506910668798508429791160349157
704823606655427754694371242037311798549538161751247717
022499271309582117026165371982235614924493938624497052
763956132172713933233621951776204763664396473407116681
441598543387523638188875971674856497044286955168449521
659704589154393137617685051431344086373525258642471427
601235866568954651132344892856185189076811465533722099
533356676905678638093375512129600237598045008846241922
470613457604578808940564818712050316256952605206375588
426995499433976770212096128346027260241553212426788880
929692728791687083689784495706953063256509789597807167
855786962419411283255536264670619508968794107457860501
738231187354552877789198318051552796386663672247955653
482367129742501156068572785952128349847498340810448633
897897147427211885818297891184957067889294983228494201
107362741129471796748221117431114614913706112491265476 4
381305726179610427578335448586641794721261209868813890
305722893884183721327340384835472347006682900575643501

789564782368054311434008835710028529816373667206896881
736955787235990938956637835164146062216575523989267015
955471344122946689253978015968440514648410266937829434
268368242992870586453615401894835332143377340556816113
262359702439561627013431433492353026860295947799535403
472793298087862189017243918672336816095653744301770344
498908482880212768078893765571632362611687488577297709
565839038182538775812536365922789996479302166032286775
561647839754728007592699791919144494996003920510168465
709513042273814255032912393514656836481478556706223932
783158520509709167213187877887677626971779676299556959
873350897439457637480265524572359453796449676946216455
622973728732932391114641868963769992957819332399840408
133623954944406713169524538285134172740327876792917116
316955500748369335539603191862724117736808828989434596
657156174998932717362474781248039563548044165103895267
611941822736641830669047201352416681580174171253200259
737316659887823791185975585517418806133055684944894486
826315222615061536593743805574035738934974419933488944
183892336419622727340519054321816318982352494168655262
586574500780415926562721796902997447086362348647921086
158298829791953626918372087966771177478221628035618893
843317608437987016637128590607

Bree won again and made Mark sing along to the cellphone ring tone version of Alanis Morissette's "Hand in My Pocket."

• • •

Greg didn't answer his phone. Just after I hung up, Dad called. "Your mother's left me for some crazed dyke."

"What?"

"You heard me. I've been ditched for Fred Flintstone's fetus."

"Dad, are you drinking rum and Gatorade on the livingroom couch with the lights off?"

He was.

"Dad, she hasn't even known the woman for fifteen

minutes. She probably went out to buy groceries and you're misinterpreting it."

"She left a note."

"She did?"

"Dear Jim, I need the passion and intimacy that only a woman can bring to my life's journey. Please don't judge me harshly. And don't forget that tonight the seedlings need their root booster growth formula."

"I'll be right over."

When I got there, Dad was in the living room, lights out, in the process of switching from orange to green Gatorade, but there were no labels on the plastic bottles. "Dad, where are the labels on the Gatorade bottles?"

"I may be pissed to the gills, but there's no way I'm going to pay full retail when I can get bulk powder at Costco."

"Jesus, Dad—are you cheap in your dreams at night, too?"

I looked at Mom's note, blotched with damp spots from melted ice cubes. A dismal and baroque scene. I'd just sat down on the sofa beside Dad when Ellen, the stalker of yore, scampered across the lawn, wearing a bright pink Gore-Tex pantsuit and shaking spruce needles off her purse.

"Just tell that pesky bitch to take a hike," Dad said.

I went to the front door and called, "Ellen, we saw you."

Her head popped out from behind an azalea.

"Ellen, today's not a good day for stalking. Dad's really depressed about something, and whatever you're up to, today's just not the day."

"Oh. Okay. I'll come back tomorrow."

"Thanks, Ellen."

I came back inside. "Did Mom say where she's staying, Dad?"

"No."

"Any phone number?"

"No."

"Did she pack a bag?"

"Nope."

I was mentally scrolling through all of Mom's infatuations, living and dead, all of whom Dad was clueless about. "If she didn't pack a bag, how long can she be planning to be away? Relax."

Dad was inconsolable. "She's been so pure and trusting all these years—and me bopping every little crumpet I share a gig with." He gulped a few shooters, then passed out, leaving me with the job of tracking down Mom. I phoned John Doe. "Hi, John."

"Hi, Ethan. What's up?"

"John, I need to track down my mom, and I think she's visiting your mother's place. Something about fertilizers."

Silence.

"John?"

More silence.

"John?"

"Oh dear."

"Why are you saying *Oh dear*?"

"I've seen this happen many a time, Ethan. You might as well accept the fact that you're soon to be my stepbrother."

"What?"

"Ethan, once my mother strikes, she becomes an irresistible force. Your mother is powerless. Oh dear, oh dear."

I faked naïveté. "You're nuts. She's simply getting information on boron phosphate hydroponic fertilizers."

John sighed.

"Where does your mother live? I've got to go see my

mother, or my father's going to pop a vessel," I finally admitted.

John gave me an address up the coast, at the end of a one-hour ferry ride. "Ethan, I'm coming with you. You'll see why when we get there."

The ferry was almost empty. We thought we'd try to get some work done at sea, but instead we bought Sunshine Burgers and slept in the car on the car deck. We were honked awake by the ferry's bullhorn.

The drive up the coast was glorious: ferns, massive cedars, a sparkling sea flecked with eagles and seagulls. I noticed that John, however, was clenching his fists. "Uh, John, what should I be expecting here?"

"I don't want to colour your perceptions, Ethan."

"Jesus, John. What are we driving into—*Planet of the Apes*?"

"Just don't try to give a clever answer on any topic at all. Any."

"Come on."

"I didn't change my name and identity for nothing, Ethan."

We forked off the highway onto a secondary road, and from there onto a tertiary road, and from there onto a quaternary road, finally ending up on a weedy, overgrown lane, which went on for a half-mile through an alder forest and ended in a small cul-de-sac covered with mulched bark chips. At its end stood a chain-smoking dwarf clad in purple nylon, her ears aglint with silver rings. She saw John coming. "Oh, it's *you*."

"Hello, Yarrow."

"Who's that?"

"That's Ethan."

"You're gay? Finally some good news from you."

"Not gay. Just here to see Mother."

"Right."

We passed the enchanting Yarrow and headed towards the house, a hundred-year-old dump sheathed in long grey planks, the structure beginning to sag into itself, and decorated with a collection of colourful nylon vaginal motif banners. What had once been the lawn was a tangled meadow. Trees didn't look so much naturalized as they did homeless.

I asked, "Is that Yarrow with a capital or lower case Y?"

"Actually, it's capitalized. Long story."

Inside the house John called out for freedom, but there was a nobody-home feeling. The place smelled of eroding fabrics and vegetarian cooking. The coloured crystals and knick-knacks everywhere highlighted my sense that here, people could stop taking their prescription medications without fear of being judged.

We looked out back and spotted a circle of maybe eight women sitting in sun-bleached Adirondack chairs. Mom was at the far end and saw me. "Ethan! Hello."

She came over to hug me. "You're so sweet to drop in unannounced like this."

"Mom, what's going on here?"

"I know what you're thinking, Ethan. I haven't become a lesbian. I just think it's really important at this point to explore my she-power. freedom is a good teacher."

freedom came over. "Can I help you?"

"Uh, hi, freedom. I just came to visit Mom."

"We're busy."

Mom said, "freedom helped me collect from that fellow who sold me bum seedlings. She didn't even use a gun."

"She helped you on a collection? I could have helped out, you know."

freedom cut in, "She didn't need you or a metal death penis—just a bit of confidence." She put her arm around Mom's waist and kissed her quite luxuriously on the neck. "Do you have business here? We need to go back to our circle."

Mom said, "It's Uterus Week. You can't imagine what I've been learning."

"I'm sure I can't. Can you at least phone Dad?"

Mom looked unsure. "No phones here. freedom says I need to be away from my stifling home environment."

"How could home be stifling? It's never stifled you."

"Ethan, you're always so critical. I know—here's an example—doors."

"Doors?"

"Doors are *very* stifling."

"How are doors stifling?"

"Inside the house here, the bathrooms have no doors, and it's a liberating feeling to be in them, it really is. Doors are nothing more than flat wooden burkas invented to keep women from feeling proud and fallopian." She looked behind her. "I have to get back to the circle. I know you'll figure out something to tell your father. Bye, dear."

Yarrow snickered as John and I walked back to the car. As we drove away, John said, "You can't say I didn't warn you. Now can you understand how I got to be the way I am?"

I grunted.

"I know," said John. "Let's go out and buy a statistically average meal from a large multinational restaurant chain. That usually fixes about seventy-five percent of life's problems."

In a weird way, eating a Whopper did feel vaguely retaliatory, but as we left the restaurant, I realized I was forgetting something. "My new coat. Crap—I left it back at your mother's house. Kaitlin'll kill me if I lose it. It was a present."

John stayed in the car, engaged in a stare-off with Yarrow, while I ran in. I looked around but couldn't see it. I called out, "Mom?"

One of the women pointed upstairs, and so up I went, taking great pains not to accidentally look into a bathroom. But when I glanced into a bedroom, there she was, naked on her stomach, while freedom, clad only in a pair of boxers, gave her a back rub.

"Oh jeez . . . sorry." I backed downstairs, with Mom yelling, "*I am not a lesbian, Ethan*!"

I found my coat on a table near the front door.

As we drove back to the ferry, John Doe insisted on listening to Top 40 on the car radio while I tried to digest the afternoon's implications.

"Isn't Yarrow a freak?" John asked.

"I can't say I disagree."

"She's my sister."

• • •

Kaitlin thought the day's field trip was a hoot.

"It's a phase, Ethan. She'll get over it."

I wasn't so sure.

We were back in jPod, staring into Evil Mark's cubicle. "It's so clean. So ordered. I bet he makes his bed every morning."

//called each frame and updates camera position based on position of its target and the current camera cut void GmMsCameraFollow::vUpdate(TReal rTimeDiff)

```
{
//	vUpdate2(rTimeDiff);
//	return;

GmMsPosKeyFrame *poCurrentDesiredKeyFrame;

poCurrentDesiredKeyFrame = m_oCurrentCut.poGetCurrentPosKey();

m_oActiveKeyFrame.vSmoothToKeyFrame(poCurrentDesiredKeyFrame,rTimeDiff);

//get a pointer to the target GmAcActor *poTarget = m_poGmAcActor->poGetTarget(); ASSERT( poTarget != NULL );

//get a pointer to the camera actor
GmAcCamera *poCamera = (GmAcCamera *)m_poGmAcActor;
ASSERT(poCamera);

if (
poPhantom &&
(RealAbs(poCamera->rGetLookVerticalDesired())< 0.2f) &&
(RealAbs(poCamera->rGetLookHorizontalDesired())< 0.2f))

g_bGoToBox = True;
\else
g_bGoToBox = False;

m_nUpdatePositionOfCameraDelay++;

AtMaPos3 oPosTarget,oPosPlayer;
AtMaVector3 oLookPos;
TBoolean bUpdateTarget = True;
//set camera offset from target and look at target
GmMsPosKeyFrame *poPosKey = &m_oActiveKeyFrame;;

//get the desired look and at offsets
poPosKey->poLocationAt()->vGetVector(m_oAtOffset);
poPosKey->poLocationLook()->vGetVector(m_oLookOffset);

//update the camera's FOV
poCamera->vSetFOV(poPosKey->rGetFOV());

//get the current vectors from the actor
vGetVectorsFromActor();

//set our initial destination position to be that of the target
poTarget->vGetVectors(&oPosPlayer, &m_oFwd1, &m_oUp1, &m_oRight1, NULL);

// BVOL prediction and Rising
{AtMaVector3 oTemp;
oTemp = oPosPlayer;
oTemp.vSub(m_oState.m_oLastTargetPosition);

if(RealIsApproxZero(oTemp.m_rZ))
// If the player's Z position hasn't changed,
// then slide the box up
{oTemp.m_rZ = rTimeDiff*400.0f;}
else
// If the player's Z position is changing, leave
```

Kwantlen College Learning Annex
Course 3072-A

Assignment: Discuss Your Notions of Good and Evil with Somebody You Consider to Be One or the Other

"Through Darkness and into Light"

by Kaitlin Anna Boyd Joyce

Mark Jackson, thirty-ish, works with me, designing videogames. He has typical geek attributes, the strangest being a need to have everything in his immediate environment be edible. He has a marzipan stapler and Post-it notes made from sour lemon chewing gum. More importantly, Mark's in-office nickname is "Evil Mark," and frankly, where there's smoke, there's fire. Let us explore this:

Kaitlin:
Why are you called Evil Mark?

Mark:
It's ridiculous. You said that my personality was boring, and so then Bree [a co-worker] decided to arbitrarily call me Evil Mark. And then last year your boyfriend, Ethan, caught me looking at something on my computer monitor, but I was able to hit QUIT before he saw what it was.

Kaitlin:
What was it?

Mark:
I can't even remember.

Kaitlin:
Oh, *please.* Something shameful?

Mark:
Why does it have to be shameful?

Kaitlin:
Sometimes you can be so sucky, Mark.

Mark:
Gee. Don't tell the media.

Kaitlin:
Tell you what—I'm going to throw guesses at you until you crumble and tell me what it was you were hiding. Here I go: cunt-o-rama, cumsicles, golden age shit-eaters sucking Satan's teat . . .

Mark:
Stop!

Kaitlin:
Getting a bit too close to the truth?

Mark:
Why does it have to be something shameful?

Kaitlin:
What planet are you from?

Mark:
I am *not* evil.

Kaitlin:
Perhaps, but then why won't you tell me what you were looking at?

Mark:
For God's sake, all right. I was looking at new treatments for . . .

Kaitlin:
Yes?

Mark:
I can't tell you.

Kaitlin:
Don't wimp out now. Kleptomania? Pedophilia? Bedwetting?

Mark:
!!!

Kaitlin:
It's bedwetting, isn't it?

Mark:
That's ridicul—

Kaitlin:
!!!

Mark:
I did it back when I was a kid. It's nothing to be ashamed of.

Kaitlin:
It's not that you wet the bed, Mark, it's that you can't discuss it, and the fact that you'd rather have everybody here in jPod call you Evil Mark for almost a year, instead of simply telling us to screw off and deal with our own problems.

Mark:
It carries such a stigma in our culture.

Kaitlin:
Maybe you could turn it around and work it to your advantage. I bet there are all sorts of people out there who'd pay for you to come visit their house for a . . . *nap.*

Mark:
Thank you, Kaitlin.

Kaitlin:
Do you think there's a connection between your childhood experiences and your disturbingly undecorated cubicle?

Mark:
Probably. I've never thought of it that way before.

Kaitlin:
What about a connection between bedwetting and your having an edible mattress?

Mark:
I doubt it.

Kaitlin:
Michael Landon, that guy from *Little House on the Prairie,* did a TV movie once about bedwetting.

Mark:
Little House on the what?

Kaitlin:
It was a 1970s TV show.

Mark:
I don't watch shows from before 1990. Otherwise, you could spend the rest of your life watching TV. The TV archives are too big now.

Kaitlin:
He was this guy with really good hair. Anyway, in this movie, his mother hung his bedsheets out the window when he was in high school, and he'd race home after class to take them down before anybody could see them. He became a championship athlete as a result of it.

Mark:
Can we change the subject?

Kaitlin:
We're supposed to discuss good and evil. How does this relate to the game we're all working on?

Mark:
In what sense?

Kaitlin:
Well, we're supposed to be building this sucky fantasy game with elves and rinkly-tinkly lucky mushrooms and stuff, but what we're really doing is secretly embedding a monster inside the game who will come in and pervert the game into a total gorefest.

Mark:
It's a great idea, isn't it?

Kaitlin:
I agree, but let's narrow the good/evil debate down to this one question: Why is gore more fun than its opposite?

Mark:
The opposite of gore?

Kaitlin:
SpriteQuest is the opposite of gore.

Mark:
That's true.

Kaitlin:
I repeat: Why is gore more fun than the opposite of gore?

Mark:
I think that beneath your question is the assumption that gore is bad. I'm not sure I agree.

Kaitlin:
Possibly.

Mark:
Look at nature. Nature is one great big woodchipper. Sooner or later, everything shoots out the other end in a spray of blood, bones and hair.

Kaitlin:
Agreed.

Mark:
Gore is Nature's way of saying, "There are too many human beings on the planet, and I'm trying to rectify this any way I can. SARS didn't work, but trust me, I'm cooking up something better. In the interim, please kill lots of yourselves."

Kaitlin:
So gore is good?

Mark:
Absolutely.

• • •

The next afternoon, Kaitlin showed me a gory new room she'd added onto Ronald's Lair.

"What's it called?"

"Dentistry."

Bree's eyes were red.

"Bree, what happened?"

"I emailed a long, scary letter to the Frenchman."

"So?"

"I've burned that bridge forever. I never should have sent it."

"Nonsense. Guys never read any email from a woman that's over two hundred words long. You're totally safe." Mark and John Doe nodded their agreement.

Bree said, "I think computers ought to have a key called I'M DRUNK, and when you push it, it prevents you from sending email for twelve hours."

Kaitlin said, "I've got another one: a key called FUCK OFF. You press it every time your computer does something annoying—in turn this would somehow force your computer to experience pain. And if you pushed SHIFT/FUCK OFF, you'd end up with FUCK OFF AND DIE, the computer equivalent of a razor being raked across your nipples."

On the corkboard by the coffee machine was a poster announcing the new Tetris season. Tetris, retro as it is, remains a big-deal game here at the company. The plan was to rig the condo lights of a tall, empty downtown tower to simulate the Tetris grid. Greg found just the right place—what a stud. He confirmed an empty tower: 156 condos owned by offshore residents, and all of its units empty. Cowboy and John Doe planned to hack a Tetris algorithm into the building's lighting system so that we could play on the building's front facade while stationed across the street in a park. Talk about stoked.

I got kind of sentimental looking at the layouts of the empty condos. It reminded me of my summer jobs in university, going into Greg's condo towers, rearranging the patio furniture and randomly turning lights on and off to make the buildings look occupied. Buyers don't trust empty buildings. It's bad feng shui. Or maybe it's just bad feng. Or shui.

Tetris Challenge
Tonight, 7:00

Folders
vs.
Crumplers

• • •

John Doe asked, "What's a folder or a crumpler?"

"Both are technical terms used by the pulp and paper industry," said Kaitlin.

"Meaning?"

"Toilet tissue manufacturers divide end users into two categories: people who crumple their paper and people who fold it. Each is fifty percent of the market."

Mark said, "What about you, Bree—crumpler? Folder?"

Bree said, "This is like the white vs. black 'Spy vs. Spy' thing."

"You're changing the subject."

"I'm a folder . . . *obviously*."

"No! I would have had you down as a crumpler."

"Surprise."

"Do geeks skew in any particular direction?" I asked.

Kaitlin said, "I suspect they're more likely to be folders."

A quick and highly viral email campaign throughout the building revealed that game builders are eighty percent folders, but the few crumplers took pride in their stance. Dylan from server maintenance said, "When I crumple my paper, in my head it feels like a particle-based onscreen effect, like an explosion. That's not just a wad of paper in my left hand—it's a non-dimensional pyrotechnical *event*."

I read that one out loud. Bree looked at me and said, "Did he really have to specify which *hand*? I mean, nobody's left-handed when it comes to toilet paper. That's just plain wrong."

That's how everybody in the office found out that Bree had set her sights on a brand new conquest. Dylan, beware.

My phone rang. It was Greg, calling from Mom and

Dad's place. "Ethan—Dad just told me that Mom's gone off the wiener."

"She's *what*?"

"She no longer digs man-muff."

I blurted out, "Mom is *not* a lesbian." I could hear my podmates' antennas rising as if commanded. "I went up the coast and visited her. She just needs time to do some kind of . . . life enhancement seminar."

"Man, it's so weird thinking of parents as being sexual, let alone dykey."

"Mom is *not* a lesbian."

"You're doing way too much protesting here."

"Okay. It appears that way."

"I knew it."

"How's Dad?"

"I don't know if it's the cheating or the lesbo part that's got him more freaked."

Greg, like my father, had no idea about Mom's flings, living or dead. But God only knows what Greg knows that I don't. Does Mom divvy out her psychoses to her children like Christmas gifts?

I remembered Lot 49. "I'm coming over right now."

• • •

When I arrived, Dad and Greg were loading up Greg's Hummer with duffle bags. It was a gorgeous afternoon.

"Hey—where are you guys going?"

"Up to Whistler. And you're coming with us. We need a change of scenery."

A perfect chance to ask Greg about fixing that real estate deal. "Where are we going to stay?"

"A client's place."

"Great."

Drunk or not, Dad was fulfilling his masculine parental duty by checking Greg's tire pressure. "Greg, your back two tires are a bit low."

"Dad, I'm not sixteen any more. Just leave them alone."

"Jesus, Greg, I'm just trying to save you some money. Boy, when I think about the two of you, gallivanting about town on your underpressured tires, needlessly accruing excess wear and tear—like you were made of money."

"Dad, I moved a hundred million bucks worth of residential space last year—"

"So I guess you're too fancy for your lousy old father, who's just trying to help you out in his own little way."

"Everyone get in," Greg ordered.

We were soon on Highway 99, headed up Howe Sound into the Coast Mountains. The alpine environment was already making me feel healthier than I really am—which I believe is the secret allure of skiing as a sport.

Dad was in the front seat, swigging from a hip flask. He was slurring his words, and finally lost the will even to berate his spendaholic children. I, however, was thrilled that he was actually using the flask, my Christmas present to him a few years back. Hip flasks are the juice machines of the alcohol world—everyone has one and it never gets used.

"So who is she? What's she like?" Greg asked.

I was about to say she looked like that old TV character, Alf, but caught myself in time. I don't really know what sort of description of freedom would disturb Greg the least. "She's, uhhh—"

"She's what?"

"Kind of average."

"In what way?"

"In an average kind of way."

Greg said, "You're the most pathetic liar, Ethan. Is she hot or not?"

Dad blew up. "Don't talk that way."

"Talk what way?"

"About your mother's—" In a blink, Dad knew that saying the word would confirm it once and for all. "Whatever. I don't feel like talking about it right now."

Suddenly we were doing a hundred miles an hour to pass a Pepsi delivery truck. "Greg—what the *fuck* are you doing?"

"Ethan, be quiet."

"Greg, slow down."

We squeaked past the truck, narrowly avoiding a head-on collision with a white stretch limousine filled with Japanese college students on a pot holiday. My nerves were in ribbons.

"There, now—that wasn't so bad, was it? I also got an extra five thousand points for an insane stunt bonus."

"You could have fucking killed us."

"Ethan, I'm a roadrageoholic, but I'm really trying to overcome it with therapy. When I lapse, could you at least try to be supportive and find some joy in my rageoholism?"

A lemon yellow Supra with all sorts of silly spoiler attachments sped past us. Greg went nuts: "I'll kill you, you little fuckhead!"

Now's not a good time to ask about Lot 49.

When we arrived at Whistler, my toes were still so clenched inside my shoes that I had to bang them on the back seat floor to loosen them. My spirits rose when we turned into a street bordering the Maui North subdivision. Our particular ski cabin was mall-sized and resembled the

Swiss pavilion at the 2020 World's Fair. "Hey, Greg—who's the client?"

"I've actually never met him or her. It's a registered offshore buyer who only goes by a number."

The keys were plasticized electronic cards, like in a hotel. We walked in the front door and turned on a light and—*boom*—we were suddenly in what seemed to be Oprah's chic Nordic retreat: everything was perfect—furniture, art and lighting. It reeked of untold volumes of spare cash. Greg said, "Okay, laddies, pick your bedroom. There are eight to choose from."

I walked up the grand staircase and selected a large bedroom with an ensuite bathroom and a magnificent view of the forest out back. But I sensed something weird going on. I couldn't put my finger on just what until I began sneezing. I looked more closely and realized that every surface in my room—and all of the other rooms—was covered in a gentle felt of dust. Sunset beams coming from the west hit windows caked in dirt, spiderwebs, birch leaves and guano streaks. Down in the kitchen, Greg was on his phone. I went to the stove, turned the electric burners on maximum and watched as the dust on them burned away.

Greg clicked shut his cell. "Ethan, what are you doing?"

"Greg, when was the last time anybody was ever actually in this house?"

"Here? Let me see—" From the kitchen counter he picked up a yellowed, desiccated newspaper. "August 10, 1993."

"Nobody's been here since 1993?"

"Why would they? On the other hand, if Taiwan or China or Singapore implodes, there'll be a family of thirty living here in a flash."

Suddenly the house felt like a coffin. "I have to go get some fresh air."

"You do that."

• • •

Sometimes what at first seems like a coincidence isn't really one at all. I say this because I decided to walk over to the Maui North project and check out the lots. I heard Lot 49 before I saw it: a roaring stream. I was walking there to have a magic moment between nature and myself, when who popped out from behind a boulder? *freedom.*

She looked at me. "Well, well, if it isn't the Penis come to rescue Mumsy-wumsy from being brainwashed."

"freedom, what are *you* doing here?"

"I might ask you the same question. Me? I'm here because I'm buying this lot."

"What?"

"Kam Fong put me on to this place. I can already taste the wattage this little trickle is going to give me. You?"

I was too confused to say anything cogent. "Where's Mom?"

"Over there."

freedom pointed to a patch of moss embedded with pine needles and chipmunks. A cinematic sunbeam lit my mother in end-of-day magic light.

"Ethan! Come feed a chipmunk!"

And then, from behind me, I heard Greg calling to freedom. "freedom! Glad you could make it." Greg looked at Mom and said, "Mom, what are you doing here?" Gathering his wits, he said, "freedom—have you met my mother?"

• • •

Before I forget, Bree came up with this new trick—how to create your name if you become a stripper. Basically, just figure out the least expensive form of sugar or sweetness you ate today . . .

"Molasses"

"Sweet 'N Low"

"Vanilla Wafer"

"Tang"

"Brown Sugar"

"The Doublemint Twins"

"Cling Peaches"

"Cinnamon"

My own stripper name is "M&M."

• • •

• • •

We decided to let Dad sleep it off while the four of us went to a coffee place that catered almost exclusively to astonishingly attractive young people from Australia and New Zealand, all of whom were baked on local weed. In the middle of the café, freedom gave Mom a lusty back rub while Mom explained to Greg, "I know what you're thinking, but I am not a lesbian. I just need to reclaim my ovarian inner landlord."

This was too much for my brother. His form of denial is to begin speaking like a real estate ad. "Lot 49's such a honey of a property—a prestigious ski-in ski-out location with Whistler Village close by—it's ideal for a luxury chalet. Think vaulted ceilings! Think river-rock fireplace and wraparound decks! Think Ultraline professional appliances and beautiful detailed log work—a chalet to be proud of!"

"Greg, you know how bored we get when you talk like a brochure," Mom said. "And besides, don't sell something that's already sold."

freedom was cackling. "I'm certainly the chalet type, aren't I? Ha! I'm going to make a box out of concrete and pack in as many plants as I can. High style is for pantywaists." Her hands were disturbingly close to Mom's chest.

"Greg," said Mom, "as a favour to me, be sure you never ever sell that lot to anyone but freedom. I know how cannibalistic real estate sales are in Whistler. Even if someone offers you twice the asking price. You promise? On my grave? And that if you sell it to someone else, it means you don't love me?"

Greg promised.

An awkward silence ensued.

I was miserable. I saw no way to get Greg to ditch the sale to freedom.

More unnerving was the sight of Mom possibly being turned on by freedom's body rub. What a mess.

freedom barked, "Okay, we need to go now. We have just enough time to make it to *The Passion Cycle of the Mons.* I'm working the breast puppets this season."

Neither Greg nor I had the will to pursue that gambit.

"Give your father my love, boys." With that, Mom was gone.

Greg turned on me. "Why the fuck didn't you tell me Mom was freedom's—"

"freedom's *what*? Her shag bag? Her meat treat?"

"Nothing."

"Let's not tell Dad about what just happened."

"Deal."

Rank
2
Skill
1579
Skill bonus
134
Total kills
585
Total deaths
245
Suicides
0
Souls crushed
4
Rounds survived
190 / 411
Life expectancy
46.73%
Kill streak
14
Death streak
5
Kills per death
2.37
Kills per minute
1.08
Kills per round
1.43
Deaths per round
0.60
Skill increase per round
1.08
Teammates killed
0
Death by teammates
0
Last man standing
4
Play time
8h59m
Longest session
1h5m
Terrorists joined
35
Killed VIPs
0
Planted bombs
33
Bombed targets
(91.38%) 31
Killed hostages
2
Killed terrorists
156
Saved VIPs
0
Defused bombs
(33.33%) 1
Grabbed hostages
9

I'm so fucking sick of Google.

• • •

In the end, the chalet's dust overwhelmed my sinuses, and I caught a bus back to the city. I was alone in jPod, looking up gory websites at which to park my brain for a few hours. Around eleven o'clock, everybody arrived back at work in high spirits.

"He's so funny, isn't he?"

"I know—it's like he has no OFF button."

"He can take anything and just *run* with it."

They saw me and clammed right up. "Uh . . . hi, Ethan."

"Don't tell me—it's Coupland, right?"

Bree went over to her desk and began Swiffering her shrine. "It's as if he knows everything about us—he listens to us and *cares* about us."

"Let me guess again—you've been at a shareholder meeting."

"Did you have a nice trip to Whistler?" Kaitlin asked.

"I would have told you about it already if you'd been around."

"Don't get pissy on me, buster, because I can tell with one glance that you've been having a gorefest. Even if I'd been here, I might as well have been a stacking chair."

She had a point.

My phone rang, and everybody dissolved into their own spaces. It was Bruce Pao: "Hey, Ethan, buddy—how did things go?"

"Hi, Bruce."

"So, how did things go?"

"I'm working on it, Bruce."

"He's not going to sell it to me, is he?"

"Nothing's final yet, Bruce."

"You have twenty-four hours or your game dies."

Crap.

• • •

I phoned Greg to plead my case. "Greg, come on—pleeeeez. This guy, Bruce—he'll top anything Mom's girlfriend pays."

"Ethan, no. Mom asked me specifically not to sell it to anybody else, so I can't."

"You'll get double your regular commission."

"No can do, bro."

Shit.

Kwantlen College Learning Annex
Course 3072-A

Assignment: Discuss Love with an
Unlikely Person

"Dial 888-LOVE"

by Kaitlin Anna Boyd Joyce

Kam Fong, thirty-four, is a friend and international businessman operating in most countries of the Pacific Rim.

Kaitlin:
Hi, Kam, thanks for agreeing to be interviewed.

Kam:
No problem.

Kaitlin:
The topic for this assignment is love. Have you ever been in love?

Kam:
No.

Kaitlin:
In like, then?

Kam:
I like people, but I have yet to love one.

Kaitlin:
Do you wonder if you're missing out on something?

Kam:
No.

Kaitlin:
How old are you?

Kam:
[Pauses.] Thirty-four.

Kaitlin:
Thirty-*four*? That's bad luck in Chinese, isn't it? Three is okay, but four is a terrible number.

Kam:
It is. Forty-four is considered the worst year of your life; thirty-four is second-worst.

Kaitlin:
When was your birthday?

Kam:
The day of the hug machine's launch.

Kaitlin:
You never told us!

Kam:
It's okay. That's why I put a quarter-pound of uncut medicinal-grade cocaine into Cowboy's cola—as a celebration of life.

Kaitlin:
That was so great, by the way. Everyone had a blast, and nobody had a clue why. I'm still finding glitter in my keyboard.

Kam:
I try to bring joy to people.

Kaitlin:
You really do.

Kam:
[Makes motions indicating he's about to do an impersonation.] *If caring about your friends is a crime, then come and arrest me right now.*

Kaitlin:
That's a perfect John Doe! [Another friend.]

Kam:
Thanks. Did you meet John's mother?

Kaitlin:
Yes.

Kam:
Believe it or not, of all the people I've ever met, I think I could actually fall in love with her.

Kaitlin:
Really? Now this interview is truly getting somewhere. You mean to say you could make it with freedom? [freedom (lower case f) is an ultra-lesbian.]

Kam:
She's a powerful, confident woman in a way that Chinese women aren't.

Kaitlin:
If things work out, freedom could end up as my mother-in-law.

Kam:
What?

Kaitlin:
You don't know?

Kam:
About what?

Kaitlin:
Ethan's mother ran off to live with freedom in a rural lesbian communal love shack with no A/C, electricity or running water.

Kam:
[No response.]

Kaitlin:
Kam?

Kam:
Really?

Kaitlin:

It's true. Ethan's dad is a mess because of it. He sits in the house, drinking rum and Gatorade with the lights turned off.

Kam:

He *did* miss dance class. [Kam and my boyfriend's father are professional-level ballroom dancers.]

Kaitlin:

In desperation, Ethan even allowed this stalker named Ellen, who's been hounding Jim forever, into the house. She got so bored that she left and quit the stalking.

Kam:

I see.

Kaitlin:

Let's go back to love. If you don't think you're capable of love, you must be doing something with all that love energy inside you.

Kam:

[Pauses.] I like to play matchmaker. If two people are right for each other, I hook them up. If things aren't working out, I can come in and help . . . ensure that things end peacefully.

Kaitlin:

So you're like the Internet then—except you're a real person.

Kam:
You flatter me. But yes.

Kaitlin:
What about your family? Where are they?

Kam:
Pffft. I don't really have one.

Kaitlin:
You're an orphan?

Kam:
In a way.

Kaitlin:
That's so adorable! You should let word get out—girls would swarm you. It's even better than walking around shirtless holding a puppy.

Kam:
I prefer the dignity of silence. I've actually made you numskulls in jPod my family.

Kaitlin:
Oh God, I'm getting teary.

Kam:
Here . . . [Reaches into pocket in search of Kleenex, finds none, then brings out wallet and removes a scarlet wad of fresh fifty-dollar bills.] Use these.

Kaitlin:

Thanks, Kam. [I blow my nose.] Hey, are these real?

Kam:

No. Pretty good forgeries, huh?

Kaitlin:

They're great. I'm impressed. My parents got hosed with a suitcase of fake fifties on this shipment they sent down to the States via Spokane. I took one look at the bills and then looked at my parents and said, "How could you be taken in by such pathetic forgeries? You deserved to be shtupped! They look like they were done by a toddler running a tonerless Lexmark Pro they found in a garage sale."

Kam:

What did your parents say?

Kaitlin:

My mom said, "Well, they had a bumper sticker that said PROUD TO BE AMERICAN, and someone had just blown up an embassy somewhere, and we felt sorry for them."

Kam:

Parents.

Kaitlin:

Tell me about it. So for Christmas that year I gave them a Samsung Model CPC 993C-1 banknote counter with built-in forgery detection system. It can do over a thousand notes per minute.

Kam:
Is that the one that has banknote-width sensors that detect undersize notes to prevent accidentally mixed notes from being counted incorrectly?

Kaitlin:
No, that's the Model OMAL 75D.

Kam:
Of course. What was I thinking?

Kaitlin:
So, if we're discussing love, we really do have to discuss your parents. Can you tell me anything?

Kam:
I was the second male child from Wife Number Four.

Kaitlin:
Is that good or bad?

Kam:
I suppose bad, because all alone I had to claw my way up and out of Beijing's unlubricated pre-capitalist sphincter, cockfight by cockfight—but, then, it was also good because I found my own way in life. I think that's important.

Kaitlin:
What about the first male child from Wife Number One?

Kam:
His life is so boring.

Kaitlin:
What does he do?

Kam:
He runs a chain of maybe five hundred massage parlours across the southern provinces. I went to one once. He cuts the baby oil with canola, and they charge you extra for a shower, and even then the water's the temperature of spit.

Kaitlin:
And he gets repeat customers?

Kam:
You'd think he'd simply offer better service to withstand a free market, but instead he kills his competitors. Where's the challenge in that? But I take some satisfaction in selling him his canola oil from here in Vancouver.

Kaitlin:
You're always helping people.

Kam:
I try. I really try.

Kaitlin:
Did you ever spend time with your father?

Kam:
No. Number One Son took care of him.

Kaitlin:
His own father?

Kam:
I know—where do you draw the line? But in all fairness, it was an accident. They were at the launch of his five hundredth parlour, and Dad showed up and got whacked out on Japanese apricot sake and some leftover date rape drug from a Chanel fragrance launch the night before in Hong Kong.

Kaitlin:
And . . . ?

Kam:
Suddenly someone wheeled out a helium canister and a stack of party balloons, and Dad thought it would be really funny to do a squeaky voice. He inhaled the helium, and all the capillaries in his lungs exploded, and he died on the spot.

Kaitlin:
!!!!!!!!!!

Kam:
What?

Kaitlin:
!!!!!!!!!!

Kam:
What?

Kaitlin:
You don't know?

Kam:
Know what?

Kaitlin:
That's how somebody from jPod died once.

Kam:
No shit. Fuck off. You're spooking me.

Kaitlin:
It's true.

Kam:
!!!!!!!!!

[NOTE: Kam excused himself here and went to his room for a few minutes. He came back in a much better mood.]

Kaitlin:
Sometimes drugs help us deal with our problems.

Kam:
I agree. Can we end the interview now? Too many painful memories.

Kaitlin:
No problem. Thanks, Kam, and thanks for helping everybody in so many ways.

Kam:
It's my job in life.

• • •

I was wondering what electrons are actually doing when they sit in your hard drive in an old laptop at the back of your closet. I mean, how does an electron sit still—is it like a cartoon M&M leaning back in a folding beach chair? Is it like an angry little steel ball bearing hovering there, just waiting to go nuts on protons? What's the mechanism that starts and stops the electron? Who's its dungeon master? And if an electron has only a negative electrical charge, how can it possibly even exist? It'd be like a bar magnet with only a north or only a south pole. A monopole. It's impossible.

I voiced these concerns in the pod one day, and Bree didn't even look up, just said, "Quarks, aisle three."

"I think I hear the sound of someone who didn't make the high school math stream," added Evil Mark.

"Gee, Mark, pass me the bong. I just had this really profound idea about subatomic particles."

"Bree, why does water feel wet?"

"Mark, why are kittens fluffy and cute?"

"I like fluffy wuffy kittens."

"Don't worry your pretty little brain, pudding, no one's going to say anything ever again to make you feel small."

"Okay, guys, you can stop now."

I felt so stupid—and I still don't know the answer! What's worse, I couldn't find the answer on Google, which always drives me nuts. Then I made my situation worse. "Do you guys think they'll ever invent some form of wireless electrical power transference?"

Bree said, "Well, actually, it exists right now, Ethan. It's called x-rays."

Then John Doe googled and found these great photos

of people standing on top of their apartment buildings in Chernobyl on the night of the big meltdown. They were a mile away, yet they were still absorbing the equivalent of ten chest x-rays a second.

"Goners," John Doe said.

• • •

Bruce Pao killed SpriteQuest today, Friday, at 4:30 p.m.

Ugh.

After everybody heard the news, it took only forty-five seconds for them to adjust. Evil Mark is already designing a new goal post for a football game, and Bree vanished to hit on guys at the local pub.

Kaitlin said, "It's as if the game never existed."

I had to agree. I felt . . . *blank*. Just blank.

intentionally blank

M

o

t

H e

R

F

uck

E

• • •

Steve refused to believe the game was dead, but there was something more going on than just denial. Around midnight he came to my place and told me to accompany him to my parents' house.

"Steve, Mom's not there. She's at her commune."

"I don't want to see your mother. I want to see your father."

"Why?"

"You'll see."

Dad was moaning drunk when we got there. Steve asked me to help drag Dad into Steve's Touareg.

I said, "Not until you tell me where we're taking him."

"A recording studio. We need to get Ronald's voice tracks laid down. Your booze-soaked heartsick dad is the dream voice for Ronald we've been searching for. I'm paying my own money for the sound session."

"What if he pukes in the back seat?" I said.

"He won't. Members of the Greatest Generation never puke. They just internalize their nausea, then squeeze it out in the form of freeway infrastructure and tightly indexed pension plans."

"Dad is a boomer, not a member of the Greatest Generation."

Dad's body was about as stiff as a garden hose, which made it hard to carry him. Just before we plunked him in the back seat, Steve gently nudged Dad's liver, and Dad parped out a hoarse, mucousy *goddammit.*

"Need I say any more? If he isn't Ronald, then who is?"

Steve was right. A drunken, utterly fucked up Dad was Ronald to a T.

Once Dad was inside with his door closed, Steve and I stood there in the moonlit darkness. The only sound was the faint roar of the Trans-Canada Highway to the south.

"Ethan, over the past year you've made crap, you've made shittier crap and you've made three-layered crap sandwiches—but don't forget for a moment that with the creation of Ronald and his Lair, *you* and the jPod crew have been making the finest form of art—a blood-soaked communion that allows weak souls and lost lambs across the globe to give vent to their inner rage as surely as Jackson Pollock threw household enamel onto raw canvas, or Jack Kerouac scrawled his druggie maunderings onto Woolworth's foolscap."

"I'd never thought of it that way, Steve."

"You, Ethan, dammit, are an *artist*."

"I am!"

"Okay, let's drive off with boozie here."

The drive downtown was uneventful. Steve needed a fix big time, but the recording studio adjoined his favourite dealer's alley—convenient. After lugging Dad into a small room covered with grey carpeting, Steve popped outside for his vein treat, and returned with a bit of zing in his step. "Let the voices begin."

I sat in the recording room with two techies while Steve circled Dad, who was slumped over on a teal-coloured Naugahyde sofa. He bent down and screamed in Dad's face: "Ronald, who the fuck are *you*?"

"Wha—?" Dad's body hopped like a cricket

"I said, WHO . . . THE . . . FUCK . . . ARE . . . *YOU*?"

I cut in over the intercom. "Dad, just say you're Ronald, okay?"

"I'm Ronald."

Steve said, "No, you're not, because the Ronald I know is *angry.* The Ronald I know is pissed off. *You,* you disgusting maggot, are a flaccid, docile fetal pig splayed out and waiting for the first incision." He whacked Dad on the back of his head.

"Steve, Jesus Christ, go easy on him."

Steve kept talking to Dad. "Ronald gets the first speaking role of his life, and what does he say? Nothing."

The words "speaking role" seemed to rouse something deep in Dad. He grabbed Steve by the neck and pulled Steve's head down to his own.

"This particular Ronald does *not* blow his chance for a speaking role. I will ace this goddam role, or I will snap your legs into slivers like the stems of cheap wine glasses."

Steve looked at me. "Did you get that on tape?"

"Got it."

From there, Ronald's/Dad's words flowed smoothly.

I am Ronald,
of Mordor,
the Mage,
the
Destroyer.

Taste the scorched fruit
inside my pies.

Chew the bitter towelette
of truth.

Die, you seedy little elves
who refuse to accept any
new menu items added
after 1975.

I scorch your loins with
coffee that sears like a
molten steel patty
flipper.

I smash your bones on
rocks of ice churned by
spews of cola.

I till your soil, steal your
potatoes, circumcise
their skins, cook
them in tallow
and tell you
they're vegan.

I shall castrate your
bulls, rendering them more
juicy and docile,
and I shall salt them with
hormones, making them
girly-cows.

***You* shall wander the**
wastelands in search of
fishwiches fallen from
the sky, frozen and plump
with weevils and sauce
of fiercest tartar.

My face is stripped of
pancake makeup,
staring at the sun,
burning, awaiting
balloons and a helium
canister that will never
arrive.

Your ears shall hear only
the sound of a french-fry
computer that beeps
eternally.

You shall remain forever
parched with a
bottomless Styrofoam
drinking cup.

You, my imprisoned
sprite servants, I shall
deprive of both minimum
wage and nutrients.
My cooker writhes
with yellow frybabies
your lips shall
never taste.

I shall pierce your being with shakes made of ground bones, nay, chalk.

You shall beg for death, but instead shall receive only laughter and choking hazards disguised as plastic toys.

In my costume of yellow
bib and coarse
enormous red feet, I will
smite you with burgers
laced with thorns.

Inside your bird nuggets
you will find razor
blades, rats and tumours.

The
only
real
clown
is
a
dead
clown.

唯一的真
正的小丑
是一个死
的小丑

I ONLY MAKE YOU FAT SO THAT YOU'LL SIZZLE WHEN YOU BURN

我只做您
油脂以便
您将烧得
发嘶声当
您烧

• • •

"Hey, Ethan, there's some really great stuff here—"

It was three a.m. Cowboy and I were listening to Dad's work.

"Thanks. Dad is such a star. Steve really coaxed it out of him."

"I had no idea Steve had all this pent-up bile. It's wild."

Cowboy was dressed in weird beltless rugby pants. "What's with the pants, Cowboy? You look like a 1982 liquor store clerk with herpes."

"Since I've laid off the sex, I've had to come up with all sorts of ideas to help me out. Allison downstairs told me about these special undergarments worn by Mormons. They're specifically designed to unflatter the body, so that if you end up with someone, they'll snuff out any urges."

"Right. How's the no-sex thing going?"

"I hate it."

"Are you at least allowed to, er, fly solo?"

"Nope."

"So what happens?"

"Meaning?"

"Meaning—can you sleep or think or anything else?"

"Nope. The thing about abstinence is that *all* you think about is sex, whereas when you actually have sex, you don't think about it nearly as much. Which do you think is the more religious option?"

"Sex."

"Thank you, Ethan. That was the permission I needed!"

Cowboy leapt up and was gone. I made a mental note to turn off my cellphone for the next twenty-four hours.

Mark came in. "Where'd Cowboy go?"

"At the very least he's gone out to stock up on Kleenex."

Mark and I worked until dawn, generating new moves for Ronald. Now that he had sound effects, it was impossible not to work on the project. Ronald had become real to us.

Kwantlen College Learning Annex
Course 3072-A

Assignment: Describe Your Life Quickly

"Ma Vie"

by Kaitlin Anna Boyd Joyce

Another day passes. Everyone picks away at minor tasks. The cafeteria makes nutritiously stylish meals. The crows arrive by the tens of thousands to roost in the alder forest across from the Willingdon off-ramp. Endless cars drone by. I once saw the Oscar Mayer Weinermobile, but never again. I say hello to people in the hallways, and they say hello to me. We all go home and watch *Law & Order.* New pairs of Pumas and Nikes arrive, and idle chat begins. The sun rises and sets and the moon changes phases. Someone comes home from Tokyo or E3 with a new electronic toy and everyone says, "Ooooh." People move from one office to another office on another floor in another building. The TVs in the lobby blare whatever league games are happening. One day is much like the next and the one after that. Somewhere along the line you buy a new sofa at a store maybe two notches above Ikea, but then its cushions get dull and have a wear pattern from your butt. Nothing's new. You wonder how much the guy you're talking to is making. He wonders if you have stock options. The guy at the cafeteria table beside me wonders if he should initiate a conversation with me, whereas I wonder if he would have been out of my league pre-Ethan.

Life is dull, but it could be worse and it could be better. We accept that a corporation determines our life's routines.

It's the trade-off so that we don't have to be chronically unemployed creative types, and we know it. When we were younger, we'd at least make a show of not being fooled and leave copies of Adbusters on our desktops. After a few years it just doesn't matter. You trawl for jokes or amusingly diversionary .wav files. You download music. A new project comes along, then endures a slow-motion smothering at the hands of meetings. All ideas feel stillborn. The air smells like five hundred sheets of paper.

And then it's another day.

• • •

The phone rang at 6:12 a.m., and I knew it wasn't going to be an ordinary phone call.

"Mom?"

"Ethan, honey, I need your help."

Oh God. "What's up?"

"I'd rather not discuss it on the phone."

"Where are you?"

"I've left the commune and I'm back at the house."

"Where's Dad?"

"Greg took him to a 'Swing-Step and Pivot' seminar in Seattle to try to cheer him up."

"Mom, it's 6:12 in the morning."

"Ethan, I need your help right away."

"Doing what?"

"Something only you can help me with. I don't want to discuss it on the phone."

"I don't want to get up."

"Don't be such a lazybones."

"I've got to eat breakfast."

"Breakfast is for losers."

"No, it's not, Mom. I know for a fact that every family on earth eats breakfast."

"Who told you that?"

"You never served breakfast because you didn't want to get up."

"That's not fair, Ethan. I've got low thyroid."

This is still a sore spot in our family history. Greg and I got all the way to high school without ever eating or being served breakfast. However, having stayed over at friends' houses, we finally realized that our family was aberrant in its rejection of a.m. dining. When we confronted Mom with the fact that everybody else eats breakfast, she was like a bird trapped in the house, trying to escape. Then one afternoon she came home with a bag of chocolate-flavoured Carnation Instant Breakfasts, plonked them on the kitchen table and said, "There, I never want to discuss this again." Greg and I figure we could have had master's degrees at MIT or Harvard if only we'd gone to school properly fed. But the past is the past.

"The last time I helped you like this, it was a pretty shitty experience."

"Ethan, don't swear. I wouldn't have called if it wasn't urgent."

"How urgent?"

Mom started to sniffle.

Oh God. "Okay, I'll come over."

"Thank you. Dress warmly and wear sturdy boots."

Boots? *Dear God.*

• • •

When I pulled into the driveway, Mom was loading shovels and turf-hedging tools into the K-car. Before I could say anything, she said, "Ethan, we have to go dig up Tim."

"What?"

"You heard me. He's got a safety deposit box key in his jacket."

"What's in the box?"

"Don't be nosy."

"Why don't you just call Kam and explain it to him? I doubt he'd care."

"I did phone him." Mom was loading a tarp. "His acupuncturist said he's down in Oregon, foreclosing on some small town that got wiped out by cheaper manufacturing costs in China. At least he won't catch us digging up his prized New Zealand tree fern."

"Do you have any idea what Tim is going to look like by now, Mom?"

"Don't be a sissy. Hasn't the Internet toughened you up at all? Kaitlin says you practically live in all those gore sites. And in any event, I packed a few bottles of Febreze to help mask the odour. So just get in the car."

"Okay, okay, already."

"I knew you'd help me. You've always been the responsible son."

We got in the wagon. "Mom, how come Greg gets to swear as much as he wants, but I can't?"

"Ethan, that sort of thing was decided long before you were born. Use your nervous energy for better purposes, like trying to figure out ways to make the world a better place. Wait a second—did I pack both plastic tarps?"

I looked in the back. "Yup."

"Good."

Off we drove to Kam's fabulously bizarre Canterbury neighbourhood, past an endless succession of homes even larger, more garish and more bizarre than Kam's. "I find it highly suspect that, of all the houses in the city, Kam ends up buying Tim's burial plot," I said.

"It's not a coincidence at all. I showed it to him when he was house hunting. I told him it had good kung fu."

"Feng shui."

"That, too. Wait a second—Ethan, *stop! Stop the car*!" Mom was screaming.

I jammed on the brakes. "What! *What!*"

"I saw a sign for a garage sale just up the hill. We can sneak in as early birds."

So we did, and Mom haggled like a Microsoft accountant over a stack of 1980s-era *National Geographic* magazines.

"Mom, why are you buying *National Geographic*s? We got rid of ours ten years ago."

"I know, and I've been sick about it ever since."

I helped her load them in the back. When she slammed the door, she said, "I got them to throw in a set of used Cuisinart blades for free."

As we resumed driving up the mountain, she said, "Your father *would* have to go AWOL the one day we really need him."

Finally, a natural point for me to ask a question or two.

"So, Mom, how is, um, freedom doing?"

"Ethan, I am not a lesbian."

"I'm not saying that, Mom, I was just asking how she is."

"She's fine. She's in Seattle today, delivering a speech."

"On what?"

There was a note of challenge in her voice. "It's called 'Revoicing Yesterday's Vagina: Towards a New Theory of Birth, Post-Industrial Economics and Clitoral Praxis.'"

I remained mute.

"I am not a lesbian."

"I'm not saying you are."

"freedom is an enlightened woman and has given me range to expand both my autoandrogyny and my hormonal slope."

More silence on my part.

"It's very scientific, you know."

I played silent.

Mom said, "If you must know, the food at that house was awful. A bird feeder has better food than there, and every bite came with a lecture. After a while I began dreaming of having potato chips and Tang for lunch in silence."

"Kam's house is over there."

We parked the car. "What if people question us?" I asked.

"Ethan, I'm a well-nourished rich-looking white woman. I could burn polka dots onto Kam's front door with a crème brûlée torch and nobody would question me."

"Good point."

And so we began to dig.

• • •

Four hours later:

"Ethan, this digging is boring, and it's going nowhere."

"I'll never make cruel jokes at the expense of gravediggers again."

We were only maybe a foot down in the blend of premium-grade topsoil, rock bits and construction debris that was Kam's front garden area. All that digging, and Kam's New Zealand tree fern hadn't even begun to list.

"Mom, we need help."

"But who?"

"I'll call Kaitlin."

Mom gave me a look. "Are you sure?"

"She's got the bone structure of a Ukrainian peasant. Her family's in the business, too. She'll understand."

"Leave out the main details." Mom dropped her shovel. "Curse it. TV makes gravedigging look so easy."

The phone rang. "Hi, Kaitlin."

"Hi, Ethan. Where are you?"

"I'm over at Kam's with Mom. I'm helping her out with something."

"With what?"

"It's probably best not to discuss this on the phone. Can you come over?"

"Actually, I've got this, uh, thing I have to go to at noon."

"What thing?"

"It's a, well—"

"It's a Coupland meeting, right?"

"Well, yeah. Ethan, we've been through this a thousand times. Stop taking your resentment out on me."

"Sorry. Who else is going to be there?"

"All the podsters."

"Okay. See you later." I hung up.

Mom asked what was happening, and I told her about the meeting. "The meeting! I forgot about it. *Phooey.*" She brushed herself off frantically, as though the dirt stains were leeches. "Ethan, you carry on. I'll be back around two-ish."

"What!"

"Oh, calm down."

"Can I come?"

"No. You have to dig."

At least if I was digging in a videogame, I might find a

piece of a puzzle or treasure. A fermented dead biker? Some prize.

• • •

I carried on digging, and by two o'clock the hole was finally up to my waist, but there was no way I was going to be able to finish the job. I got out my PDA and was trying to locate a place where I could rent a Bobcat or some other kind of tractor when I heard jPod voices coming towards me from up the driveway.

"Ethan?"

"Guys?"

"Ethan," Mom said, "your friends are going to help you dig for a while."

This alarmed me, for obvious reasons. "*What?*"

"Not the entire hole. Don't worry. I stopped by the house and got some more digging tools for everybody."

"Uh, great."

Kaitlin said, "It's so sweet of you to swap Kam's tree fern for a Himalayan windmill palm. You're such a good friend."

"And digging the hole your*self*," Cowboy added. "Now *that's* friendship, and *that's* commitment to being Green."

Tim's corpse weighed heavily on my mind. "You know, I thought I might get a tractor and dig it that way. I don't think I'll need any help."

"Nonsense, Ethan," said Mom. "We're all adults, and we all care about Kam. Digging will be fun, and you young people all need some fresh air and exercise. Poor John Doe here looks like a telethon child."

"Thank you, Mrs. Jarlewski."

"Well, it's true, John."

I asked Mom if I could speak to her in private. We went to her car.

"Mom, what are you doing getting everyone to help us? Are you insane?"

"Don't be such a worrywart. Once we begin to smell Tim, I'll have everybody leave."

"I'm going to rent a Bobcat."

"Over my dead body you will. What if it accidentally cuts through Tim's body? Have some respect for the dead."

And so the gang jumped in and digging began, but it was slow going. There were only two real shovels. Bree had a spade, Kaitlin had an edging tool and John Doe was using this pole-shaped thingy Dad had bought off the Shopping Channel during a three a.m. rum jag. Bree looked at the pole and said, "I think it also French braids your hair if you hold it upside down."

An hour later we decided to trash the fern. The six of us (with Mom as overseer) managed to lug it out of its pit and roll it across the adjoining rockery. I wondered what Kam was going to make of this. It wasn't going to be pretty.

Everyone was being friendly and co-operative, and despite our sad little tools, the hole came along nicely. Cowboy, for once, wasn't off in a corner, contemplating death (or brokering a quickie skankwich); John Doe was full of vim and revealed to us a heretofore unknown talent for mimicking dial tones; Bree was describing her doomed second date from the previous evening ("You think you know somebody, and then all of a sudden they start talking about crop circles. . ."). Mark, bless him, was happy simply to be doing a disproportionate share of the work.

Mom made a snack run to Whole Foods, and I couldn't

remember the last time I'd had so much fun, but then suddenly the amount of fun we were having made me suspicious—and only then did I figure out why they were being so jolly. My blood turned to Freon. I put down my wheat grass smoothie and glared at them: "You're all quitting the company—aren't you? *That's* why you're all being so nice to me."

Silence.

"It's *true*. Come on, now—tell me."

Everybody lowered their tools and looked at Kaitlin.

"Ethan, uhhh—"

"I *knew* it."

Kaitlin said, "Ethan, this has nothing to do with how any of us feel about you. Working for Doug is going to be the best gig ever. We'd be nuts not to move."

"Doug, Doug, *Doug*. Could you at least tell me what that fatuous prick's idea is?"

"Ethan, I've told you a thousand times already, we signed nondisclosure agreement forms. You know they're sacred. And let me state in public that I don't want Kam thinking I was the one who spilled the beans."

Curse Kaitlin.

"When are you leaving?"

"Effective today."

"I'm sure your friends will out figure a way to bring you along once they get settled in. Won't you?" Mom said.

The others nodded just a bit too agreeably. I felt like the last dog remaining at the SPCA.

"Don't be such a gloomy Gus, dear, and besides—" Mom was fishing around her brain for something, anything nice to say. "Learn to take pleasure in life's little accomplishments. Just look at how much progress you've made digging this hole!"

Kaitlin was heading to a tap to rinse off her hands. "Ethan, we'll discuss this tonight. Bree and I have to go get facials."

The guys bailed, too. "It's new shoe day. Some limited-edition Adidas are coming in from Argentina. We have no free will here, Ethan—we have to leave. Sorry, buddy."

It was back to Mom and me.

"Dear, don't sulk. It gives you a second chin."

"Mom, for the love of God, why can't you just break the stupid NDA form and tell me what this—"

My words were cut short by a syrupy waft of decomposed flesh scent.

"Mom, I think we've just found Tim."

"I'll go get the Febreze."

• • •

Fifteen minutes and two bottles of Febreze later, we'd scraped enough dirt away to reveal a few square inches of the rolled-up carpet from Dad's den.

"Ethan, all you have to do is yank on the carpet and we're done. It couldn't be simpler."

"Mom, it's not going to come away in one little tug. The whole torso needs to be lifted."

"What's your point, Ethan?"

"Mom! *I'm* the one who has to do this, not you."

"That's right, Ethan, but *I* was in love with him."

I poked the carpet with the blunt end of my shovel. Mom asked why I was doing that. "I don't know—I suppose to see if he's crunchy or chewy."

"I suspect probably more on the chewy side, dear. Bones take a long time to decompose. Those steak bones I put in the azalea garden for calcium back in the 1980s are still hard as quartz."

I looked more closely at Tim's back. "He's not bloated, is he? It looks like the weight of all that dirt kept him quite slim."

"You know, Ethan, maybe if we thought of Tim as a science project we might move along a bit faster here. I think we're being too fussy."

Mom's purse farted. "Excuse me, dear—cellphone." She began rummaging, then checked the number of the incoming call. "It's the Vietnamese fertilizer dealer. I really have to answer this."

I prodded a bit more at Tim's cocoon. From out of the blue above us came an extended manga-like shriek from hell.

上帝！您異教徒的豬做了
什麼的母親對我心愛的結構樹蕨?

(Mother of God! What have you heathen pigs done to my beloved tree fern?)

Of course it was Kam—Kam and a short fire plug of a blonde-wigged woman in white go-go boots, Jackie O sunglasses and a tasselled white leather jacket who resembled a hooker I saw in Las Vegas a few years back. She was buying twenty-four boxes of Sudafed in the Albertsons on Sahara Boulevard.

"freedom?" I exclaimed.

"freedom?" Mom squeaked.

"Hello, Carol. Hello, Penis."

Kam's language became more intelligible as his first burst of rage died down. "What the fuck have you people done to my baby?"

Mom was taken aback by freedom's new look; she

viewed Kam's temper as might a nursery school teacher a toddler's wail. "Now, Kam, don't be angry. There's a good explanation for this."

"There'd better be, and you'd better tell me right now."

Mom remained distracted. "freedom, I thought you were delivering a speech in Seattle today."

"I was going to—until Kam phoned."

"Carol! *What about my goddam tree fern!*"

"Kam, cool down, I'll buy you a new one."

"What the hell are you doing digging up my front yard?"

Mom and I swapped glances. I wasn't going to be the one to break the news.

"Kam," said Mom, "last year I had a fling with this biker chap I did business with. And then he refused to pay me, and push came to shove, and he was accidentally electrocuted, and so I buried him here. Except I just realized he has a safety deposit box key in his pocket, and I need it rather badly."

There was a pause.

"Why didn't you say so?" Kam said. "I could have had some of my, uh, travel associates come here and dig it up for free in ten minutes."

Kam and freedom walked around to the other side of the hole. Mom said, "freedom, I barely recognize you."

freedom actually blushed and then giggled. It was a dreadful thing to see. "Kam told me that if I wanted to be a true radical, there was no point in fogging my bourgeois inertia under a mist of stillborn and archaic dialogues from the twentieth century."

"Did he?"

Kam smiled as if to say, *Look, fools! You think you're so smart and politically correct and all of that, but the Chinese mastered the art of jargon-twisting-to-get-what-you-want back before your sweet Jesus was a holy zygote.*

freedom went on. "Oh yes. A truly radical act on my part would be to infiltrate and hyperbolize the concepts I consider to be my opposite. Hence this new look."

What is it about lesbians and jargon?

freedom continued. "Next week we're off to Palm Desert for a brow lift, a nose softening, an eye lift, fat removal from the cheeks, a breast augmentation, tummy tuck, removal of fat from the thighs and calves . . ."

Kam completed the sentence: " . . . and fourteen Da Vinci porcelain veneers."

"Isn't that rebellious, Carol?" freedom had become a thirteen-year-old girl in search of approval. "Oh, and my new name is Kimberly."

Mom mouthed the word "Kimberly," but no noise escaped her throat.

Kam asked, "Ethan, have you reached that guy's body yet?"

I tamped the patch of carpet with my shovel. "Yup. I should have Mom's key within the hour."

Kam said, "Do me a favour. Just put a little bit of dirt on top of him once you're done. I have a few things I might as well put down there while there's a hole happening."

"What kind of things?"

"Don't you worry about that. I'll get one of my, uh, associates to fill in the hole after that."

"Thanks, Kam."

"Excellent."

Kam bowed to Kimberly/freedom, and then took her arm. "Very well, then. Kimberly, shall we go kick up our heels?"

Kimberly tittered. Small birds in the sky witnessed this and fell to the ground, dead.

Kam and his new girlfriend walked in the front door. Mom still stood in the hole, mute.

"Mom?"

No response.

"Mom?"

"Ethan—"

"Yes?"

"Ethan, I . . . I think I might be a lesbian."

"Mom—listen to me—Mom? *Mom?*" I grabbed her by the shoulders and shook. "Look me in the eye. Okay?"

She did.

"Here's the deal. You are not a lesbian. You do not have a crush on Kimberly. You will go home right now. You will cook Dad a hot, nutritious meal, and you will watch an episode of *Band of Brothers* on DVD with him, and you will enjoy that episode. And life will be just like it was a few months ago, and you will feel free and happy because of that. Okay?"

"Okay."

Mom teetered towards her car, bits of dove-grey soil trickling down the hole's edge in her wake. After she'd driven off, I remembered that she was my ride.

And so I toughened myself up and pretended Tim was a particularly well-designed gory website. I must agree that everything experts say about the Internet and violence and games is true—it *does* make you a little bit callous—the first gore makes the second gore easier. But the stench!

I retrieved Mom's key and tossed a bit of dirt back Tim's way. And then I simply sat at the hole's bottom, wondering about life, wondering about death and wondering about curious raccoons passing through the neighbourhood on their nightly rounds, snacking on Tim's remains.

And then I sat thinking about nothing.

Finally I heard a car pull up, a door slam, and someone approaching.

His face appeared above the hole, his dead eyes and his cruel mouth. Coupland. "Well, if it isn't the happy wanderer. Trying to dig your way back to China?"

"Fuck off and die."

"Temper." He was dressed like a 1960s TV father—glen plaid jacket and matching wool pants. He was holding, of all things, a pipe.

I said, "Kam's inside."

"That's nice. So, tell me, Ethan, why are you digging a hole, and why have you trashed Kam's tree fern?"

"That's not your business."

"Isn't it?"

I picked up a shovel, realizing that there was a part of me that wanted to whack this guy on the skull. "Just go inside."

"Maybe *you're* the one I want to speak to."

"Huh?"

"Come on. Ask yourself if there's some practical reason why I might be here to see you."

"You've lost me."

"Why don't we go for a ride?"

I did need a ride. "Okay."

I got into his Jaguar XJ12 ("Take your shoes off first, and don't touch any of the knobs or dials! Jesus Christ, you've got ants crawling off you"), and we drove down the mountain. I was tired and just wanted some peace and quiet.

"Where are we going?"
"North Van."
"Why?"
"There's something there you need to see."

Term	Type	Meaning
Bsh	Cmd	Sound made when CD ejects from burner
Execle	Fct	Discontinued Popsicle flavour
.osc	Cmd	C++ (indicates that file contents have received an Academy Award)
Diff	Cmd	Rhymes with piff
PPP	Prot	Larger than normal urination
Qdaemon	Cmd	Nomeadq spelled backwards
Scanf	Fct	Misspelling of skank
Eval	Cmd	Opposite of goad
Glob	Misc	Biannual Windexing of monitor screen
.i	Ext	Low self-esteem version of “I”
ARP	Prot	Your seal needs a herring

• • •

We ended up at a building near the Second Narrows Bridge that, until recent currency fluctuations, had been a film studio used primarily for TV movies. The signage near the roof had been removed, leaving an off-white rectangle behind it. The offices up front had the stripped-to-the-bone feel of commercial space undergoing a total overhaul.

"Welcome to the offices of Dglobe."

"Dglobe? Can you spell that?"

"Capital D, lower case g, l, o, b, e."

"What does the D stand for?"

"Doug, you dumb shit. Dglobe is where your friends are coming to work."

"Some friends they are."

"*Tsh, tsh.* Nobody gets rich on software in the twenty-first century. The only money remaining is in hardware, and only hardware made offshore at that, preferably in some unregulated, uninvestigated Asian backwater where you can get a day's labour and a hand job for the cost of a bag of Skittles."

"So, then, what happens here in Vancouver?"

"Here is where the Dglobe gets its *soul.*"

"All I see is a big empty heap of a building. Show me something real."

"With pleasure. Come this way."

We stepped over a pile of removed drywall and a tangle of beige phone cables. The carpeting was stained and lying in piles—bright orange steak restaurant carpeting from the 1970s. The rooms smelled like a cold, dank used bookstore.

"This way, if you will." Coupland opened up a set of double doors leading into what was once a fair-size sound stage. In the centre of the room was one small light, enough to illuminate veritable kelp beds of abandoned electrical cords on the concrete floor. Leaning against the wall across the space were dozens of pieces of scenery, stacked like toast slices.

Coupland turned to me. "There, in the centre of the room—that's the Dglobe."

We walked towards it: a beach-ball-sized globe lit from within. "Big deal."

"Fair enough. But watch this."

Coupland pulled a key fob from his pocket and clicked it at the globe. Suddenly the continents vanished, and in a blink the globe reconfigured as one big land mass. "Look closely at—"

"That's Pangaea . . . continental drift."

"Yes, it is."

Pangaea began separating into continental chunks, all of which began moving away from each other. Over the course of sixty seconds, I witnessed the creation of the world as the land masses dragged across long-vanished oceans. Some of them collided, some of them barely moved. South America and Africa crept away from each other. After two minutes the Dglobe showed Earth as we currently know it. And then—and then—the continents *kept* moving. And moving. California touched Alaska; India smushed itself into oblivion into the concertina'd ridges of the Himalayas; South America rested in the middle of the Pacific.

Coupland said, "That's Earth three billion years from now. Hey—let's look at it again in fast motion!" He clicked the fob, and we watched the continents form across a thirty-second span.

I said, "Again."

We watched it again.

Doug said, "Gee, Ethan—I wonder what Earth would look like if Antarctica melted completely? Why, let's find out! And let's do it in sixty seconds."

Before me Earth's land masses lost their familiarity. Florida vanished, as did much of Asia and all the planet's coastlines.

"Do it again!"

"With pleasure."

The continents submerged once more.

"Show me more stuff!"

"*Hmmmm* . . . I wonder what the most recent Ice Age looked like from start to finish."

"Show me the Ice Age!" I shouted.

"With pleasure."

Bingo! Fifty thousand years squished into sixty seconds.

Coupland said, "Gee, Ethan—how about an instantaneous real-time picture of all the weather on Earth at this moment?"

"You can do that?"

"Watch me." With a click, the Dglobe turned into Earth as seen from thirty-two geosynchronous weather satellites. It was stunning.

"Let's go back thirty days and see a whole month's worth of weather leading up to the present moment." With a click, the Dglobe showed thirty days of weather, with the planet rotating to show night and day, the cities of Earth twinkling when cloud cover permitted.

He said, "Let's see what happens if we throw a class 5 hurricane towards Florida . . . yeehaw! Disaster! Better still, what does Mars look like?"

Earth became Mars.

"What does the moon look like?"

I saw the moon.

"The sun? Flame on!"

Next came a succession of morphings: a glitterball; a mirror image of Earth; a graphics light show; political maps of the planet in various languages; a colour-coded slow-speed mapping of human populations on the planet since 5000 BC.

I looked at the Dglobe up close. "How does it work?"

"By using a spherical liquid crystal screen programmed with proprietary 3-D cartographic algorithms. They're going to be made in China . . . obviously. And your friends are writing and designing the globe's various uses."

"How does this particular model here work?"

"It's a mock-up with internal projectors. It cost me a bomb."

I asked, "How come you're hiring jPodders? Why not get eggheads from Yale or Stanford or India?"

"Because it's not that hard to program, so I might as well have fun people doing it instead of robotic geeks."

"And you really *can* make these globes?"

"Yes, I can. And every school on earth is going to want one. And anyone with a kid is going to want one. What am I saying—everyone in the *world* is going to want one."

"I want in."

"I knew you would."

"I also know you're evil, Coupland, so what's the catch?"

"There's no catch, but there *is* a price."

"I knew it."

"I want your new laptop, the one you bought after you returned from China. No erasing allowed—if you mail-ordered a DVD of *Sandra, the Living Chunnel,* I want to know about it. And I also want all of your files from work. *All* of them. Business and personal."

"Hang on a second—you already have my old laptop. Why do you want my new drives so badly?"

"Because my contract says I have to write a book, and it's easier just to steal your life than to make something up. So I need to find out what happened in your life after China."

My life a story? "Really?"

"You have ten seconds to make up your mind. One, two, three—wait! I think I hear marketing phoning with a new idea on how to dilute your latest game ideas with crap—four, five, six—wait, none of your friends are working there any more. You're alone in jPod—seven, eight, nine—"

"It's a deal."

"Good. You're living in Doug's world now."

"Not yet. I want your word on paper."

"Fine. No problem." In the parking lot Coupland handwrote an appropriate document, then handed it to me. "By the way," he added, "you're going to be filling in that hole tonight, aren't you?"

"Kam's people are doing it tomorrow morning."

"Do you think Kam would mind if I threw in a couple of things of my own?"

"Not at all. Just chuck them in and cover them with a tarp or a bedsheet so nobody can see what they are."

"Marvellous."

Three Months Later:

And so here I am. Dglobe is a blast. Life is good—so good, actually, that I have to ask myself, why do I worry so much? In fact, everybody in my universe seems happy, including our glamorous new receptionist, Kimberly. Kam is happy, Mom and Dad are happy, Kaitlin and I and all the ex-podsters are happy. Woohoo! Happy, happy, happy!

As for Steve, my old employer decided it needed to enter the gore sector of gaming, and wouldn't you know, Steve had our Ronald package all ready to go. He's golden and is going to turn around yet another company. He also got us all paid as consultants on the project, and we earn money doing sweet fuck all. *Wheeee!*

Yesirree, life sure is good.

Yesirree, nothing could possibly go wrong with everything being so good.

But of course, in books, good is boring.

Good is a snoozer.

Good makes people close the covers and never reopen them.

But you know—you'd think that just *once* when life finally started going my way, that cosmic writer out there would allow me and all of my co-characters to simply enjoy things for just a little while. I mean, what kind of a prick would end a book just when everything's going so well?